SOUL
MIЯRORS

SOUL MIRRORS

WILEY A HAYDON III

SCRIVENER BOOKS

Editorial work and production management by Eschler Editing
Cover design by Steven Novak
Interior print design and layout by Sydnee Hyer.
eBook design and layout by Eugene Woodbury.

Published by Scrivener Books

First Edition: June 2018
Printed in the United States of America

10 9 8 7 6 5 4 3 2 1

978-1-949165-02-9 (Softcover)

For Janelle. Forever.

ACKNOWLEDGMENTS

I've worked on this book for years and sometimes wondered if I'd ever finish it. The fact that you're reading it is owed at least in part to the generous people who contributed their time, energy, and encouragement to get me to this point.

Thanks to my early fans, particularly Scott, Kyle, Jeff, Kris, not-my-friend-Chris, Cheri, Paul, and Rocky. Your feedback and support have been invaluable. Words can't express my appreciation.

Thanks to my editorial team: Everyone at Eschler Editing (EschlerEditing.com) who contributed, but especially Sabine, Angela, and Michele. They were diligent in helping make this novel better and patient as I struggled to write with a day job and writer's block. Also to Becca and Katie at Loving the Book, who helped a shy, introverted engineer navigate the world of promotion and marketing.

Thanks to my family: my dad, my mom, John, Kimmy, David, Kristin, and Travis. They have been excited for the book even when I've been too nervous to share in their enthusiasm.

Especially I owe thanks to my wife, Janelle, who fits all three of the above categories and so much more.

Finally, a big thanks to you, the reader. I'm glad I'm able to share this book with you, and I hope you enjoy it.

—WILEY

— PART I —

Twelve Years Old—First Reflection

In our age of media and information, it is easy to forget that a rare event is just that: rare. News outlets cover the unusual ad nauseum, citing every possible example so long as its novelty still makes it even mildly intriguing. Constant coverage dulls us to the utter improbability, and eventually the unique is rendered banal. That which is rare, by miracle of attention, seems suddenly commonplace.

Thus, I find it essential to start this lecture with a well-known— but apparently misunderstood—fact: Mirror births are rare.

The likelihood of any given pregnancy producing a Mirror is approximately one in 750,000. That almost certainly means nothing to you. Humans understand better through relative measurements than absolute ones, so I will compare it with a similarly unusual event. According to the accepted calculation, a natural pregnancy has a one in 729,000 chance of producing quadruplets.

Thus, if you found out today that you or your significant other were pregnant, you are more likely to welcome four normal children in nine months than you are to birth a single Mirror.

Depending on your point of view, that fact either makes Mirrors seem mythically rare, or quadruplets terrifyingly common. In truth, it's somewhere in between. Mirrors are rare, but even at that rate, we still see an average of five or six such children born each year here in the United States.

At this point we still don't know if these variables are independent. It's possible genetics or environment or some other factor plays a role and would increase the odds of multiple Mirrors in a family. It's always hard to be certain, though. In the fifty-two years since the first Mirror birth in Norway, we've never had two Mirrors in the same extended family, let alone the same birth.

Until now.

—Excerpt from a guest lecture by Dr. Cole Bryant at Harvard University shortly after the birth of the Ross twins

— CHAPTER 1 —

Ashley Ross finally decided she wasn't going to get any more sleep. Even after accepting that revelation, she kept her eyes tightly shut. Pulling her right arm from the warmth of the blankets, she reached toward the nightstand. Blindly searching with splayed fingers, she identified three hair ties, a pack of gum, and a screwdriver before she finally found what she was looking for: her glasses.

A familiar mix of comfort and distaste washed over her as she slid the glasses on. With a practiced motion, she flipped the spring clips behind her ears. The cool metal locked into place, providing a reasonable guard against the glasses accidentally coming free. Safeties engaged, she ran her fingers along the rim where frames met skin to ensure there was a tight seal. This pair had been made based on measurements taken only three months ago, so they were still a good fit.

Finally sure her gaze was locked away from the world, Ashley opened her eyes.

A tiny night-light burned on the other side of the room, but its already meager light was dampened further by the heavily shaded lenses. Shadows cloaked her room, and she could barely see anything. She'd spent her whole life behind special glasses, though, and functioned well in the dark.

Still keeping as much of her body under the blankets as she could, she twisted to look at the clock on her nightstand. She could just barely make out the dull-green numbers. Ten after five. She'd last checked it at about one o'clock before finally drifting off, so four hours' sleep was the best-case scenario.

Trying not to think about that too much, Ashley pulled herself up to sit, legs swinging off the bed. After a month, she was almost used to the extra weight on her right leg, but she still frowned down at the ankle monitor. She knew her special glasses protected her from the world and vice versa, but she'd never gotten a clear answer as to why she had to wear the tracking device. Maybe that would change today.

Sliding from her bed with a shiver, she flicked on the bedside lamp. She glanced over at the closet and considered her next course of action. She'd have to get dressed soon enough, but for now she wanted to see her brother. She paused long enough to grab a blanket off her bed and wrapped it around her before heading for the hallway.

Ashley gave only the most peremptory of knocks on Thomas's door before slipping in. He always complained when she did that, but this morning she was pretty sure he was asleep. If she waited for a response, she might lose this chance to see him before all the chaos started.

"Hey, wake up!" she hissed as she closed the door behind her.

"Huh? What? What time is it?"

"Quarter after five."

Her twin groaned. "I don't have to be up for another fifteen minutes. Go away."

"I couldn't sleep."

"Well, I can. Go away."

"Come on, I want some company."

"Can't you just let me sleep?"

"No."

Thomas gave an angry grunt, then went silent. Ashley waited for a moment then reached out and poked him. Thomas give an exaggerated sigh.

"You're still here?"

4

"Yup."

"Are you safe?" he asked, using the family shorthand for "glasses on."

It was a stupid question, and she told him so.

When his lamp clicked on, Thomas was sitting up in bed, his own eyes uncovered. He regarded her with a decidedly grumpy look, which she answered with her sweetest smile. That earned a grunt of a laugh at least.

"You're not safe," Ashley said sternly, dropping the grin.

"You have yours on."

"And if Mom or Dad opened the door?"

Thomas's sour look deepened, but he did slide his own glasses into place. Ashley relaxed as he flipped the ear clips, securing the dark shades. She'd known him her whole life, all twelve years, but she could count on both hands the number of times she'd seen his eyes uncovered. She decided suddenly that he looked weird without the glasses.

"You're really excited about today, aren't you?" he asked.

"Yeah."

He shook his head. "It's not Christmas, Ash."

"Well, yeah, but this is what we were born for, right?"

He didn't respond to that, so she chose a different topic.

"It may not be Christmas, but it *is* our birthday."

That finally earned her a real grin. "Okay, *that* I'm excited about."

"You're always excited about getting presents," she teased.

"That, and getting out of the house." His smile slipped suddenly. "Normally, anyway."

"You get to fly on an airplane, though!" She was jealous of that. "You've got to tell me what it's like. Promise."

"Okay."

"You have to promise."

"It's not that big a deal."

"It is to me. Come on."

5

He didn't respond immediately. Instead, he turned around and began making his bed. With gentle care, he tugged his blankets back into place and arranged his pillow neatly at the head.

"Why does it matter?" he asked. "You'll probably fly out to your Reflection next week."

"Because I know we'll both be tired tonight, but I want to hear about it. I want something to look forward to after this is all over."

"All right," he said finally. "I promise."

Ashley bounded up happily and pulled him into a hug. She expected him to immediately pull back—he did that about half the time these days—but this morning he returned the embrace.

A knock on the door drew their attention. Thomas called out, "Come in," and Mom looked in. Her eyes were closed, and she said, "Time to wake up."

"I'm up and safe," Thomas replied.

Mom opened her eyes, and Ashley noticed the bags beneath them. Ashley had heard sounds from the office up until she'd fallen asleep last night and figured at least one of her parents had been awake. She wondered now if Mom had slept at all.

"Oh, you're both here. You could have slept in, Ashley."

"I want to see Thomas off."

"Well, right now he better get ready. Mr. Barton'll be soon."

"I know," Thomas said, and Ashley could hear the eye roll she couldn't see.

Mom ignored his tone and turned to Ashley. "Well, since you're up, you can get ready too," Mom said as Ashley brushed past her into the hallway. "What about that red dress of yours?"

Ashley stuck out her tongue. She was *not* wearing a dress today.

"I'm going to wear my silver sweater." Mom frowned, and Ashley hurried on. "I mean, it goes with my eyes and everything."

"Only one person's going to see your eyes."

"Yes, and he'll see that they match my sweater."

Mom opened her mouth but then closed it with a shake of her head. "Fine, as long as you're dressed when your Shepherd gets here."

"Yes, ma'am," Ashley said dutifully.

Back in her room, Ashley picked her way across her floor, stepping carefully to avoid treading on any of the various piles of clothes and assorted debris. Opening the closet, she pushed against the wave of stuff she'd shoved in there the last time she'd cleaned her room; the tide of junk pushed back threateningly. She reached in, grabbed the sweater she'd mentioned, then quickly slammed the door.

Returning to her dresser, she instinctively picked up the rainbow striped knee-length socks resting on top. These were her favorites, but even as she grabbed them, she let them go again. With the tracking device on her leg, they didn't fit right anymore. Frowning, she opened the top drawer and pulled out a pair of white ankle socks instead.

She gathered the rest of her clothes and dressed quickly, careful to avoid snagging her glasses in the process. If she took them off, she'd probably be okay for the brief period of time it took to throw her clothes on, but the proscription on being unsafe ran strong. Still, once she was ready, she stood in front of her full-length mirror and, after a quick glance at the door, released the metal clips on her earpieces and pulled the glasses from her face.

Some might call her eyes gray, but that description did them no justice. Her eyes were a brilliant, shining silver so crystal clear they actually reflected images like a mundane mirror did. Dr. Bryant had even told her that the eyes were the inspiration for calling children like her Mirrors. Leaning in close to the mirror, Ashley saw herself reflected in her own eyes, scratching the surface of infinity.

A knock at the door interrupted her musings, and she hurriedly pushed her glasses back onto her face. She locked them on and was safe by the time she scurried over and opened the door. Mom stood in the hallway, slowly wringing her hands.

Ashley noticed the motion with a frown, and her stomach lurched with sudden fear. Even though today's events had been explained to her at least a dozen times, she still didn't feel like she had a full grasp on things. She'd only ever Reflected one person, her father, and that was before her ability had matured a few weeks ago.

"Mr. Barton just pulled up," Mom said, then turned away.

Fear and exhilaration swirling uncertainly, Ashley followed.

— CHAPTER 2 —

Daniel Ross had first met Thomas's Shepherd a few months ago. Sam Barton was a broad-shouldered black man in his early fifties. He'd told Daniel he had been a chemist in the years before he joined the Department of Justice, but Sam was well-muscled and moved with a deliberate grace that made Daniel wonder if he'd served in the military prior to his career in science. As Daniel admitted him, he noted that the Shepherd wore a pressed suit, gray fedora, and Mirrors' glasses this morning, just as he had each previous meeting.

To ensure the children were acquainted with their guides before that first fateful Reflection, the Mirror Review Board mandated a series of meetings in the months before a Mirror's power matured. The first such meeting with Sam had been awkward. It would be easy to blame the Shepherd for that, but it wouldn't be fair; Sam had been open and honest from the start. Then again, maybe that was the problem. For the most part, the Ross family had couched today in the vaguest terms and euphemisms, and the Shepherd's frank approach threatened to put a dent in those comforting obfuscations.

Despite the tension of that first visit, Sam's personality had proven infectious. The man was warm and sympathetic, with a great sense of humor and a booming laugh. Daniel had taken to him quickly, and he thought Ashley had come to like the Shepherd as well. Unfortunately, Sally and Thomas had never come around.

If he had to guess, Daniel assumed they disliked the man's role rather than the man himself.

"Morning, Sam."

"Morning, Daniel."

"I just realized I should offer you coffee, but then I also realized I didn't make any. I'm not thinking straight this morning."

Sam waved a hand dismissively. "First time's always crazy." He cracked a grin. "Just don't forget it next week."

"Deal."

Daniel glanced toward the back of the house. "I thought he'd be ready by now. I swear that boy is meticulous with everything except his time."

"It's fine. Any last-minute questions I can answer?"

Daniel shook his head. "No. Not now. Maybe tonight. Maybe once it's all over."

"Fair enough. My flight home doesn't leave until tomorrow morning, so I can stay as late as you need tonight."

"Thanks."

"Any last tips for me?"

"What do you mean?"

"Anything that you think would help me get to know him better. Every time I've visited, Thomas has been withdrawn. I don't feel like I got to know him. They call me a Shepherd for a reason. My job is to care for Mirrors, and I can do that better if he's willing to trust me. More immediately, it'll be easier on him if he doesn't feel he's spending every Thursday with a total stranger."

"I guess that makes sense." Daniel thought for a moment, trying to think of anything that hadn't come up in those prior visits. "He likes sports, particularly football. He loves building things—everything from Legos to model planes. Despite their differences, he and his sister are closer than any two siblings I've ever known. He's very organized, and very smart, but he can also be lazy if he thinks he can get away with it. He's prickly about being told what to do but will obey if you put it firmly enough."

"Good. Anything else?"

"He has some basic education, but nothing formal. He's good with math and science, but . . . uh . . . we didn't teach them to read."

Sam nodded. "On Bryant's suggestion, I assume?"

"Yeah. He said it would be easier to control information."

"That's one of his standard procedures. He and I disagree on that one, but I don't think it makes a major difference."

Daniel blanched. "We didn't want to fight Bryant's rules. He told us . . ."

Footsteps from the back hallway interrupted their conversation, and Thomas shuffled disconsolately into the living room. Sally followed closely behind looking harried, and Daniel was surprised to see Ashley trailing her mother.

Thomas stopped just inside the room, hands tucked into pockets and head down. He shot just one surreptitious glance at Sam, then studiously ignored him. He held that position of disinterest even as Ashley joined him.

Sally skirted the two, moving over to join Daniel. She shook her head and said softly, "I wasn't sure I'd even get him out of his room."

Daniel suppressed a sigh, then took a step toward his son. Sam placed a hand on his arm, though, holding him back with gentle pressure.

"May I?" Sam said quietly. "I'm the one he has to spend the day with; let me see if I can bring him around."

Daniel glanced at Sally. His wife, in turn, looked back at their children, then shrugged. Daniel nodded to the big man.

"Good morning, Thomas," Sam said, crossing the room and extending his hand. Thomas reluctantly slid a hand out of his pocket to take it. "Nice to see you again."

"Yeah."

"Nervous?"

"No," Thomas answered immediately. It was an obvious lie.

"Good," Sam said, seeming to take the answer at face value.

He smiled confidently. "I've done this a thousand times. We make a quick hop over to Memphis, take care of business at the police station, and then fly back. If the planes are on time, you're home before dark. Nothing to it."

Thomas nodded slowly. "Yeah." He pulled his hands from his pockets and stood up straighter. "I can do that."

Sam clapped him on the shoulder. "Good! I knew I could count on you."

Turning to Sally, the Shepherd asked, "Do you have some snacks packed for him?"

"No, Bryant said not to feed them before the Reflection."

"He and I agree on that. And it's unlikely Thomas will be hungry afterward, but I prefer to be prepared.

"I can pull something together really quick," she said, moving to the kitchen.

"Cookies are always good," Thomas offered, warming a bit.

"No, you're having cake tonight," Sally countered. "I think we have one apple left, though."

Both twins followed her into the kitchen, Thomas pressing the cookie issue and Ashley apparently trying to claim that last apple. Daniel smiled in spite of himself. For that moment, it felt like a normal day in the Ross house.

Daniel's buoyant mood deflated as he turned back to Sam. As much as he liked the man, the Shepherd's presence here today meant everything was about to change. Even though he'd spent the last twelve years preparing himself for today, part of him still ached at the coming storm.

"I've read everything I can find on Reflections," Daniel said quietly to Sam. "I know it's going to be a horrific day for them. You know it too. Why lie?"

"When they were little, did you tell your kids that getting a shot hurts? Or did you focus on how quickly it's over?"

"That's hardly the same. Everything changes today. I know it."

"And Thomas? Does he?"

Daniel hesitated. "Not . . . entirely. We went over the basics. Ran through the procedure, explained why they were doing this. About the Reflection itself, well, we didn't go into details."

"Exactly," Sam said. "I don't want to hide it from him, but I don't want to terrify him, either. Today's going to play out the same way whether he knows what's coming or goes in with just the barest knowledge. I've tried it both ways. They're always crushed after the Reflection, but I feel that ignorance allows them to enjoy those last few hours as much as they can. He'll know it all afterward, anyway."

"I . . . okay. You're the expert."

The sounds from the kitchen began moving closer, and the two men stepped apart.

By the looks on their faces, Ashley had gotten her apple, and Thomas hadn't gotten his cookie. Sally handed the brown paper sack to the Shepherd, who promised to tuck it into his carry-on.

Everyone stood around for a moment, waiting. With everything taken care of, it was now time to go, but no one was moving. Thomas stared at his shoes. Sally shared a look with Daniel, and he felt his stomach drop out. It was time. The day he'd always known was coming had arrived, and he still wasn't ready.

Suddenly he couldn't find the words. His mouth was dry, his heart pounding. He'd been acting this morning on instinct, taking care of things because it was what he did. He'd gotten lost in the rhythm of preparation, and now that everything was done, he found he'd not equipped himself for the flood of emotions.

"Come on, Thomas," Sam said. "Let's get this over with."

"Fine."

Thomas started forward, hands in his pockets and head down again. Sally reached out to give him a parting hug, but he ducked at the last second and shot his mother a frown.

"Come on," Sally prompted. "Give me a hug goodbye."

"No. I don't want to do this."

Daniel opened his mouth to say something, but Thomas spun on him.

"Let me guess. You're going to say I don't have a choice. Yeah, I got that."

"At least say goodbye," Sally pleaded.

"No. You're letting them do this." His voice was rough, and Daniel thought he might be fighting tears. "If you want a hug, then don't make me go."

"We don't have a choice either," Daniel said.

That was mostly true. They'd had a choice twelve years ago. Today, though, their hands were as bound as their son's. That wasn't comforting as he watched Thomas angrily back away.

"Well, then, I guess I'm leaving," Thomas said, turning toward the door.

"Wait! It's not *my* fault!"

A blur shot past Daniel, and Ashley crashed into her brother with a hug that almost lifted him from his feet. Her momentum probably would have driven them both into the grandfather clock, but Sam caught them with a steady arm.

For a long moment, Thomas seemed at a total loss. The angry sneer had left his lips, and he stood stock still, hands at his sides. He cast a wary look at his parents, then at Sam, then finally returned his sister's exuberant embrace.

"You have to tell me what it's like to fly. You promised." She invested that final word with a wealth of meaning.

"Okay."

Thomas turned to go, and something in Daniel snapped. He couldn't let his son just walk away to hell without saying goodbye. Motioning for Sam to give him a minute before leaving, he darted into the kitchen, grabbed one of the cookies Sally had baked yesterday, and tucked it quickly into a plastic bag.

Rejoining everybody in the living room, he tossed the treat in a soft underhand to Thomas, who plucked it out of the air with a surprised look.

"What's this?" Thomas asked suspiciously. "A bribe?"

"I'm pretty sure it's a cookie."

Even through the dark glasses, Daniel could sense the long-suffering eye roll. Thomas did give a grudging smile, though, as he looked at the snack.

With obvious reluctance, Thomas marched back over to his mother and let her embrace him. To Daniel's surprise, he did return the hug, if only barely. He was no more enthusiastic in his farewell to Daniel, but considering it was a small miracle he'd gotten anything, Daniel decided not to be picky.

"I love you, son," he said as he released his boy. "We'll see you tonight."

Thomas shrugged, then turned on his heel. With a sullen huff, he wrenched open the front door and stalked out without looking back.

— CHAPTER 3 —

Thomas slouched in one of the seats at gate 9, sunk low enough that his head barely crested the seat back. His shoulders slumped, and he held his hands pressed between his legs. Mom always griped at Thomas about bad posture. She wasn't here, though. If she wanted him to sit up straight, she should have come along.

Given the early hour, Thomas had been convinced the airport would be nearly empty. Who woke up this early to fly somewhere?

The answer, it turned out, was *everyone.*

Plenty of people had steadily filled the area around the gate as he and his Shepherd waited, but none of the gathering travelers sat close to them. Now, only minutes from boarding, Thomas hardly believed it mere coincidence that he and the big man each had an entire row of seats to themselves.

Mr. Barton sat directly across from him. Leaning forward ever so slightly, the man rested his chin on his thick, steepled fingers. Thomas had spent the last fifteen minutes slumped here, watching the Shepherd watch him.

On the car ride to the airport, the man had tried to engage him in small talk, but Thomas had rebuffed every attempt, and Mr. Barton had finally lapsed into silence. Once they'd gotten to the airport, the only words he'd spoken had been to help Thomas with the unfamiliarity of the security screening. Since reaching the gate, neither of them had said anything.

"Are you asleep?" Thomas asked.

"No."

Thomas paused, then finally asked the question that had gnawed at him since his first meeting with the Shepherd. "Are you a Mirror?"

"No."

"Why are you wearing those sunglasses? Those are Mirror grade. Besides, nobody wears sunglasses inside except Mirrors."

"If your glasses come off, I don't want to have to close my eyes."

Thomas mulled that for a second. "Would that work? I thought I had to wear the glasses."

Mr. Barton shook his head. "Either person can. As long as there is a break in the connection, the Reflection doesn't happen. Have you ever looked at your sister when one of you wasn't wearing your glasses?"

He'd done just that as recently as a few hours ago, though he wasn't sure if he should admit such a breach or not. He wasn't supposed to be around anyone with the glasses off. Still, the Shepherd's tone wasn't judgmental, just curious.

"Yeah. A couple of times."

"And nothing happened, right?"

"Yeah, I guess."

He considered that and frowned. "So why do Ashley and I always have to wear them? Why can't our parents wear them occasionally?"

"That's something you'd have to ask them, but I'd guess to protect you both. Your situation is unique."

"Unique? There are other Mirrors."

Mr. Barton shook his head. "Yes, but never two in the same family, let alone in the same birth.

"I suppose that makes sense," Thomas said grudgingly. Still, it didn't help his mood. He hated wearing the shades.

Overhead, the speaker burst to life, and a woman's voice crackled throughout the terminal. "First call for flight 9606, nonstop service to Memphis, Tennessee. This is a Justice Department flight; general boarding will begin immediately after government assets are secured."

"That's our cue," Mr. Barton said, rising.

"I'm a 'government asset'? Why not just say 'Mirror'?"

"Euphemism. You'll find a lot of what you do is wrapped in it. People don't know what Mirrors do. For the most part, they don't want to." He held out a hand to Thomas. "Come on. We don't want to hold up boarding."

Personally, Thomas didn't care about inconveniencing these people. Their surreptitious stares irked him. Mr. Barton's posture was insistent, though. With a sigh of mingled resentment and reticence, Thomas pushed himself to his feet. He didn't take the Shepherd's proffered hand, though. He could walk just fine on his own.

"May I have your ticket, please?" asked the lady near the door. Thomas thrust the thick piece of paper into the woman's hand, then blinked in surprise.

She was smiling at him. She even met his gaze levelly through his darkened glasses. That wasn't normal. People at McMurray's always looked away when he and Ashley entered. Even the pediatrician tended to speak just to the side of them. To have someone here, a stranger, willing to meet his gaze and even smile caught him off guard. Did she know what he was?

"Good luck, Thomas," she said, handing him back the stub of his ticket. He took it, his eyes never leaving her face, but she had already directed her attention to Mr. Barton. Thomas only followed the hallway away from the terminal once the Shepherd pushed him onward to the plane.

Thomas would have dropped into one of the nearest seats, but Mr. Barton pointed to the rear row of seats on the left-hand side and said, "Those are ours." Together they threaded their way back. "Take the window seat; it's a much better view."

"Thanks." Thomas forced the word, not quite managing to keep the irritation out of his voice.

He dropped into his seat and disconsolately stared straight ahead. To his left, Mr. Barton pulled a thick curtain around their two seats, putting them out of view of the rest of the cabin. Once they were cut off, the Shepherd settled into his own seat next to Thomas.

Turning away from his companion, Thomas stared out the window. Clouds hid the rising sun, but the world was shedding its dark carapace nonetheless. A foggy gray settled across the lightening airport, a dreary image that suited Thomas's mood just fine.

"Buckle your seat belt," Mr. Barton commanded.

Without looking away from the window, Thomas felt across the seat cushion until he lit upon strips of rough fabric tipped by cool metal. The device was somewhat unfamiliar, but if it was like a car's restraints, then he could fasten it without having to look. He fumbled for a moment but secured the clasp without breaking his line of sight.

"Pull it tight," Mr. Barton said.

Sighing with annoyance, Thomas scooted back until the seat pressed his shirt firmly against his spine. Gripping the loose strip of cloth in his right hand, he pulled until the belt drew taut around his waist.

"That lady who took my ticket smiled at me," Thomas said abruptly. There wasn't anything to hold his attention outside, and getting questions answered ranked higher on his list than boredom. Besides, gleaning information from the man didn't mean that he had to like him. "And she wasn't afraid of my eyes."

The Shepherd glanced down at Thomas. "I'd guess she appreciates what you're doing."

"I don't understand."

Mr. Barton hesitated. "Most people don't understand what Mirrors do. They don't understand what Mirrors actually are. They're afraid of you, afraid of your power. Some, though, like the ticket agent, really believe in Mirror justice. Usually people like that lost a loved one to a crime and a Reflection provided closure."

"There don't seem to be a lot of them," Thomas said bitterly, running through his memories of times outside his house.

"There aren't. I wish there were."

"So you agree with them? You think I'm doing something great?"

Mr. Barton's face split into a broad smile. "I know it, Thomas. You're the superhero here. I'm just your sidekick."

Thomas stared for a long moment. He stood two inches under five feet and hadn't yet cracked one hundred pounds. Meanwhile, the Shepherd had to be over six feet, with the muscles to match. The idea of this mountainous man as not just a sidekick but *his* sidekick was such an utterly ridiculous image that a laugh escaped before he could stifle it.

"I guess we should get you some tights," Thomas said before laughing again.

"You first. The hero's ensemble sets the theme."

"I've got an old pair of dinosaur pajamas. I think you'd look amazing in dinosaurs."

Mr. Barton opened his mouth to respond, but a thump from the front of the plane caused Thomas to jump. He looked out the window, but nothing seemed out of the ordinary. He turned back to the Shepherd, who raised a hand in a calming gesture.

"Just closing the door. Totally normal."

The plane began a slow retreat, confirming Mr. Barton's assessment. The moment was gone, though. Thomas's lighthearted mood faded, and he leaned away from the Shepherd, resting his head against the window.

"How long's it gonna take to get there?"

"Almost three hours."

Thomas groaned. "And there's nothing to do but sit here the whole time?"

"If we drove to Memphis, it would take all day."

Over the speakers, a terse voice barked, "Flight crew, prepare for takeoff."

Waves of noise rolled from the wings into the cabin, and Thomas jumped. Instinct drove his first nervous glances out the window to the roaring engines, but just as quickly he spun back to the Shepherd. The man showed no fear, so this must be normal.

"First time's always the hardest," Mr. Barton said. "Some of the boys say that looking out the window helps. The ones who don't just close their eyes."

No time for consideration was given. Outside the window, the terminal was already sliding from view, slowly at first, but then with frightening rapidity. The acceleration pressed him into the seat. Exhilaration kept his eyes glued to the scenery speeding by outside, but fear locked his arms, and he dug his fingers into the armrests with such force he felt pain.

Beyond the window, the horizon suddenly tipped at an angle, and Thomas felt his stomach lurch. He wrestled down a scream that ultimately passed his lips as a startled squeak. Trees and houses dotted the land below, shrinking as they fell away beneath the plane. Houses melted into views of entire city blocks, and those blocks into neighborhoods. Cars, barely visible now, drifted almost lazily along highways that split the city into a colorful, if misshapen, patchwork.

"Where's my house?" Thomas asked suddenly.

"Don't know," said the Shepherd, leaning closer to watch the shrinking city over Thomas's shoulder. "We might not even pass over it. If we did, you'd never recognize it."

"Is the whole flight like this? This isn't so bad."

"Something like it. Most of the time we'll be over open land. Impressive, but nothing like the cities."

Sure enough, the neighborhoods and parking lots soon gave way to geometric patterns of what Thomas assumed was farmland. Eventually, even those were lost when a roiling layer of clouds overtook the view. He watched the unbroken plains of white for a couple of minutes, then turned away.

"Do you like sports?"

The Shepherd's question caught him off guard, and Thomas didn't respond immediately. Was this a trap? Why did the big man care?

He wavered a moment, then shoved the doubts down. He was already bored, and he guessed there were still a couple hours to go.

"Yeah. Dad and I watch the football games every Sunday during season." Thinking about Dad stirred the embers of homesickness, and Thomas fought down a mix of tears and anger.

"You've found my favorite game. Who's your team?"

"Denver," Thomas answered immediately. "Duh. Gotta root for the home team. My dad cheers for the Bears, though. He's from Chicago." He paused and then added, "Has a Mirror ever played on a pro team? I asked Dad once, and he said no. I thought he was holding back, though."

"No. Never been a Mirror on a pro team."

"Even after they finished Reflecting? Huh. Maybe the glasses?" Thomas mused. "I'll bet they'd come off when you get tackled, even with the safety clips."

"That's certainly a concern."

"Yeah. Still, I think it would be fun just to play. Maybe I'll be the first Mirror on a pro team. Dad and I used to toss the football around in the backyard; then he almost knocked my glasses off with a bad throw and . . ." He trailed off. "My stupid eyes ruin everything. They probably don't even let Mirrors try out, do they?"

"There's no rule preventing it."

"Really? I really could be the first Mirror in football, then." The daydream was pulling together; he could see the fans screaming his name as he heaved the ball down the line. With just seconds on the clock, everything depended on his pass. "I could be a quarterback for the Broncos. We'd go all the way to the Super Bowl, and when we'd won it once, we'd go again. It'd be great. You a Denver fan?"

With a guilty grin, Mr. Barton said, "Well, I grew up in Kansas City . . ."

"No!" Thomas laughed.

The Shepherd spread his hands apologetically and admitted, "Sorry. Chiefs fan."

Despite his best efforts to keep the man at arm's length, Thomas found himself drawn in by the Shepherd's sincerity. Eventually the conversation slipped from football to basketball before Mr. Barton took Dad's side and tried to convince Thomas that golf was a fun sport. For the first time in days, Thomas's mind drifted fully away from the coming task. Blissful ignorance might be impossible now, but an hour of conversation without the words "Reflection" or "Mirror" was a joy all its own.

—CHAPTER 4—

Sally waited on the love seat, her eyes flicking to the grandfather clock on the far wall yet again. It was now 9:23, a grand total of two minutes since her last furtive glance. That meant that, like the last few times she'd looked, it was still at least a half hour until Ashley's Shepherd was scheduled to arrive. Wrenching her gaze back to the room, Sally promised herself she would *not* check the time again. Carol would arrive when she arrived.

Waiting for Carol might actually be preferable to the woman's arrival. Unlike Sam—whose affable demeanor sort of made up for the fact that he was a government escort—Carol Raines had always been cool and businesslike. Sam dressed formally; Carol lived it.

Despite her dispassionate mien, the woman had clearly managed to earn Ashley's respect over their handful of meetings. Ashley had spoken on various occasions about the Shepherd, and the commentary was always glowing. She'd told her parents how she was sure she was in good hands come her first Reflection. This morning, though, that optimism seemed distant.

Across the room, hunched down on the couch, Ashley sat idly picking at the lint on her sweater. Sally had tried to convince her daughter to switch into one of her dresses after Thomas had left. Ashley had agreed, but in the end she'd been so pathetic about the whole thing Sally finally relented.

"Why don't you go play?" Sally suggested for what must have been the third or fourth time.

Ashley shrugged without even turning to look at her, which wasn't new, then actually spoke, which was. "It's no fun without Thomas. I mean, we've always played together, and without him it's . . ." The girl trailed off, then stuck out her tongue and blew a raspberry. She shrugged again and seemed to sink deeper into the sofa.

"Oh."

9:27.

Wrenching her eyes from the clock, Sally sighed. There had to be something to do that was better than sitting around waiting for the end to come. Maybe she should suggest working on a puzzle or playing cards or something.

Ashley turned to face her and said, "Mom, you're rubbing your hands again. You're making me more nervous than Dad."

Indeed, Sally gripped her left hand in her right and was wringing it fiercely. Distracted and nervous, she hadn't even noticed. Frowning, she thrust her arms to her sides.

It was an embarrassing slip since she had rather forcibly pushed Daniel into the master bedroom after she'd decided his incessant pacing was upsetting their daughter. She'd been determined to set a better example. So much for that.

"Do you think Thomas has landed?" Ashley asked quietly.

Sally glanced at the clock. *This time it's legitimate*, she told herself. "Yes. About fifteen minutes ago. They're probably on their way to the police station."

"And that's where he'll Reflect someone?"

"Yes."

"And I'll be at a courthouse?"

"Yes."

"Why am I not at police station?"

"Because every state gets to choose where the Reflection takes place. Tennessee chose police stations, and Colorado chose courthouses."

"Right."

26

They'd gone over all of this as a family, of course—first when the twins' abilities had matured a couple weeks ago, and then again once their first assignments had come in. Sally was certain Ashley remembered that; both children learned quickly and forgot slowly. Perhaps she'd underestimated her daughter's desire for communication.

"Mom, you're doing it again!" Ashley complained from the sofa, and Sally jerked her hands back to her sides.

Three firm raps upon the door drew the attention of both mother and daughter. Sally glanced at the clock. 9:34. Carol Raines was early.

She rose from her seat and walked hesitantly to the door. Ashley slid off the sofa and stood expectantly, that look of eager anticipation returning to her face.

Opening the door, Sally revealed a tall woman in her sixties. The Shepherd's gray hair was pulled back in a tight bun, and, like Sam Barton, she wore her own pair of Mirror-grade sunglasses. A heavy black coat covered a finely cut dress, the color of which matched Ashley's sweater almost exactly. The woman presented a warm smile to Ashley before sweeping imperiously past Sally without waiting for an invitation.

"Good morning, Ashley," Carol said smoothly. "I love the sweater; I'm sure it matches your eyes perfectly."

Ashley nodded and smiled, obviously pleased. Sally frowned at the comment; why reference the very feature that made her a Mirror? Before she could object, though, Carol continued.

"You've been sitting here awhile, I think. Why don't you go freshen up and run a brush through your hair one last time? Looking sharp always makes me feel better."

As with most of the Shepherd's comments, the words were crisp; Carol Raines was a woman who expected to be obeyed. Sally frowned at the command, but Ashley gave a quick, "Yes, ma'am," and slipped quickly from the living room.

The instant Ashley was out of earshot, Carol turned to Sally, pulled off her glasses, and shot her a penetrating glare.

"Stand up straight and stop wringing your hands," the older woman snapped.

"Excuse me?" Sally blurted.

"When you opened the door, I thought you might start sobbing at the mere sight of me," Carol continued with a grunt of disgust. "Ashley does not need a reed bending in the current; she needs a rock. What she will experience in the coming hours is enough to make even the strongest child cry. That's fine; she'll have earned those tears. You, however, must be solid. If you waver, so will your daughter. If you collapse, so will she. For her sake, do try to display a little backbone."

With that, Carol deftly slipped the dark glasses back onto her face and locked them with a flourish. Fury boiled inside Sally, but it was tempered by a measure of stunned confusion. What just happened?

"I'm ready," Ashley announced as she returned. She wore a genuine smile, but her hands kneaded her jeans in fear.

"Good girl," Carol said with a nod. "You look very professional."

"Are we leaving already?" Ashley asked hesitantly.

"There's some traffic this morning. We don't want to be late to your first Reflection."

"Oh. Right." She paused. "Can I say goodbye to my dad?"

"Of course," Carol said.

Ashley walked toward the master bedroom, her gait stiffer than when she had left the room to brush her hair. Sally felt a stab of regret; she wished desperately that she could do something to remove that growing fear. She wanted to simply hug her daughter and never let go.

"Show her strength and expect strength from her. It really is that simple," Carol said. "At least at this stage."

Anger rose within Sally again. In front of her daughter she had muted her response, but with Ashley out of the room, her restraint crumbled. Hands balled into fists, she turned to confront the Shepherd.

"I don't need your advice on how to raise my daughter," she spat.

Carol smiled at the outburst. "That's promising. I hoped you had some fight in you. Your daughter shows remarkable resilience, after all; she had to get it from somewhere."

"Don't patronize me! I don't need you—"

"Think carefully before finishing that sentence," the Shepherd interrupted. "I've been escorting Mirrors to Reflections for thirty years, and I know exactly what brings out the best in these girls. Do you want your daughter to make it to eighteen? Good. So do I.

"You have two choices, Sally. You can fight me every step of the way because you dislike me. Understand that it won't bother me in the least, but it will have a detrimental effect on your daughter. Alternatively, we can work together. You put up with me, and we make sure Ashley lives long enough to find a life beyond Reflections. Your choice, dear."

Before Sally could reply, Carol's features regained their pleasant cast. Ashley had just swung around the corner into the living room. She walked less enthusiastically, perhaps, but she still bore none of Thomas's overt terror. She didn't hesitate as she pulled on coat and gloves, and even gave Sally a small smile as she came up for a hug goodbye.

Ashley paused, stopping as she stepped into the embrace. "Mom, are you okay?"

"I'm fine," Sally lied, pushing down her anger. "Make me proud."

Ashley nodded resolutely, then stepped up for a long embrace. Sally felt a tenseness in her daughter, but there was no sobbing.

With a final squeeze, Ashley released the hug, stepped back, and approached Carol. The Shepherd gave the girl's shoulder a reassuring squeeze. Then they stepped out the door and were gone.

With both of her children sent on their hateful missions of justice, Sally's own resolve fractured. She walked back to the couch, wringing her hands, and stole another of the day's many glances at the softly ticking grandfather clock.

— CHAPTER 5 —

"How much have you been told about the subject of today's Reflection?" Mrs. Raines asked as Ashley closed the door of the Shepherd's silver Lincoln Town Car and dutifully buckled her seat belt.

"Some, but I have questions."

"As is natural," the woman said, shifting the car into drive. "All right. You remember what we're going to do today?"

"I'm going to take off my glasses and look into the eyes of someone accused of a crime. Then I'll tell the lawyers whether or not he's guilty."

Mrs. Raines nodded as she turned left, leaving behind the collection of suburban homes. She merged onto a busier street lined with businesses. Ashley couldn't read any of the signs, but she recognized logos of the fast-food restaurants where her parents occasionally bought dinner. Her stomach rumbled in anticipation, but no breakfast was forthcoming. Clearly the Shepherd had heard Dr. Bryant's advice about forbidding food before the Reflection.

"And you looked at someone before your power matured, correct? Your father?" Mrs. Raines asked.

"Yes," Ashley said quietly.

Years of fervent prohibitions had been erased that day. From her earliest memories, the twins' entire existence had been dominated by those shaded lenses. The harshest punishments her parents had doled out had been for stubbornly reaching for those frames, and the overt worry that action inspired in her parents had infused her at the deepest level. When Dad had pulled her into the study and told her to uncover her eyes, Ashley had protested for ten minutes before finally relenting.

All she'd known to that point was that her eyes were dangerous. Both parents had been intentionally vague as to which party would actually be harmed by her gaze, a fact that had helped reinforce obedience. She remembered how much she had trembled as her hands had slid the glass and metal shield from her face. It was the first time she could recall actually being unsafe in front of someone else. Even once she'd pulled the glasses off, it had taken her a long time to draw enough courage to finally open her eyes.

Her father had been waiting, directly in her line of sight. Before she could second-guess her decision, their gazes locked, and her world suddenly collapsed. A terrible moment passed, an instant where she lost herself completely in a foreign scape. An image flickered, something stolen from that alien world. Then she stumbled, grabbing the desk for support as Dad had looked away. She had gasped, knees shaking, as she suddenly realized what had happened.

She'd been given a memory.

Morning sunlight streamed into the kitchen on a warm summer day. The dishwasher lay open with Sally frozen beside it, a recently washed bowl clutched in her hand. Pink flowers in a glass vase adorned the windowsill over the sink, and their scent was just lightly detectable in the air. Thomas, six years old, stood at the door to the dining room, sticking his tongue out at his sister.

At her.

It was the scene as her father had lived it. She'd gained every sight, every smell, every emotion buried in that stolen second of his life. In those first minutes his view of the event was particularly strong. It was not "Mom" by the dishwasher, but "Sally," and the love for her was that of a husband, not a daughter.

It had taken only a minute or two for the initial intensity of the vision to fade. Ashley's own experiences had strongly pushed back to the forefront, and her world seemed to right itself. She could recall the image, view the experiences through her own filters, but her dad's interpretation of events was still there, nestled in the back of her mind.

She'd shoved her glasses back on as soon as she could.

Shaking free of the memory, Ashley asked Mrs. Raines a question of her own. "Can . . . can you tell me more about Reflections?"

"Of course. What do you want to know?"

Ashley let out a long sigh of relief. It was the first time she'd broached the subject with an adult and not immediately sensed hesitation.

"What will happen when I look at someone now?" She already knew the answer to that one, but Dad's explanation had been abrupt. She wanted a thorough treatment.

"You receive an entire life. Every action, every thought, and every emotion will be yours. You don't simply see these, though; you'll live them. A Reflection won't simply play out the other person's life like a TV show. Instead, you'll be the one taking those actions, living those choices.

"At first, that life will override yours," she continued. "During the Reflection, you will lose all sense of who you are. It will come back, though, over time. The immediacy of what you experience will fade, and you'll be able to look at that life through your own eyes instead of theirs."

"What happens to the other person?"

Mrs. Raines turned to give her a reassuring smile. "Don't worry, you don't steal their memories. You simply take them on. In doing so, you show their lives back to them, as if they were an outsider looking in. It's one reason you are called a Mirror."

This was all a review, a confirmation of things she'd been told but had only half considered until now. It was her next question she'd been leading toward, the question that really mattered to her.

"Do I make a difference?"

"Absolutely," Mrs. Raines answered immediately.

Ashley felt her enthusiasm from earlier in the morning bubbling back to the surface, smothering some of the uncertainty that had been building. She'd been afraid that her Shepherd would hesitate or stutter. She'd worried that she'd be taking on these other lives for nothing.

"Mirrors provide stability and certainty to the justice system," Mrs. Raines continued. "You ensure the innocent go home to their families and the guilty are punished for their crimes. Since Mirrors entered the system, we know for a fact that we haven't executed the wrong person in capital cases. We can convict serial offenders who might have escaped due to lack of evidence. In short, Ashley, Mirrors make more of a difference than anyone else could hope to."

Mrs. Raines looked over at her for a moment, smiling proudly, and Ashley felt like a warm fire had been lit inside her. The cold fear melted away, and she returned the grin.

"Who am I Reflecting today?" she asked, a thrill rushing through her.

"Spencer Duncan. He's a twenty-three-year-old man from a wealthy family."

"What did he do?"

Mrs. Raines hesitated for the first time, and Ashley felt some of her elation melt away. "You're going to tell us whether he kidnapped and killed a little girl."

—CHAPTER 6—

Defendant is named Dennis Carson. Some kind of engineer," the police officer walking ahead of Thomas and Sam explained as he led them through the halls of the police station. "Accused of killing his wife with a cleaver. Nasty case. I assume you've been briefed?"

"We have," Sam rumbled in his throaty bass.

This was at least the fourth time Thomas had been briefed. Sam had filled him in on the basics of the case on their trip from home to the airport. The officer who'd picked them up at the airport had given them a rundown. The sergeant who'd met them at the station provided his own spin. And now the dark-haired man leading them through a maze of offices seemed intent on going over it again.

Thomas did his best to pretend to pay attention. He wanted to be anywhere else. He thought of home, of Ashley, of his parents. He thought of being someplace warm with a beach. He'd never been to a beach, but he thought he'd like it. It would certainly beat being here.

"Good," the officer said. "Carson and his attorney were here before you were, but the DA had trouble getting away. That's why we had to leave you sitting so long. Sorry for the delay; she's here now."

"Not a problem," Sam replied.

"I was bored," Thomas said, and the officer looked back over his shoulder at him.

"Huh. He talks," the man said with genuine surprise.

"He's not a robot," Sam said irritably.

"Well, yeah, but I've been here for a few Reflections, and I never heard them say anything. I mean, they're *Mirrors*. It's hard to think of them talking."

Sam pulled the officer to a halt as his face twisted into a too-smooth grin. "You think Thomas is just a tool? You think he's a hammer? Picked up when needed, does a job, and then goes calmly back into the toolbox, right?" Sam put a hand on the other man's shoulder, still smiling widely. "Well, I think you should stop talking before I get angry."

The nameless officer studied the Shepherd's overwide smile for a moment, seemed to realize that he was probably outweighed by a good fifty pounds, and then gave an enthusiastic—but thankfully silent—nod of assent. Sam looked over at Thomas and shook his head as if he couldn't believe the stupid things people said. Thomas shot him a brief grateful smile.

They walked the rest of the way in silence. Their movement attracted attention, though, and people stared at them wherever they went. Conversations died as they approached and restarted as mumbled whispers after they passed.

This wasn't really new. It was like this every year when the family went to McMurray's for the twins' annual birthday lunch. It had been like this at the airport this morning. A few stared openly, gawking at the unusual sight, but most simply hid their eyes from him. Whether a spectacle or a horror, the majority of the world treated him as something other than a person.

Thomas decided that he hated them all.

The officer stopped abruptly. He gripped the knob of a door and swung it inward. "This is it."

Sam gripped Thomas's shoulder and nudged him forward. Jerky steps carried Thomas into the room, and his heart sank a little as the door clicked shut behind him.

A large wooden table split the room. Five people waited. Two were uniformed officers stationed on either side of the door. One of the assembled must be Dennis Carson. Based on what he'd heard, the other two must lawyers for each side.

A woman next to the door suddenly grabbed Thomas's hand and gave it a firm shake. "Hello, Thomas. I'm the district attorney, Jennifer Hallman. This is Dennis Carson, and his council, Kyle Dallas." She indicated each man in turn. Thomas nodded stiffly. "Have you been briefed?" Another stiff nod. "Are you ready?"

The DA didn't gawk, and she didn't look away. She even shook his hand without hesitation. Part of him warmed at the contact, and he appreciated that she treated him like a human being. That small pool of gratitude paled next to the gulf of his anger and frustration. Whatever niceties she doled out today, she was still a part of the machine that had dragged him here. He pulled his hand back with a jerk and regarded her sullenly.

If she was insulted or hurt by his behavior, she gave no indication. Instead, she eyed him calmly and repeated, "Thomas, are you ready?"

He didn't have an answer. Was he ready? How could he know? He'd never done this before, and he wasn't sure he *wanted* to. He certainly didn't want to Reflect a violent stranger, of all people. He had no choice, though. Perhaps best to get it over with? To finish his job so he could go home?

"Can we get this over with?" Mr. Carson demanded. "I'm going to enjoy watching you sign that kid's statement, Hallman. After the hell you've put me through, I'm . . ."

"Dennis, enough," Carson's lawyer interrupted warningly, and the man stopped his tirade midsentence. He grimaced, though, and slumped back in his chair with his arms crossed.

Thomas shivered. He wanted this over. He wanted to leave these people and go home. It made him feel like a little kid, but he really wanted his mom and dad and sister. He wanted a hug and a piece of birthday cake and presents.

"I'm ready," he managed.

Behind him, Sam squeezed his shoulder again. Thomas guessed it was supposed to be encouraging.

Hallman nodded. "Face Mr. Carson, but don't take your glasses off until I tell you. While they're off, look at no one but the defendant. After this is over, we'll ask you some specific questions. You'll provide answers to those and nothing else. Then you'll sign some papers. After that, you can go home."

Thomas felt his cheeks redden. He didn't actually need to read often; the menu at McMurray's for the annual birthday celebration was usually the limit. By now he knew what he wanted and could simply pretend he'd read it. There was no avoiding this, though.

"I . . . I can't write . . ."

"Okay. Don't worry about it," the DA said, not even missing a beat. "It'll be fine."

Thomas paused at the disinterested response, uncertain whether he should feel indignant or relieved that the woman didn't seem to care. He was still pondering when a gentle nudge from Sam pushed him forward.

Suddenly remembering the task at hand, Thomas balked. Another gentle push propelled him forward, and he somehow managed a half-dozen halting steps before finding himself directly across the table from Mr. Carson.

Thomas studied him quietly from behind the safety of the dark glasses for a moment. Slightly overweight, Mr. Carson's deep-brown hair was thinning in front and graying elsewhere. A pair of thin-rimmed glasses rested near his elbow on the table. His tie, black slashed with a deep royal blue, was rumpled slightly, and even his suit showed signs of wear. Lines of anger, or perhaps impatience, creased the man's face. After a few seconds, Carson noisily cleared his throat and spread his hands in a "What are you waiting for?" gesture.

"Whenever you're ready, Thomas."

Hands that had threatened to dissolve into anxious trembles found stillness at the final moment. Gripping the glasses from both sides, he unlocked the frames, then cautiously slid them over his ears and off his nose. Light exploded unhindered around the plastic, and he winced. Head tilted down so that the accused man was just out of his sight, Thomas finished pulling the dark covers from his face and set the glasses on the table. Drawing a final, tense breath, he looked up.

Thomas's silver eyes locked abruptly with Mr. Carson's deep brown, and the world lurched.

Memories exploded into Thomas's mind, racing past so quickly he understood little more than a blur. Emotions accompanied the incomprehensible olio of thoughts and drilled his mind with a fury that made him gasp. Anger. Joy. Fury. Lust. Sorrow. Love. Hate. Despair. Pain. Loss. Each barreled past with the speed of a bullet train, hammering his mind. Some he had never truly felt before, certainly never so fiercely, and some he never wanted to feel again.

A single moment was all Thomas had claimed when he'd looked into his father's eyes. This was a life. Every event, dramatic and mundane, noble and ignoble, hidden and plain, rushed from man to boy along the invisible connection between them.

Crushed by the sheer magnitude of the memories he received, his identity began to fail. Forty-three years of life swept over twelve and swallowed them whole. Worse, Thomas remembered those twelve years with imperfect clarity, while the new memories he received were flawless in their construction. All five senses were engaged. He saw Mr. Carson's first car, his wife, his children. He heard the shouts of the man's father, the ringing of the phone, the church bell. His tongue absorbed fine food and alcohol. He smelled smoke from fires burning on cold nights in winter and smelled perfume that burned fires of passion. Finally, he felt carpet beneath bare toes, the gentle touch of a woman's lips on his own. Feelings erupted with every new sensation, woven seamlessly into each memory. To recall was to relive.

Drowning in the flood of another man's life, Thomas held on to a single thought: *I am Thomas Ross. I am Thomas Ross. I am*

Thomas Ross. Even as the words echoed against the walls of his mind, the meaning slipped from them. The torrent continued, and Thomas found himself unable to separate them from himself. Dennis melded into him, consumed him, and he knew no other self.

"Come here, boy!" The words rang with fury and echoed slightly in the small room. Striding toward him was his father, drunk and sneering, arm stretched back and—

He felt the blow; the memory of it was so powerful his cheek burned. Tears stung the corners of his eyes; that show of weakness earned him another cuff from the angry man and a slew of obscenities. His father swung back for another hit, but the flow of thoughts pressed the scene away.

Another swept in immediately. A teenager now, he relaxed in his room, music blasting on the stereo. His hands were clenched into fists around a piece of paper. Long, sweeping strides carried him back and forth across the carpet, and he bit his upper lip in frustration. Anxiety shredded his nerves, and his hands shook. He wanted a cigarette but didn't dare smoke in the house lest his father find out. Unfolding the paper, he stared again at the seven numbers scrawled in a hasty but neat script across it. Kathy's looks had been inviting, but he was risking it all to call and . . .

The tide marched on. No pattern forced the sequence, and he jumped backward in time just as frequently as forward. There seemed no rhythm to the timing. He jumped from a teenager to a toddler frightened at the circus, then to a business meeting nearly thirty-five years later. No memory forged to the front of the pack long enough to play out in its entirety, but each was crystal clear and precise.

Memories of his wedding to Kathy surged just long enough to forge fear and joy before melting into more terrified memories of his father's ire. "Tell them you fell down the stairs," a stern voice commanded, and he remembered nodding stiffly, trying hard not to cry and earn another painful reason to "be a man."

Going to college meant escape and freedom from home. He remembered the drinking and the parties, and he remembered the moment he found his reason to work hard. Staring slack-jawed at the first semester's report card, he realized that if he failed out, he'd have to go home. Nothing curbed the late-night antics entirely, but he maintained Bs and Cs after that.

He grunted with surprise when a scene of college graduation cut directly into him and his wife arguing. A stupid argument over who should drop the kids off at day care the next day, the scene unfolding right as his anger peaked. The tingling in his hand as his wife reeled backward burned with an all-too-familiar fire that still tinged his cheek. A part of him shrieked in horror: *I've become my father!* Another part fought it: *I'm not him! She deserved this!* The latter part won. She stumbled back, stunned, even as he pointed his finger and commanded . . .

A baby's cries broke the air. Kathy laughed amid the tears glistening on her face, and joy and pride surged stronger than almost anything he had ever felt. Every wail from Alan's tiny body boosted his spirits, and the tide seemed strong enough to sweep away his strongest despair.

Thank God he's not a Mirror. The news was still buzzing from the birth of the Ross twins two months ago. He felt bad for their parents; the kids would likely be dead by sixteen.

The mists of life swirled around him, and he found himself in the Memphis police station. He was arguing with his lawyer, Kyle Dallas. Dallas claimed they had a tight case, but the DA wasn't willing to budge, citing that too much evidence pointed to his guilt. It had been Dennis's idea to request the Mirror, but Dallas had opposed it from the start. "You're just worried about your fee," he had snapped at his lawyer.

Dallas shook his head solemnly. "You don't know what you're about to do to this kid."

"Screw the kid. This is his job, and I want my freedom." He stabbed a finger at the DA "And I want to rub my innocence in her face."

Dallas frowned but said nothing before his face melted into that of a child.

Four-year-old Alan ran up to his chair and held out his arms. "Hold me, Daddy!" the boy cried delightedly, and strong arms reached down to sweep the boy into his lap. Young Alan giggled as Kathy looked on with a smile.

Swept into the mists again, the room was the same, but everything else was changed. He stood in his living room, his son opposite him. Eight years old, the boy's eyes squinted in frustration, and his mouth twisted petulantly. Throwing a temper tantrum that would have made his three-year-old sister proud, Alan whined at his father, demanding to go to the pool with his friends. Instinct bred in anger lashed again, and he felt the muscles in his arms extending, reaching. Alan, caught unawares, barely had time to flinch before the force of the blow snapped his head back and sent him tumbling. *Not uncalled for! He needs discipline!* he screamed silently, but that cold ice in his stomach belied the ease with which he'd dismissed his action.

Another lurch, and shock and terror assaulted him. Dried blood coated the body of his wife as she lay naked on the bed. Brownish-red stains marred the sheets and carpet. Kathy's eyes stared blankly at the ceiling. A deep slash across her throat left no doubt as to how she died.

Confusion, rage, and fear mingled in a mind broken beyond coherency. All reason left him, and he ran to the bed, grabbing Kathy's arm. Cold, dead flesh greeted his touch, and he dropped it with a start. Dabs of half-dried blood oozed against his hand and in horror he unthinkingly wiped them on his jeans. A large knife rested next to her. So stunned he wasn't thinking clearly, Dennis grabbed the blade and stared blankly at it. This was a dream. It must be.

"Dad?" Alan stood in the door, his face ashen.

"Go!" he called. "Call . . . call an ambulance! Now! Go!"

Alan hesitated but eventually ran from the room, tears staining his cheeks.

Somewhere deep inside a voice whispered that this was the answer justice demanded, but the Reflection didn't halt. Memory after memory rushed in; the connection couldn't be broken until the whole story was told.

An entire lifetime had been given, but the room's clock, old and dusty, hadn't swept even a full second from the time the Reflection started until it broke. As the connection shattered, an empty husk of a boy collapsed to the ground, lost in the details of the world he'd just absorbed.

— CHAPTER 7 —

Fatigue swept in suddenly as the Reflection ended.

Spencer Duncan's life swirled inside the fractured shell of a person. This shell wasn't Spencer, but it wasn't anyone else, either. An identity lost in the rush of Reflection fought to reassert itself, to be recognized, but it was like trying to climb a sheer cliff with bare hands.

The shell was in a room, a place of fluorescent lights and tables. There were people; some were talking. One of them, a white-haired woman with sharp features, slid a pair of dark glasses over the shell's eyes. Then a dark-haired woman in a dress leaned down close and asked a few questions. The shell answered. The words were reflex, nothing more than an automatic response.

The memories of Spencer Duncan ebbed, slowly losing their power, a sea of personality receding like tide waters, draining away to reveal a rocky protrusion in their midst. As the waters fled, that stony node in the seas reasserted itself; this was the core that had been—and was again—Ashley Ross.

As she regained awareness of herself, Ashley released a sobbing scream. Tears welled immediately, spilling from her eyes and pooling in her glasses. Shaking, she drew breath to yell again but was drawn up short as her stomach rebelled. She gagged, stomach heaving. She pulled her arms tightly around the knees she'd drawn up to her chest. She wanted to pull in on herself and simply vanish. Instead, she sobbed in agony at the thought of what Spencer had done to a little girl named Jessica Graves.

Ashley's stomach rebelled again. She wretched, sobbed a bit, then wretched again.

A hand gently stroked her hair. A voice whispered soothing words. Ashley latched on to these, on to the tenderness behind them.

"It's all right. I'm here," her Shepherd said, voice calm and level.

Everything from the Reflection burned in her head. She knew who she was again but felt Spencer's memories clawing at her soul. She twisted in revulsion at the smallest part of his depravity, but that disgust was only part of her reaction. Another part, a very large part of her mind now eaten up with Spencer's essence, remembered the ecstasy at the same memories. This expectant pleasure, even more than his actions themselves, made her wretch again.

Her body eventually quit shaking, but a long, wail poured from her, reverberating off the walls and echoing in the tiny room. Clammy tendrils of hate and horror rippled up and down her arms. Her skin crawled, and the hair on the back of her neck stood up. Hoping to blot the world from her mind, she squeezed her eyes shut. A small whimper escaped her lips, and her eyelids snapped open; Jessica's still form and blank eyes waited in the darkness.

"Come here, Ashley. Up." Mrs. Raines' voice was soft but firm. Her hands gripped Ashley's arms, and Ashley was gently pulled to her feet. Her legs swayed weakly, but she was able to stand, barely, by leaning on her Shepherd.

Ashley's eyes fell on Spencer Duncan, and she winced. He was staring at her, wide-eyed. Tears ran down his cheeks, and confusion and shame painted his face as clearly now as desire had when she'd entered the room. He stared at her for only an instant before ducking his head and shielding her from view with his hand.

The torture of what he had done to Jessica Graves burned in her mind and fueled an angry fire that burned so hot it lit her cheeks with red fury. Spencer's life still rang as loudly as her own, though, and she still felt that burning lust as he'd leered down at the girl; she still felt the ecstatic anticipation as he toyed with her. Those memories incited her stomach to lurch again, but this time Ashley fought down the urge to vomit.

Am I a monster now? Am I like Spencer?

Spencer looked around the room. "I did it," he said hoarsely. His lawyer began to splutter, but Spencer cleared his throat. His voice was still soft but noticeably stronger when he continued. "I did it. I raped her. I killed her. I did it. I'll sign whatever you want. I . . ." He broke off. "I . . . I . . ." He shook his head angrily and then dropped it onto the table, sobbing.

"Well, that'll expedite matters," said the well-dressed man Ashley now recognized as the district attorney. He was watching Spencer with a mix of disgust and relief. "We'll still need Ashley to sign the typical Mirror papers, of course."

"I . . . I can't . . ." Ashley began, but cut off abruptly with a sharp intake of breath.

Behind the man, a black sign loomed high on the wall. Unreadable symbols melted into letters, and the letters into words.

"Please . . . do not smoke . . . in this room," Ashley read slowly, her voice shaking. The DA turned around to glance over his shoulder and shrugged when he saw the sign. "I can read," Ashley explained quietly.

All of Spencer's memories played in her head, burned there against her will, but in memory there was knowledge. Spencer had never paid much attention in math and science, but the bits and pieces he picked up stood head and shoulders above anything Ashley had learned. Every book he'd ever read, everything he'd ever learned she also knew. Even how to read. The knowledge of a lifetime had been donated amid the pain.

Spencer's lawyer was talking hurriedly to his client, and Ashley heard him hiss, "Don't sign anything. You're in shock from the Reflection. Once it wears off, you'll regret . . ."

"Shut up." There was no strength in Spencer's voice, but there was conviction. Spencer opened his mouth to speak again, but shut it without another word, and he shivered. Lust had fired the young man's eyes as Ashley had walked in; horror washed over him too fully now to hold much room for anything else.

"Sign the affidavit," Mrs. Raines said to Ashley as the DA slid a stack of papers onto the table. In his hand he extended a pen.

Tired legs allowed no more than halting steps, and Ashley made the journey only with the support of the Shepherd. Each step brought her closer to Spencer, and that made her stomach roil.

Still shaking, Ashley gingerly lifted the pen from the DA's grasp and wrapped her fingers around it, the muscles in her hand moving stiffly, arcing around the pen with exaggerated unfamiliarity. In her mind, holding a pen came naturally, but her body was unused to the grip. Ink rolled onto the page, affixing a shaky signature to the attestation of Spencer's guilt.

A finishing flourish marked the second *s* in her last name, and Ashley dropped the pen back onto the table. Studiously avoiding Spencer's eyes, she looked up at her Shepherd. Words bubbled in her mind, but none escaped, and she settled for staring nervously up at the woman.

"I think we're done here. A pleasure as always, Carol," the DA said brightly. Turning toward the table, he said, "I still need that statement from you. We can draw up the documents elsewhere." Spencer nodded dully while his lawyer threw an irritated glance between the DA and his client. The DA made his exit briskly.

The movement from the defense's side of the table was more sluggish. Spencer didn't look as worn as Ashley felt, but he pulled to his feet with obvious effort, and it was halting, shuffling strides that followed in the DA's wake. His lawyer was still talking.

"As your counsel, I strongly advise against this. You haven't signed anything yet. We can chalk up your confession to the stress of the moment, the uncertainty of what that girl did to you . . ."

"I told you to shut up, Warren," Spencer growled just as the two men disappeared from sight beyond the door.

Ashley and Mrs. Raines were alone. Silence reigned for a moment until the heater rumbled to life, casting its monotonous whir into the room. A blast of warm air brushed Ashley's face, but she barely noticed. Twisting her head around to gaze up at the Shepherd, the girl swallowed hard and whispered, "Can I go now?"

"Just a few minutes," Mrs. Raines promised. "Sit down and rest. You don't want to push too hard." Even as she spoke, she guided Ashley to an unused chair. Ashley collapsed into the padded seat, sighing with relief as she did so. Mrs. Raines claimed the seat beside her.

"Do you want to talk?"

Ashley shook her head, though she did so without much conviction. "I'm . . . I'll be okay."

Mrs. Raines leaned back, tapping a finger thoughtfully on her lips. "I can count on one hand those who've shown even that much resolve after the first Reflection. You're tough, which is good; you'll need every scrap of strength you can muster." Ashley shifted uncomfortably and turned to gaze out the dingy window. Mrs. Raines rested a hand on her arm. "You're not Spencer Duncan, you know."

"But I am!" Ashley insisted. "I've got his whole life up here!" She gestured to her head and slumped wearily into the chair. "I remember all sorts of stuff. I remember what he got for his eighth birthday; I don't even remember what I got for my eighth birthday, and that was only four years ago. Everything he did, or felt, or wanted. I've done those things, or felt those emotions, or wanted those . . ." She trailed off and licked her lips nervously. "I can still see Jessica lying there . . ." That wasn't any easier and even set her insides lurching. Drawing all the strength she had, Ashley said, "I didn't *see* Spencer kill her, Mrs. Raines—I killed her."

Straightening, the Shepherd snorted. "I spent a few years teaching before I started as a Shepherd, and one thing my students learned quickly was that I don't tolerate much nonsense, certainly not from a girl as bright as you." Ashley managed a weak smile at the compliment, but the grin slid away quickly. "Spencer Duncan killed Jessica Graves, and for better or worse, you have his memories. Regardless of what you now remember, though, you're still Ashley Ross. Spencer Duncan will build no new memories in your head; you have everything of his you'll ever have."

"But . . ."

Mrs. Raines waved her to silence with a stiff gesture and plowed on. "It's not perfect, I know. Everything about his life is so vivid now. That makes it hard to ignore." She shrugged. "Vivid or not, though, you're a far better person than Spencer."

"How do you know?"

Mrs. Raines smiled. "Because unlike him, you're agonizing over Jessica's death, the senselessness of it, the horror of it."

"Spencer felt bad afterward. He hated that part of him; he felt out of control."

"I'll bet he still told himself he didn't deserve to go to jail, though. He may have felt bad for her, regretted what he'd done, but he never made amends. He never felt he deserved to be punished for it, did he?"

"Not really." She paused, considering. "So why did he confess?"

Mrs. Raines sighed tiredly. "The power of a Mirror is to take on a person's entire life and show it back to them. Spencer received, as vividly as you, the entirety of his life in the breadth of seconds. But you took it on and played his role. His experience was more confusing. He didn't see it as you did."

Ashley wrinkled her forehead in confusion. "I don't understand."

"Like the rest of us, Spencer could only evaluate himself through his own point of view. That's all any of us can do unaided. But Mirrors do more than simply gain a person's memories. Today you showed Spencer his life in a way he'd never seen, and in a way, quite frankly, he wasn't ready for. He saw it as someone else would. He watched it as a neutral observer."

Ashley shrugged. "Why does that matter?"

"We all tell ourselves we're unbiased, but it's a lie. It's one of the many lies we tell ourselves. We pretend we're thinner than we really are, or prettier, or happier, or younger"—she gestured to herself—"than reality says. Over time, the lie takes hold, and we can almost believe it. The bathroom scale, or the mirror, or protesting joints are all reminders of the truth we're ignoring, but practice makes perfect, and life makes for plenty of practice in ignoring facts.

"I'm sure," she continued, "that Spencer told himself plenty of those lies. That he wasn't really going to hurt Jessica, or that he deserved that moment of pleasure, or something equally absurd. And, given time, he could at least pretend he believed it.

"But a Mirror is an unusual thing. Your eyes can feed no deception. When you play back a life for someone, you show them as they truly are. All delusions of grandeur or importance, of youth or wealth or any other construct we lean on is stripped away in those beautiful silver eyes of yours. Having every excuse shattered is like pulling every support column from the lobby of a skyscraper. Spencer had more, or at least worse, lies than most, and the effect upon him from the collapse was staggering."

Ashley swallowed. "You sound like you know."

"When I said your sweater matched your eyes, I wasn't guessing. I've met a Mirror's gaze twice in my life, both times while working, and I wouldn't do it again for any amount of money." She paused as if sizing up her young charge, then said, "I don't envy your talent, Ashley, but I envy the strength that allows you to use it."

"Thank you," Ashley responded quietly, dropping her gaze to the floor. "But I don't want to ever do this again."

Mrs. Raines smiled sadly. Ashley braced herself, expecting more lectures on how she would find the strength, or that she had no choice in the matter. When the Shepherd spoke, though, the topic had nothing to do with the coming Reflections. "I know you want to get home. Are you ready?"

Ashley hesitated at the question, and Mrs. Raines added, "Best to get going now. Waiting won't make these feelings go away."

"Yeah. I want to go home."

Mrs. Raines extended a hand to Ashley and pulled her to her feet. Her legs still shook uncertainly, but Ashley could stand unaided. As long as the pace was slow, she could even walk alone.

She didn't have to, though. All the way back to the car, and even into her house, her Shepherd never left her side.

— CHAPTER 8 —

Cole Bryant stood in a small-town hospital watching his subject from just inside her room.

Amy Langley, sixteen years old, lay collapsed in the sleep of utter exhaustion. Her dark hair was splayed about her head in tangled strands, and a thin string of drool fell across her pillow. Her breathing was so soft as to be inaudible; the gentle rise and fall of her chest served as the only indication of life. Thirty-one hours of labor exhausted a person—or so Bryant had been told.

"Amy." His first attempt at rousing her was soft, but he grew progressively louder as she slept through his calls. It wasn't until his fourth try that she finally stirred.

The girl's eyes opened, and her face displayed several emotions in rapid succession: shock at her sudden awakening, horror at her disheveled appearance, discomfort with his unexpected presence, and, finally, curiosity. She looked past him to the door, which had been left open only a crack, then looked at the call button. She reached for it with fumbling fingers but stopped just shy of pressing it.

"Who are you?"

"Dr. Cole Bryant. I'm the Mirror specialist."

"Oh." She paused, clearly working through this information. A sudden recognition dawned. "I know why you're here."

"That makes this easier," Bryant said calmly, pulling a nearby chair next to her bed.

"I don't want to talk to you. I want you to go away."

Cole ignored this, taking his seat. "There is paperwork that must be signed when a Mirror is born."

Amy looked away, her gaze directed toward the window. "I'm not going to sell him to you."

This was the usual response. By now everyone in the country knew who he was and ostensibly what he did. That they were mostly correct in their assumptions hurt his cause, but he'd been practicing his pitch for close to thirty-five years now. He knew where to push on people and where to back away. He had a natural feel for it all by now, but preparation always helped.

Nowadays a simple test could determine whether an unborn child might be born a Mirror. Even a highly accurate test fell victim to the false-positive paradox, though, and that meant only one in every twenty or so positive results actually led to a Mirror birth.

Every potential positive was passed along to the Mirror Review Board, and the board's researcher, Maria, dug up data on all of them. She assiduously pursued every possible lead and compiled all that information into a dossier. Her data wasn't perfect, but with her preparation, his close rate had climbed over the years to just above 50 percent.

Today was different. Afraid to tell her parents, Amy had gone most of her pregnancy without any kind of prenatal care and thus missed that crucial test. When Dillon Langley entered the world at 3:34 a.m. and was definitively identified as a Mirror, it had come as a huge shock to Amy, the hospital staff, and the Mirror Review Board. In a frenzy of early morning activity, the board's logistics expert, Peter, had booked flights and rental cars for Bryant, while Maria had started what research she could. She was very good, but even with the bits she had managed to assemble, there were large gaps.

Bryant had been visiting new mothers of Mirrors for years now, and he'd learned to quickly evaluate a situation. Sometimes, if rarely, Maria's information was incorrect or incomplete, and he'd had to adjust on-the-fly. He'd learned to read visual cues and could tell a lot from tone of voice and phrasing.

He loved the logical aspect of all of this. He loved figuring out what made a person tick. Every such interaction was a chance for him to solve a puzzle. He'd always been better with concepts than people, and focusing on the inherent riddle in these interactions made it a far more enjoyable experience. In that way, he appreciated these unplanned visits for the challenge they presented.

Even today he wasn't completely bereft of guidance, though. Maria's hasty research turned up that Amy had voluntarily left her house when she eventually told her parents she was pregnant. She'd bounced between friends' homes a bit before finally moving in with one of her aunts. That act of kindness had earned the aunt in question a vitriolic series of confrontations with Amy's parents.

Ultimately, Amy's story implied a strict upbringing that included little tolerance for disobedience or mistakes. By Maria's account, though, Amy Langley had been a good student who got along with her parents, was active in her church, and wasn't seen as a troublemaker at school.

Amy's body language and appearance confirmed much of Maria's research. She was clearly distressed but not argumentative. She was reserved, perhaps a little shy. Cole didn't notice any overt signs of rebellion, either; her hair wasn't dyed an unnatural color, and he didn't see any unusual piercings. The only decoration she wore was a silver chain around her neck with a cross on it.

Cole himself wasn't religious, but he did appreciate religion.

All in all, everything he saw reinforced his initial assessment: she was a generally compliant kid from a controlling family, a kid who had gotten caught up in a moment of passion.

No, there was a problem with that reasoning: if she was so willing to surrender, why had she left home?

"The question of guardianship is important to you," Bryant answered smoothly. "Many new parents wish to start there.

Unfortunately, my focus cannot be so narrow." He reached down, popped open his briefcase, and pulled out several thick stacks of paper. He gently placed the first on the tray beside her bed. "Start with this. It's an overview of the Mirror phenomenon. It includes scientific perspectives as well as the response of most major world religions."

"Religious responses?" Amy asked, leaning forward.

"Some people want to know what God's supposed response to Mirrors is." His usual impulse was to dismiss it as meaningless, but he fought down that urge today. Amy had come from a devout Christian home where her father was some kind of leader in the church. Dismissing her faith out of hand would probably be the quickest way to end this meeting. Instead, he said, "I confess that is not my area of expertise; another member of the board assembled that."

Amy nodded slowly, and Bryant moved ahead. "The second section of that packet includes the laws and statutes currently governing Mirrors in this country. Included are descriptions of their work in the justice system as well as explanations of the legal portions in layman's terms. This includes a list of common questions among new Mirror parents."

"Finally, at the end are forms that must be filled out. Whether you choose to turn him over to the government or to keep him, we need the documentation."

"I'm keeping Dillon," Amy said immediately.

Bryant regarded her sternly. "Read through the documentation first."

The first hint of fire burned in her eyes, but she eventually broke the gaze and glanced away. She frowned, swallowed hard, and began to read. Bryant left her to find a cup of coffee.

It took him longer than expected, and by the time he returned, she was busily working her way through the papers. One stack, flipped facedown, rested at her right elbow, while the remainder awaited her attention at her left. She had managed to procure a highlighter from somewhere and it bobbed up and down in her mouth as she chewed it gently. Occasionally she would reach up, pull it free, and mark a section of text before popping it back between her teeth.

When she finally noticed him, she nodded back to the chair he'd pulled over earlier. Her eyes were clearer now. She hadn't shaken off the torpor entirely, but there was a clarity there he hadn't seen before.

Amy flicked her eyes to his cup, then asked, "Is that for me?"

"I didn't know you drank coffee."

"I gave birth this morning after more than thirty hours of labor. I definitely drink coffee."

"Of course. My apologies," Cole said, holding the Styrofoam cup out for her. "My bedside manner has never been good."

Amy greedily took the cup. Cole let it go, carefully maintaining his poker face; he didn't want her to see how irritated he was at surrendering his drink. Still, it was the proper choice. Even small seeds of compassion could reap returns in these negotiations.

Cole briefly considered going out in search of a replacement but immediately rejected the idea. Amy was almost to the crux of matter, and he wanted to be here when she reached it. So he sat, sans caffeine, and watched as she took small sips of black coffee whenever she pulled the highlighter from her mouth to mark a passage.

This continued until she stopped suddenly. Her mouth dropped open, and the marker fell into her lap. A thick line of neon lime blazed onto her hospital gown as it fell. She blinked once, turned to look at Cole, then did a double-take as her gaze whipped back to the paper.

"That . . . that is a lot of money," she said in a whisper. "Like winning the lottery."

Cole nodded solemnly. "In a typical year, the United States will welcome six children with Mirror abilities. Even if all of those children were given to government care and raised to be part of the justice system, we'd still be unable to meet the requests for their services. As you might expect, though, parents are unwilling to surrender their children. In the end, less than half of Mirrors we have end up with the Justice Department, and many of those come from broken homes."

Or were born to young single mothers, he added silently to himself.

"No matter the sum, the money offered is an inefficient lure. Most people perceive it exactly as you do: a purchase. Or a bribe. That's not how I see it, though. These people are giving their children to the country, to justice itself. No price we pay can assuage that loss. We can't put a dollar value on justice, and we definitely can't put one on your child's life. It's all we have, though.

"We're not buying children, Miss Langley, we're thanking you for giving them up to a greater good."

Amy frowned. "It's just semantics."

"Of course it is. I frame it as best I can, but there's no escaping the taint on it. If I had my way, there'd be no money involved at all."

That was a lie. He'd fought hard to get the offer as high as it was. However, by downplaying it, he'd managed to play to people's nobility. As long as they saw the money as a bribe, they treated it with the same disdain. Pretending that the money wasn't important helped nudge the decision from the realm of economic considerations to social ones.

Tell someone you wanted to buy their children, and no amount of money was enough. The idea was so repugnant they wouldn't even hear you out. But if you could frame it differently, point out the social advantages of the deal—particularly for the children themselves—people would at least consider the issue. It was a fantastic mix: social pressure and financial grease. It was a tricky maneuver, but Cole had gotten good at it.

"So you think people would give you their kids for nothing?"

"Not 'nothing,'" Cole said. "You haven't finished reading.

"Every Mirror dies young," he continued. "All of them. Every mother wants to believe her child is the exception, but . . ."

"Wait. What? All of them?" Amy's eyes were wide, her hands gripping the blanket with white-knuckled fists.

"Every Mirror dies young," Cole repeated, baffled. This was one of the two facts everyone he spoke to knew: he came with money, and Mirrors lived short lives.

"I thought it was just the government ones. The ones who Reflect criminals."

"No. Average life expectancy for all Mirrors is just over fifteen years. In fact, over the course of . . ."

"So he's going to die anyway."

This last was delivered in a whisper, and Cole almost didn't catch it. She wasn't speaking to him, instead staring out the window at the gently falling snow. Her shoulders sagged, and he saw the reflection of tears welling in her eyes.

Her words rang in Cole's head. *He's going to die anyway.*

Anyway.

Suddenly all the pieces fell into place. Cole knew what made her tick, why she'd left home, and what might compel her to give her son over to the state. He fought down a smile as a surge of adrenaline hit him.

"You really want what's best for him, don't you?"

Amy nodded, a tear running down her cheek.

"It can't have been easy for you. Being pregnant in high school in a small town. When it came out, I'm sure you suffered your fair share of finger pointing and insults. And I'm sure your parents were disappointed."

The girl huddled down, wrapping her arms around herself. This was a dangerous game. Push too hard and she might simply break. He had to use just the right amount of pressure.

"I believe many girls in your shoes would have chosen to simply avoid the teasing. A simple medical procedure, and no one would have to know."

She was crying in earnest now, her forehead resting on her right palm while her fingers gripped her hair. Her left hand gripped the cross she wore.

"You didn't, though. Why not?"

"Abortion is murder," Amy answered instantly, even through the tears.

"Your parents taught you that?"

"Yes." She hesitated, then shook her head. "They lied, though. They don't really believe it."

Cole feigned shock. "They don't?"

Anger replaced tears. "My dad's an elder in our church. He's respected by the town. He wants to run for state legislature. He gave me all kinds of excuses for why it would be best for me, but I knew what he really meant. He didn't want people to look down on him. He didn't want to lose his position because of a disobedient daughter.

"But I knew it was wrong. I told him so. Told him he was being selfish and that I wouldn't kill my baby for him." Her voice cracked again, and the tears began anew. "And then he told me that as long as I lived under his roof . . ." She swallowed hard and shrugged. "So I left.

"It doesn't matter, though. Dillon is still going to die. It doesn't matter."

Someone more empathetic might have leaned in and hugged her or whispered comforting words. Sadly, the remark about his poor bedside manner was the truest thing Cole had told Amy. While he'd gotten good at wrapping his case in a blend of truth and lies, such sympathy would be crafted totally of artifice. It was, unfortunately, who he was.

"It matters to him."

Amy rubbed a sleeve across her eyes and looked at him curiously.

"It matters to Dillon. He's not dead yet. You made the right choice. He's alive because you stood up for him. Even though it was hard. Even though it cost you your home. Why, though? Why do you believe so strongly in it that you were willing to destroy your own life?"

"Because God knows us before we are born. Because he has a plan for us."

"And how exactly has that changed?"

Amy opened her mouth to respond, then closed it again. Her eyes went wide, and she gasped.

"You think I was given Dillon so he can help people?"

"I cannot claim to know the workings of God," Cole said, spreading his hands. "But it makes sense. Plenty of girls in your shoes would have chosen the convenient path. You stood strong, and now he's here. Alive. And he has a purpose."

"I . . . I need to think about it."

"Of course," Cole said. "It's a lot to absorb."

He moved toward her door but stopped at the threshold. "I'm going to get a cup of coffee. I'll be back in a bit. I don't want to rush you, but the law says we have to get all the paperwork signed by tomorrow."

Amy nodded thoughtfully. He thought he heard her praying as he strode away.

The negotiation wasn't over, but Cole was convinced this one would go his way. Amy's son would be alive and cared for even if she wouldn't be raising him. Amy would get the money she needed to live a life independent of her idiot parents and could easily afford college if she wanted. In the end she'd even get the warm fuzzy feeling that came with furthering "God's will."

Yes, Cole Bryant didn't believe in God, but he definitely appreciated religion.

— CHAPTER 9 —

"Come on, it's time to go." Sam's words were barely more than a whisper, but his deep voice seemed to boom regardless of volume.

Huddled in a chair at the airport, Thomas sat with his knees pulled to his chest, arms wrapped protectively around his legs. He'd buried his face in the gap between his arms, hoping to shut out the rest of the world. There'd been a sort of respite, if not quite freedom, in the shadowy cavity there.

The Shepherd's words were an intrusion into that solitude. They were a reminder that an entire universe existed outside the dark vacuum he had created. He didn't want to return to that world, so he closed his eyes, huddled deeper into his protective crouch, and ignored the call to rejoin reality.

A thick hand gripped Thomas shoulder and gave an encouraging squeeze. "No stalling. It's time to go home."

What if I don't want to go home?

In the confused dance playing out in Thomas's mind, that thought had pushed its way to the forefront on several occasions. Home brought warm thoughts of his family. These provided warm feelings of strength and love but also made his cheek burn with the remembrance of pain.

That wasn't my dad! The thought was desperate, almost pleading. That it was also true didn't seem to matter. Thinking of "Dad" brought both the love Thomas Ross felt and the fear and disgust

Dennis Carson felt. The two opposing realities swirled into a confusing blend that left a queasiness in Thomas's stomach.

Worse, while Dennis's emotions toward his father played havoc on Thomas's feelings, it was Dennis's own reactions that haunted Thomas the most. Thomas remembered how his cheek burned but recalled the throbbing of his hand just as clearly. The fury that drove the man to strike his son rang as true as the fear of his own dad. Thomas bore several recollections of hitting Alan, and there were numerous memories where Dennis's anger seethed just under the threshold of his self-control. It was the only glance into parenthood granted to Thomas.

Dad had never hit him like that, but he'd seen his father angry. Like Dennis, was Dad letting his anger burn just below the surface? Was he going to push the man too far one day?

"They're waiting to board, Thomas."

"Can't we just stay here for another day or two?" It was a stupid question, but he waited for the answer anyway.

"I'll bet Ashley's looking forward to seeing you."

His sister's name calmed the spike of anxiety that thoughts of his parents had generated. She might understand the confusion he felt, the revulsion pouring through him. Maybe he could talk to her. His spirits lifted just slightly at the image of his sister waiting for him.

"All right," Thomas said. Raising his head from the sheltering cocoon, he uncurled his limbs and slid to the floor. He stood unsteadily, swaying on feet half asleep. Sam reached out an arm to steady him, and Thomas gripped it instinctively.

Thanks," he muttered, his voice barely audible. The Shepherd didn't speak but nodded appreciatively.

Shepherd. The word burned in his head for a moment, seeking connections. Memories from Dennis sprang to the front, fighting for prominence.

Seven years old, he was dressed in a robe and bore a curved stick in one hand and a stuffed lamb in his other—a shepherd in the church's Christmas play. His stomach roiled in nervous fits even though he had no lines and did nothing more than move across the stage following the 'head shepherd,' an older boy in the fifth grade. Dennis's eyes scanned the darkness, searching the shadowy pews for his parents. His father had come to see the play, and he certainly didn't want to screw up the whole affair.

Thomas mentally shoved the scene aside, frustrated how easily the other man's memories rushed to fill the gap of any inquiry.

He followed his Shepherd down the plane's aisle, heading for the seats at the back reserved for Mirrors and their keepers. Thomas slid in first, claiming the window seat again. Sam closed the curtain that separated them from the rest of the passengers, then sat down and secured his seat belt.

"Shepherd," Thomas said quietly, another string of memories rising with the word. This time those stolen experiences played closer to his world. "It's your title. It's an insult, too. People who don't like what the government does to Mirrors."

Exhaling sharply, Mr. Barton released the mechanism and turned to look at him. Licking his lips, he opened his mouth twice before finally speaking.

"Liberators can be cruel."

"Liberators?"

"It's what people who oppose Mirror justice call themselves."

Thomas nodded, realizing that Dennis Carson knew that. That Thomas knew it. Was there a difference anymore?

The big man continued. "In their fight against Reflections, the Liberation movement needed to paint an ugly picture of the process. Displaying ingenuity, if not exactly kindness, the Liberators grabbed the positive image of a shepherd caring for his sheep and twisted it into a negative. They use the name Shepherds to imply that we are leading lambs to the slaughter."

Thomas swallowed. "Isn't that what you're doing?"

Sam's face fell, and he looked genuinely sad. "Is that what you think?"

65

Outside, the terrain began to glide slowly past the window. Thomas afforded the sight only a passing glance. Thanks to Dennis Carson's penchant for travel, Thomas now possessed enough flying experience to satiate even his eager curiosity.

"What am I supposed to believe?" he demanded. "Six more years, and that's if I'm lucky. "I'm gonna lose my will to live. I'm gonna give up. Every Reflection is a step closer to despair so great it'll kill me." Thomas swallowed, trying to fight back tears. "Does it help you sleep at night knowing that you're not the one pulling the trigger? Is that what you tell yourself after each Reflection?"

Over the speakers, the pilot announced the coming takeoff. Acceleration pressed Thomas into the firm foam padding, but he kept his gaze unwaveringly directed at the Shepherd. That odd sadness played at the corners of the man's mouth. He let the angry questions hang unanswered for a moment, and the jet was angled up into the sky before the man spoke.

"Escorting Mirrors never made a man wealthy, and I doubt it ever will. If you don't take a job for the money, then it should provide satisfaction. Instead, this is the most thankless, draining, difficult job I've ever done."

"Then why do it?"

"That's a question I ask myself almost every day. I suppose I could hand in my resignation, leave this behind, and trade back my suit and tie for a lab coat. But even if I went home tonight a free man, you'd still be scheduled to Reflect next Thursday.

"Nothing I do, either as Shepherd or not, will change your lot in life. You're going to Reflect criminals even if I'm mixing chemicals in a lab somewhere. Of course, if I'm not here, someone else will step in to take over.

"To that replacement you may be nothing more than a tool, and the Reflections nothing more than a way to put food on the table and pay the bills. I've seen a few like that in my time, and they hurt more than they help. If you're looking for Shepherds leading lambs to slaughter, I nominate them."

Sam leaned forward conspiratorially. "Thomas, I do this job because someone has to, and I'd rather it be someone who cares about the Mirrors he's charged to protect." He sighed and leaned back. "I care. I care about you. It may not look like it, but I do this because I really want to make a difference."

Thomas frowned. That made no sense. How could you hope to change something by being a part of it? If Sam really wanted to do something, he should have become a Liberator.

"You're a coward," Thomas said quietly, huddling up against the window. "You're too afraid to be a real Liberator, so you do this instead. You tell yourself you're helping when you're just making it worse."

Sam grimaced, and his whole face seemed to crumple with the motion. Thomas expected him to turn away, but he didn't.

"I know it's hard to believe, but I'm here to help. I'll do whatever I can to make this easier."

"Then let me go."

"Go where? You won't get far with that tracker on your ankle."

"Then just . . . stop doing this."

"And someone else would take my place."

"Just . . . just make it better!"

What did he mean? He didn't even know. It just hurt. Everything hurt, and he wanted someone to fix it.

Thomas curled up, pulling as much into a ball as he could. He felt tears in his eyes but fought them down. He'd always hated crying with his glasses on; the frames trapped the tears inside. Today, though, he didn't want to show weakness to his jailer.

He felt Sam's hand on his shoulder and tried to jerk away but couldn't get any farther from the man. He settled for burying his face away, hiding in the dark hollows of his hands.

"I want good things for you, Thomas. I want good things for Mirrors. I want you to live a long life and find happiness."

"Won't happen," Thomas shot back. "I'm going to die in a few years. You know that."

"You're not dead yet, are you?"

"The glass is always half full for you, isn't it?" Thomas asked, turning back to glare. "I guess it's easier to be an optimist when it's not your glass."

"You're right. I'm sorry."

Lines of regret creased the big man's forehead. The two stared at each other a moment more before the Shepherd nodded sadly to himself and released Thomas's shoulder. Thomas sighed tiredly and let his head drop over to rest against the window; his eyes scanned the countryside as it crept slowly past, but he couldn't really make himself focus on or care about what he saw.

Given the delays waiting for a plane and the time spent in the station after the Reflection, Thomas guessed it was after three o'clock now. Middle of the afternoon on November 12th. There were no celebrations today, and likely no meal at McMurray's. He didn't feel like making the annual visit to the restaurant even if his parents decided there was time enough this evening.

Unlike his sister, Thomas had never anticipated today's Reflection. The unknown had terrified him as much as it intrigued her. Through it all, though, he'd held on to the celebration of their birthday as something exciting.

It seemed insignificant now. More than four decades of another person's life rattled around inside his head. What was a twelfth birthday when you'd known forty?

He frowned. Did those memories make him an adult? Did remembering the life of a grown-up make you one?

In the immediate aftermath of the Reflection, Thomas had assumed it did. As he stumbled weakly from the stark room in the courthouse, he'd held on to the belief that what he'd done today had turned him all grown up. All the memories, all the thoughts, all the remembered lessons surely made it so.

Only it didn't.

He remembered how Dennis Carson, at forty, had barely noticed the passage of each birthday. At the end, maybe he'd even hated each one a little. That was the adult perspective on it. That was how grown-ups saw it.

Thomas wanted his birthday party. He wanted the cake and presents. He wanted his family. He wasn't grown up; he wasn't even sure he wanted to be.

His tears started falling, finally, manifesting as nothing more than a stinging wetness that prickled the eyes and blurred the countryside passing thousands of feet below. He shoved down hard on that misery, fighting to keep the tears locked away.

Beside him, Sam dug around in his pocket for a moment, then pulled out the cookie Dad had tossed over that morning. Holding it out he said, "Hungry?"

Something in that simple gesture destroyed the little resolve he had left. Pushing away from the window, Thomas buried his face in the Shepherd's jacket, stifling his bone-deep wailing against the big man's chest. A part of him still hated the man, resented what he did for a living, but he was also the only port in this storm.

As Thomas wept into his Shepherd's shoulder, the man stretched an arm around him and whispered, "I'm here."

Thomas felt the man's fingers unlatch his glasses from behind his ears. His training kicked in, and he stiffened, but Sam said, "Don't worry. We're isolated, and my glasses are on."

Needing no more invitation, Thomas pulled the glasses away from his face and buried himself in the Shepherd's jacket. He cried so hard he could hardly breathe, but he needed to talk, needed to share what had happened. Between gasping breaths and shudder-ing sobs, he managed to piece together what he'd experienced and how it all made him feel.

Relating memories of abuse, both received and given, sent him shaking violently. He had to stop more than once to regain enough composure to go on. Every word of those revelations burned like the fires of hell in his veins, but an odd relief swept him as he dragged the unspeakable into the air.

It wasn't for his Reflected subject alone that he cried, though. From the abuse he moved to the confusion of his own impending death and the mystery that surrounded it. He knew he would die now; no Mirror escaped that fate. Sobbing into the chest of his companion, purging himself of the day's misery, Thomas could almost understand why older Mirrors ended their lives. Almost.

Longer and longer the cathartic discharge poured forth. With every word the fury of tears assuaged a little. Pain still wracked body, mind, and heart, but the tears dried. Sniffling occasionally, he related as much of his mind's confusion as he could before the plane landed.

— CHAPTER 10 —

Daniel paced in the living room, unnerved by the silence in his house.

Most days in the Ross household were boisterous affairs. As well as the twins got along, they still found plenty to disagree on. A typical day provided Daniel and Sally practice being judges while the children got practice being lawyers. These adjudications were tedious at times but part of the heartbeat of life in the Ross family.

Of course, even when the two agreed, there was noise. They were creative; they had to be since they had been cooped up in this house their whole lives. That imagination manifested in the card and board games they made up, the short plays they performed, and the crazy new sports they devised.

He'd once caught Ashley running through the house with a jump rope knotted around her waist. The other end had been tied securely to a stuffed elephant. She'd been wearing a cape and wielding a croquet mallet while Thomas had chased her wearing one oven mitt and swinging a butterfly net with wild abandon. As near as he could figure, the goal had been for Thomas to catch the elephant. Daniel hadn't figured out the purpose of the mallet or oven mitt before he'd banished them to their room for nearly breaking a half dozen things in the chaos. After he'd ended the game, he couldn't decide whether to shake his head, laugh, or take four aspirin. He'd done all three.

Perhaps the insanity here was aided by the fact that their lives were so abnormal. For their part, Daniel and Sally needed no jobs. Their agreement with Dr. Bryant twelve years ago meant they received a government paycheck each month for being the children's caretakers. Unlike the payment they'd have received for completely signing their children over to government control, this arrangement didn't make them wealthy. They'd invested wisely with what they had, though. Neither of them would need to work again, even once the government money dried up.

Thomas and Ashley, meanwhile, wouldn't be accepted into any normal school. That was mostly irrelevant since the Reflections today would have rendered any classroom work redundant. Why send them to special schools for years when they would eclipse all the knowledge in the literal blink of an eye?

The old grandfather clock announced the hour, five long, resonant chimes, and Daniel paused in his pacing to glance at it. As the tones faded, the cloak of silence settled back into his bones. Daniel shivered; the stillness just wasn't right.

He'd hoped things would change when Ashley came home. Instead, she'd stumbled through the door leaning on her Shepherd. Carol had helped the family get situated, said goodbye to Ashley, then left without fanfare. Ashley had cried some, hugged both of her parents weakly, then cried some more. When she'd moved toward her room, she'd wobbled on unsteady legs. In the end, Daniel had wrapped her in his arms and carried her to bed. That she had held on tightly to his neck rather than protesting only highlighted just how draining the day had been.

He'd wanted to stay by her bed, to tell her it would be okay. To be sure that she *was* okay. She'd asked him to go, though, so she should cry without the tears filling up behind her glasses. He and Sally had retreated reluctantly. If there were any mercy, she'd be asleep by now.

A key rattled in the front door lock, and the dead bolt released with a sharp click.

This had to be Thomas. Daniel adjusted his stride, shifting momentum from peripatetic stress relief into productive motion for the first time in hours. He called for his wife and heard a door open deeper in the house.

Thomas and Sam shuffled slowly into the entryway. Like Ashley, Thomas slumped brokenly, his posture suggesting he stood only with his companion's aid. Unlike Ashley, though, Thomas's demeanor was one of tense wariness. Where his sister had stared at the floor while biting off sobs, Thomas kept his eyes up and stood on the balls of his feet. When those dark glasses shifted to Daniel, Thomas's muscles tensed, and then he pulled away slowly, putting Sam between himself and his father.

"Thomas." Sally called softly from behind Daniel.

That single word worked like a spell. Daniel stepped reluctantly away from the door, clearing a path between Sally and their son. From the doorway, Sam gripped Thomas's shoulder encouragingly. Thomas shuddered once, barely stifled a quivering sob, and slipped past Daniel to Sally.

She pulled him into a hug, and Thomas returned the embrace limply. Daniel heard his wife's gentle whispers trying to draw out the day's pain like poison from a wound, but Thomas clearly wanted none of it. He shook his head a few times, then shook it more firmly before pushing himself free of his mother's touch.

He took a step toward the back hallway, then turned his eyes back to Daniel. Daniel instinctively reached a hand out to his son and took a step forward. Thomas responded by drawing back again, his face going ashen.

Thomas finally said, "I . . . I'm sorry. But Dennis . . . he . . ." The words trailed into unintelligible murmurs, and Thomas shuffled his feet nervously.

"Today wasn't supposed to be like this," he continued. "Is Ashley in her room?"

"Yes."

With that, he was gone.

"Should . . . should I go after him?" Sally asked, watching the empty doorway.

Sam shook his head. "It's a bad idea."

Daniel expected the answer. Carol had said the same thing. Sally hadn't liked it then, either. "Why? Why should I abandon him?"

"Because I've seen it over and over again," Sam said. "The first Reflection is the hardest. It scrambles everything these kids know, even down to the most basic. After remembering being adults, the parent-child relationship is skewed in their minds. They'll remember how they saw you this morning, but even fresher in their minds will be the recollection of their Reflected. It will work itself out to some extent in a few days, but right now you'll only confuse them. Particularly Thomas. His experience is the worst kind of first-time scenario."

Daniel stepped closer. "What happened? Is that why he shied away?"

"The man Thomas reflected today was beaten and abused by his father and passed the same treatment on to his wife and son. Your son's confused. He's fighting the fear that he'll get the same treatment from you."

"I would never—!" Daniel began angrily, and Sam raised his arms in a gesture of surrender.

"I know," the Shepherd interrupted. "I know. Thomas told me that. But your son also has another man's life inside his head now. He has twelve years of thinking of Dad as the man you are and forty-plus years of seeing Dad as the man who hits you when you need it. He's had several hours to process, and he's actually better. Not much, but sleep and time will help that a little."

Daniel shook his head, dumbfounded. What could he say to that? How did you fight something that changed the most basic way you saw the world? Ashley's return had already set him on edge, but this was worse. Was it over already? Had they lost the war?

"Can . . . can you stick around for a bit?" Sally's question was hesitant but obviously hopeful. Daniel felt foolish for not asking it himself; they needed to talk to someone knowledgeable, and Sam had mentioned this possibility earlier that morning.

Sam nodded and gave a small smile. The Shepherd moved into the living room and took a seat on the couch. In those few seconds his entire demeanor had changed; the nervousness melted away, and he was again in his element.

"I'll get you something to drink," Sally offered. "Tea? Coffee?"

"Coffee, thanks. Black."

Daniel settled into the old wooden rocking chair across from their guest. Sam regarded him stoically, and Daniel wished the other man would remove his sunglasses. Sam's face was open now, his posture relaxed, but he still seemed locked away with the reflective glass blocking his eyes.

"You wanted to stay," Daniel said simply. "You were afraid we wouldn't offer."

"I almost always get the invitation after the first Reflection. Most of the government-hired guardians don't last long in the job, so this is usually their first time as well. They feel helpless, and all the preparation for this day suddenly isn't enough. I'm the expert in their midst, and they need to know what's happening. They want to know why a child they thought they knew recoils from their touch. They want to know how everything changed so completely in one day.

"I don't have all the answers, but I can at least be sympathetic. I can tell you the mistakes I've made with the kids, and the mistakes I've seen other caretakers make. There's no magic solution that will make it all better, but there are pitfalls that can make it worse. I just want to help you avoid those."

"So why not share all that this morning?"

"Not enough time, for one."

Daniel shook his head. "I don't buy it. You could have come earlier. Or mentioned it in previous meetings. So why keep it quiet?"

Sam sighed. "Because people can't understand. Not until they see it. You knew what was happening today. You've spent the last twelve years preparing for it. Is it like you expected?"

"No."

"It never is. Even after eight years of this, it still shocks me how poorly I judge each kid's reaction. Thomas opened up to me on the ride back; I didn't expect that."

"He talked to you, but he won't talk to us?"

"Today it's easier to talk to me. As I said, his understanding of parents and children is all askew. That's a normal reaction, but this is worse because of Dennis's acts of violence. Today's experience linked a whole bunch of emotions to the concept of "Mom" and "Dad" that he's still working out.

"I'm a wild card, though. Dennis Carson had no strong emotions or thoughts on Shepherds, so he had nothing personal to transfer to Thomas. The way Thomas views Shepherds—and me specifically—was almost unaltered by the Reflection. It's unfair that it works out that way, but it's why Cole Bryant first pushed for the Shepherd program. He knew the Mirrors would need someone unaffiliated.

"Don't worry, though, it will get better."

"When?"

"Not soon enough," Sam admitted. "The next few weeks will seem like the end of the world. Then, slowly, your children will reassert themselves. They'll push down the lives they've taken on and move toward something approaching normalcy. For the next couple of years, every week will get a bit better."

"And then?" Sally asked, standing at the edge of the kitchen. She held a mug in her hands, and it shook slightly as she held it.

"Then," the Shepherd said slowly, "you remember the good times."

— CHAPTER 11 —

Thomas pushed away from the confusion that played out in his living room. He shoved down hard on every memory that sprang up, trying desperately to think of nothing. He wanted to simply exist, to float free without associating anything he saw with anything in life. It didn't even matter at this point whether those recollections were from his life or Dennis's. He wanted to be free of it all.

What he wanted didn't matter. His brain linked thoughts, sought to remember things all on its own. He couldn't escape his brain, and his brain was confused.

Hours after the Reflection, he was finally managing to erect some very basic walls. He could toss Dennis's memories into a corner all their own. He pictured dropping them into a dark pit or throwing them into a box and locking it shut. The imagery helped, he thought. It made it feel like he was fighting back.

To recognize any given memory as Dennis's, though, he had to examine it first. So as he walked down the hallway, other similar treks sprang to mind. Some through this hallway, some through places he'd never physically traveled. The latter he kicked away into the abyss, but not before he processed them, drew on them, and felt the horrible strangeness of experiencing another person's world.

He needed clarity. He needed help. He needed the only other person he knew who could understand.

Thomas wanted to simply burst into his sister's room but forced himself to knock instead. At first he thought there was no answer, but when he knocked a second time he caught a reedy voice admitting him. He slipped in quickly, shutting the door behind him.

Ashley's overhead lights were off. Fading sunbeams left long, creeping arcs of orange splayed across the carpet but did little to illuminate the room. Behind his dark lenses, Thomas could make out shapes, but little more. His hand drifted to the switch at his right.

"I'm going to turn on the lights, okay?"

If his sister actually waited somewhere in the room, he couldn't pick her out against the shadowy forms. His question fielded no answer, either. Taking her silence as tacit acceptance, his finger flipped the switch. The gray mist of shadows evaporated in a rush of light.

With darkness banished, the room snapped into clarity. Blurry specters coalesced into comfortable familiarity, and he scanned the room anxiously. Dirty clothes overflowed from a plastic laundry basket to spill unceremoniously onto the floor, and a trio of stuffed animals held an impromptu meeting atop the chest of drawers next to a pair of rainbow socks. His sister lay in bed, blankets tucked up to her chin. When he saw her, his breath caught, and he flinched. Pulled from her face and folded neatly on the bedside table sat Ashley's sunglasses.

Thomas stepped closer, watching his sister cautiously. He'd never seen her unsafe before.

Ashley didn't move, even when tears leaked from the corners of her eyes to slide down her cheeks and drop to the sheets. Her gaze was directed toward the ceiling, but her eyes were unfocused, staring at something beyond vision. Thomas drew up next to her and knelt beside the bed. No words came to mind, so he sat quietly.

"I . . . lived it," she said finally. "I felt him rape her. I felt his lust and fear, and I felt the thrill of his absolute power over her." She shuddered. Rolling away from him, she twisted beneath the blankets, drawing herself into a ball. "I stared into that mirror on my dresser for a long time this afternoon; I wanted to Reflect myself. I wanted to know that I wasn't like him, that I couldn't do the things he did, but . . ."

". . . Mirrors can't Reflect themselves," Thomas finished quietly.

Ashley nodded to the wall. "I understand why people rape now. I understand why people murder." Tremors shook her voice, rendering it almost indistinguishable; Thomas struggled to understand her. "I didn't want to know. I don't want to know."

For a long time, he said nothing. What could he say? Dennis Carson had been beaten by his father and beaten his family in return, but the man had never raped or murdered anyone. Though Thomas and his sister had both taken on lives, their respective experiences were quite different. He guessed she couldn't understand the abuse Dennis had endured, but maybe . . . maybe she could identify with something else.

"A whole lifetime in seconds," he said in a whisper. Ashley didn't respond. "I saw everything. Lived everything. I thought I was . . ." He broke off, then, grimacing, said, "It's clearer now, but for a while it felt like I was him. It felt like he had wiped away everything inside me. I thought I was going to be him."

Ashley finally moved. With a tired sob, she rolled over but didn't bother sitting up. Those silver Mirror's eyes watched him tearfully. She stared at him, meeting his shaded gaze for a long moment before finally nodding.

"You could Reflect me," she said. "I could see myself. Know that I'm not him."

Thomas exhaled sharply. "It would kill us." That was one of the first things he remembered their parents explaining. He'd never even considered meeting Ashley's eyes on purpose. The very thought sent a shudder down his spine.

"I . . . I know." Ashley let out a sob. "I don't want to die. I just . . . it's not fair. I just want to know who I am, Thomas. I want to scrub away Spencer; I want to see *me*. I've seen him, Thomas, and I don't want to become him."

"You won't." The words were forceful, but Thomas felt hollow saying them.

Idle dreams were no more than fleeting hope, but he had dared to dream about this conversation. Riding home, he had constructed an impossible scene. Meeting Ashley, she would smile and hug him, welcoming him back. Then she'd proceed to tell him that her Reflected was innocent, that he was good and kind, and that his arrest was a mistake. She'd act like she had this morning: excited and happy to have played her part.

He usually liked ribbing Ashley for being stupidly optimistic, but he realized that today he'd fallen into the same trap. No one could endure what they had lived today and smile about it. For once, though, he wished she'd been right.

"Did your guy do it?"

Thomas looked at his sister's red-rimmed eyes, and he could see hope in them. She wanted to believe Dennis's innocence would make everything better.

Something in Thomas's gut wrenched. She still believed that he could make it better. That he could tell her it was all right, that Dennis was innocent and the hell she'd lived would suddenly all be worth it. Even after all she'd seen, she still wanted to be that optimist he despised.

If he gave her that hope, then wasn't she right? He could tell her that Dennis didn't do it, that he was innocent and that he'd gone free. He could tell her that an innocent man was with his family tonight and she'd feel like the hero she thought they were. And, then, by extension, wouldn't it give him exactly what he wanted? Hadn't he just wanted her to be right?

He sucked in his breath, opened his mouth to tell her, then closed it again.

But she was wrong.

"Dennis hit his wife," he said softly. "He said she deserved it, that it was the only way she would learn, but it was more that she said things he didn't want to hear. I don't know why she stayed with him; Dennis didn't really know either.

"That's not all." His words came in a harsh whisper. Thomas hated Dennis's dark secret, but there was still enough of Dennis's thoughts to attach an intense fear to the act of confession. "He hit his son, too. Hard." His palm tingled and he began to rub it with his other hand. "But I couldn't tell the lawyers that. They only wanted to know if he killed Kathy."

"And he did?" Ashley asked, eyes wide.

"No," Thomas said bitterly.

Ashley's brow furrowed. "I don't . . ."

"He's a bad person, Ash," Thomas said harshly. "It's all a lie. It doesn't matter that I proved he was innocent of the murder. Dennis Carson is going to keep beating his kids because he didn't kill his wife.

"We're not heroes," he continued angrily as she opened her mouth. "They've lied to us. We're not bringing justice. We're giving people the illusion of justice."

"But Spencer did rape . . ."

"I'm going to my room," Thomas said, cutting her off. "I need to think. Or not think. Maybe I can sleep."

She reached an arm out to him, but he ignored it, pushing away from her bed. Switching off the light, he snubbed her pleas.

It was all a lie. And it was going to kill him.

He pushed into his room and shut the door behind him. Sliding to the floor, he ripped off his glasses, buried his face in his hands, and cried.

—CHAPTER 12—

How can I help?" Sam asked, setting his coffee on the end table beside his chair.

Sally's hands shook as she took a seat opposite him. "What can we do? Can we fix this?"

Sam arched an eyebrow. "That depends on what you mean by 'fix it.' They're going to Reflect every Thursday from now until they die or turn eighteen. That's the standard Mirror contract. It's pretty clear."

"Can we get them to eighteen?" Daniel said.

"I'll be honest; your odds aren't good. Here in the States we've only had two make it that long."

"So it's possible," Daniel pressed.

"Not like you're thinking," Sam said somberly. "I don't want to set up false expectations. Even if they survive that long, their quality of life will be low. Both of the Mirrors who survived to eighteen didn't make it past twenty-one, and their lives were anything but normal in the intervening time.

"I've found it's best not to focus on longevity; look at quality of life instead. We have to move from 'How can we keep them alive?' to 'What can we do to make the last few years of their lives the best they can be?'"

"And if we're not willing to give up on keeping them alive?" Daniel asked, casting a glance at Sally.

"Then you still want to listen to me. Mirrors don't die because their bodies fail. You know this. Thomas and Ashley are going to kill themselves.

"Eventually it becomes too much. Everything they've experienced weighs too heavily on Mirrors, and they simply can't take it anymore. If you can keep them engaged, help them forget the daily struggles, then maybe they make it a little longer before they give in.

"Improve the quality of their life and you lengthen it as well. It's not a cure, though. You're going to lose your children before this is over."

Daniel frowned, then turned to look at his wife. Sally didn't respond, instead sitting quietly. He reached out to take one of her trembling hands, but she yanked it away and stood.

Turning toward Daniel, she pulled her shaking fingers into fists. "No. I refuse to believe that. We saved them." Then she spun and fled the room.

Daniel's heart sank as he watched her dash from the room. He took a step to follow, then stopped. It wouldn't matter. They'd had this argument plenty of times over the past twelve years. Tonight, between exhaustion and raw emotion, it would only go worse than normal.

Sighing, he dropped down onto the couch and faced the Shepherd. Sam stared into the depths of his coffee mug, politely ignoring the brief spat. Upon seeing Daniel take his seat, the other man reached up, flipped open the lock on his glasses, and pulled the protective gear from his face. He set mug and glasses on the table.

Daniel thought the Shepherd looked kinder without the silvered glass hiding his eyes. He was clearly more tired than he'd let on, though. More than just the wear and tear of an early morning, this was an exhaustion that clung to his very soul.

"No matter what we do, they're going to die," Daniel said simply.

The Shepherd nodded sadly. "I'm sorry. I thought you understood what was coming."

"We did. Sort of. We knew Mirrors killed themselves, but we'd hoped that by keeping them with us, it would help. You know, maybe if they were raised by their own parents . . ."

"I'm sure it'll help. This is definitely a better environment than the government housing with revolving-door foster parents."

Daniel frowned. "But not enough?"

"Mirrors die young, Mr. Ross. Nothing changes that. I know it's easy to blame Cole Bryant for this, but he's right. Mirrors in the system do live longer. The two who made it to eighteen were actually part of the Justice Department program."

Daniel knew that. He'd spent a lot of time thinking about it. "But don't you wonder if those families did something wrong? That if you could do it, maybe you'd fix it? Do it right?"

Sam smiled sadly and shook his head. "Not anymore."

"So what *can* we do?"

"Let them know you love them. Support them. Make sure they understand that they're not the people they've Reflected."

Daniel sat frozen for a long moment, thinking back over the homecomings they'd seen today. Ashley's quiet despair and Thomas's refusal to come anywhere near him. Their behavior had been so aberrant, so different from what he'd expected, that it left him wondering.

"Are you sure they're not?"

"They're not," Sam said firmly. "They've seen a lot, but they're not the criminals they've seen. That influence will fade, and they'll seem more like themselves as the days go by."

"Until they do this all again next week."

"Yes." Sam's look was sympathetic. "This never becomes easy, but it will become routine. You'll learn how to deal with every day as it comes. Fridays will be different from Mondays, and you'll automatically know how to approach each. As I said, each week will get better as they figure out how to cope."

"And then?"

"Don't worry about what's after that. It'll come when it comes. Find out how to enrich their lives, and help them enjoy each day."

Daniel sat for a second, absorbing the advice. "Okay. Thank you."

"What else can I do?" Sam asked.

"You said that the man Thomas Reflected . . ." Daniel paused, searching for a name.

"Dennis Carson."

"You said he hits his son?"

Sam sighed. "Yeah. It complicated things for everyone today."

Daniel arched an eyebrow. "Complicated?"

"Poor choice of words," Sam acknowledged. "Let's see if I can explain. Did you ever study Mirror legal precedents?" Sam asked.

"It's been a few years."

"Do you remember the Constitutional challenge? It was being argued that Mirror Reflections violated the Fifth Amendment. Self-incrimination."

Daniel nodded slowly. "Yes. It went all the way to the Supreme Court. There was strong public opinion on both sides. Protests in most major cities. There were even some violent clashes between the two sides. I remember seeing news footage."

"To say it was a contentious decision is to understate it dramatically. In the end, though, the justices decided that Mirror testimony wasn't governed by the Fifth Amendment but instead by the Fourth."

"It's been a long time since I took civics," Daniel admitted.

"The Fourth Amendment states that search and seizure require a warrant issued with probable cause. The court basically stated that a person's memories were property. If probable cause existed, those memories could be searched by a Mirror and then used as evidence in a court of law."

Daniel frowned. "A nice refresher, but what does that have to do with Dennis?"

"It turns out that those warrants speak to specific instances. Today, for example, the warrant was to look specifically for memories related to the murder of Kathy Carson. Mirrors can't see *just* that, though. So, they receive the whole life, but anything they see beyond the scope of the targeted memories isn't allowed as evidence."

"So, Thomas couldn't legally tell anyone."

"Yes. He tried, but the DA knows the law. Thomas was silenced before he could say anything important."

"And Dennis Carson keeps beating his son," Daniel said darkly.

Sam shook his head emphatically. "I'll put in an anonymous call to CPS tonight. I've done it before. I know Carol's made similar calls on evidence from her girls."

"Is that enough?"

"Honestly? No, but it's what I can do legally."

"I don't like that he could get away with this," Daniel said.

"Neither do I. Neither does anyone, really. It's particularly hard for Mirrors since they have actually lived the crimes. I've never worked with a kid who handled it well. I'm willing to bet it'll be even worse for Thomas since it's his first. It's probably at least part of why his reaction tonight was so strong."

Daniel nodded. "I'll tell Thomas know you're letting someone know about Dennis."

"I already did, but I'd appreciate it if you'd remind him."

They lapsed into silence again before Daniel stood up. "It's been a long day. We should all get some sleep."

"You don't have any other questions?" Sam asked, obviously surprised.

"Dozens," Daniel admitted. "But I don't think I'm in the right state of mind tonight."

"All right. I can understand that." Sam handed him a piece of paper as he stood. "That's my phone number. Call if you need anything. I'm here to help."

The Shepherd moved to the door, taking his coat from its hook. He nodded to Daniel as he pulled on his gloves and stepped outside. He waved over his shoulder, and Daniel returned the gesture. No mention was made that Sam would be back in one week to pick up Thomas; they both knew.

— CHAPTER 13 —

Wind blew the trees outside Ashley's window, casting eerie, trembling shadows across the floor. She sat on the bed with her back braced against the wall, surveying the darkness. Sleep threatened to pull her eyes shut, but she fought that end with every ounce of her failing strength.

From the bedside table, the clock proudly glowed the hour: ten minutes shy of midnight. She couldn't hope to stay awake forever, no matter how tempting that goal, but she wanted to at least finish out and see the close of this day.

Spencer Duncan was going to jail. He wouldn't be able to hurt anyone else the way he had Jessica Graves, and for that alone she could have laughed with joy. Thomas might doubt what good he had done today, but Ashley could not. Without a Mirror to give definitive testimony against him, he might well have gotten away with murder. Ashley gave a sudden literal shudder at the thought of Spencer Duncan walking free.

She hated the memories inside her head. She hated the lust and the selfish fulfillment. Her life had been altered forever, and this was only the first of hundreds of Reflections. Absorbing Spencer's life had shown her the fate that awaited all Mirrors, and she could understand why they wanted to die. A tiny part of her still wished that Thomas hadn't been wearing his glasses when he walked in. If they'd looked at each other . . .

No. She wasn't ready to die. Not yet.

Spencer had only been the first of many. More evil waited, and more justice was needed. She had the power to put men like him behind bars, to protect the world from their ravages. If she failed, if she fell, wasn't she just as responsible for their crimes?

Just because it was necessary didn't make it easy. Nothing about the Reflection had been easy. She couldn't shake the memory of Spencer standing over Jessica. She remembered leering down at the girl while Jessica whimpered piteously. The memory seared Ashley's brain and chilled her to the bone.

It wasn't the only memory that haunted her, though.

Six years old, lost in a department store and separated from his mother, a panicked Spencer cried inconsolably. Desperation and fear filled him so completely that reason vanished in their wake. He ran aimlessly, confusion alone driving his steps. Terror threatened to eat him entirely, and Ashley shuddered as she remembered that moment of absolute surrender. Collapsing to the ground, he wailed wordlessly, unable even to move. It was the most vulnerable moment of Spencer's life.

Seeing him rape Jessica horrified her, but this other scene destroyed her. The brutality of his crime made it easy to view him as a monster, but the memory of Spencer as a lost and frightened little boy made him all too human.

That moment of petrified terror, washed in confusion and vulnerability, was far too close to Ashley's own feelings. After today, she knew what it was to be alone and scared; she knew what it was to be uncertain and susceptible. The one memory was the most jarring because it was the one that gave her the strongest connection to the man toward whom she wanted to pour out unbridled hate. But in light of that connection, the heat of her fury waned. That scene of vulnerable terror reminded her that as hard as she tried, she couldn't reduce Spencer's entire life to a single evil act.

With that option barred to her, how could she cope? She knew his evil in a way that still made her insides lurch. Just because he had once been a terrified little boy didn't alter that. It was the same question she had danced around all evening, and it was threatening to tear her apart.

Her doubts stripped her of energy, sending her to seek the comfort of her bed. That comfort was a lie, though. The solitude of her blankets offered no answers.

The sudden knock on her door was so unexpected she almost fell out of bed. Acting out of habit, she threw on her glasses and locked them into place.

"Come in."

Thomas stepped inside, shutting the door behind him with a soft click. He moved slowly, picking his way through the clutter of her room to the chair by her bed. He pulled the chain on her lamp with a lazy motion, then collapsed in his seat.

"It's really boring," Thomas said without preamble.

Ashley blinked in confusion. "What is?"

"Flying."

"Oh, yeah. I know. Spencer did it all the time."

Thomas shrugged and nodded as if it were the answer he'd been expecting.

Ashley smiled wanly. "You came back."

"I had to tell you about flying," Thomas said with a shrug. "You made me promise."

"I did. I should have made you promise to tell me everything else."

Thomas paused, clearly haunted. He shot her a searching look, then took a deep breath. "Well, let's pretend I did."

Ashley's smile deepened, and Thomas even managed a thin one of his own.

As he started his tale, the grandfather clock in the entry way rang out the new day in long, somber tones.

PART II

Thirteen Years Old—Confessions

The science behind the Reflection mechanism is still a mystery. This lure of the unknown has drawn much conjecture over the years but few facts. Current theories range from the rigorously scientific to the ridiculously magical. One of the former postulates that "patterns in the eyes trigger an autonomic response in the cerebral cortex." One of the latter is as vague as "the eyes initiate an unfettered connection between two souls." The first sounds far more scientific, but how it sounds is irrelevant since no one has managed to rigorously test it. Even if proven, that result would only create more questions as it addresses only one-half of the equation.

If anything, Mirrors show us that we are still infants in our grasp of biology and physics. Their ability is so far beyond our ken that it makes a mockery of our best attempts to categorize and comprehend it. Ultimately, I don't expect any of this to be answered in my lifetime, and while that disappoints me on an intellectual level, it doesn't hinder my work.

This seems counterintuitive to some people. I've been asked how I can advocate using Mirrors to deliver justice if I don't understand how their abilities work.

The answer is simple. I don't need to understand how electricity powers a cordless drill to bore a hole. In the same way, I don't need to understand the Reflection mechanism to make use of Mirrors.

Fortunately for us, they can fulfill their role even if we never figure out exactly how they do it.

—Excerpt from a guest lecture by Dr. Cole Bryant at Harvard University

— CHAPTER 14 —

Morning was not quite gone, and rays of sunshine bathed the Ross home in golden light. The past two days had been unseasonably warm, a brave, final reproach against the chill of mid-fall. Meteorologists cited today as the end of that trend, but the promised denouement waited, the sun still noticeably blunting November's chill. Thomas, in a concerted effort to catch as much of this summery reprieve as possible, basked on the front steps.

If he were being honest, though, a desire to be alone prompted his escape outside as much as the pleasant weather.

When he woke up that morning, Thomas had noticed blankets folded next to the couch. Blankets next to the couch meant that Dad had slept in the living room again after another fight with Mom. And, like always, the fight was played off as "something you don't need to worry about." Also, like always, Dad hadn't slept well after a night on the sofa, and his back was acting up. Grumbling was common when the man was tired, and it still made Thomas nervous. After a year, the fear that his father might hit him in an angry moment had faded significantly, but it never truly vanished. Whenever Dad was extremely touchy or grumpy, Thomas preferred to simply stay away.

Mom wasn't much better, but that was quickly devolving into an all-the-time problem as opposed to the occasional "sofa-night" dilemma. She smiled frequently and broadly but never sincerely. Those wide grins of absolute confidence never touched her eyes, and when those eyes came to rest on either of her children, a hollow look painted her whole face. Thomas knew that death waited at the end of this road, but try as he might, it was something he couldn't fully wrap his mind around. His mother could. He could see it in the furtive, pained glances she shot him when she assumed no one was watching.

Ashley, his final option, generally proved the best company of the three anyway. Unfortunately, Dad's flu from the previous week had migrated, and she had spent the past few days either sleeping fitfully or lying awake in misery. That was a pain he had no desire to share, and so had left her to her quarantine.

Upon finding himself spending all his time alone, the mitigation in fall's standard chilly fare had proved an inestimable boon. Two days ago, he had enjoyed the sunshine in the backyard. Yesterday, he finally screwed up the courage to venture out to the front steps by himself.

When he'd wandered outside yesterday afternoon, there had been a group of children playing on a lawn a couple of houses down. Even as he'd lowered himself to the porch's top step, the kids' parents had herded them roughly inside. Thomas obviously had no desire to Reflect any of them, but they apparently didn't know that. How could they know it hurt him as much it would hurt those he Reflected?

Today's story was slightly different. School was still in session so there were no frightened children to run off with his presence. No one dared wander outside to talk to their neighbors, though.

Across the street, he occasionally saw the blinds part as the lady of the house peered out. Those surreptitious glances brought him a guilty pleasure. He'd been trapped in his house for thirteen years because people were afraid of him; it seemed only fitting that same fear now kept everyone else on his block prisoner.

Imprisoning his neighbors did nothing to weaken the bars of his own jail, of course. His ankle monitor meant that without prior board approval, he was trapped at home. He'd grown to hate the thing even more over the past twelve months.

The exception was Thursdays. Every week, the world opened itself to him, embraced his presence just long enough for him to dispense justice, then insisted he return to his quiet oblivion.

His grasp on sanity was helped by the rare ray of light penetrating his dungeon. Every Mirror was granted two weeks off a year, provided they met the proper stipulations. Those weeks had to be scheduled a month in advance, required the approval of the Mirror Review Board, and couldn't be redeemed consecutively. Mom had handled all the arrangements. One of those reprieves had been the Thursday before Christmas. The other had been yesterday.

Movement drew Thomas's attention; the lady across the street was spreading the blinds again, her eyes surveying to see if he was still waiting on the steps. In a fit of cruel impulse, Thomas smiled and waved avidly at the woman with one hand. He raised the other hand to his face, his fingers brushing the metal frames of his glasses. Snapping closed with a sudden jerk, the gap in the blinds disappeared entirely. Grinning impishly, Thomas dropped his hands back to his side.

He congratulated himself on his clever taunt, then froze in surprise. While he was pranking his neighbor, a dark sedan had pulled to a stop in front of his house. Thomas frowned uncertainly; no one visited the Rosses. Moreover, who would stop willingly in front of a house where a Mirror stood guard?

Creaking, the driver's side door opened to reveal a broad-shouldered man. "Outside?" boomed a familiar voice. "You're getting brave."

"Sam!" Thomas was off the steps in an instant, running toward the Shepherd. Sam closed his door and walked around the front of the car, meeting Thomas at the end of the walk.

It was the first time since he'd started Reflecting that Thomas had seen him outside their weekly Thursday rendezvous. Dark glasses still hid the big man's eyes, as always, but over the past year, Thomas had grown to accept them as part of the man himself. Other seemingly static bits had changed, though. Gone was the suit Sam wore for every Reflection, replaced by a deep-red polo shirt and khaki slacks. Even the professional edge Sam maintained was dulled; he didn't stand stiff straight but instead leaned casually against the car.

"Hey, Sam," Thomas said, the grin returning, "Didn't you hear? I've got the week off."

Sam laughed. "Nothing like that. I'm just here to wish you a happy birthday."

"That's quite the trip for a simple greeting." Thomas smirked as he added, "They make these devices called telephones. You might have heard about them. You can talk to people all over the world, and they're way cheaper than a plane flight."

Sam ignored the good-natured jab. "I heard your sister was sick, and I thought you might be looking for a chance to get out of the house. Being stuck at home on your birthday's no fun."

Thoughts tripped through Thomas's brain at lightning speed. For the past eight days he had sought a means of escape. A mission had presented itself to him after the last Reflection, but it was something he could never ask his parents to understand. Moreover, with the ankle monitor, he literally *couldn't* do it. And now, Sam had arrived, hinting at the impossible.

"I didn't think I could go anywhere without prior approval from the board," Thomas said.

"That's true," Sam admitted. "But I'm a government trained agent specifically tasked with dealing with Mirrors. If I say I need you somewhere, I'm authorized to get you there. Nothing says I can only take you to Reflections."

Thomas smiled. "Awesome. Let's tell my parents and then take off. I'm bored out of my mind here."

It took far too long for Sam to come in, say hello to his parents, perform all the necessary small talk, and finally get back outside. After an agonizing fifteen minutes, though, he was finally free.

"Come on! Let's go!" Thomas urged.

Sam held up a finger, then bent down and pushed a button on his keychain. The little light on Thomas's ankle monitor blinked from red to green.

With an exhilarated laugh, Thomas ran to the car. He waited as patiently as he could, but every step Sam took was an agony of eternity. Thomas's heart beat like a machine gun; he was exhilarated at the prospect of time beyond the walls of home and free of Reflections but terrified at the thought of how he intended to spend that time.

As the Shepherd approached, the car let out two shrill beeps. The doors unlocked with a click, and Thomas barreled inside. Sam followed within seconds, sliding behind the wheel. He hesitated starting the car, though.

"Do you know where you want to go?"

"Yes." The word was firmer than Thomas had thought he could make it.

Sam waited a moment for something more, but when Thomas said nothing, the Shepherd spread his hands in a "go-ahead" motion. Thomas wanted to speak, but the muscles in his throat constricted. Now that he had reached the pertinent moment, telling Sam was proving little easier than telling his parents would have been.

"I could drive us," Thomas said.

"Nice try."

"Hey, I've got more driving experience than you."

"You *remember* more driving experience than me. That's not the same thing."

"It's close enough."

"Thomas, where do you want to go?" Sam's tone was clear: the day had plenty of time for games, but this wasn't one of them.

Closing his eyes, Thomas managed in a barely audible whisper, "Church of the Holy Cross."

"What?"

"Church of the Holy Cross," he repeated louder, then opened his eyes. The words burned in his mouth. "It's a Catholic church. I can guide you there."

For a long time, Sam's shaded gaze studied him. Thomas felt the confusion behind those shielded eyes. Given the option to go anywhere, to pick any of the myriad things he'd never seen with his own eyes, and he'd picked a church. He knew the questions would come. Mom and Dad always asked, even when they sensed they shouldn't.

Sam didn't ask. Instead, he shifted the car into gear and pulled away from the curb.

"Thanks," was all Thomas could manage to say, and he meant it as much for the lack of prying as for the ride. The Shepherd nodded solemnly but didn't respond.

Conversation drifted to other subjects, broken occasionally by Thomas's need to provide directions. Sam deftly navigated the streets, and Thomas knew his instructions were infallible. They had been gleaned from a man whose life he had absorbed only eight days ago, and Reflections that recent left memories almost perfect in their clarity.

This intentional focus on a stolen life was rare. The key to surviving the Reflections—as he had learned in those first precarious months following last November 12th—was to ignore the lives he had seen. Following that initial Reflection, Thomas had been sure he would drown in the sea of pain that swelled higher with each passing week. By Christmas, he was uncertain he would survive to the following summer, let alone fifteen.

The oblivion of sleep was the only break in those first few weeks. Every hour awake was torture. He found himself sleeping most of each day or lying in bed trying to sleep when his body would accept no more. Six days of each week were spent trying to lose himself in the imperfect cloak of unconsciousness and the seventh in the baptism of more unwanted images.

It wasn't until January that he finally began to pull ahead. Before that, he had gravitated to the pain in the lives he had had seen. Catharsis was a strong impulse, and though he sought it with all his heart, he could never fully purge the remains of one Reflection before the next came calling. He wasn't sure he could have done it even if he were granted a year between each.

It was after the second Reflection of the new year that he finally fought down the pain. Instead of accepting the grief of the life, instead of trying to work past it, he strove only to ignore it. Immediately after each Reflection, it was impossible. Each memory was too fresh in his mind; no amount of willpower could draw his focus away. By Saturday morning, though, the first rays of light pierced the dungeon, and Thomas drew himself out of bed to do something—anything—that would keep other thoughts away.

Staying busy was the greatest boon and the easiest way to forget the unforgettable. He'd taken up model building, and cross-word puzzles, and painting, and sketching, and any hobby he could find, so long as it drew his mind away. Ashley did the same, and together the twins assembled a rickety scaffolding on which they could climb above the river of emotions.

Nothing was perfect, and this precarious grasp on sanity stretched pretty far from that mark. Busy or not, cautious or not, it was impossible to continually avoid his own mind. Minor events, seemingly unconnected, could trigger a recollection and the scaffolding would collapse. Music was a particularly powerful connector, and both he and his sister had sworn off certain bands because of the emotional confusion they provoked. Smell was even more closely linked to memory. Thomas dreaded the smell of fresh-baked cookies, and one of Mom's cleaning products had left Ashley vomiting every time the house was cleaned. Mom had changed brands, but not even Thomas knew what connections his sister had made; he'd asked, and through her tears she couldn't manage to tell him. He'd never asked again.

Those inevitable moments aside, the past ten months had proven far better than the first two. Life wasn't 'normal'—at least not if he ascribed 'normal' as pre-Reflection—but it now scaled above unbearable. Thrusting away the memories of others and keeping himself occupied helped assuage the weekly crush. After discovering this small measure of peace, he'd been content just to ignore the other lives he'd gained.

Until Michael Pater.

"Is this it?"

Sam made a final turn, and the car scrolled slowly past a large white building. Thomas recognized it immediately. From the high reaches of the bell tower to the trees which spread bare branches over the main pathway, Michael knew this place well. As of eight days ago, so did Thomas.

The memories here were so strong Thomas was suddenly lost in the swirling mists of Michael Pater's world. Emotions swept through him at the sight of the main doors, and though Thomas fought bravely to keep them from overwhelming him, the flood consumed him before he could breathe. Joy and peace came first, the feelings of a boy who had found comfort in these walls. These were quickly replaced by the resentment of teenage rebellion, before finally melting into the fear of an adult. The exchange was swift, powerful, and confirmed to Thomas that this was indeed the place.

"Yes," he managed. "This is it."

The sedan swung a hard left into the near-empty parking lot. Pulling as close as possible, Sam veered into a space and pulled the gearshift into park. His hands brushed the keys, but before turning off the car, he asked, "Do you want to go in alone?"

Yes. The answer came immediately to Thomas's mind, but he shoved it down. What he had to do would have to be done alone, but the man's presence was a comfort to Thomas. He'd been there for the most stressful moments, and he'd never yet broken under the strain of Thomas's weakness. Having him along, if only for moral support, was better than wandering alone.

"No. I'd . . . I'd like you to come."

"All right." Sam cut the car's engine.

They strolled up the path together. Every step brought back more memories. This was a particularly odd sensation, since he knew they weren't really *his* memories. It was the first time he'd traveled somewhere one of his Reflected knew intimately, and it sent weird chills down his spine.

Seemingly sensing his uncertainty, Sam reach out and gripped Thomas's shoulder encouragingly. Relaxing a little, he shot the big man a smile.

Once inside, Thomas knew instinctively where to go and set off immediately down the aisle to his left. He stopped in front of a confessional, turned to Sam, and said, "I need a few minutes, okay?"

The big man hesitated, then nodded solemnly and stepped back to wait in one of the pews. Drawing a deep breath, Thomas opened the door and slid into the booth.

Forgive me, Father, for I have sinned. The opening lines of the verbal dance burst into his mind, and he felt his lips working, mouthing them. He made no audible sound, though. Sitting down silently, he sought the words that could explain what brought him here. Seconds strayed long, and finally, simply to break the silence, he spoke the first words that came to mind.

"I'm not Catholic," Thomas whispered.

There was a pause from the other side of the screen, and for a moment he wondered if he would receive an answer at all. His gaze strayed to his feet, barely visible in the darkness behind his glasses. A weary sigh escaped his lips, and he thought, *I shouldn't have come*, as he stood and opened his mouth to apologize.

Before any words came out, he heard the voice of the old priest on the other side. "The sacraments are usually reserved—"

"Yeah, I know." The words were tired and regretful but not bitter. "I just thought that . . . I don't really know what I thought, but I was Catholic when . . ." Thomas stopped, not quite willing to divulge precisely why he considered himself part of a religion he had never experienced firsthand.

Curiosity had obviously gripped the priest, though, because instead of rushing him out of the confessional, he gently said, "Continue, son. I'm listening."

Thomas hesitated, hand still on the door, debating whether to leave. "I was Catholic eight days ago for an instant . . . for a lifetime. I'm . . . my name is Thomas Ross."

There was an intake of breath from the other side of the screen, and Thomas knew he had been recognized. He still stood, not having bothered to retake his seat, and with a shake of his head he moved to exit.

"Wait." The sound was quiet, barely audible, but Thomas heard it and froze with his hand on the smooth wooden door of the confessional. "Why did you come?"

Waves of joy, or perhaps simply hope, since he was still unsure if he should be happy at all, washed over him, and he relaxed, letting his arm drop to his side as he slumped back into his seat.

"I'm a Mirror," he began unnecessarily, but it felt easiest to start with that. "Last week I Reflected a man accused of murdering his wife and child. He grew up Catholic, grew up here, but he hasn't been to church or confession in about five years, and I think he probably should have. Well, he did it, the murders I mean, and I felt that, since I was him for that moment, and he was Catholic, and he didn't confess, that maybe I should because it should at least be confessed, and I want to do it for him, his soul I mean, but I also want to do it for me, because I don't know if I should confess for myself since I committed the crime too since I *was* him for a time and . . ."

Thomas stopped abruptly, snapping his jaw shut. His teeth clacked together, and his lips curled into a rueful smile. "I'm rambling," he apologized. "My mom says I do that sometimes when I get nervous."

"That's understandable," the priest said. Thomas thought this phrase was supposed to make him feel better, but it didn't. He didn't want what he was experiencing to be deemed normal, he simply wanted it all to go away. He wanted answers, he wanted absolutes, and had instead found what he wanted least: a patronizing adult.

"Thanks for the chat, but I should get going."

"Wait."

"Why? Are you going to tell me that it's okay to feel confused and hurt? Everyone's done that, and it hasn't solved any problems. I came here for an answer. Do I need to confess for either my part or on behalf of Michael Pater?"

"As you're not Catholic, I can't take your confession, and as you're not Michael Pater, you can't give his. However, if you'd like to talk about something, nothing bars me from doing that."

Thomas nodded slowly. "Can we do it somewhere else, though? It's a little cramped in here."

"An excellent idea. Give me a few minutes to finish up here, and we'll meet in my office."

Gratitude flooded Thomas. Maybe today was the day he'd finally get some answers.

He suddenly wished he knew the right questions.

— CHAPTER 15 —

Ashley woke up coughing. Her body convulsed with every hacking drive until the muscles in her stomach ached. She coughed until she gagged, and then lay breathing raggedly, her lungs burning with exertion. Groaning softly, she summoned the little strength she had and rose slowly to a sitting position.

From the window, thin rays of golden sunlight played through the blinds, tripped across the foot of the bed, and spilled onto the cluttered floor. Her bedside clock glowed the hour: three past noon. Folded clothes still lay on top of the dresser from two days before. She had pulled them out after waking that morning but had crawled back into bed immediately after breakfast, never dressing for the day.

Sharp rapping at the door drew her attention. "Ashley?" Dad's voice was muffled through the wood.

"Hold on." Her motions lethargic, Ashley reached out to the nightstand and grabbed her shades. Slipping them onto her face muted the world and shut out the little sunlight seeping through the blinds. Plunged into comfortable darkness, she answered.

"I'm safe."

Dad opened the door, hovering in the threshold. "You all right, kiddo?"

"I'm still sick."

"I know. I heard you coughing. You're due for more medicine any-way."

Ashley made a face. "It tastes terrible."

Dad ignored the commentary. "Are you hungry at all?" Ashley shook her head. "All right. I'll get your medication."

He turned to leave, but Ashley spoke up. "Wait." Dad paused. "Can you bring me the paper?"

"Okay."

He was gone. Scrubbing her running nose on the sleeve of her pajamas, Ashley collapsed back against the pillow, staring blankly at the ceiling.

Fatigue still racked her mind as much as her body. Suffering through the physical aspects of the flu had proven taxing enough, but it was the drain on her mental energy that hurt more. Thoughts of doing anything more than lying in bed were met with apathy. Willpower left her, and for two days she'd slept—slept or traced the patterns on the ceiling.

Setting aside the typical childish frustrations with inaction, the previous two days might not have been too bad. She'd certainly wanted nothing more than to lethargically bask in dreamless respite. In activity's hiatus, though, waited the specters of her mind.

Keeping the mind occupied never extinguished the Reflections' impact, but it certainly assuaged it. Fighting the flu blurred Ashley's mind to bored apathy and let the flurry of Reflected images run unchecked. Worse even than the myriad physical symptoms of illness had been the two tortured days of hazy remembrance.

Mists still clouded the edge of her mind, and she didn't want to do anything more than recline listlessly, but forcing herself to action promised a happier course than another day focusing on other people's miseries. So when her father returned with paper and pills, she would accept both as their own special form of medicine.

In the weeks since the first Reflection, she had come to hate the newspaper. Cursory glances at the headlines in those following days had finally shown her why Mom and Dad had never taught them to read.

"Twin Mirrors Complete First Reflections" the headline had blazed in all capitals after the first day. The subheading, in lowercase but bolded letters, read, "Girl Evokes Duncan Confession; Memphis Man Cleared by Boy." Ashley hadn't even bothered to read the article. Instead, she'd shoved the paper away, stumbled back to her room, closed the door, and pulled the covers over her head. She'd spent the rest of that day in bed, and most of the next two as well.

The focus of a Mirror story relied heavily upon the Mirror's verdict. Those not guilty of the crimes listed received glowing adoration from the paper. The wrongly accused was a good husband, an excellent father, a volunteer for community service and a little league coach. He was a boon to the community, and the execution of proper justice would finally return him to his rightful place. The guilty gained no such benefit. Often they were played as deranged, or simply cruel. For murderers, it was the victims who received the star treatment, showing what sort of model citizen this brazen criminal would cut down.

Regardless of how the accused was handled, the Mirror always lost. Barely mentioned in most stories, the few articles that spared any space for the children did so only as one might explain the use of a tool. No one ever reported what actually happened at the Reflections; Ashley doubted most people knew. The paper could spare no sympathy for the Mirrors; they were simply doing their job, even when it killed them.

Tara Peterson overdosed on sleeping pills three weeks after Ashley and Thomas pulled their first Reflections. Tara was from North Carolina, but it hardly mattered. The *Denver Post*, along with most other major papers in the States, devoted almost an entire front page to her. Or her Reflections, anyway.

"Mirror Tara Peterson Dies at 16" the top of the page heralded in bold letters. The article consisted primarily of a list of every single Reflection she had completed during her tenure. Date, name, crime, and verdict of every case were all laid out in bare detail. Not quite two hundred names strong, the collection spilled past the front page and completely covered A11.

Though it was sparse on details about Tara herself, Ashley had tried to construct a beautiful story from it: braver than her young years should have allowed, Tara had marched to certain death knowing it would make the world a better place. It was a beautiful myth, and Ashley wanted desperately to believe it. Viewing fellow Mirrors as valiant martyrs softened the final stroke. Purpose gave an otherwise senseless death meaning and filled Ashley with a measure of hope.

No one else seemed to believe it, though. Every police station and courthouse were filled with people who ignored her. The final narratives the news media constructed for them hammered this viewpoint home, after all. The Mirror who died had received practically no discussion in her own obituary, instead focusing on the people whose lives she had affected.

Dad's knock broke that train of thought. She accepted the paper with no resistance, accepted the medicine with only a little, and then began digging for the daily crossword.

Ignoring the front page, she passed the entire section to the floor with a careless toss. Her loathing for the journalistic tendencies of the papers had not really been assuaged in the past months. She ignored the news portions as a rule. While she understood the business section, she found it boring and usually skipped it as well. Life and Arts held some interest, but it was the crossword that truly drew her in.

As she reached for the pen she kept beside her bed, Dad sat down in the chair opposite her. He immediately hopped back up to pull some dirty clothes from beneath him. Giving her an exasperated look, he tossed them into the hamper by her door.

Retaking the now cleared seat, he paused. Dad frowned slightly, eyebrows drawn down in concern. Ashley's stomach knotted. Did he have bad news? "What?" she asked, hands clenched tightly around her pen.

He frowned, then seemed to come to some sort of decision. "I want to ask you something, but I'm not sure if I should. It's kind of about the Reflections."

He waited, watching her. Ashley hesitated, considering. Dredging up those memories was rarely enjoyable, but neither parent had asked much of import in the past year. Anything to do with the Reflections was couched in layers of double-talk and euphemism. Originally she thought this was for her and Thomas, but she had since overheard her parents talking among themselves the same way; the topic made them uncomfortable too. Because of this, they'd struggled to help the twins cope with their new life in any meaningful way. Mom and Dad didn't understand what was happening, and neither she nor Thomas wanted to start the conversation.

It was time to end that. With a deep breath, Ashley steeled herself and motioned for him to continue.

"What is it about the crossword that interests you?" Dad asked carefully. His tone was soft, and he spoke slowly as if hoping he could cut off the question if it started to go south. "I know you don't like to focus on your Reflections, but, well, isn't that where most of your knowledge comes from?"

"It's complicated," she said. "I like them because there's always something new. Something different."

As expected, Dad's look was quizzical. This was hard to explain.

"Sometimes it feels like I can't have unique experiences. Through my Reflected I've read thousands of books. If there's a story worth reading, I probably know it. I was excited when I found out I could read last year, but I've discovered there's almost nothing worth reading that I haven't already experienced.

"The same is true with movies and music. I would guess I've seen about a third of the movies ever made. By the time they make it to video or TV, I can probably quote any that are worth seeing, and plenty that aren't.

"It's that way with everything. Everything reminds me of *something*. Sometimes that's a trigger to horrible revelations."

She paused, not sure whether to continue. At her left, Dad was leaning forward, listening intently. Ashley felt warmth bloom at his genuine interest. Part of her had wanted to share her life with her parents the way she did with Carol, but they had never seemed open to it.

"That's why I broke down last Christmas. Remember?"

"Yes. I remember," Dad said quietly.

Mom had arranged for Thomas and Ashley to spend the holiday week as their first vacation. Christmas had dawned as a frozen wintry morning; she could read in her parents' eyes the hope for a holiday miracle. Instead, Ashley had broken down crying beside the tree and spent the next two hours curled up on the couch, wavering between sobs and blank stares. She had confided in neither parent the private hell that had triggered the episode.

"Victor Mercer lost his wife and three kids on Christmas Eve. I still remember him sitting down with a bottle of vodka the next morning. He plugged in the tree, dropped onto the couch, and drank until he passed out.

"I saw that Christmas tree, and it just . . . I . . . the loss . . ." Ashley broke off and dropped her face into her hands. "It was pure pain. That Reflection was only a few weeks old, and I could still recollect some of Mr. Mercer's more . . . tragic . . . days better than I remembered many of my own. As I sobbed on the couch, I wanted that alcohol. I wanted the oblivion it brought.

"But I never lost a wife and three kids," Ashley continued. "It was Victor Mercer's family who'd died on Christmas Eve so many years ago, but I couldn't keep his life from invading mine.

"I can think of the Mercers without crying now, but I still see that December morning I spent weeping on the couch for four people I never actually met.

"Those are the worst triggers. They're brutal and strike with no warning at everyday experiences. The longer it's been since the Reflection, though, the less likely they are to pop up unbidden.

"They're not always devastating, though. Practically everything I do has a shared origin with someone else. No matter how I choose to pass the time, it seems I'm sharing that experience with an uninvited guest. There are so few things I do that are uniquely mine." She held up the crossword. "Then there's this. Yes, a lot of this knowledge came from my Reflected, but most of it is emotionally neutral. It's hard to get emotionally connected to a five-letter word for 'all gone.' I'm not saying there aren't clues that trigger me, but they're pretty rare.

"Even better, if I'm lucky, there's a few clues here that are new to me. A bunch of Reflected have worked puzzles in their past, but every day is a new challenge. I particularly like the weekend ones; they have enough obscure trivia I can be sure I don't know it all. Then, when I solve those clues, I feel like I have a bit of knowledge that's really mine. Something that *I* learned."

Dad leaned back, watching her thoughtfully. "I hadn't thought of that."

She shrugged. "It's kind of silly. I mean, who cares if I know about some obscure Russian tsar?"

"It's not silly," her father said emphatically. "It makes perfect sense to me."

Ashley gave him a small smile, then erupted into a coughing fit that probably ruined her expression of gratitude.

With a hug, Dad left her to her distractions. She returned to the solitude that had marked the past couple of days. As she watched him go, though, she thought he'd displayed a sense of purpose that hadn't been there when he'd come in.

Summoning the first smile in days, she picked up her pen and let it hover over the crossword. She didn't start writing, though; her gaze was fixed on the door. Dad's understanding had lifted her spirits more than she would have thought.

— CHAPTER 16 —

Father Sean Murphy stood barely five foot five, walked with a slight limp, sported thick, close-cropped white hair, thin-rimmed spectacles, and a warm smile. He spoke crisply and clearly, his voice betraying the practiced English of an educated man. Calluses and partially healed cuts ran along hands that, despite their weathered appearance, moved with practiced gentleness.

The limp was an injury from some unnamed war, the speech a mark of many years of college, and the calluses and cuts a gift from his love of carpentry—a hobby he had taken up in his twenties to follow in the footsteps of the one he humbly called "Lord."

All of this had rushed to Thomas as soon as he saw the priest emerge from the confessional booth. Michael Pater had known Father Sean for many years, and though they had last crossed paths four years ago, the images gleaned from the condemned criminal matched almost exactly with the present.

There had been brief introductions between Sam and the priest, then small talk as they'd walked to Father Sean's office. Sam had done most of the talking on the way, something Thomas appreciated. He was still working through his emotions. When they finally arrived, though, Thomas had timidly asked the Shepherd to wait outside again. He wanted to do this alone. As always, Sam had given an understanding nod and said he'd wait in the nave.

As Thomas entered the priest's office, he noted that little had changed since Michael's last visit. On the far side of the room, twin bookcases stretching ceiling to floor framed a broad window facing a garden. A dark, lacquered desk crafted by the priest himself dominated the center of the room, while crosses and various religious works of art adorned the off-white walls. Rays of sun spilled into the room, spreading enough light to warrant keeping the desk lamp unlit. Two chairs sat near the door, and it was to the closest of these the old priest motioned Thomas upon their entry.

Father Sean walked in his uneven gait to the other chair. Thomas took a seat as his host did, and for a long moment the two did nothing more than exchange appraising glances. The priest broke the silence first.

"Would you like some tea?"

"No, thank you."

"Then perhaps you could tell me what I can do for you."

Thomas squirmed uncomfortably. "I was hoping you could tell me."

Father Sean's brow furrowed, and he leaned forward. "I'm not sure I understand."

"Do you know anything about Reflections?"

"Only the basics. I know that your eyes allow to you see the truth."

"Not exactly." Thomas leaned forward now, the words flowing easily from a speech he had prepared in his mind for more than a week. "I can't give you a perfect description of what I do; trying to explain the Reflections to you would be like trying to explain color to a blind man. I could lay out the foundation, maybe even give him an idea, but until he sees for himself, he wouldn't really understand."

Father Sean contemplated briefly on that statement, then nodded.

"My eyes force me to live the lives of those I Reflect. Their every act and thought becomes mine. I know if criminals are guilty, but I don't know it because I've seen them act; I know it because I've committed their crimes.

116

"I've absorbed fifty lives over the past year and tried to reconcile fifty different worldviews and value systems with my own. Every new acquisition is another paradigm shift, and it's tiring trying to hold on to myself while drowning in the worlds of those who are simultaneously complete strangers and intimate confidants. I don't feel I really know Dennis Carson—the only time I met him was when I cleared his name last year—but his life still rests up here." Thomas tapped the side of his head with a finger.

"I don't receive just the pertinent facts to which the Reflection is attuned, Father, I receive everything. I know these people as even their most trusted friends never see them. I've seen the 'innocent' stand as evil more times than I can count. A man may not kill his wife, but he cheats on her. He may not lie, but he does steal. He may not rape, but he does abuse.

"Some people say I've been given the gift of insight. But I don't want this 'gift.' Worse, this 'gift' is going to kill me.

"For a year I labored under the delusion that I had been randomly chosen by Fate to live and die as nothing more than a tool of justice. My life was doomed to be painful and my death ultimately meaningless. My life was to be traded for those whose lives would be wrongly cut short without me.

"And then I Reflected Michael. He grew up believing that good, bad, or whatever, the god he served would right the wrongs in the end and that all things happen for a purpose. I want to believe that. I want to believe that there was some reason I was born a Mirror and that something more than random chance assigned me this death sentence.

"I came to you, Father, because, well, Michael respected you. I think he wants to confess what he did. He's scared, though, and I don't know that he will. I took on his crimes; I lived them, and I didn't know if that made them mine to confess . . ." Thomas trailed off, shrugging. "That's why I came for him, but the rest of it . . . that's why I came for me. I want to know why I'm cursed with this."

Thomas gestured angrily to his glasses and, frowning, slumped back in his chair.

"Do you believe in God, Thomas?" The priest's question was quiet, his face calm.

"I don't know. Make your case."

Father Sean smiled weakly. "You're not going to start easy on me, are you?"

"I've waited a year for answers, and you're my first real hope. I'm a bit anxious."

"My dear boy, I'm afraid you place far too much faith in me. However, I will do the best I can."

The old priest cleared his throat, then continued. "Make a case for God—that's the starting point, right?"

Thomas nodded.

"That may actually be the easiest. You can choose to believe or not believe. If you choose the latter, though, nothing I have to say will make sense."

Father Sean leaned back in his chair and began studiously cleaning his glasses. Thomas waited patiently for more, but the priest seemed unperturbed by the stretching silence.

"That's it?" Thomas demanded.

"What did you want?"

"Explanations! Reasons! Proof! Something more than your simple 'here it is' trick."

Replacing his glasses, Father Sean fixed Thomas with a steely gaze and a slight frown. "I'm old, Thomas, but I'm not a fool. Your brief explanation of Reflections told me that you already have all those things. Despite your youth, you've seen more years than I have. Thomas, the average thirteen-year-old boy does not use the term 'paradigm shift' in conversation, but you did.

"You *learned* from those Reflections, and I doubt that your knowledge is restricted to vocabulary. You have searched for answers over the course of the past year, and in that same year you would have heard almost every argument for the existence of God available. I know that to be fact since you reflected Michael, and I taught Michael most of them personally.

"So we can rework old territory, plow those fields again, and reach no more conclusion together than you have reached alone. Or you can let me know what you've decided and work from there. I'll warn you now, though, that if you're firmly decided against God's existence, there are few answers I can give—my view of the world's workings requires His presence."

"So either I say I believe in God or you won't help me?"

Father Sean shook his head emphatically. "Not won't. Can't. Not about this. I'll help in whatever other ways I can, but without God's presence, I can't make the world make sense."

"This isn't what I expected. I mean, you gave Michael reasons to believe."

"I did . . . when he was a child. We all need to learn the supports for belief, but those reasons cannot force it. Men smarter than I am have heard the same arguments I would make now and still say there is no God. Other men, again smarter than I am, hear them and believe. Well-reasoned arguments do not always equate to belief."

"But shouldn't they?"

"What should and should not be are usually not what is. I wish that every well-reasoned argument led to instant conversion; life would be much simpler, though probably more boring. But people don't work that way. We have prejudices and desires. We come into most arguments knowing what we believe, and little can sway that. Some who lack that predilection for one side or the other can be swayed to the first side they hear. And some are swayed back and forth by whichever case they've heard most recently. In short, human selection is as important to this process as human reason. If you choose to believe in God, then the arguments for his existence will make sense and will stand solid. If you choose to disbelieve, then you will always find holes in them. I can tell you which option I think best, though you already know. What I cannot do is make that decision for you."

"Okay, for the sake of argument, let's assume I believe."

"All right."

"Why would God do this to me? To anyone? And don't give me any of the 'his ways are mysterious' or 'we grow through pain' stock answers, either. I've heard those, and they don't answer the question."

Father Sean arched an eyebrow. "I believe they answer more than you're willing to let them, but I agree that they hardly provide comprehensive explanations. Unfortunately, the explanation I can give is no more helpful and likely to frustrate you."

"That won't be new. What's your answer?"

"I don't know why God would inflict such pain on one so young."

Frustration at playing mind games had burned throughout the proceedings, but this final response proved too much. Any hope of answers vanished, and with an angry sigh, Thomas rose. "Yeah, in that case, I'll be leaving."

He started toward the door, but the priest's hand shot out and snagged his wrist. Thomas struggled futilely against the hold. The old man might look frail, but his woodworking hobby kept his hands strong, and Father Sean's grip held firm.

"That's not all I have to say, Thomas."

"Let go of me, Father." The words escaped as a hiss. The pressure lessened, and Thomas wrenched his hand away with a furious twist. "I'm done playing games."

"Then sit down and listen to me."

"Tell me why I shouldn't just walk out."

"If you leave, you'll never hear what I have to say. I might be wrong, I might be a crock, and a liar, and a snake-oil sales-man. I could be another lunatic spouting nonsense, and you'd be absolutely right to ignore me. But I could also have the answers

120

you need. You can make that decision, Thomas, but you can only make it if you don't leave."

"Will you stop playing word games?"

Father Sean shook his head. "I don't mean to play games."

"You said you don't know why God would do this."

"That's no game. I don't know."

Growling softly, Thomas turned and seized the doorknob.

Standing now, the old priest made a final request. "Explain the Reflections to me again. Give me details; help me understand what you feel. Maybe I can help you if I understand."

Shaking his head, Thomas wrenched open the door. "I told you before, I can't do it. Explaining color to a blind man. Do you remember that? You just wouldn't get it. You couldn't get it. You can't wrap your mind around it, Father. It wouldn't matter what words I gave you. Nothing I tell you would give you more than a fleeting impression of the power and pain delivered to me every Thursday. I could spend all day talking and you *still* wouldn't understand the tiniest part of it!"

He was already striding angrily into the hallway when Father Sean's voice followed him. "And yet I am supposed to explain so simply the mind of God?"

Thomas almost lost his balance. The old priest's words finally pierced the veil of frustration, and for the first time since he had stepped from the confessional, Thomas believed that Father Sean might be able to help him.

"I can give you ideas, vague impressions," the voice behind him continued, "or even a simple structure of God's intent. I can lay out the basics as I understand them and show you His fingerprints in your world. To use your analogy, Thomas, I am a blind man trying to see the colors of God.

"I can't give you all the answers. If I implied I could, or if Michael believed I could, I'm truly sorry. I want to help you, but I can't do it on those false pretenses. I can guide, instruct, counsel, and sympathize, but I can't tell you the things only God knows.

"If that's not enough, then I understand. There are days when I shout at the sky and demand the reasons for pain, and poverty, and loss. I want the answers that I can't have, but I've also learned to live without them."

"How?"

"Through patience garnered from years of living."

Thomas finally turned to face the priest. "I may not have years. I'm going to die soon."

Father Sean stood in the doorway of his office. Lines of concern creased his tanned face, and a sad certainty dimmed his eyes. He nodded slowly, as if thinking, before motioning Thomas back into the room. Reluctance fading, Thomas obeyed and slumped tiredly into the chair nearest the door. Father Sean hesitated just long enough to close the door before joining him.

"So God taught you what you needed to know over the course of your life," Thomas began quietly, "but I won't have that time since I'll die young. According to your view, God chose me for the life of a Mirror, and that means he condemned me to never understand."

Father Sean shook his head. "I've been unclear again. I'm sorry. Thomas, it was the experiences of my life that taught me, not the years. You have the potential to learn more, and understand more, than any save other Mirrors. That, I confess, I envy."

"You don't want my ability, Father."

Shaking his head ruefully, the old priest said, "No, I guess I don't. But in all I've learned from my seventy-two years, I've left so much untouched. No matter how much you gather in a single life, it's never enough. There is so much I wanted to learn and won't, and so much I wanted to master and didn't. And you've lived only thirteen years and done many times what I will ever accomplish."

Thomas shrugged. "To what end? If I die, I'm not helping any-one, least of all myself."

"Is death your only aim?" Father Sean's eyebrows knitted curiously, and wrinkles furrowed his forehead. He leaned forward, rubbing his chin thoughtfully as he did so. "Why must that be the beginning of all of your queries?"

Thomas snorted angrily. "Because it's the most important consequence of my Reflections."

"That's like saying that death is the most important consequence of living." Father Sean stood and walked in his stilted gait over to the bookshelf at the far side of the room. Thomas remained in his seat, watching as the priest pulled a book down, thumbed through it, and drew forth a yellowed sheet of paper folded into thirds. Carefully—almost lovingly—Father Sean carried it back to the pair of chairs and extended it to Thomas. "Look at this."

Gingerly, Thomas accepted the frail piece of paper from the priest's fingers and unfolded it.

Scribbled in faded colors was a child's rough sketch of a very simple church—little more than a box with a tower and a cross, beside which stood a stick figure dressed as a priest. A pale-yellow sun adorned the upper right corner, while a pair of drooping V's served as birds in the upper left. Written in messy cursive script along the bottom were the words "Thank you, Father Sean."

"What is this?" Thomas asked finally, folding up the paper and handing it back to the priest.

"That," he replied as he retrieved the paper and took it back to the far side of the room, "was a gift from a girl not much younger than you from many years ago. She battled leukemia from the time she was six until shortly before she turned ten, when it finally claimed her life."

"Evidence of another senseless premature death," Thomas said. "I don't get it. Why show me that?"

"That little girl was no Mirror, but even if she had been, she'd never have made it to her first Reflection. You may still make it to eighteen and be free from government control. Some have. Alternatively, you may die in a couple of years, but the same could be true of me. I'm old, and there are no guarantees of tomorrow at my age. She was dying young from disease of the body. I'm dying old from failure of the body." Father Sean hesitated, then with a sigh concluded, "You're dying young from disease of the mind.

"Thomas," Father Sean said as he resumed his seat, "the difference between dying and dead are facts of medical science, but the difference between dying and living is nothing more than a choice of purpose. That small girl was living right up until the moment she died. She touched lives, mine included, both in life and death. I intend to live that way as well.

"You, meanwhile, wait for death. You anticipate it and have formed your life around it. Everything you see swirls around that central point. You're afraid to truly live because you think it will make death more terrifying. It doesn't matter, though. Like everyone else in the world, you're slowly dying. Being afraid of it, or angry about it, or bitter about it won't change that simple fact."

Thomas paused. The speech about death and dying triggered thoughts of his mother. In some ways, Father Sean's observations matched closely with what Thomas thought about her view. Dad knew that he and Ashley would die; Mom knew her children were dying. It made a difference in how they acted and reacted. Dad wasn't perfect, but he still tried to engage them; they talked and played games with him. Mom, though, saw each day as one more step to death and nothing else. Every sunset was another wasted memory, every sunrise the harbinger of another poisonous dawn.

"Maybe I understand," Thomas began slowly. "Maybe. I mean, nothing you've said changes my fate . . ."

Father Sean's face grew sad, and he abruptly cut off that train of thought. "I have been as gentle as I know how, but you are fixated on this point. You must not focus on your fate, only on your life."

"That's easy for you to say," Thomas shot back.

"Is it? I am an old man. There is a reasonable chance that you will outlive me. What is to prevent me from whining about my situation as you do?"

"You've lived a full life! You got fifty-plus years that I won't get!

How is that supposed to make me feel better?" He paused, then added, "Whining?"

Father Sean leaned forward intently. "Dig through those memories of yours, Thomas. Look at all the lives you've experienced and find their outlook on death. How many of them are better prepared to embrace that end than you are?"

Thomas licked his lips. Six months ago such a request would have been impossible; he couldn't separate out the memories well enough to find such specific information. With practice, though, he'd gained a measure of control.

Tentatively he reached out, searching through the fifty lives he'd absorbed. He still picked up the stray bit of emotional detritus as he scanned, but fortunately he could filter out enough to keep it from burying him.

One by one, he methodically parsed the worldview of his subjects. The older Reflections, like Dennis Carson, were fuzzier, but he retained enough to find what he needed. In the more recent collections, the emotions were sharp . . . and familiar.

"You're right," he said slowly. "They're no more ready than I am."

"You have received a terminal diagnosis," the priest said gently. "Many children your age will get one this year for one reason or another. You actually have more time than some of them will. Moreover, as you've just seen, that diagnosis does not necessarily grow easier with age."

"I . . ." Thomas trailed off, at a loss for words.

"You have to accept this. Until you do, your life will be dominated by it; you cannot live as long as you are waiting to die."

Silence blanketed the small office. It was too much for Thomas to take in all at once. He agreed with some of it, but his heart still clenched at the thought of his own end. Part of him wanted to cry, but he fought the tears back; sobbing into Sam's arms a year ago had been hard enough. He didn't want to break down in front of a virtual stranger again.

At the thought of the Shepherd, Thomas looked at the clock on the wall. "I should probably be going. Sam's been patient, but he didn't come here today so he could sit in a church."

He stood to leave but stopped to ask one more question.

"If the board agrees, can I come back sometime? Talk again?"

The priest smiled and nodded. "Anytime."

— CHAPTER 17 —

Thank you again. You don't know how much this means."
Daniel heard the click on the other end of the line and was hanging up when Sally walked around the corner.

"What was that?" she asked.

"I've rented out a movie theater for a matinee next Monday." He gave a nervous laugh. "I'm going to take the kids to see a movie."

Sally blinked in surprise. "What? Will the board even allow that?"

"Yeah. I called them first. They were a bit reluctant but came around as long as I could find a theater willing to allow it. Turns out the board was the easy part. I had to call around to a few places before I found someone even willing to entertain the idea."

His wife shook her head as if trying to clear it. "You rented out the entire thing?"

"Well, one screen of it. He was afraid that other people wouldn't want to watch a movie if there were Mirrors in the theater, so I told him that I'd purchase every available ticket."

"Why?"

"We've been approaching this all wrong," he said with a grimace. "We've been trying to deal with this as we would have before, but they're not the same kids they were a year ago. A hug and some ice cream isn't going to fix anything.

"I was talking to Ashley earlier, and I think I finally understand what I can do. They need something that is truly theirs: a memory they don't have to share with anyone."

Sally shook her head. "We give them those. No one has been in this house. Everything we do here as a family is ours alone."

"No, those are the same experience over and over," Daniel said. "They need *new* experiences. They need something unique."

"I'm sure their Reflected have all been to a theater," Sally said wryly.

"Of course, but there have to be movies in the theater that they haven't seen. It would be something novel for them, even if only for a little while. They can hold on to that memory as something that is only theirs, or at least theirs first."

"This is ridiculous. It's just a movie, Daniel."

"It's not stopping at just a movie. I'm going to the mall next. I'm going to buy a bunch of new releases of every kind and bring them home, and then I'm going to try to find every way to make their world new and exciting."

Sally frowned, her brow furrowing. "And how much is all this going to cost?"

"I don't know," Daniel admitted honestly. "As much as it costs, I guess. I'll pay it."

"Is it really worth wasting all that money?" Sally was fidgeting, dry-washing her hands. "We've had everything budgeted for years. We knew exactly how much we could spend every year to stretch it all the way through our declining years."

"This isn't really about the money, is it?" he asked gruffly.

"It's just one thing to consider . . ."

Daniel closed his eyes and fought the urge to sigh. This was the way every discussion about the children went. He had hoped this would be different since he had finally found a way to expand their lives. He wanted his wife to join him in making the Ross family's final years more palatable. Instead, she was retreating from reality, throwing up walls so she wouldn't have to acknowledge that anything had changed.

"They're going to die," he whispered.

"Don't say that!" Sally snapped.

"Just because you can't face it doesn't mean it's going to change. They're going—"

"No!" Sally shot back, pointing an accusing finger at him. "They're not! Our family is different. We're going to beat this."

"We can't ignore reality, Sally. We can only mitigate it for them. For us."

"Fine! Do what you want."

Before he could fire back a retort, she stalked from the room.

Deciding not to let her irritation rub off on him, Daniel grabbed his keys off the kitchen counter, intending to head out to the mall. Instead, he froze with his hands just above the countertop when the doorbell pealed.

Sam and Thomas had been gone a couple of hours; they were the most likely candidates. His son had a key to the house, but as he rarely used it, he might have forgotten it in his haste to escape.

Instead, when Daniel yanked open the door, he found himself face-to-face with Dr. Cole Bryant.

"Oh," Daniel said, not hiding his irritation.

"It's customary to invite guests in," Bryant said dryly after fifteen seconds of tense silence.

"It's also customary to announce your visit before you arrive on the doorstep," Daniel shot back.

"True." There wasn't a hint of apology in the specialist's voice. "Since today is the children's birthday, I was worried you might try to push me off with excuses. By coming in person, I avoid that eventuality."

It was true. Part of the paperwork they had signed upon the twins' birth had required them to allow the expert "reasonable" access to their children. Had the doctor tried to arrange an appointment, it would have been simple enough to push him off for a day or two. Managing such a feat with him on the front stoop was less likely.

"All right," Daniel said grudgingly. "Come on in."

The Mirror expert strode confidently into their house. Setting down his battered leather briefcase, Bryant unwound his gray scarf and shrugged out of the matching coat. He draped both over an unused arm of the nearby coat tree before retrieving the briefcase and striding solemnly into the living room.

"Thomas isn't here," Daniel said. "He's out with Sam."

"Then I'll start with Ashley," the expert said, striding to the back of the house.

"She'll be thrilled," Daniel whispered to the man's disappearing back. Shaking his head, he looked around for Sally. She'd vanished to either the study or their bedroom. Deciding to avoid further confrontation, he stormed from the house without another word.

—CHAPTER 18—

Ashley perked up immediately at the rap on her door. Looking up from the crossword, she muttered around the pen in her mouth, "Come in!"

As the door opened to reveal Dr. Bryant, she slumped back down and muttered, "Oh, goody."

He couldn't have missed her reaction to his presence, but he said nothing. Instead, he moved into the room and set his briefcase atop the only clean space on her dresser. Crossing his arms in front of him, he loomed on the far side of the room.

These visits followed a pretty standard pattern. Bryant would open up with a series of questions about her mental health, eating habits, activities, and so forth. She imagined it was supposed to give him some kind of insight into her current state of mind, but it seemed a waste of time. She usually tried to answer honestly, but she knew that Thomas hated him enough to give whatever answer he thought would get rid of the man the quickest.

She and Thomas had been forced into these meetings annually growing up, but the onset of their full power had added at least one extra visit each year. During her most recent evaluation, she had been one day removed from the Reflection of a murderous white supremacist, and her thoughts had been so muddled she'd barely been able to speak. Today was a different story, and Ashley had a question of her own.

A year had passed since she'd Reflected Spencer Duncan, and time had dulled those memories some. Part of her still remembered the aftermath of that experience, though. She'd needed to know who she really was. Regular mirrors didn't work, and trying with another Mirror would kill her. That desire had lost much of its urgency in the intervening year, but she still yearned to see her true self.

"How are yo—?" Dr. Bryant began.

"Why do we die if we look at each other?" Ashley interrupted.

The Mirror expert paused midword. For a moment he gave no reaction, simply staring at her. Eventually he shook himself, mouth snapping shut with an audible click of the teeth. Idly, Ashley wondered if it was the subject of the question that had shaken him so, or if it was simply her temerity in asking a question at all.

"I'm not sure," Dr. Bryant replied eventually. She could tell the admission frustrated him.

"You have to have theories," she pressed.

He nodded slowly but hesitated again before he finally spoke.

"We know that the brain of a Mirror is different from that of a normal person, even if we don't yet know how. When a Mirror Reflects, the brain attempts to accept the other person's entire existence. It's not just memories that it absorbs but physical cues as well. The heartbeat shifts, trying to match the rhythm of the subject, and the muscles twitch in response to the other person's commands. Any Reflection would be extremely dangerous if it lasted longer than a fraction of a second."

"I didn't know that. I don't feel it," Ashley said, confused.

"As I said, it's over too quickly. Your heart may skip a beat or two, but your own autonomic nervous system returns to its job the moment the connection is broken. Other changes can have lasting consequences, though, and give this theory some credence."

"Like what?"

"Mirrors who Reflect frequently tend to see puberty delayed and shortened. We assume that the body receives signals from their Reflected subjects that adolescence is over and thus the release of specific hormones for growing up are delayed or frequently interrupted. Additionally, since most of the criminals Reflected are men, we've found that female Mirrors tend to have lower output of estrogen than their peers. We're seeing some very limited success with hormone treatments, but the effects are too variable to combat effectively. Ultimately, as is always the case, we simply do not have enough data.

"So the people I Reflect really do change me? Do they change the way I think? Or act?"

Bryant cocked his head, thinking. "Yes and no. Yes, they produce a detectable change in the way your body works, but only on a physiological level. Note that puberty is delayed and shortened, not eliminated; a Mirror's body is confused by the conflicting signals but is not transformed. Further, all my research has shown that a Mirror's mind is still her own. She has absorbed a wealth of information, but that's all it is. The scenes you have grabbed do not shape you unless you let them. They are filled with powerful emotion and complex thoughts, but they impact your decisions in the same way a well-crafted novel or movie would."

Ashley returned to her original question. "So why do Mirrors who look at each other die?"

Bryant had relaxed over the course of this discussion. Given the chance to lecture, his demeanor was more open than Ashley had seen before. His words were smooth, his face thoughtful. In distraction, he almost managed the sympathy that evaded his most ardent conscious efforts.

"As I stated, any normal Reflection would be dangerous to a Mirror if it lasted longer. All the evidence suggests it is the Reflected subject who somehow breaks the connection between the two of them. With two Mirrors, that connection is not disrupted until they are physically pulled away. By the time that has happened, the Mirrors' brains are entwined somehow. Their bodies are receiving input from two minds. Severing that connection causes problems;

the heart is seeking the input of a source that has vanished unexpectedly. For some reason, the body can't recover on its own; by that point, it believes it needs a second mind to function."

Ashley swallowed. There was nothing in that to help her defuse the risk. If Dr. Bryant was right, then looking at Thomas would kill her, and neither of them would be able to do anything to stop it. She would never be able to see herself as she wanted; whatever reassurances she received, there would always be that nagging doubt about how much people like Spencer had changed her.

She might have asked other questions, but in the time it took her to digest what she'd learned, Dr. Bryant had recovered from his initial shock. The ease that had accompanied his brief oration was gone, consumed by the reserved uncertainty she usually associated with the expert. She didn't even bother to stifle a groan as he began his list of questions.

Ashley endured the interview as best she could. She hated the probing questions almost as much as she hated the apathetic specialist, but as it only happened rarely, she figured it was better than the weekly horror that the Reflections were. Bryant spent an hour bouncing from topic to topic; she'd heard most of them before, but there were a few surprises. The end, however, was always the same.

"What drives you?

This had been the final question of every meeting she'd ever had with this man. He had asked it even before she'd known what a Reflection was. She'd never managed to assemble anything close to a reasonable answer. Before her last birthday she hadn't understood the question's intent. In the visits since, she'd not given a cogent answer; she endured simply because that was less terrifying than dying.

Today she had something else. She spoke of Tara Peterson's obituary, of the myth of the brave Mirror martyr. She remembered Jessica Graves sobbing as Spencer Duncan raped her. She ran through the list of all the criminals she'd convicted over the past twelve months. It was a jumbled mess of an answer, practically incoherent, but there was real emotion behind it. Ashley rambled, bouncing from memory to memory as she tried to assemble it all into something meaningful.

When she finally trailed off, she hitched her shoulders uncomfortably. It felt odd to dig so deeply for this man who never gave anything back. She worried she'd said too much, looked foolish. Embarrassed, she scrutinized Dr. Bryant's face for some kind of response. Was this what he had been waiting for, or had she poured out her soul for nothing?

A long silence passed between them, then Dr. Bryant gave the barest nod. Ashley blinked. How was she supposed to interpret that?

With the steps of the ritual completed, Bryant picked up his briefcase and moved to open the door.

"Wait!" Ashley said suddenly. She was surprised at the force in her voice. Even more shocking, the specialist obeyed, pausing with fingers on the door knob. She quickly barreled on before he could change his mind. "What drives you? Why do you do this?"

Hand still gripping the knob, Dr. Bryant stood frozen. He didn't turn to look at her, but he didn't open the door, either. He seemed to be wrestling with himself, trying to decide what to say, or maybe whether he should say anything at all. Finally, he glanced back, shook his head, and spoke so softly she almost couldn't hear him.

"Why should I tell you?"

"Because you keep asking why I stay alive to keep doing this, even as horrible as it is. I've done my best to find an answer. Now I want to know why you'd make me keep going, even knowing how horrible it is."

Bryant processed that for a moment, watching her behind his own shaded glasses.

Ashley sighed. "You don't care about me. I get it. I'm a tool for justice. That's great, but you don't suddenly decide to throw away a bunch of kids' lives simply for justice. Something has to drive you.

135

A desire to right some wrong. I just want to know what it is. I think I deserve that much."

"No Mirror has ever asked me that before."

"Then every Mirror's afraid of you, because I guarantee we all want to know."

Bryant finally released the door knob and turned back into the room. "So you're not afraid of me?"

"Terrified, but I'm curious, too. I'm told it's a dangerous trait."

Bryant actually smiled wanly. "It's definitely that. Still, it's one I can respect."

Sighing, he set down the briefcase again and crossed his arms in front of him.

"A Reflection likely saved me from conviction. Without Mirror testimony, I'd almost certainly have gone to jail."

"What were you charged with?" She knew. There weren't enough Mirrors to waste on lesser crimes, but she needed to hear it.

"Murder."

Ashley fought down a shiver. He said it so matter-of-factly, just like everything else. Even this was just another fact for him, another piece of a bigger puzzle.

"So you didn't kill him?"

"No, I did. Reflection merely proved it was self-defense." He turned back to the door but paused to regard Ashley again.

"I suppose I do this because I know for a fact that Reflections save innocent lives."

Ashley shook her head, thinking of the hell she went through each week. "You're not innocent, Doctor."

He watched for a long minute, apparently trying to judge her reaction. In the end, he shrugged and opened the door. Before he left, though, he whispered, "I never said I was."

—CHAPTER 19—

Chocolate chip cookie dough ice cream dripped steadily from the rim of its container to pool in a sticky mound on the plastic tablecloth. Of the twenty-six birthday candles, eight remained nestled in Ashley's cake, five rested beside it, with the bottom third of each still wrapped in frosting, and the rest—all thirteen of Thomas's—were stacked neatly on his paper plate, the frosting licked away. Shreds of brightly colored wrapping paper dotted the table; the gifts they had hidden now deposited safely in the twins' rooms.

Daniel was in the kitchen scrubbing dishes left over from the evening meal, and both kids were in bed for the night. Sam had left before the cakes and ice cream were presented so he wouldn't miss his flight. Cole Bryant had, thankfully, departed before dinner. That left Sally alone in the dining room, staring blankly at the tattered shreds of chaos left over from the celebration.

It galled her to admit Daniel had been right. She had shopped for presents for the twins over the past weeks, but it was his last-minute additions that gained the most excitement. Brand-new hardcover books, collections of insanely difficult puzzles, and the latest releases of music had brought wide smiles to their children's faces as he had explained his reasoning. Their joy at the chance to see a movie in an actual theater had brought them to almost literal squeals of delight.

The temptation to shrug and leave the entire mess until the morning was strong. She might have done so, but the ice cream would certainly melt in the night; that, at least, had to be remedied. Of course, the cakes needed covering, and leaving the crumbs would attract ants. Fighting down a tired sigh of protest, she marched to the table.

Starting the process lent rhythm to the chore, and confident that routine would attend the task, she let her mind drift.

Once, these birthday parties had sown happy memories. With a little effort, she could still recall most years' festivities. These images ran together, though, lacking any defining lines to mark where one birthday ended and another began.

In the Ross household, one year had been almost identical to any other. It was always just the four of them; there were no school friends to join the children, and neither side of the family had been particularly open to the twins. Visits from Daniel's and Sally's parents and siblings had been almost nonexistent to begin with. By the time Thomas and Ashley were old enough to wear glasses, the visits stopped completely.

After she was done cleaning the table, Sally wandered to the office. On the tallest bookcase rested a row of photo albums. She reached up and grabbed the one farthest to the left. The fauxleather cover had once been white, but time and use had worn it to a dull cream color.

This was the oldest of her collections, and the first page of pictures made that abundantly clear. Two pictures, one of each Mirror as a baby in the NICU ward, dominated the page. Strapped to each child was a device almost like a muzzle; there were plenty of different straps to pull on to ensure a proper fit, and a glassy, dark mask covered both eyes. Various versions of these would cover her children's faces until they were old enough to accept the responsibility of sunglasses.

Spurred by that thought, she grabbed another album from behind her. A blue cover marked this series; painted on the front were growing vines sprouting multicolored flowers. Recorded inside were her children as she most often thought of them: old enough to be rid of the constraining headgear but young enough to avoid the horrors that awaited them.

She'd pulled down these albums several times a week over the past year. What would start as a simple desire to remember better days usually ended with the shelf emptied and the office cluttered. She'd fallen asleep here more than once, clutching a book of photos to her chest. Daniel had frowned and scolded her on those mornings as she shook sleep from her eyes, particularly when the room's debris included an empty bottle of scotch.

Retreating to the solitude here didn't solve anything, but it was so tempting to lose herself in better days. Flipping through page after page, she could pretend that nothing had changed. In these moments, she felt she could almost touch that halcyon past.

Unconsciously, her hand reached out and pulled down the most recent of these collections. Even without opening the cover, she knew what she would find here. Normally the opening set of photos grew from a birthday celebration, but because of last year's chaos, there were no such records. Instead, the first pictures here were drawn from a couple weeks later.

Sally had tried hard to assemble this album with the same care she had lavished on the previous incarnations. It hadn't worked, though. When she flipped through the pages, all she noticed was the hopelessness that darkened every picture. Her eyes were inexorably drawn to the tight-lipped grimaces that had replaced the carefree smiles.

With an angry grunt, she tucked the leather-bound book under her arm. Stalking across the room, she opened the old cedar chest. Trying not to think about what she was doing, Sally pulled out the memories she had stored there over the course of her life. When her fingers finally scraped bottom, she tossed the photo album in. As it thumped against the wooden floor of the chest, she released a long breath. Within moments, the offending pictures were buried deeply, the lid closed.

Taking her seat back at the desk, Sally let a small smile cross her lips. Daniel had taken pictures today, but a part of her now knew that they would never make it into an album. There was no reason to preserve these painful years.

Remember the good times. It had been Sam's bit of advice on how to accept the hard times. So she retreated here, her sanctuary of good memories. Flipping idly through her evenings, she'd work through a different album every night, clinging to better times. She missed those days but clung to her conviction that if she never gave up hope, never surrendered her belief in something better, then maybe they'd come back.

It was all she had left.

— CHAPTER 20 —

Sean Murphy inhaled deeply, the crisp tang of night air burning his lungs. He had hoped the meteorologists' predictions would prove incorrect and that the pleasant warmth of the past few days would continue. Instead, he was wrapped up in a coat and wishing for a hot cup of tea. An evening walk was the best medicine for a clouded mind, though. This was a truth he had embraced as a much younger man, and it still served him well.

He regretted that so many of the constellations he'd once known were now lost among the flush of bright city lights. Even the moon, nearly full overhead, seemed dimmer. On other strolls this might have drawn his thoughts off into unrelated tangents, but his focus was solid tonight.

Thomas Ross's visit had been short but eventful. Even after the young Mirror had left, Sean had spent the day returning to their discussion. Sometimes he regretted how he had phrased things or wished he had said more. More often, though, he tried to figure out how to incorporate the pain of Mirrors into his worldview.

So intently was he considering this problem that he almost ran into the dark figure waiting on the sidewalk. Shadows hid the other man's face, and Sean's muscles tensed; for once he actually found himself wishing the city lights were brighter. Then the stranger shifted, and the glow of a nearby porch lamp bathed the broad form in its yellowish glow.

"Sam Barton, is it?"

The shadowy figure nodded. "We should talk."

Sean walked up the steps to the door and opened it. He motioned his guest inside and said, "Tea?"

"Would love some."

"How long have you been waiting for me?"

"A couple minutes, I guess. Long enough to know you weren't here. I was trying to figure out what to do when I saw you come around the corner."

Sean limped into the kitchen, where he began filling an old, dented kettle with water. As he threw open a cabinet and pulled down the small box containing various loose-leaf teas, he said, "I thought I would see you again. Your mannerisms implied you wanted to speak with me but were hesitant to do so in front of your young charge."

He turned back around in time to see the large man nod appreciatively. "Very perceptive."

"So, what brings you here?" Sean's eyes flicked to the clock on the wall. "As I recall, your flight would have been leaving right about now."

"I want to make sure you know what you're getting yourself into. I want to prepare you for what's coming."

Sean paused in his search for the perfect tea blend. "You imply that I did more than converse with a troubled young man today."

Sam grimaced. "Mirrors are watched over very carefully by the government. They're considered a valuable resource, and the board worries constantly about them. They keep their foster families monitored. The screening process for my job is rigorous, to put it mildly. Your sudden appearance will worry them because you're a complete unknown."

"Meaning?"

"You can probably expect a phone call from the board in the next couple of days. If Thomas wants to visit on a regular basis—something he mentioned on the ride home—I imagine Cole Bryant, the vaunted Mirror expert himself, will take an interest.

It may even be as soon as tomorrow; he was in town today, and I don't know if he's flown out already. They'll also run background checks and generally do whatever they feel necessary to minimize the risk you present."

Sean laughed. "Risk?"

"They'll want to know if you're a Liberator. If you are, then expect access to Thomas to be very limited; at the very least it would be available only with some kind of chaperone."

Silence fell over the kitchen, and Sean regarded the other man intently. Behind him, the tea kettle began to whistle shrilly.

"Are you here to help me avoid that fate or to act as the board's first ally in the vetting process?"

"You seemed to connect with Thomas today. He was quiet on the ride home, but it was a thoughtful quiet as opposed to the sullen side I was afraid I'd see. If you can raise his spirits, then I consider you a friend."

Shuffling to the small dining nook, the priest set down the cups of tea on opposite sides of the table. Pulling back a chair with a soft scraping, he gestured to the seat across from him. Sam took it with a respectful nod.

"How much do you know about Mirrors?" Sam asked.

"As much as I could learn on my own, plus what I was given by Thomas today," Sean answered honestly. "I decided to educate myself on the subject when I saw that Michael Pater had been Reflected last week."

A sad sigh escaped his lips. He had always liked Michael, always wanted to find a way to help him. In the past few years he had wondered if there was anything else he could have done to prevent the tragedy the young man's life had become.

"That's why you knew who Thomas was," Sam said. "You didn't tell him that."

"I wanted his perspective. I was worried he might not be as open with me if he felt I was sympathetic to Michael's position."

The larger man paused with the cup of tea halfway to his lips, then gave a slow nod. "You might be right."

"After speaking with Thomas, though, I wonder if the entire point is moot. My research was quite limited by the resources I was able to secure, and fifteen seconds with the boy was enough for me to recognize just how ill-informed I actually was. There must be people out there who understand Mirrors, but they are clearly keeping that knowledge to themselves."

Sam waited a moment, not even tilting his head in acknowledgment. Finally, he replied casually, "Perhaps they cannot find a suitable means of distributing what they know. Perhaps the people they work for do not want that information dispersed."

"Ah. Valid points," the priest replied thoughtfully. "I assume you speak with insight." As expected, this also elicited no response, not even the twitch of a cheek, so he changed the subject.

"So, they will do their best to curtail my influence if they determine I am a Liberator? I hadn't realized that the situation was that grave. What exactly are they worried I will do?"

"Try to flee the country, mostly. Mexico and Canada will both extradite Mirrors under the current agreements, but it takes time. The board hates losing those potential Reflections."

"I thought they wore ankle monitors."

"They do, but the board still worries. The ankle bands are a deterrent, but they're hardly foolproof. It may seem an overreaction, but keeping Mirrors from escaping is vital, so paranoia is allowed, even encouraged."

Sipping his tea, Sean's mind raced. There were layers to this phenomenon that he had never even suspected. The arrival of Mirrors to the world was a recent event; the first had been born within his lifetime. His work had been focused elsewhere, though, and he was woefully unprepared for the arrival of one of these children into his life.

"I will be honest with you," Sean said carefully. "I am unsure whether I am a Liberator. They seek to prevent any Mirrors from

Reflecting criminals, but I know almost nothing about them beyond that fact. Ultimately, I have far too little information on their beliefs to carry their banner. Something tells me, though, that I'm unlikely to agree with their position."

The man across from him arched an eyebrow quizzically, and Sean continued.

"I can see from the way you talk about Thomas that you care for him. More generally, and this is just a guess, I would think that you care for all Mirrors.

"This is problematic. Having spoken with Thomas, I can see the pain that Reflections push onto these children. On a purely emotional level, I cannot imagine how someone who feels such strong affection for one of them could be anything other than a Liberator.

"By your own admission, though, if you *were* a Liberator, then the government would have certainly discovered it by now. If they're going to go to so much trouble vetting an old priest, I can only imagine what the process is like for one who is actually trusted with a Mirror on a weekly basis.

"So, there are a few options." Sean held up three fingers and began to tick them off. "First, you have managed to fool the board and are actually a Liberator. Second, the compassion for your young wards is feigned. Third, you are not a Liberator for reasons that are not obvious to an outsider like me."

"I think I like you," Sam said with a smile. "Insightful, organized, and to the point."

"And I think I like you," Sean replied, "even if you're a bit evasive."

"You understand why my position is precarious."

"Absolutely." He took a sip of hot tea as he pondered the situation. "You're clearly hindered legally or are worried this is a trap. So let's see if I can work some of this out on my own. That way you're not at fault for letting anything slip."

Sean sat back, thoughtfully tapping a finger on the side of his teacup. He'd already given this topic some thought but wasn't really prepared to present his case. Normally he'd be frustrated by the amount of conjecture in his analysis, but he'd been honest earlier: gathering facts about Mirrors was difficult.

"I think the first option is the easiest to dismiss. You may harbor some Liberator tendencies, but if you had any major contacts with them, I can only assume the government would know. You're one of the few people in this country who can take a Mirror wherever you want with no prior arrangement. Based on my study of the current laws, not even Daniel and Sally Ross have that liberty.

"So, your life has been thoroughly examined, and I imagine that this screening is a continuous process rather something that happens once and is forgotten. Thus, if you are a Liberator agent, then you're under such deep cover you rarely speak to any of your compatriots. Not completely out of the realm of possibility, but to what end? Shepherds would have influence with their Mirrors since they see the children frequently, but you're likely to have little influence with the board, Cole Bryant, or Congress, since you're never in DC. Moreover, you're unlikely to move up to a position on the board even after serving your time as a Shepherd."

Sam arched an eyebrow at this last part, but Sean didn't explain. He'd hit that point in a minute.

"All said," he continued, "there's little long-term strategic value for the Liberator movement in placing one of their own in your role. Also, I suspect that those who espouse its philosophies wouldn't be comfortable acting as a soldier for the Justice Department without some ulterior motive. In the end, I can safely say you're not secretly a Liberator.

"So, we move on to the second option: you don't really care for the boys you work with each week.

"On the surface, this one may be harder to disprove. I saw compassion today in your interactions with Thomas, but actions can be faked. Perhaps you see your role as Shepherd as simply a paycheck and feign concern merely to maintain satisfactory job evaluations from your superiors. Or you have other motives for maintaining an illusion of empathy.

"It's a reasonable question, but I doubt that is the case. Based on my research, I think your motivations go much deeper.

"Thirteen years ago, barely a week before the Ross twins were born, a young Mirror named Adam Barton committed suicide in his home in the suburbs of Kansas City. His obituary stated that he was survived by his two sisters, his mother, and his father, Sam."

This was a gamble. It could all be an incredible coincidence. He'd wanted time to dig deeper into this, to confirm his suspicions, but hadn't had the time. The Shepherd's unexpected appearance tonight had denied him that.

"How do you even know about that?" Sam asked, obviously nonplussed.

Maybe this hadn't been the right tactic. It was too late to back out now, though. "When I started my initial research, I discovered a paper on the average lifespan of Mirrors. Some enterprising grad student wanted to know whether Mirrors raised in government foster homes actually lived longer than those raised by family. His appendix included a list of every Mirror he used in his calculations. Adam Barton was one of those."

"And you looked up his obituary?"

"Not until this afternoon. When Thomas introduced you, your last name rang a bell. I became curious."

Sam frowned. "How did you even remember Adam's name? Since Mirrors started appearing fifty-two years ago, there have been more than 350 children born in the United States with the condition. Surely you don't remember them all."

"Well, this was written about ten years ago, so there were fewer. More importantly, though, Adam was an outlier. Even for a Mirror raised at home, he died young."

Sam's grip tightened around his mug, and Sean worried for a moment that the man might crush it in an act of anger. He then wondered what he might do to the man who had brought up such

147

memories. Sean did his best to feign poise. He also tried to project his sympathy for the Shepherd's plight, which he fortunately didn't have to fake.

"I tried to be a good father," Sam said, his voice tinged with regret and frustration. He thankfully eased his grip. "I just didn't know how to help him."

Sean leaned across the table and gripped the other man's arm firmly. "I'm sorry. I didn't mean to tear at old wounds. I was trying to find answers, but I dug too deeply. Forgive an old man who pries too much."

Sam shook his head. "It's all right. Nothing to forgive."

"But . . ."

"People in the government know my history, of course. Most of the ones in DC, the board, for example, don't want to talk about it. My experience humanizes the children. They want to see Mirrors as tools, and I make that harder.

"The house parents, though, the ones who actually raise the Mirrors? They know too, but they do want to hear more. They want to know how to cope with the shift in personality, and ultimately the loss of a child. I've gotten plenty of experience sharing my story over the last nine years."

"Still, I could have been more tactful," Sean admitted.

"Mostly I was surprised you knew. My story is well-known in the circles I travel, but almost no one outside remembers. Even the Rosses didn't know until I mentioned it a few months ago."

Sean frowned. "How did you manage to get this job? The board would have every reason to suspect that you are a Liberator, given your history."

"They did. And they really didn't want to hire me because of that. In the end, though, I survived almost a year of background checks and interviews. They couldn't ignore the fact that I *wanted* to work with Mirrors, that I had experience with one, and that after my son died I studied everything Bryant had ever written. Even then, I think my hiring was contentious.

"You're right about one thing, though. I'll never move up to the board, despite those qualifications. They've decided I'm good with the kids, but I'm not allowed anywhere near policy. Maybe that's for the best."

Sean nodded to himself. "Well, I think I can safely say that you care about Mirrors. So that eliminates option number two.

"Which leaves us with our final possibility: you're not a Liberator for reasons I don't understand."

"You're doing well so far," Sam said. "See what you can piece together."

"I confess I'm running out of ideas. I was hoping at least for a hint."

"Start with Adam."

Sean nodded slowly. That did seem a good place to begin.

Adam Barton had been a Mirror. Specifically, Adam was a Mirror who hadn't been part of the Justice Department's toolbox. Sam was the parent of a Mirror who hadn't been given to the system. As such a parent, wasn't he a de facto Liberator? After all, he'd had the chance at Adam's birth to allow his son to Reflect and chosen not to.

The Liberators seemed the perfect movement for someone like Sam to join officially. He didn't want his son to Reflect, so why not work with the group that wanted that for every Mirror? The Liberators should have been a strong match for his ideology.

Sean was running in circles. By everything he could see, Sam should have joined the Liberators. It just made sense.

Of course it did. It would make perfect sense if it were true.

"You *were* a Liberator," Sean said, comprehension dawning. "When your son was alive. He still died young, though.

"That's why you ended up reading everything of Bryant's you could find. You were trying to see if his way was actually better."

Sam nodded sadly, looking down at the table. "When Adam was born, I heard Bryant's spiel about his Mirrors living longer, and I rejected it as nonsense. The Liberator way made so much more sense. It was easy to believe that their way was better and that if we could find a way to free all the Mirrors, they'd live full lives."

"And then when Adam died, you realized that wasn't the case."

Sam nodded. "It was the start. It guided me to the questions I should have asked in the first place."

"Such as?"

Given how cagey the Shepherd had been to this point, Sean wasn't really expecting an answer. Sam obliged him, though; apparently he'd figured out enough that the Shepherd was willing to fill in the cracks.

"There are a couple of major ones. First is whether to let the government use the children at all. Not every country uses Mirrors in the criminal justice system, you know. The second is whether they should Reflect so young."

"And what did you learn?"

"The second question is actually easier to answer. I found that it's the age of a Mirror more than the number of Reflections that seems to kill him. Older Mirrors handle it worse than the kids. Maybe the young ones are more resilient or they simply process it better. I don't know. The sad truth is that if they're going to be used for justice, then starting them young actually maximizes their potential Reflections."

Sean rested his elbows on the table, thoughtfully steepling his fingers. "Which leaves the bigger question: should they be used this way at all?"

"Exactly. So, I studied how Mirrors are treated around the world.

"In Norway there are no compulsory Reflections, but the public can petition the Mirrors themselves for one. Convicted criminals and their families do so assiduously. Of course, it only takes one such Reflection before they understand how horrifying the experience is. Still, most Mirrors keep giving in to the teary-eyed requests of the victim's grieving family members. In the end, they meet the same fate as the ones here. The few that choose not to Reflect end up locking themselves away from the public, becoming hermits. Either way, their lives tend to be short and bitter.

"France has taken an even tougher stance. They have outlawed all Reflections, so there is supposedly no such pressure from the populace. Mirrors are not unaware of their situation, though. Some are eventually persuaded to Reflect people, but since the evidence is inadmissible in court, they will never see any kind of reward for their sacrifice.

"There are worse consequences, though. Use of Mirrors has gutted organized crime within the United States; France, meanwhile, has one of the strongest mob presences in the world, and the dons have found a use for these children. Kidnapped Mirrors are common there; Reflections are used to prove the loyalty of their underlings. It's a horror far worse than what happens in the United States.

"I understand what Liberators want, but they aren't ready to answer the difficult questions about it. Mirrors around the world die young regardless of the political climate. I think the better solution is to make their lives the best they can be. I think they need people who care about them as children instead of as tools."

"And Thomas?" Sean asked.

"When my son died, I felt lost to the world. I didn't want to know about anything else; I wanted to focus on my grief. Instead, the birth of the Ross twins shattered my sanctum. No matter how much I wanted to wallow in self-pity, I knew there was another family who would be living this nightmare twice.

"I wish I could claim it was altruistic, but I needed something to keep me going. I needed a purpose, and I latched on to the idea of helping Thomas Ross. Everything I've learned has been bent toward that end. It's stupid, but I feel if I can help him, maybe it'll erase some of the guilt I carry from Adam's death."

Looking down at his teacup, Sean asked quietly, "What is it you hope to do for him? Are you hoping to help him survive?"

"I'm not fooling myself. He's going to die. I just want to make his life as fulfilling as possible. I want him to have the opportunities Adam didn't. I want . . ."

Sam shook his head. "I don't know. I wish I had set better goals, but all I have is this nebulous idea that I need to give him purpose. It's not much to go on, I guess."

"It seems you want to improve a boy's quality of life by giving him something to live for," Sean said with an encouraging smile. "That seems a pretty good start to me."

"And if I can't figure out more than that?"

Sean waved a hand dismissively. "Don't overthink this. Focus on the goal: if you can give Thomas a purpose, something that makes him feel like his existence is worthwhile, would you consider it a victory?"

Sam thought for a moment, then nodded emphatically. "Yes. Yes, it would."

Sean's smile broadened. "Then we fight."

— PART III —

Fourteen Years Old—Promises

We risk it becoming too easy for the opposition to downplay the efficacy of Mirror Justice. By focusing on the emotional rather than the demonstrable, they are succeeding in altering the narrative. Reclaiming the upper hand in this debate starts and ends with disseminating the relevant facts of Mirror work.

Since the inception of this program, homicides are down more than 50 percent, and conviction rates are above 99 percent. Since the addition of sexual assault to the list of Reflectable offenses, we have seen marked decrease in those crimes. Convictions are increasing as well.

Some alarmists have noted that reported sexual assaults have risen recently. On the surface, this rise might seem problematic, but further study has revealed a more positive trend. The suspected number of assaults has actually decreased in recent years; the number of reported incidents has increased because victims now believe that the possibility of a Reflection implies a better chance for justice.

Perhaps the greatest impact of the Mirror program, though, is the dismantling of most of the organized criminal elements of the United States. From the local street gang to the powerful mob bosses, the Mirror program has gutted these organizations.

Though rare, our interventions into the world of white-collar crime have reaped results far beyond anything we could have hoped.

We've shut down corrupt boards at several companies and through those events removed a handful of corrupt congressmen from office. While this has made us some enemies on the Hill, it's caused a significant uptick in public support for our work. Individually, political representatives may feel threatened by our work, but as long as their voters approve, they will keep supporting us.

All this, of course, is supported by a trickle-down effect. More murders are getting solved, and those cases are wrapped up with nigh-incontrovertible evidence. This frees up resources from both the law enforcement and legal frameworks and allows them time and energy to tackle other crimes. The final result of all this is that we've seen a double-digit percentage decrease in crime across the board, even in crimes completely unconnected to Reflections.

This is just a snapshot of what we do. It's the most easily quantifiable list of our successes, but it is only the precis of a far greater story: Mirrors change thousands of lives for the better, including people they touch only tangentially.

The Liberator movement is growing stronger, but it does so only because they give a face to the suffering. If we could easily personify the untold masses who have benefited from our work, we would bury their position under a mountain of emotional connection.

Don't waver in your devotion to this work. When you see their pamphlets with dejected-looking children, or when you hear of the death of another young Mirror, think back to today. Remember that the Liberator propaganda portrays only a single battle in a vaster war. Hold on to your convictions; your victories are worth literally hundreds of theirs.

—Excerpt of Dr. Cole Bryant addressing the collected members of the Mirror Justice Program

-CHAPTER 21-

Renewing tradition brought Daniel a profound satisfaction. McMurray's itself was a welcoming respite from their new normal. Years ago, the owner had offered the small private dining room in the back of his restaurant for their annual celebrations. The first eleven of the twins' birthdays had been celebrated in this room, and being back here was a respite in its own way.

In many ways it seemed that time had forsaken this space. Every picture adorning the wall rested where it had on their first venture here thirteen years ago. Even the table was the same, the deep gash near one of the corners unmistakable.

Daniel had always felt an odd sense of peace here. Even as his children grew up before his eyes, this place had been stable. Every birthday had been a mixture of joy and anxiety for the parents who watched their children inexorably approaching the end of innocence. Even for that, he had looked forward to these celebrations. In the midst of a life that was often boringly familiar, these excursions were sparks of color and excitement. Today was all that and more; where all previous birthdays had been a quiet family affair, today the walls almost shook with the cacophony inside.

When it became clear that this year would see them return to McMurray's, Ashley had insisted on inviting Carol Raines. Sally had worked diligently to talk her out of it, but their daughter had proven adamant. Sally had wanted to simply deny the request, but Daniel had made it clear that such a refusal was nothing but self-serving egotism. That had won him points with Ashley but meant he and Sally had barely spoken over the past week.

Upon learning of the invitation, Thomas hadn't wanted to be left out. With Carol invited, he had made his own plea for Sam to attend. Sally was less unsure about this, but that may have been born of a belief that the man wouldn't be able to make it. He lived out of state, and traveling on Thomas's birthday two years in a row was a bit much to expect; the board didn't pay for his flights when he wasn't working. Sam had been delighted, however, and made it clear that the plane fare was worth the cost.

Those two would have been enough to dramatically change the usual festivities, but two days ago Thomas had decided he also wanted to extend an invitation to the priest he visited.

In retrospect, he and Sally should have expected that invitation. Thomas had fought hard to get regular access to the man, even writing several letters to the board. It had taken six months, but they'd finally approved weekly visits. With that emotional investment, it was surprising it had taken that long for Thomas to bring him in.

Daniel wasn't particularly religious; he had grown up in some long-forgotten branch of Protestantism but hadn't been to church in years. This led to some deep-rooted but vague guilt that made conversations with Father Sean awkward. To his credit, the priest had never even brought up religion in their meetings.

In the end, he had decided it was Thomas's birthday, not theirs, and had put his foot down. The priest didn't have a vehicle, so Daniel had picked up the man at his church; Daniel wasn't sure Sally had forgiven him for that, either.

At the moment, Carol sat across the table regaling Father Sean with stories about her Mirrors. The man listened intently, nodding interestedly as she spoke. Sam, Thomas, and Ashley were excitedly discussing the current football season, which wasn't really surprising.

Ashley had started showing an interest in sports about six months after the Reflections started. Since the competitions were live, sports would always be an event she could experience before seeing it in Reflections. If he had asked about her sudden fascination in baseball at its onset, he might have been able to start creating new memories for them months earlier.

Today that delay didn't seem to matter much. His children's moods had steadily improved over the past year, climbing to the peak Dr. Bryant called "the two-year bounce." Apparently, every Mirror learned a measure of control over their experiences at around this point in the cycle. Life didn't suddenly revert to the way it was before the Reflections, but there was a brief respite from the horror here. Nothing lasted forever, though, and as these defenses failed, the Mirrors would fail with them, tumbling faster than they had before.

Thomas and Ashley were enjoying a monumental bounce. No other Mirror had shown this level of adaptation at this point. They still didn't smile as much as they used to, but when they did, the emotion was clearly genuine.

Daniel started as the waiter placed a salad before him. Looking around, he realized that the scene had changed while he'd drifted off into contemplation. Sam and the priest were discussing religion while Carol listened. Sally, unsurprisingly, eschewed the conversation, instead staring wistfully at the twins.

The children, meanwhile, were playing their favorite game, something they had named Stibium. Stibium was all about obscure trivia. The game had a couple of forms. In the rarer version, one child would start with the first word in a list. They'd alternate back and forth, each providing the next item, until one of them answered incorrectly or simply didn't know. In the past year, he'd heard them list off Heisman Trophy winners, films that won Best Picture Oscars, films that *didn't* win Best Picture Oscars, Russian czars, and several others.

Usually, though, they played simple trivia. One of the two would start, usually Ashley, by firing a single question at the other. If the interrogated child answered correctly, the questioner continued asking questions about the same topic until finally hitting upon a question the other couldn't handle. Upon failing, they switched roles and the game continued.

"Whose law states that the potential between two points is equivalent to the current times the resistance between them?" Thomas asked.

"Ohm's Law. Come on, that's easy."

Daniel let the conversation drift away. This wasn't the first time he'd heard the kids spouting off impressive-sounding facts. It wasn't as stunning anymore, particularly since finding out they weren't sure what exactly to do with the information. Given values for each term, they could plug in the numbers and find an answer, but they didn't always possess the logic to properly manipulate the principles they quoted.

Not that what they remembered wasn't impressive; it was. He wasn't sure how any one person could know so much, let alone two fourteen-year-olds. They admitted that plenty of information faded after each Reflection, which was the only thing that made the game any fun at all. Knowledge that had been held dear or important or particularly interesting by one of their Reflected stuck about much longer, though. As Ashley had once put it, "People know what they love." Then pointing to Thomas and herself, she'd added, "You wouldn't forget our names, would you?"

They practically ignored their salads to play the game, but that may have been more about the greens and less about the competition. Ashley missed a question about pressure, and then Thomas answered about a half-dozen baseball questions correctly before missing a query about a Triple Crown winner Ashley dubbed "an easy one."

"Fine. What New Testament books are missing from the Chester Beatty papyrus?" Thomas replied, smiling with a smug certainty.

"The pastoral epistles," Ashley replied without missing a beat.

Thomas paused, fork halfway to his mouth. "Wait. I had that serial molester preacher, but who did you . . . ?"

"Jealous, hatchet-wielding seminarian," Ashley said.

"Oh yeah!"

Both children abruptly burst out in riotous laughter. Across the table, Sally looked absolutely scandalized, but the waiter removing their salad plates joined in with a barely stifled laugh of his own.

"Ashley, you invited Mrs. Raines to join you today; don't you think you should play games later? It's not polite to ignore your guest." Sally's tone was mild, but Daniel knew the desperation in that request. If she was telling Ashley to spend time with her Shepherd, she was truly discomfited. Then again, he wasn't sure how comfortable he was with his daughter laughing about murderous seminarians.

"Oh, let them have fun," Carol said. "We talk every week, but I don't often get to see her smile."

Ashley turned an exuberant grin to the woman, and Sally made a terrible attempt at a smile herself; she looked like she had eaten a rotten tomato.

"For heaven's sake, stop pretending," Carol said suddenly, shaking her head. "You're going to strain something." Then, turning to Daniel, the older woman said pleasantly, "Now, I understand you're from Chicago?"

He opened his mouth to answer the question, but his focus shifted to the priest. Sean Murphy was leaning over toward the twins, a sort of mischievous smile twitching at the corners of his mouth. His eyes twinkling, he said, "I'm intrigued by your game. Would you mind letting an old man join in?"

Thomas looked taken aback, but Ashley nodded. "Sure. We don't just do Bible stuff, though."

"I know. I've been listening with half an ear for a while. I admit that I'm not as versed in the sciences, but I think you'll find me up to the challenge."

"Okay," Ashley said with a nod, and Daniel bit his lip. He had thought about playing with them a couple of times, just to show them that their father wasn't stupid. He had decided against it after realizing that it would have the opposite effect.

"We'll start easy on you," the girl continued. "Thomas said you like baseball, right? We can do that first."

Her brother nodded, taking the initiative. "All right. Who was the baseball commissioner during the Black Sox scandal?"

An arched eyebrow from Ashley said she didn't think that was necessarily a friendly opening, but the priest didn't even pause. "Kennesaw Mountain Landis."

Intrigued, Daniel sat back to listen, but Carol Raines wrangled him into conversation. She had been born in Chicago and shared how the city had changed within her lifetime. He was just beginning to tell about his own childhood when a delighted laugh from Ashley drew his attention back to their game.

Father Sean was still answering questions, and judging by the look on Sam's face he was doing so with literal jaw-dropping accuracy. A broad smile painted Ashley's face, but Thomas wore a deep frown, and his fingers were drumming on the table.

"Biology," Ashley said, introducing her next contribution. "What are the only surviving monotremes?"

Apparently the older man had proven so knowledgeable that they had departed from a single-subject approach, instead peppering him with queries from any number of fields. He'd never seen them do that before.

"Let's see. Monotremes are egg-laying mammals, and I believe the only living examples are the platypus and several species of echidna."

"Geography," Thomas snapped. "Deepest lake in the world?"

"Lake Baikal in Siberia, at just over a mile deep."

Ashley shot her brother a slight frown before proceeding. "Entertainment: who has been nominated for the most Oscars?"

"Walt Disney. I don't know the exact total, but I believe it's about sixty."

"Yes," Ashley said, shaking her head in disbelief. "It's fifty-nine, by the way."

Thomas made a dismissive gesture. "Art History: Dutch artist with a painting of children teaching a cat to dance."

There was no mistaking Ashley's frustration now. Leaning over, she put a hand on her brother's arm. "Remember rule two!"

Daniel had heard them mention rules before, but it had taken him a while to figure out what each rule was. The topic was only broached when they disagreed on whether something was actually a violation. Over time he'd puzzled out that rule two could probably best be stated as "The answer to any given question must be instantly recognizable to the average person." It didn't mean the average person had to know the trivia, just that they would have heard of the person, place, or thing the question referenced. It was amusing to Daniel that what the two Mirrors considered common knowledge wasn't always what a normal person would actually know. In fact, the name of the game, Stibium, came from a heated argument about whether that answer was rule-two legal or not.

This apparent violation of what would be commonly known didn't even slow the priest, though, who smoothly answered, "Jan Steen." Daniel had never even heard the name, but as neither child corrected him, it was probably the right answer.

"Uh . . . history," Ashley began, but Thomas spoke over her.

"History! Who assassinated Archduke Franz Ferdinand?"

"Thomas! That's a clear rule-two violation!"

"Gavrilo Princip."

Almost sneering, Thomas quickly asked, "Who assassinated the Prime Minister of Sweden?"

"That's rule four! Stop it, Thomas!" Ashley seemed genuinely upset by her brother's side-stepping of the tacit strictures. Even Daniel was a bit surprised; rule four made trick questions illegal.

161

Given how his children had treated this rule, he had assumed it was the most sacred.

"I assume you mean Prime Minister Olof Palme?" Father Sean asked, clarifying the question. "Trick question. His murder is officially unsolved."

Visibly shocked, the boy sat still for a moment. Just as he was leaning forward to launch another volley, Ashley's hand darted out and firmly grabbed his shoulder. Pushing him so that he had to look at her, she gave him a disapproving grimace and said, "Enough. You couldn't get him even when you were cheating."

"No," Thomas shot back fiercely. "He admitted he's weak in the sciences. Quick, think of something to throw at him."

"Thomas," Daniel said firmly. "I think you need to let it go."

His son opened his mouth to protest, but Daniel raised a finger and the boy slumped back in his chair, sulking. Ashley shot her father a grateful look, then turned to Father Sean and said, "That was amazing!"

"Thank you."

Before anyone could press the issue, lunch arrived. Sally dug in immediately, apparently happy for the distraction. Sam and Carol were only slightly behind her. Ashley directed several more queries at Father Sean, but these were personal instead of competitive. Upon discovering that he'd briefly lived in Europe, the two went off into a short private discussion in German that ended with both laughing.

Thomas picked at his food at first, but after many furtive glares at his sister and the priest, seemed to decide not to let this defeat spoil the only meal he ate out all year. He chewed his steak silently, though. Snatches of talk wandered across the table for the rest of lunch, but Thomas didn't break his silence, even after blowing out the candles on his cake.

Only after chairs had scraped away from the table and good-byes were being tendered did he finally rejoin the world. That return was clearly grudging, and he kept his hands thrust deep into the pockets of his windbreaker even as he mumbled farewells. He'd quite obviously saved the priest for last but did approach the man without needing any outside pressure.

Father Sean spoke softly, and Daniel couldn't make out any of the words passing between the two. Thomas's anger turned to embarrassment before eventually melting into an uneasy acceptance. The aloof stance didn't change, but he did give the man a quick embrace before leaving the private dining room.

Daniel would have intervened at this point, but the two had clearly come to some sort of understanding. More importantly, the priest would still need a ride back to the church, and that would provide plenty of time to question the man's motives in private.

Once outside the restaurant, the knot of people began to unravel. Carol offered a few polite departing words before striding imperiously to her large sedan. Sam and Father Sean held a short conversation before the big Shepherd headed for his rental car. Sally and Thomas were already walking over to the family's station wagon, leaving Daniel with the priest and—unexpectedly —Ashley.

"Why don't you go ride with Mom?" he said. "I need to talk to Father Sean."

"I know," she replied simply. "That's why I'm riding with you. I want to hear what he says."

Daniel opened his mouth to order her to the other vehicle but stopped short. His daughter's demeanor was calm and confident; she understood what was about to transpire and wanted the same answers her father wanted. Even amid the trappings of a birthday party, it was easy to forget just how quickly she was growing up.

"All right," he said reluctantly. If nothing else, her presence might help him keep his temper in check.

Silence dominated the first few minutes of the drive. Father Sean seemed perfectly at ease watching the passing scenery with a peaceful smile. Daniel, meanwhile, felt his stomach pitching wildly; arguing with a priest wasn't exactly how he preferred to spend his time. Glances in the rearview mirror showed Ashley watching him anxiously; at least she seemed to share his discomfort.

Finally, drawing a long breath, Daniel demanded, "What was that all about?"

"Pardon?"

"That demonstration back at the restaurant. Were you trying to drive my son crazy?"

"A little, yes."

Daniel balked, suddenly taken off guard. It strained credulity to believe that the priest had missed Thomas's increasing fury while they played their game, but Daniel had expected the man to dissemble.

"You thought I would lie to you." the older man said. It wasn't really a question.

"Uh, yes, actually. Most people don't admit to actively baiting a child."

Father Sean gave a weak laugh. "Lying is a sin, but teaching a boy humility is not."

"Is that what you think you were doing?" Heat was rising in Daniel's voice. "Did it occur to you that you might be taking something precious away from him? The knowledge that he gains from the Reflections makes him feel special; he revels in the fact that he knows more than any non-Mirror. You destroyed that all in a matter of minutes."

"Pride in trivial knowledge is a terrible foundation for one's life," the other man replied, his voice firm. "I've come to care for Thomas over the last year, and I won't have him believing that his worth comes from how much minutiae he can recite. He deserves better."

"Does it matter? If he finds joy in being smarter than everyone else, what difference does it make?" Daniel shook his head angrily. "I've worked hard over the past year to give my children whatever measure of happiness I can. Thomas has found something he likes, something that actually makes him smile, and for you to casually strip it away is petty."

"An old man with a good memory shouldn't be able to destroy your sense of self-worth in a matter of minutes," Father Sean said placidly. "I want him to find purpose in something meaningful."

"Oh, I forgot. You're the religious leader, the expert on life. Well, how do you know that his way is so frivolous?"

Father Sean paused, turning to cast a weighing glance at Daniel. Before he could answer, though, Ashley's voice cut the tension. "You knew the answers. *All* the answers. Some of those were pretty obscure."

Memories of lunch rushed through Daniel's mind in an instant. He had been so focused on Thomas's reaction he had missed the obvious question. Ashley was right, though. The average person might have known some of those, but his son's last few attempts delved well beyond the realm of common knowledge. For someone to have a grasp of so many different subjects . . .

Slowly, Daniel said, "You have a photographic memory."

"Close enough, I suppose. Age is stealing more every year, but I have retained enough.

"I speak from experience, Daniel. Knowledge is a beautiful thing, but it shouldn't be the underpinning of one's entire existence. It promises much but delivers only an empty life."

"Maybe that's true for you, but it might not be true for my son. Did it occur to you that it might be enough for him?"

Father Sean paused, a finger raised to tap thoughtfully on his lips. "Did it seem enough at lunch? If I can strip it away by simply knowing more than him, then don't you think it's a weak foundation? A life's purpose should be something you can draw strength from while languishing in the deepest of pits. I'm not sure trivia qualifies."

In the backseat, Ashley was nodding approval. Daniel gave her a frown, but she didn't seem to notice. Her attention was directed solely at the priest.

"Even if that's true, there must be subtler ways to point it out. Destroying his birthday party wasn't necessary."

Father Sean turned a flat look at Daniel. "Thomas has never been one to appreciate subtlety." At this, Ashley's nod became more vigorous, and the corners of her mouth twitched up in a hesitant smile. "Frankly, neither have I. I honestly think it's one of the reasons he likes me.

"Still, I have broached the subject with him on several occasions over the last few months, but my arguments have left no impression. I'm not willing to give up so easily, though."

"Why?"

"Thomas has told me of your efforts to provide new experiences from him and his sister. I applaud you for that; their lives are rife with suffering, and offering any respite from that is a worthy cause. Where you and I differ is whether that is enough to sustain a person.

"You cannot simply string together a series of blissful memories and call it a life well-lived. We crave more than that. We need a purpose to make us strong. As today's foray into trivia proved, anything less than that will collapse under stress. Being the smartest person you know is a weak salve to the pains of life. Particularly since there is always someone smarter.

"Right now your son sees himself as a puppet, dancing about at the behest of a government board he's never seen. He sees no more value in his life than he does in his death. I disagree strongly with that sentiment; until death claims him, he can have a purpose. Until he draws that final breath, he can be a person of worth and value."

"What do you expect him to do?" Daniel almost added, "He's a Mirror," but was conscious of his daughter's presence. Whatever this man might hope for Thomas, the opportunities afforded the boy were few and far between. What the government didn't expressly forbid, society would. It wasn't a truth he wanted Ashley to dwell on, but he wouldn't lie to himself about their fate.

"Ashley," Father Sean said, turning toward the backseat, "what is your greatest accomplishment?"

There was no hesitation. "Reflecting Spencer Duncan."

"Why?"

"Not him alone; it's just that he was first. I still remember most of his life because it ran through my head so often those first few weeks, before I learned to shove it down." She drew a shuddering breath, obviously steeling herself. "The people I'm called to Reflect are those who would likely walk free without my help. Spencer was dangerous, a monster who thought he could get away with anything. Jessica Graves would not have been his last victim; I know it. I saved those girls, the ones he would have raped had he walked free."

"If you could be rid of your powers at the price of voiding all the convictions of the criminals you have reflected, would you accept that bargain?" Father Sean's tone had changed. No longer was he proving a point; he now seemed genuinely curious.

This time there was obvious reluctance. Ashley scrubbed a hand nervously through her hair, then massaged her forehead. "I don't know. I want to believe I wouldn't turn my back on everything I've done, but to be free of this . . ." She trailed off.

Father Sean smiled at her warmly. "I respect an honest answer. That you would even consider abandoning a normal life proves just how powerful your purpose is. This is what I want to give your brother."

"I understand." She turned her attention to the rearview mirror, catching Daniel's eye. "He's right, Dad."

That was too much to absorb so quickly. Instead, Daniel hastily pulled into a parking space near the church's front walk.

Father Sean swung the door open and managed to climb out rather nimbly despite the bad leg. He made a final show of gratitude for the ride, then turned toward the large stone building. He didn't make it two steps. Ashley had popped outside too, hurrying around to the passenger side. The priest gave her a surprised look as she drew up short.

"Thank you," she said in a quiet voice. Daniel could barely make out the words. "I always wanted to believe the official story that Mirrors are brave martyrs who give their lives to make the world a better place. Maybe it's not a lie. Not if I live it like it's true."

A smile split the priest's face. "Hold on to that and make it your own." He paused. "Perhaps you'd like to come with Thomas some time? Ich habe kaum Chancen Deutsch zu sprechen."

Ashley gave a small laugh. "No one I know speaks it either!" She then gave a sad shrug. "I would, but he can get pretty possessive. He sees you as *his* friend and might not want to share. I'll stay away so you can keep working on him."

"Agreed."

Ashley moved to open the passenger-side door, but the priest called her back before she could slide in.

His face was serious now, and he spoke with emotion. "Your brother is a troubled young man, but if there's anything in his life that he truly cares for, it is you. He tolerates—maybe even appreciates—Sam and me, but you may be the only one he really loves. You can use that. Bind him to something meaningful; make his life matter."

Father Sean gave her a final smile, then waved before hobbling up the main walk toward the heavy wooden doors. Ashley turned back to the car, claiming the vacated seat for herself. Buckling herself in, she watched the dark-robed man disappear inside the church.

As he maneuvered the car back toward the highway, Daniel looked over at his daughter. "I don't get it. With that memory, he could be anything he wanted."

Ashley gave him a quizzical look. "Dad, he was trying to tell you that he already is." She turned back to glance at the structure vanishing behind them. "I like him."

Daniel wasn't sure he shared that conviction.

-CHAPTER 22-

Ashley stepped outside, sliding the glass door closed behind her. Long shadows stretched across the hardwood deck, creeping up the side of the patio furniture and shading its normal white into a mottled gray. Cruel wisps of November wind licked the air, tugging at her loose hair and tossing it across her gaze. With a cut-off sigh, she dug into her pocket for a scrunchie to make a hasty ponytail.

Vision clear, she surveyed the yard. Behind the ubiquitous tint of the sunglasses, the world was fading rapidly into indistinct patches of darkness, but even through the dying light, she could make out the red of Thomas's windbreaker against the deep-brown stain of the wooden fence. He stood halfway up, feet braced on the center crosspiece and fingers wrapped around the top of the slats, staring west to the setting sun. If he had heard the door open and close, he gave no indication.

Ashley stepped toward him. "There you are." He offered no acknowledgment. "Mom says dinner's about ready."

"Come watch the sun set."

"I've seen it, Thomas."

"Not like this."

Ashley shrugged. "What? From the fence? It can't make much difference."

"Just come here. I want you to see."

"All right."

Her footsteps echoed off the hardwood planks of the deck as she strode to join him. Her short, quick clops shifted abruptly to the quiet *shif-shif* of dead grass underfoot before she stopped at the fence. She gripped the top of the slat with both hands, placed a foot on the center crosspiece and hoisted herself up to stand next to her brother.

Resting low in the sky, the sun lay halfway hidden behind the mountains that formed their horizon. Light spilled through the breaks between peaks, and the shadows they cast loosed the first dark harbingers of night into the yards and streets.

"It doesn't look any diff . . ."

The words died in Ashley's throat. She'd pulled her gaze from the setting sun to look at her brother and for the first time understood what he meant.

Gone were the black frames and reflective lenses that formed practically every memory of his face. Thomas was unsafe, his silver eyes searching the horizon with an almost reverent intensity. He never turned to look at her, never broke his gaze from the failing fire in the sky, but she knew he felt her confused stare. Brandishing one of those coveted genuine smiles, he said softly, "It's better without them."

"And if someone walks outside and meets your eyes?"

"It won't make the sunset any less beautiful."

"Thomas . . ."

"I don't care if I Reflect someone. This is my moment. Let *them* wear the glasses for once; let *them* live trapped in shadow. This sunset is mine." He paused, nodded to himself, then said, "No. Ours. Take off your glasses, Ashley."

Guilt welled in her even before she complied. She'd wanted to see the world unhindered for so many years. So fervent were the lessons of her childhood that she always felt awkward without the protective lenses. Deep inside, though, burned a desire to see the world as it truly was. She'd lived that world through her Reflected. In reality, she'd seen only a handful of places outside her own home and the occasional police station.

Turning back to the sun, she gritted her teeth and seized the fence post tightly in her right hand. With her left she unlocked and pulled the dark glasses from her face.

Light streamed into her now-uncovered eyes, and she shied away instinctively. This was not the soft, yellow light of her bedroom or the warm fluorescent of the Reflection Rooms. Evening light blazed with a different fire. Still bracing herself with her right hand, she threw up her left to block the harshest of the fading rays.

"It's unique," Thomas acknowledged. She could see him out of the corner of her eye. His head never even twitched in her direction; the glowing horizon held his focus. "And seeing it like this isn't like seeing it through someone else's eyes."

Slowly, almost unwillingly, she forced herself to look. Painfully brilliant, her eyes avoided gracing the sun directly, but the sky around it held sufficient wonder. Purples, blues, oranges, and reds splayed out in a final tantrum against the night's imminent victory. Clouds hovered above the sun, glowing with the same moribund spectrum as the sky.

Childish as it sounded when Thomas voiced it, he was right. She'd seen sunsets through a hundred different sets of eyes, but to stand here herself, with the wind slashing her face and whistling in her ears, it seemed better.

"Another day gone." Surprisingly, Thomas's words weren't bitter. They were regretful, though. "Two years, maybe three? It doesn't seem enough."

"I thought Father Sean told you not to focus on that." She knew this might be a sensitive subject after lunch that day, but she wanted an answer. She needed to know what was on her brother's mind.

"He doesn't understand. He talks to me like I'm dying of cancer or something. He tells me to live rather than just be alive and that death is only the end of the journey, not the destination." Thomas sighed. "But I'm not dying of cancer. I'm dying of a loss of hope. I'm going to die because I reject life, not because it's taken from me."

Ashley frowned and instinctively tightened her grip on the boards. "We're doing okay. Life's better than it was two years ago, not worse. I think we'll make it."

"Make it to what, Ashley?"

Mouth open, Ashley stopped abruptly. About to answer simply, "Eighteen," she instead froze. Mrs. Raines talked about living to eighteen all the time. It was the milestone that promised freedom from all these Reflections. As she considered Thomas's question, though, Ashley balked.

He must have sensed her confusion, because he picked up the thread of conversation. "Why does it matter? Even once we stop Reflecting, we'll still have all these memories. You know that the few who make it to eighteen still kill themselves. I think it's just too much. We're not designed to hold all those lives, all that sorrow. We *will* die. It's inevitable."

He paused, shifting his weight on the fence, and the boards creaked. Ashley wanted to say something, to oppose him, but she wasn't even sure where to begin.

"We're a twist of the head away from death right now. I look right, you look left, our eyes meet." He sighed. "But I'm not ready. I've nothing to live for, nothing to really hope for even now, but I'm still not going to do it."

Ashley bit her lip, thinking. Father Sean had been right. Whatever Thomas derived strength from clearly wasn't enough. Even today, their best day in the past two years, he wasn't alive because he wanted to live. Instead, he was still too afraid to die.

On the other hand, Ashley knew her purpose.

"I want to stop people like Spencer."

Thomas tilted his head in a barely perceptible nod. "For how long? How long can you bring yourself to become Spencer to stop people like him?"

She tried to speak, but he cut her off. "Life is better right now, Ashley, but it's not perfect. Every Mirror hits the two-year bounce. You know that. I've heard Sam and Carol both talking about it. It gets better, and then it gets worse. Much worse."

"I know."

By now the sun was no more than a thin sliver above the mountains, and the purplish livery of night's servants crept closer to the horizon. Dinner was probably ready, or at least close enough to warrant returning inside, but neither Ashley nor Thomas moved.

Ashley fidgeted, uncomfortable. Even in a life with purpose, she had come to accept that it wouldn't last forever. Eventually the Reflections would weigh her down and she would embrace the only option left to her. Thoughts of that final moment terrified her. Not just that her life would be over, but something that scared her even more.

"I don't want to die alone," she whispered in a rush.

"What?"

"I don't want to be alone when I die."

"Mom and dad won't abandon us . . ."

Ashley frowned and almost bounced on the fence with frustration. "We'll abandon them, Thomas! You know this; you've told me."

"I trust Mrs. Raines, but I know some Mirrors don't at the end. I think I could always lean on her, but I don't know that I will. I don't know what my final days will be like. She's so important to me, Thomas, and I want her to always be that important, but . . ."

She trailed off as the last glimmer of the sun vanished completely behind jutting peaks Twilight claimed the world, though slivers of sunlight would battle for a time before finally conceding to their eternal rival.

"That leaves . . . me." Thomas's acknowledgment came slowly.

"Yes."

"You don't know that you won't abandon me at the end."

"I won't abandon you if you won't abandon me."

"You can't promise that."

Eyes still riveted forward, her head never swaying even an inch in her brother's direction, Ashley wiped away a tear. "I can. I will! I promise I won't leave you to this alone. I promise that as long as you are willing to fight, I'll stand at your side. As long as you're willing to live, I'll live too."

Only silence met her pledge. Thomas's head never even twitched, and she dared not look at him to see if she could piece together his thoughts. She waited, the wind throwing its errant gusts against her face and hands. Her ears began to burn with chill, and she was sure her cheeks shone red, but she couldn't leave yet.

The last golden hues were fading from the sky before he finally responded. "It doesn't matter. You'll be a different person then; so will I. That promise won't mean anything to you."

"It means something to me now."

Thomas released a pained sigh, a long and tired sound.

Streetlamps flickered on, bathing the world in their dim, unnatural illumination. Dipped down out of sight, the sun existed now only as the last failing tint of orange. In that creeping darkness, the wind seemed suddenly colder, and Ashley shivered. Still, she held on.

From behind, the shuffle of the sliding glass door opening crossed the yard, followed only seconds later by Mom's call that it was time to eat. She never saw their uncovered eyes and shut the door without another word.

Thomas slowly withdrew his glasses from his shirt pocket. Flipping them open with a snap, he stood a final second gazing at the evening. Ashley followed his lead, securing herself into almost total darkness as the shades locked over her ears.

Thomas hesitated. "Words now are a poor substitute for actions later, but . . ." He hopped down from the fence, landing on the grass with a muffled thump. Ashley kept her perch, watching him as best she could by the dim light of the streetlamps. He turned his uncovered eyes upon her shaded ones, nodded ever so slightly, and whispered, "I promise."

—CHAPTER 23—

Cole Bryant closed the door behind him, flipped the dead bolt, and dropped his keys in the small ceramic bowl on the bookcase in a series of practiced motions. He traveled so often he'd boiled the details of coming and going down to an art. These actions were merely the first steps in an intricate dance he'd performed hundreds of times.

Carry-on bag momentarily left at the door. Briefcase to the office, and computer turned on. Back to the kitchen to check the cat food, his answering machine, the mail his landlady had left on the table. Toss 90 percent of the mail immediately, then return to find the computer booted up and ready to go. Print documents to replace the ones he'd given out on his trip. Return to the carry-on, unpack it, pack it again, make it ready to go at a moment's notice. Take the freshly printed documents and slide them into the proper pocket of the briefcase.

He moved by rote. It was tedious and dull, and he appreciated every boring step. His trips were always a chaotic series of inter-actions with people who never wanted to see him; coming home to a silent apartment was a reprieve rather than a disappointment.

Returning to the kitchen, he pulled open the fridge. Cole stared at the contents for a long moment, then shut it without taking any-thing. Days like today made him wish he drank.

No, he amended silently, days like today made him wish he trusted himself to drink.

With only a little regret, he loaded up the coffee machine and set it brewing. It was only 11:00 p.m. Still plenty of time for caffeine.

Returning to the office, he slipped into his chair, woke the computer up again, and created a new file. Pulling his small recorder from his briefcase, he set the machine on his desk and hit Play. He copied his notes on the first birth to his computer for fifteen minutes, paused his recording long enough to pour a cup of coffee, then finished.

About the time he was wrapping up the first stop on his trip, he felt an insistent force against his left leg. He completed that section of notes before reaching down to acknowledge his pet.

"Good evening, Inspector," he greeted as the black cat flipped over to present his stomach for rubbing.

It was probably unkind to keep a pet. Between winning new Mirrors for the Justice Department, visiting existing Mirrors for psychological profiling, and providing the occasional guest lecture, Cole was gone at least as much he was home. Inspector didn't seem to mind; in fact, he probably appreciated Cole's absence more than his presence. Cole strongly suspected that the landlady who checked on things while he was gone did her best to spoil the "adorable kitty."

Cole turned back to his typing, and Inspector hopped up onto a corner of the desk kept cleared specifically for him. He stood a moment, perhaps hoping for another round of scratching behind the ears. He meowed once, waited another few seconds, then gave a disgruntled glare before curling up and closing his eyes.

"Overall, it did not go well, Inspector," Cole admitted, leaning back in his chair. His cat cracked open a single eye to regard him.

He'd decided long ago that talking to his cat was a ridiculous habit. Apparently, that hadn't dissuaded him. Now these conversations were practically a nightly occurrence when he was home.

"Won the first fight. Easy sell. They signed over their baby within the hour. They were already well-off, so it wasn't the money. Maybe it was the longevity. I don't know."

That normally would have made for an excellent week. Every Mirror committed to the system was cause for celebration. If that had been it, the week would have been much shorter.

It was his common practice, though, to drop in for his regular visits to government Mirrors in the area after he went to negotiate for a child. Peter had booked him to Seattle for the sales pitch, then LA, Phoenix, and Denver. Exhausting but efficient, he was more or less used to the schedule.

Then he'd gotten snowed in at Denver. When the weather cleared up two days ago, he'd gotten paged at the airport right before he got on the plane. A second Mirror born in one week. Peter had already made new airline reservations to Milwaukee.

"Second one seemed to go well. Ideal candidate. Already a mother to three kids. No husband, and the boyfriend is completely out of the picture. She definitely can't afford to raise a Mirror.

"I knew playing up luxuries was a bad idea, so I stuck to the banal. Feed your kids, make sure they have clothes for school. She was listening, nodding along. She understood.

"Then she changes her mind at the last minute. Decides to keep her daughter. I'm not sure who she spoke to, but I'm guessing someone convinced her that she would be a terrible mother if she gave her child up for money."

Cole released a long breath and shook his head regretfully. Picking up his mug, he wandered into the kitchen to pour a fresh cup of coffee. Inspector raised his head curiously as Cole left, but didn't follow. When he returned to his chair, the cat was standing expectantly on the desk corner.

"It was as clear a win/win as I've ever seen," Cole continued, fondly rubbing the cat's ears. "And now? Her whole family suffers in abject poverty when they could be living in luxury. For what? So she can claim that she didn't make her daughter a pawn of the government. She's shaved years off the girl's life and almost certainly denied her other children necessities.

"The universe is insane. I'm not sure how evolution can produce a species simultaneously so brilliant and so stupid. We are so smart that we can do all kinds of complicated calculus but can't work simple addition when it conflicts with our emotional wiring."

He didn't expect any sympathy from Inspector, which was good since the cat was now studiously ignoring him. Cole sighed and turned back to his recorder. Before he could hit the Play button, the phone rang.

"Bryant speaking."

"It's Maria. Sorry to call so late." The Mirror Review Board's head only called at this hour for one of two reasons.

"Birth?" he asked, hopeful.

"No. Sorry."

"Damn it. Irena?"

"Slit her wrists."

He paused, thinking. "Well, she's within one standard deviation of my most recent estimates of her longevity, so a point in favor for the predictive modeling. Anything you need from me?"

"No. House parents are prepping funeral arrangements, Peter is reassigning her Reflections, and Beverly is gathering her cases so that Norman can send them out to the media. I'm just letting you know."

"All right. Thank you."

"No problem. See you tomorrow."

There was a harsh click as Maria hung up, and Cole replaced the phone with a long sigh.

Irena's death wasn't a shock. She was seventeen and had been on a strong downward trend last time he'd seen her. Still, he also remembered the little girl she'd been. She was one of the few who'd smiled at him every time he came to visit. At least until the first Reflection.

Elbows on his desk, Cole cradled his head in his hands, eyes watering. He felt the horrible wrenching pain that had become so familiar over the years. These feelings were irrational; statistics indicated Irena would have been dead years ago without his intervention.

That didn't matter. Her death still hurt.

It seemed even Cole Bryant was bad at emotional calculus.

— PART IV —

Fifteen Years Old—Hard Losses

Perhaps the most difficult question I study is "Why do Mirrors Reflect?"

In this context, I'm not speaking to the actual mechanism of Reflection but instead of to the psychology of Mirrors. What drives a child to take on another human being's entire life? What compels them to do it again, even after the devastation the first one inevitably brings?

Curiosity clearly plays a role in the first Reflection. No matter how well the process is described or how furious the proscriptions, it is impossible to fully impart the horror of the experience to the uninitiated. To be told that what makes you terrifying is also what makes you powerful tends not to encourage restraint but, instead, experimentation. After all, everyone believes that they are the exception to the rule: what destroys others will spare me.

It is the following incidents which are harder to explain. Even among Mirrors outside government control, it is unusual for them to perform only a single Reflection before ultimately taking their own lives. Many Reflect a trusted family member, then seek out a second or third as well, provided the family has not taken precautions against further such events.

Within the justice system, it gets murkier. Mirrors complete hundreds of Reflections, then kill themselves. However, despite vociferous protests and a clear desire to be free of our control, out-right refusal is rare. We have never had to hold them down and pry their eyes open at the police stations.

I believe they are searching for something, that every Reflection is another piece in a puzzle they hope to solve. It is not a problem they work at willingly, but one they feel compelled to study.

I believe Mirrors are born with a psychological need to Reflect other people. Much as an alcoholic may have a need for a drink, these children find themselves drawn to the act. They cannot help themselves. Given the opportunity, they will take it.

I speak only of compulsion, though. Whether they actually want to Reflect is another matter entirely.

—Excerpt from an APA Convention speech by Dr. Cole Bryant

–CHAPTER 24–

Pulling her coat tightly around her, Ashley stepped from the warmth of the rented sedan into the writhing tempest of snow flurries. The wind tugged at her hair and lashed at the exposed skin on her face. She shivered at the chill air blowing across her legs, and silently cursed the ankle monitor that kept her from wearing hose or leggings or *something*.

Mom hurried up next to Ashley, and without pulling her hands from her pockets motioned toward a building that seemed much too far away. Mrs. Raines, striding resolutely from her own vehicle, caught up to the pair as they shuffled along. Stung by the blowing snow, none were talkative. Occasional words of encouragement rang from the Shepherd, but for the most part, the trio approached the Justice Department's main building in silence.

Ashley had desperately hoped their final approach would offer conversation, if for no other reason than to pull her mind away from what was ahead. She'd brooded over this meeting enough already, and any distraction would be welcome. Instead, she fretted over her preparation: running again through the information Mrs. Raines had provided over breakfast and rehearsing her answers one more time.

Of course, even the trepidation that left her ill was welcome in its own way. All too often she struggled to feel anything.

This transformation hadn't descended all at once, of course. Instead, the emotions that had flown so freely during the two-year bounce had ebbed away slowly. Happiness had fled first, but time had stolen the rest just as surely. As summer began to wane, even anger and sadness became strangers. More and more frequently, she felt . . . hollow.

She preferred the days of depression; at least then she had wanted something. Her sobbing was born of a desire for a better life, for the chance to find peace in her battle. The emptiness that threatened to consume her was worse. It wasn't just living a bad life, it was not living at all. This apathy didn't grip her every day, but she knew that this void was the seed of destruction; when it bloomed, she would take her own life. In light of that, even the roiling terror in her stomach was cause for celebration.

Just as she wondered if she might freeze to death before she had the opportunity to commit suicide, the front doors of the Greco-Roman behemoth rose up before her. Mrs. Raines yanked one open, and Ashley and her mother gratefully rushed into the welcoming embrace of light and heat and noise.

Ashley looked around a minute, confused as to where to go now. As always, it was Mrs. Raines who rescued her. With a firm but gentle push on Ashley's back, the woman strode forward imperiously. In a habit ingrained over the last three years, Ashley's feet slid into motion, trailing the Shepherd. So often after Reflections, it was hard to think, and following Carol Raines had become a matter of instinct; the older woman was her port in these storms.

They went through security, then wandered down a hallway until Mrs. Raines gestured at what seemed like just another door and said, "Here." Mom paused, visibly paling, but Ashley refused to be cowed. She strode in without hesitation.

A massive table dominated the room, but it was the six people waiting at it who drew Ashley's attention. The five strangers comprised the Mirror Review Board. Beside them was a man she knew all too well: Dr. Cole Bryant, the Mirror specialist.

Everything Mrs. Raines had managed to impart over breakfast came rushing back in that moment. Ashley's eyes flicked quickly over each of the unknown, matching names to faces and judging how sympathetic each might be.

At the left edge of the table was a hard-faced woman with piercing blue eyes and snow-white hair that hung loosely past her shoulders. This had to be Dr. Beverly Urich, and the displeased glance the woman shot at Mrs. Raines only confirmed it. The animosity between the two had been clear in the Shepherd's stories. Dr. Urich was the one who approved cases for Reflection. Today she was clad in a dress the color of pitch, and the only jewelry she wore was a large onyx stone on a silver choker. With a shiver, Ashley decided the woman looked better suited to attend a funeral than a hearing.

To her right was a bald man with gold-rimmed glasses. Peter Lane was in charge of logistics. He determined which Mirror Reflected which case and did all the scheduling for flights and the like. Mr. Lane's face was disconcertingly blank, as though he fought to keep any emotion from showing, positive or negative. He didn't even spare a look at Mom or Mrs. Raines, instead watching Ashley intently. Before Ashley moved to the next board member, though, that mask of indifference flickered, and she caught a genuinely curious look in those brown eyes.

Maria Perales, a pretty woman in her late forties, was the current head of the board. She sported a soothing smile that actually made Ashley relax a bit. In sharp contrast to Dr. Urich's dark dress, Ms. Perales wore paler, almost bright colors. They seemed a bit out of place on the cold November morning, but perhaps their presence was intended to convey a contrast between her outlook and that of her dour-faced colleague's. Ashley hoped so, anyway.

Fourth down the table was a large man with a round face and thick brown hair. He offered no friendly grin, but there was an openness to this man's manner that Ashley drew comfort from. Mrs. Raines had told her that Dr. Hanover had been a pediatrician before being appointed to the board, and Ashley had no doubt that the man had used that calm aura of control to set his young patients at ease. His role on the board was mostly one of public relations and media.

The last member of the board was also the newest. A retired Air Force officer, Colonel Ethan Dyer had risen to this post within the last six months. Everything from his close-cropped hair to his stiff-backed posture trumpeted his military heritage. It was the calculating look, however, that chilled Ashley. This was a man searching for a way to best use a tool, and that was in some ways worse than Dr. Urich's open hostility.

"Miss Ross, please have a seat."

Ashley hesitated, caught off guard. She had always known her last name, but until now, no one had used it to refer to her. To Thomas, Dad, and Mrs. Raines, she had always been nothing more than Ashley. Mom called her that sometimes but also slipped into nicknames such as 'sweetie' or the insufferable 'baby.' Even Dr. Bryant eschewed the use of 'Ross,' though that was mostly because he almost never named her. As a result, it took a long moment for her to realize she was being addressed. Once she did, though, it drove home the magnitude of the hearing.

Tremors of tension threatened to seize Ashley's hands, but she fought them down, drawing her fingers to absolute stillness. With as much calm certainty as she could muster, she pulled out the closest chair from the long table and sat. Mom and Mrs. Raines followed suit on the left and right, respectively, but while the Shepherd effortlessly struck the same stoic confidence Ashley tried for, Mom's actions were marred by fidgeting hands that clearly portrayed her fear.

"Miss Ross, I'm Maria Perales, head of the Mirror Review Board," the woman continued. Ashley knew this but didn't interrupt. "These are my associates, Dr. Beverly Urich, Peter Lane, Dr. Norman Hanover, and Colonel Ethan Dyer. You, of course, are familiar with Dr. Cole Bryant, who serves as an adviser to this board."

Behind the safety of shaded glass, Ashley rolled her eyes at the last statement but said nothing. She was 'familiar' with the doctor in the same way one might be 'familiar' with a particularly ill-placed blister.

Unable to see Ashley's expression of distaste for the doctor, Ms. Perales continued smoothly, "Miss Ross, you know why you are here?"

Ashley nodded slowly. "For Reflecting Calleigh Kershfeldt."

"Do you understand the severity of what you did?"

"I think so."

Dr. Urich arched a thick white eyebrow questioningly, and Ashley vented a short sigh before continuing.

"I saw the chaos at the airport. I saw the horror on people's faces. They started talking about what should be done with me even before I left. Some wanted me fined. Some wanted me jailed." She paused and shrugged before adding, "Some wanted me dead.

"The media is billing Calleigh's Reflection 'mind rape,'" she continued levelly, "and the mere mention of the term is enough to start heated arguments about what to do with Mirrors. I know there's a Congressional bill that would confine all Mirrors to their home cities, instead ferrying all criminals to them; the House votes tomorrow, and the Senate votes on its version next week.

"The Liberators say Calleigh's Reflection is proof that we need to be free, and everyone else says that this is exactly why we can't be free. I've even heard there's support for drugging all Mirrors leaving their houses until they reach their destinations, or for dark-lensed muzzles with locks only the Shepherds would carry keys for. Basically, no one can agree on the best course of action, or even a 'good' course of action.

"In fact, the only thing people agree on," Ashley finished quietly, "is that the Mirror Review Board has to send a harsh message by making an example out of me."

Uncertainty and surprise flew in the looks the board quickly cast at each other, and Ashley wondered idly if any of them had ever actually spoken to a Mirror. If they had expected her to enter as a confused innocent, they knew nothing about the children whose lives they so callously reigned. That thought gnawed at her, and an angry fire filled her stomach.

Despite his many faults, Dr. Bryant did indeed know more about Mirrors than any of the board members and took Ashley's summation in stride. Ignoring the board's momentary confusion, he asked, "Do you know why this Reflection caused such uproar?"

Ashley nodded. "The government, particularly this board, has worked diligently to keep all knowledge of extra-judicial Reflections from the public. While Mirrors often Reflect family or careless Shepherds, these encounters are in private. Keeping these events secret heightens the illusion of absolute control over Mirrors and insures that the people feel insulated from the 'danger' we represent. I reflected someone seemingly at random, and now people wonder if they are 'safe;' they're afraid I'll do it again or that another Mirror will."

If Ashley had harbored any lingering doubts about the board's complete inexperience with Mirrors, she didn't now. Dr. Urich, stared openly while the friendly-seeming Dr. Hanover scribbled notes hastily on a legal pad. The rest were exchanging startled gazes.

With his colleagues still struck dumb, Dr. Bryant continued. "A concise and astute assessment. Well done, Ashley."

The compliment was so unexpected Ashley almost gaped. He'd even used her name! To her right, Carol seemed just as taken aback. Across the table, the specialist continued as though he had said nothing outside the ordinary. "You have found the key issue: people want to know, and thus this board wants to know: what made you decide to randomly Reflect a . . ."

"I did *not* 'randomly Reflect' anyone," Ashley replied tersely. "It just seemed random to everyone else."

"Then why Miss Kershfeldt?" Ms. Perales had finally found her voice.

"Calleigh was sick," Ashley began, but before she could go on, Dr. Urich stepped in.

"Why does that matter?"

Dismissing the interruption with the barest shake of her head, Ashley continued. "I was trying to help her."

Mr. Lane had removed his glasses and was massaging his right temple. "Start at the beginning, please. It's the only way we're going to understand."

"I was in Detroit on November 1st, reflecting Haltom Morrison." Pain burned at that memory, and despair flooded her insides, muting the fire inside. Frowning, she pushed on anyway. "I'd finished the Reflection—guilty—and was in Detroit Metro walking to my gate. I was still tired, but I could walk without Mrs. Raines's help by then.

She closed her eyes, for once letting the images bouncing inside her head take shape. She could see the airport terminal, hear the click of Mrs. Raines's heels against the floor, and feel the chill in the air. She remembered the way people had veered out of their path, most never looking directly at them. A couple of passersby smiled and waved encouragingly. Sometimes she had even mustered the strength to return their silent well-wishes.

With her eyes still closed, Ashley continued. "We stopped at a departure screen to check the status of our flight, and the Kershfeldt family was there. They weren't really checking flight times so much as arguing." Ashley frowned; so engrossed in argument was the family they hadn't even noticed the Mirror and Shepherd stride right up next to them. "Mr. and Mrs. Kershfeldt—" Ashley paused, opening her eyes and trying to pin her thoughts back to the present. The memories were still stiflingly close, even eleven days later. It felt awkward to call them anything other than Mom and Dad; that was how Calleigh thought of them.

"Mr. and Mrs. Kershfeldt," she repeated, "were arguing with their oldest daughter, Calleigh." The argument was quiet, and Ashley had not wanted to overhear, but she was still so tired at the time that moving or interrupting or doing anything other than standing listlessly next to her Shepherd seemed too much work.

Her mind was swimming now, the separating of her own past from Calleigh's becoming increasingly difficult. She felt both the other girl's bitter resentment toward her parents' interference and her own frustration and grief at overhearing Calleigh's problem.

Apparently, the flux in her brain quieted her too long because Ms. Perales gently asked, "What were they arguing about?"

"Calleigh wasn't eating again. That was the first thing I heard her mother say."

"Wasn't eating?" This time it was Dr. Hanover.

"She was anorexic. I could tell once I knew what I was looking for. She was thin. Not emaciated yet, but definitely too thin for healthy."

"I still don't see what this has to do with why you Reflected her," Dr. Urich said coolly.

"Have you ever been Reflected?" Ashley asked. The woman shook her head fiercely and pointedly looked away, as if the question had been a threat.

Stifling a sigh at the woman's reaction, Ashley continued. "I didn't think so. If you had, you'd understand. Reflections don't leave room for lies. They show people as they truly are. We're not so young or so kind or so smart as we pretend. No Reflected person can hold on to those lies."

Out of the corner of her eye, Ashley caught Mrs. Raines nodding; across the table, so was Dr. Bryant. They both understood the truth of that.

"Calleigh was lying to herself about her weight, about how she looked. Not intentionally, but she was." Ashley paused a moment, then added, "She's better now."

"That is not so clear," Ms. Perales stated calmly.

Ashley considered for a moment, then amended, "Well, I bet she's not anorexic anymore."

"Whatever you intended to do, your actions have potentially destroyed the life of a teenage girl," Dr. Urich countered. "If you revealed truths, then you revealed more than she was able to handle. She's emotionally unstable and possibly suicidal. Your reckless decision may yet claim her life."

Flames finally roared inside Ashley, melting the last shreds of icy apathy that bound her. "Don't lecture *me* on what a Reflection is," Ashley snapped. "I know that an honest evaluation of life shows pain. I've lived that for three years now at the insistence of this board. Calleigh Kershfeldt is struggling with the vagaries of one life; I've got over 150 now and will add another later this week. Somehow, though, this board doesn't find *my* impending suicidal tendencies to be of much consideration."

Ashley slumped back into her chair, arms folded across her chest. She scowled at the members of the board and especially at the white-haired doctor. For their part, those opposite her looked abashed, or at least discomfited, by her outburst. Bryant frowned, but it was more worried than displeased.

For a hopeful moment, Ashley thought her heated outburst might actually end the hearing prematurely. Several of them looked ashamed, as if realizing the hypocrisy of their stance. That the board was spending time worrying about Calleigh's state of mind while forcing the destruction of Ashley's was almost unbearable. Maybe someone *should* Reflect them.

Mrs. Raines rested a hand on Ashley's shoulder, and when she turned, the Shepherd gave her an encouraging smile. Clearly she understood the irony of their position; given her personality, it wasn't hard to imagine Mrs. Raines had been trying to do just that for years now.

"Can we, perhaps, deal with the matter at hand?" Colonel Dyer's voice cut through the chatter, and he leaned forward intently. "Calleigh's current situation is irrelevant."

"Why do you say that?" Bryant's question seemed one of genuine curiosity.

"Would it honestly change the situation if Calleigh suddenly began espousing Ashley's praises for her decision? Public perception would still be very negative, and the board would still have to act. As Ashley herself noted, people at the airport were terrified of the Reflection even before the end results could be known. We are not deciding whether Ashley's actions were beneficial; we're trying to calm the public because of their fear of Reflections."

"I believe Calleigh's state is relevant," Dr. Urich said firmly.

"The colonel has a point," Ms. Perales rebutted gently. "If our decision today is made based on this girl's state of mind, we leave it open to reversal in the future. What if a year from now Calleigh is grateful for Ashley's intervention? No, we need to act on what is most important: maintaining an image of control."

Peter Lane nodded. "I agree. Previous unscheduled Reflections have had negative consequences on Shepherds or on the family members of Mirrors, but the board has never involved itself directly in those matters. The only reason we are meeting today is because this was done in public, not because we are concerned about Miss Kershfeldt."

"Your motives," Mrs. Perales said, turning back to Ashley, "were noble. I don't think any on this board question that, but the act itself has generated backlash against the Mirror Review Board and against Mirrors themselves. You've made life more difficult and dangerous not only for us," she gestured to include her fellow members of the board, "but for yourself, for your brother, and for all Mirrors.

"The use of Mirrors in criminal matters is not in danger here. Reflections will continue whatever this board decides; that's up to Congress, and they've already made that clear. However, the actions we take today may mitigate the reaction against you. If the public sees we have acted, perhaps it will curb some of the politicians' more drastic measures."

Just that quickly they had moved on. Ashley almost shook her head ruefully. She had waved her imminent death in their faces, and after the initial shock had worn off, they had immersed themselves once more in the bureaucracy. Perhaps it was a coping mechanism; if they avoided facing it, they could pretend it wasn't happening. If that was the case, then it was almost certainly the reason they had never met a Mirror.

Part of her thought about yelling again, but she doubted it would draw the same reaction a second time. No, if these people were content to live in their ivory tower, it would take more than one angry teenager to shake down their walls. Worse, that likely meant that whatever they did would be executed without the slightest concern for her; if she wasn't worth their attention, she wasn't worth their compassion.

"So what do we do?" Dr. Urich's tone was irritated. "We've heard her explanation, and it doesn't mitigate the situation."

"I think it does," Dr. Hanover replied. "Had this truly been a random occurrence, it would have been more troubling. Instead, she acted on a logical chain of thought. I disagree with her decision, but I think education will fix that."

Dyer frowned. "That might prevent a repeat of these events, but it doesn't address the public outcry. Even if she acted without malice, people are terrified that we can't control Mirrors. That's what must be addressed."

The white-haired doctor was nodding along with the colonel. "He's right. We have to make it clear we have the situation well in hand." She paused, running an eye over the trio opposite her.

"I think we need to understand what caused this," Mr. Lane said. "The United States has been using Mirrors for decades, and this is the first time one has ever Reflected a person unknown to them. Is this mindset unique to Ashley Ross, or is this a problem we'll see in other children?"

This last question was directed at Dr. Bryant. The specialist was staring into his coffee mug, a grimace just barely twitching down the corners of his mouth. The hearing had finally come to a topic that touched on his expertise, but he now seemed oddly hesitant. Drawing a long sip of the dark liquid, he finally faced the board.

"This board knows what I have reported on the Ross twins for the past three years. Their progression through the stages of the Mirror life cycle are aberrant and somewhat unpredictable. Both showed remarkable resilience early on, mastering the ability to push down their collected memories almost a full six months ahead of the curve. At fourteen years old, both showed an exceptionally powerful two-year bounce that left them almost psychologically identical to their pre-Reflection states.

"By fifteen, they should be clearly showing signs of the slow decay of will that has marked all Mirrors by that age. Ashley has hints of that; our last meeting was only four weeks ago, and there are cracks in the armor. Relative to her cohorts, though, she's surprisingly whole. The few overt signs of atrophy she displays are all what I would expect from a child beginning the descent from the top of the two-year bounce. That should have come six months ago at least, and as many as eight or nine months ago for many children. Her state of mind at this juncture is astonishing; she is, relatively speaking, untouched by her Reflections, and with the exception of her brother, is unique in this quality."

Ashley frowned. *Untouched? Life isn't as kind as three years ago. Or even one year ago*, she thought bitterly.

"After isolating as many factors as I could, I've determined there are two potential causes to which I could trace this almost preternatural resistance. First is that they, unlike other Mirrors, have been raised by their birth parents. And while that is possible, I've come to believe that it is far more possible that it is her relationship with her brother. Buoyed by her friendship with another Mirror, Ashley has found a support group unavailable to any other Mirror in the country.

The colonel cleared his throat. "Are you suggesting we place more Mirrors together? That seems dangerous. If they Reflect each other, it will kill them, and we lose those assets."

"When they decide to die, they have that option. Until they reach that point, Mirrors still show all the normal signs of self-preservation," Dr. Bryant said.

Dr. Urich snorted loudly. "If putting Mirrors together gives them strength to defy the board, then we must do everything to keep them apart. In fact, the Ross twins must be separated immediately."

Pandemonium erupted. Members of the board began speaking over each other, some indignant, others defensive. Mrs. Raines was pointing a finger at Dr. Urich and saying things that Ashley was certain she wasn't supposed to hear. Mom simply gaped, apparently unable to process this latest twist. Dr. Bryant also said nothing, his face impassive as his gaze rested on Ashley.

Heart thumping in her chest, Ashley's mind raced. She should have expected this possibility; on his last visit, the specialist had even told her much of what he had just relayed to his colleagues. It wasn't a stretch to assume her connection with Thomas was what gave her the strength to defy all social convention and Reflect an anorexic girl. Moving from that premise to Dr. Urich's conclusion was so obvious Ashley should have seen it herself.

It made sense, and the board would have to see it too. Relocating Ashley to a government facility would not only remove her troublesome source of support but would send the heavy-handed message the public needed. The other members of the board were fighting those conclusions, and might continue to do so out of a desire not to tear a family apart. In the end, though, logic could still prevail over sentimentality. Using Mirrors in justice was already a very utilitarian approach, and sacrificing one little girl to save the rest of the program fit very much in line with these people's philosophy.

Thoughts of saying goodbye to Thomas flooded to the forefront of her mind, and tears stung her eyes. Her emotions had grown increasingly dull over the past year, but the anxiety of being separated brought them roaring back with a fierceness she wasn't prepared for.

"No!" she shouted. "Don't do it! Please don't do it!" She reached across the table, arms extended, pleading.

All conversation cut off abruptly, and every eye in the room turned to her. Into that sudden silence, Mrs. Raines muttered, "Don't worry, Ashley. They don't have the authority."

"That's not true," Bryant said slowly. "The modified paperwork the Rosses signed at their children's birth made them government employees. If the board deems it necessary, we can assign Ashley to another employee to raise."

Ashley's panic increased. She wasn't sure exactly why her parents had let them Reflect, or even what they'd signed all those years ago. It made sense, though, that the board could do this.

"I'm sorry!" she cried. "I wasn't thinking. I just wanted to help Calleigh! I won't do it again, I swear. Can't you tell everyone why I did it? Isn't that enough?"

Dr. Urich shook her head fiercely. "That might make it worse. You'd be asking people to expect random Reflections simply because a passing Mirror thinks it is in their best interest. That's a lot of faith in the judgment of a fourteen-year-old girl."

"Fifteen today," Ashley shot back. Some of her sorrow and fear burned into rage, watching the woman. "The country supposedly trusts *your* judgment, and you had never even met a Mirror before today. Why are you qualified to pick my subjects but I'm not? It's *my* power!"

The gift of Reflection—this accursed, hateful, baleful "gift"— was tolerable only as long as she was helping people. She could imprison the Spencer Duncans of the world and free the Calleigh Kershfeldts, and that was reason enough to keep breathing, to keep moving . . . to keep Reflecting. It was incentive enough to keep going through the motions even if it rarely proved enough to induce her to actually *live* anymore.

"Forcibly removing a child from her home is an extreme measure," Dr. Bryant interjected before his colleague could respond. "I am certain it's one this board would prefer to avoid as it might embolden the Liberation movement. Though we have the legal capacity to do so, stripping the girl from her family may well fracture our power base; not everyone will agree the situation war-ranted this strong a response."

Ashley's heart leapt with a surge of hope even as a surge of gratitude bloomed for the specialist. He'd done very little during her life she liked, but this alone bought him forgiveness for numer-ous slights.

"I am guessing you have a better option," Mrs. Perales prompted.

Bryant paused, shooting Ashley an unreadable look. She returned a quizzical glance, and then everything clicked into place. She knew what was coming now and felt her insides freezing. All the goodwill he had just established flashed away, vaporized in a split second.

"Shepherds were created not only to protect these children from a world that fears them but to protect the world from their power," Bryant said solemnly. "We can argue why she did all this after the fact, but the truth is, it should never have happened. Her Shepherd should have stopped it."

To Ashley's right, Carol suddenly went stiff, and all eyes swiv-eled to regard the woman. In that collective gaze, Ashley could see they agreed: Carol Raines would make an excellent scapegoat.

— CHAPTER 25 —

Father Sean's study had barely changed in the two years Thomas had known him. A few more books dotted the shelves, perhaps, and a new wooden chair rested opposite the desk, but otherwise, Thomas would swear nothing in the cozy office had changed.

As near as he could tell, neither had its occupant. Father Sean might have another line under his eyes or another crease in his forehead; his limp might be a bit more pronounced, or his hands a little more scarred, but Thomas didn't notice. The priest's face was just as open as that first day, his smile just as broad. Thomas slipped through the door, closing it behind him with a soft click.

"Ah, Thomas," Father Sean said with a grin, rising stiffly to greet him. "If my memory serves, I should wish you a happy birthday. Correct?"

Thomas nodded silently, crossing the room to meet his old friend.

"Happy birthday, then."

"If you insist," Thomas replied, collapsing into the wooden chair. Father Sean had made the chair himself the previous year, and it had served as Thomas's weekly throne for these meetings since then.

Retaking his own seat, the priest grimaced. "What's wrong?'

"Ashley's hearing is this morning," Thomas replied plainly. "Besides that, the usual."

The "usual" covered practically everything associated with life as a Mirror: apathy, fear, pain, shame, confusion, death. Father Sean, over the course of two years, had heard it all. Thomas's complaints had changed little since he started coming, but Father Sean always listened patiently. Thomas knew his moods had darkened, that the small hopeful burst that had drawn him here two years ago was gone. He snapped at the priest more and smiled less.

He missed smiling. Missed laughing even more. There was a time when the priest could make him laugh, could draw out the poison from the wounds of the Reflections and let him relax. Even after Mom and Dad lost that ability, Father Sean still had that gift.

Little good it did now. Pressed down ruthlessly for three years, the Reflections were finally escaping their shoddily tethered prison. After two years of practice, he'd perfected shoving down the memories, forgetting they were there and leaving them alone. But after three years, it seemed the buried Reflected had learned how to escape.

Thomas couldn't be sure why that was. He wondered often if there were simply too many. He felt as though his brain had run out of storage and they were slowly leaking out from behind the walls. Ashley had suggested that even pressed down, almost forgotten, they had still seeped their poison. Though untouched, perhaps they had still slowly shaped his and Ashley's lives, the refuse of confusion and despair polluting the landscape of their minds.

Or perhaps, Thomas admitted silently, *I simply understand them better.*

At twelve, he couldn't fully fathom why Marcus Vale had raped and murdered three women. Three years later his body was finally lurching its way into puberty, and the flood of hormones let him understand the lust that could drive a man to such violence.

"Your sister's hearing. I'd forgotten that was today," Father Sean said, obviously choosing the easier of the two topics Thomas presented.

"She was nervous when she left last night." Thomas's voice was flat. "She'll be home tonight. Not that I'll have to wait until then to find out what happened. I'm sure it'll be on the news."

"You sound like you don't care."

He shrugged. "I guess not. It won't change anything. Not really. Whatever they decide to strip away, she's still flying to Cincinnati next Thursday and Indianapolis the next. The Reflections will continue. They're all that matter."

"You still believe that?" The priest asked.

"You still don't?"

For a long moment the priest watched in silence. Thomas sighed. "They're rewriting me, Father. It's not just about death anymore; it's about life. Look at me. I'm not Thomas anymore. Not the one you met two years ago. I keep asking myself how much these Reflections have poisoned me."

"We all change, especially the young."

"Not like this. I feel like I'm not . . . me. I'm not just Thomas. I'm bits and pieces of everyone I've seen. I feel that, and I worry I'm becoming like them."

Across the broad wooden desk, Father Sean opened his mouth, but Thomas stood and walked away a few steps, behind the familiar wooden chair. As he began pacing, the old priest closed his mouth, and Thomas spent long minutes working his thoughts even as he worked his feet.

"I can't lie," he said at last, stopping directly in front of the desk. "What?"

"I can't lie after a Reflection. Not for a minute or two anyway." He resumed pacing, but this time he fought the urge to fall silent. "I'd wondered. Wondered a lot. My testimony would be no stronger than any other, regardless of what I see, if I could lie. Worth less," he murmured, "since Mirrors turn dark and brooding so quickly."

"How did you find out?"

Thomas shrugged noncommittally at first. Then, deciding it

didn't matter, he launched into his explanation, staring at his feet the whole time.

"You remember a couple of weeks ago? When we talked about Jayce Ragen?" He didn't wait for an answer, didn't look up to see if the priest nodded. He knew Father Sean remembered. "Grisly murder of a family just a mile or so from here. Botched burglary when the family arrived home early. They bound them, executed them . . ." Thomas cut off, closing his eyes and clenching his fists as his steps faltered. "It was evil, Father."

"I remember. You said that Jayce was normally part of the crew but was away that night. He was never in the house. His associates didn't even tell him about the murders until the next day."

Thomas nodded bitterly, his throat burning. "He would have killed those people if he'd been there. I know it, Father. I *know*, because I'm a Mirror! I don't just know what he did, I lived it! He's a sociopath; he'd have killed them without a second thought! But the laws don't care about it."

"You said the same three weeks ago. You didn't tell me you tried to lie."

"Tried and failed," Thomas said bitterly. His hands unclenched, and he opened his eyes, craning his neck to stare at the ceiling in despair. "He's dangerous, Father. He'll do something like this again, but he's getting released. Without me, they felt they had an airtight case. He'd have gone to death row. But as soon as I saw what happened . . ." He hung his head.

"And so you tried to lie."

"I've seen evil in those the legal system calls innocent. Abusive fathers, dishonest employers . . . you've heard me talk."

Thomas began pacing again. He pulled his arms across his chest and rubbed his shoulders as if cold. He shivered, but it was nothing to do with the windy weather outside.

"This was the clearest, though. I'd told myself for the last year, that if I met a case as clear as this one, so obviously evil . . . I couldn't stay silent.

"If I could even tell them what I've seen without violating Constitutional protections, I'd do that instead. But I can't. The only way to bring justice would be to lie. He deserves death, Father."

"Thomas . . ." the priest began, but Thomas cut him off.

"I wanted to do it, but it's not like that. I take on a life, and it's so . . . real. So perfect. In those first moments afterward, every detail is vivid, as clear as this instant right now with you. My own life is a lit match beside a bonfire; a single raindrop beside the flood. I lose myself in them, and I forget who I am, forget what I want.

"I'm not living their life after they look away. That connection is broken, but I can't really remember myself in that first minute. I barely know my name, and I can't remember why I would want to lie, or why I hate life, or people, or anything. I'm gone, buried. And then, as the moments tick past, the bonfire fades, the flood abates, and Thomas Ross breaks through again. I'm still lost, confused, but I'm me enough to remember what I *should* have done . . . what I wished I'd done. What I'd promised I would do."

He scrubbed an arm angrily across his eyes, fighting the burning there at the corners. "It was almost a minute and a half before I realized what I'd done. Three minutes for me to regain enough of myself to realize the opportunity I'd lost."

"Maybe it's better this way. If you could lie, it would overturn the entire system. Imagine the chaos . . ."

"Don't tell me that!"

Thomas swept a hand across one of the nearby bookshelves in anger, spilling books to the floor. Yellowed pages flew out of a couple of them, and the entire mess made a thunderous boom as the spray of tomes hit the ground.

"Jayce didn't kill them, but he would have! He *will* kill some-day! And I've let him!"

"You don't know that, Thomas. You can't know the future. He *was* innocent of the crime."

"There *are* no innocent! I've seen too many lives to believe that myth anymore. Just varying degrees of guilt."

Father Sean cleared his throat. "I know another who taught that."

Thomas willed himself not to forcibly empty another shelf. Instead, he settled for hissing through gritted teeth, "Not today, Father. I don't want your religion. Your God hates me as much as I hate him, and as I've gotten deep and personal with several of his servants, I'm okay with that."

"All right, Thomas. I'm sorry."

"Unless, of course . . ." Thomas's voice was a whisper. "You'd let me . . ."

The statement hung unfinished as he raised a trembling hand to his face. It took two tries with his quivering fingers, but he finally managed to strip the glasses from his face and let them fall away. They bounced across the pale tile floor with a ringing clatter before skittering just beyond his sight. The room grew still. He kept his head down, arm resting on the emptied bookshelf as sweat prickled on his forehead and ran down his back.

"If I thought that I could help," Father Sean began deliberately, "I'd offer my life to you in a heartbeat." Thomas closed his eyes, braced against what was coming. "Nothing I could show you would help you. My life has dishonesty, too. I'm not perfect, Thomas." He sighed bitterly. "Though I wish I were. I wish I were."

Thomas straightened, his unhidden gaze locked on the bookshelf. "I would send every last person I've Reflected away if it were up to me. Guilty or innocent by the law, I'd lock up most, and the rest I'd send to die."

He turned to face Father Sean. Eyes lowered to stare at his desk, the old priest studied his calloused hands with feigned interest. Thomas watched him dispassionately, counting the seconds. Ten. Twenty. Thirty. He waited a full two minutes, but Father Sean said nothing more, never raised his head.

"So you're no different from the others I've seen," Thomas said.

An overwhelming sense of loss poured over him. He'd hoped he'd finally found someone worthy. Everything he'd seen from the priest had been exemplary. Everything Michael Pater had seen, too. Was it all a lie?

"Thomas, I . . ."

"Are you a criminal?" The words turned harsh as his disappointment turned to anger, but the priest never flinched. "Have you broken laws?" This man was supposed to save him! To make him believe that some people might be worth saving. "Is that what you don't want me to see?"

Father Sean offered no defense. His head sank a little lower, and Thomas snorted derisively.

"You've lectured me for two years on doing what I must, on being strong in the face of adversity, but you're just as weak as the rest of them, aren't you? That's what you won't show me, isn't it?"

"We've all been weak . . ."

"Is that all we have to look forward to? Weakness? If I'd never Reflected, if I could have lived a normal life, would that be all I could expect of myself? To hurt my family like Dennis Carson? Or kill them like Michael Pater? Or ignore them like . . ."

"Thomas, please."

Abandoning the list of failures, Thomas switched tracks. "If that's really life, then I understand why we die. We Mirrors alone see it all. The whole rainbow of lives laid bare before us, and not a good one in the spectrum."

Power returned to Father Sean's voice, and though he spoke forcefully, he still did not lift his gaze. "You see any weakness and count the soul as lost, but that leaves no room for hope. Can you see no good in people?"

"Really, Father? You were the greatest man I know. Kind, calm, patient, and willing to listen weekly to the incessant pessimism of a scared little boy; I thought you must be good. But you're so ashamed of who you are that you won't meet my gaze and show me what goodness is."

Thomas glanced at the clock to his left. "My time's almost up.

I think I'll go walk the garden until my dad gets here. Goodbye, Father."

He snatched his glasses from the floor and slid them over his eyes, securing them with a harsh click. Then he hesitated a moment, studying the scattered books on the floor. Pages lay bent or pulled from old spines and cast loose among the debris. Some seemed to have come wholly out of their bindings, lying as pale stacks of paper amidst the colorful array of their still-bound brethren. The urge to stop and pick them up briefly crossed his mind, but he shoved it down. It was his turn to be selfish and weak.

"I'll leave you to clean this up," he said, reaching for the doorknob.

"Thomas." The priest's voice was still, and Thomas hesitated. No doubt the old man was about to berate him for leaving without cleaning, and Thomas prepared his own angry retort, but instead the priest asked simply, "Can I expect you next week?"

No malice marred the request. Instead of anger and disgust for the child who had just angrily trashed his study, the priest's voice held hope. Hope that Thomas would come back again for this weekly conversation.

Angrily, Thomas shot out, "No." Then he grimaced and shook his head.

Turning to face the priest, he saw Father Sean had pulled his gaze up from the desk, and concern brimmed in those eyes. Images of two years of meetings rushed back to Thomas. Conversations with Thomas shouting and Father Sean sitting quietly, with Father Sean lecturing and Thomas sitting quietly. He remembered times he'd cried on the priest's shoulder and plenty more where he'd wanted to plunge his fist into the man's face. They'd argued, but Thomas had never once doubted that the man opposite that wide wooden desk cared for him.

"Never mind," Thomas said. "Never mind. I'll be here."

Father Sean beamed.

—CHAPTER 26—

Stretched out on the bed and propped up on one elbow, Sally flipped idly through the channels in her hotel room.

Carol's firing was the major news story of the day, and part of her wanted to revel in those accounts. Ashley had often begged Sally to give the woman a chance, but Carol had never made that easy. The Shepherd's smug superiority and terse commands had always proved sufficient reason to justify Sally's hatred of the older woman. Seeing Carol stripped of her position and told to stay away from the Rosses was nothing but a victory.

Sally wasn't alone, though, and her daughter certainly wouldn't appreciate rehashing the morning's events. Ashley had cried hard when the board delivered their judgment. Between the angry outburst and those tears, Ashley had showed more emotion today than in most of the previous month. A final hug from Carol had stilled some of that, and by the time Sally had pulled their rental car into the parking lot, the sniffles had faded into the stoic mask Ashley wore so often these days.

News aside, there was little airing that interested Sally. Skipping past soap operas and game shows, she finally gave up on finding anything of value. Shutting off the television, she reached for the complimentary newspaper the hotel had provided and scanned the headlines. She'd already read everything she wanted to, but she needed something to keep her occupied.

Originally, they were supposed to fly out immediately after the hearing. The plan had been for them to fly in, meet the board, then fly back. Except then the board had stripped Carol Raines of her position. Now there was no Shepherd available in DC to fly back with them. Sally had offered to fly her daughter back solo, but in light of Ashley's recent incident, they had demanded an approved representative accompany her.

Her new Shepherd, Julie Morse, was being flown in from her home in Houston to provide a government escort on the plane ride back to Colorado. So, in the meantime Sally and Ashley were cooped up in a hotel room a half mile from the airport. The board hadn't even let them wait in public without Julie there.

The room was more comfortable, certainly, than the airport, but they were basically locked up here. Sally had been told not to leave Ashley alone until Julie arrived, and Ashley had been confined to the room. They couldn't even head down to the restaurant for lunch. She'd been told that ordering in food was acceptable, but only as long as her daughter stayed out of sight when it was delivered.

At the moment, Ashley lay sprawled on her back on the other bed. She hadn't said anything for an hour now and little of note even before that. Sally knew the girl was seeking comfort after having one of her pillars torn away so abruptly, but it was hard to muster the necessary response. Rather than try to force some mockery of sympathy into her voice, Sally had simply stayed quiet. It wasn't perfect, but she thought it better than the alternative.

Three sharp raps upon the hotel door split the stillness, and Ashley sprang up from the bed. After three years, they both recognized Mrs. Raines's specific knock. A wave of fury ran through Sally at the sound. "Wait . . ." she called, but Ashley ignored her, practically leaping off the bed.

Wrenching open the door, Ashley froze. Even Sally paused, her words dying on her tongue. As expected, Carol waited on the other side of the threshold, but the older woman's shoulders sagged. None of the customary pride and vigor remained, and for the first time since Sally had known her, Mrs. Raines looked as old as her years. The former Shepherd managed a smile for Ashley, a thin and pained gesture. "May I come in?"

Sally frowned. "You know the answer to that. You heard the board."

Ashley glanced over her shoulder and frowned. "Mom . . ."

Mrs. Raines interrupted. "I won't take more than a minute of your time. I just want to say goodbye properly."

"Please, Mom?"

Sally's lip twitched irritably, but she didn't respond immediately. An outright refusal would probably embolden Carol and upset Ashley. As it was, allowing a goodbye would provide closure and might even buy Sally some respect from her daughter.

"Fine," she replied finally. "But make it quick."

Mrs. Raines nodded peremptorily and stepped inside with a hurried gait as though afraid Sally might change her mind. Ashley ran over to the woman and hugged her. The Shepherd returned the embrace, her face regaining some of its strength as she did so.

"I'm so proud of you," Carol whispered. "You're going to be fine without me."

"I need you," Ashley said, voice trembling with emotion. "I can't do this alone."

Carol broke the contact and set Ashley at arm's length. Deliberately, the woman reached up and stripped the ever-present sunglasses from her own face. Blue eyes, softer now than Sally had ever seen them, stared back at the girl. "You can. And you will."

"I'm sorry. I shouldn't have done it." Ashley sobbed. "I shouldn't have Reflected her. I didn't think they'd punish you. I didn't think about it. I'm so sorry!"

Carol pulled her in and hugged her again. "Oh, child. You may have saved her life, even if the board can't see it. She'll work through the confusion and be better for it."

"But they're right. I didn't ask. I just Reflected her, and it scared people."

209

"You saved her life," the former Shepherd insisted. "If she'd been about to jump off a bridge, you'd have grabbed her, wouldn't you?"

"I . . . well, yes." Ashley frowned, though, and opened her mouth to say something else before shutting it again. She then turned and looked at Sally. "Is it really the same?"

It wasn't. Not to Sally, anyway. Saving someone from an imminent death through a simple grab was a far cry from rending someone's soul to save them from a possible future.

Carol didn't give her the opportunity to share that disagreement. "You saved a life. You helped a girl deal with her inner demons. Sometimes people won't understand, but you did the right thing."

"Are you sure?"

"Do you feel you did the right thing?"

"I . . . I don't know. Maybe I should have asked first?"

"Well, you can ask next time. Regardless, I'm proud of you."

"Thank you."

Sally's insides roiled. This just didn't feel right. Ashley was visibly buoyed by the older woman's praise, but Sally couldn't justify the words. Wasn't there something wrong with Reflecting someone against their will?

"I don't think so," she said softly.

Carol and Ashley both turned to look at her. Ashley's face held a mixture of relief and confusion while the ex-Shepherd's was decidedly irritated. Sally quailed under those stares. This had been a mistake. She should have just let the other woman say her piece and leave.

As Sally shut her mouth, though, Carol gave her a satisfied smile. It was a look she'd seen often. It conveyed such contempt, such superiority. It was a silent reminder that Carol Raines knew everything and she knew nothing. Therefore, she should shut up and get out of the way. It was insufferable, and every time Sally had seen it, she'd wanted to punch the woman's teeth right down her throat.

Today was the last time she'd see Carol. The last time she'd endure that horrible certainty. She knew, though, that if she let the day go by without making her case, Carol would think she'd won.

"You shouldn't Reflect other people without their consent."

"So you think I was wrong?" Ashley asked, face falling.

"I think your heart was in the right place, but you shouldn't have Reflected her without asking."

"And just let her die?" Carol asked. Her tone implied that Sally was clearly an idiot.

"So saving her life overrode everything else?" Sally shot back.

Carol shrugged and gave that fake smile. "Shouldn't it?"

Fury burned in Sally. Three years of that condescension, and she'd never stood up to this woman. She'd always let Carol win every argument without a fight. Even now she wanted to just throw up her hands, fall back onto the bed, and flip idly through the TV channels again.

"Face it, Sally," she continued, "saving a life trumps a little personal space."

An idea struck Sally. "Maybe you're right. You know more about Mirrors than I do. More than just about anyone except Bryant."

Carol waved a hand dismissively. "He has a lot of clinical knowledge, but I know these girls better than anyone else."

"And that's why your Mirrors live longer," Sally pressed.

"Yes. I know what to say, how to act. I'm the best resource anyone can ask for."

"I . . . I could have that," Ashley said suddenly, turning to gape at her former Shepherd. "I could Reflect you."

Sally grinned darkly at Carol's shock. The older woman had gone pale, her mouth dropping open. She licked her lips once, eyes fixed on Ashley, as she shook her head ever so slightly.

"Her life is on the line," Sally said simply. "You've just admitted you have the best chance of saving her. Why not?"

"I don't think it would help," Carol said, her composure

slipping further. She looked even more uncertain than when she'd first walked in. A thrill of blissful spite shot through Sally.

"She couldn't use that knowledge herself. She'd need a guardian who . . ."

"She can relay it to me. Or Julie Morse," Sally interrupted. "It would have to be better than the alternative: letting all your knowledge go to waste."

"Yes." Ashley was almost pleading. "I want to live. I want to help people."

"No," Carol said, regaining some of her color. She cleared her throat and firmed her voice. "No."

"Weren't you saying she should take what she needs, though? After all, what purpose does it serve to preserve personal space at the cost of a life?"

Carol stared at her, suddenly understanding the trap. She could still say no, but it would weaken Carol's position with Ashley. The situation here and the one with Calleigh weren't perfectly aligned, but there were enough similarities to make the leap. Since Carol would never agree to be Reflected, she'd have to concede Sally's point.

Ashley hesitated, looking back and forth between the two of them. She half raised one hand to her glasses, then let it drop again, obviously unsure. She frowned, then looked long and hard at Carol again, her fingers shaking.

Carol watched Ashley for a moment, then looked back at Sally. Fear swam there, but as they locked gazes, a sudden fire burned in them as well. The older woman drew herself up, set her jaw, and turned back to Ashley with a radiant smile.

"She's right. I said that, and I meant it. I'll do it to save your life."

Ashley moved forward to hug the woman again, and Carol directed a venomous glare at Sally, but her mouth was turned in a victorious smile. Sally gaped, stunned by the sudden reversal. It was insane, but Carol was willing to be Reflected just to prove a point.

Then Sally caught the barest hint of fear still lurking in that gaze, and the truth hit home. She wasn't willing. It was just another move in this dance.

It was a good one, too. However much Sally might want to win this argument, she'd never intended to let her daughter Reflect the woman. The normal Reflections did enough damage; this one might kill her prematurely.

"Maybe it's not such a good idea," Sally admitted with a defeated sigh. "It's been an exhausting day for everyone."

"No, Mom," Ashley said. "You're right. She knows a lot. I'll bet she could help me."

"The board would never approve."

"We don't have to tell them. This one's not in public."

From behind Ashley, Carol wore that smug look of self-certainty. She'd won. She'd bet that Sally would never allow it, and she'd been right. It galled Sally to no end to surrender like this, but she wasn't willing to sacrifice her daughter's well-being just to win the argument.

"No. I was just trying to make a point, sweetie. I really don't think Reflecting Carol is a good idea."

Ashley seemed to absorb that for a second. Sinking to the bed, she dropped her head into her hands and sighed. "You said you didn't want me to Reflect someone who wasn't willing."

"I don't."

"I know, but Mom," Ashley said, head coming up, "Mrs. Raines said it was okay."

Sally and Carol realized what was happening too late. When Ashley had dropped her head down, she'd pulled her hands up to her head. Her words had covered the sound of her flipping the locks open. As she pulled her face up, she was unsafe.

There was barely time to even gasp. Across from Sally, Carol's eyes went wide. The former Shepherd hurried to pull her gaze away, but she was too slow. Ashley had known exactly where the woman was and had been too quick to give Carol the chance to look away.

In the space of a second it was over. Ashley wavered a moment before slumping sideways into the bed. Her muscles were limp, and she slid listlessly to the floor. Across from her, Carol fell backward toward the door, barely getting out a hand to brace against the wall.

Sally stepped over Ashley to Carol and wrenched the door open. "You've said goodbye. Now go."

Carol stared at her for a moment, looking absolutely haunted. Then the older woman nodded tiredly. On shaking knees, Carol Raines hobbled out of the Ross family's life.

Sally slammed the door behind her with a satisfying crash.

—CHAPTER 27—

Daniel stood at the front bay window, eyes surveying the shadowed landscape. Even at the best of times, gray days like this one had been a burden to the soul. Three years into his children's dark journey they seemed to demolish any hope he had managed to secret away.

A piercing buzz from the utility room roused him from maudlin recollection. Everyday life continued, even in the face of the abnormal. Today, that meant providing clean clothes.

Large but cluttered, the laundry room sported numerous piles of dirty clothes, boxes of detergent, and several bright plastic baskets. Reaching for a couple of the latter, Daniel set them beside him before prying open the dryer. This load consisted exclusively of the twins' clothes, and he preferred to sort them here.

His mind drifted again as he relegated various bits of dark apparel to their proper baskets. When he finished, he tucked a plastic container under each arm and strode toward the back of the house.

Since she was gone, he dropped Ashley's basket just inside her door. Knowing his daughter, she'd simply dig through the pile of clothes each day to find what she wanted rather than bothering to hang up or put any of it away. When she was younger, such behavior was actively discouraged, but these days he hardly noticed.

Thomas's door was closed. Daniel knocked loudly.

"Yeah?" His son's voice was muffled through the wood.

WILEY A HAYDON III

"Laundry."

"I'm safe."

An afternoon nap wasn't uncommon for the twins, but today Thomas was awake and at his desk. Bits of a model kit, a Corvette, if Daniel wasn't mistaken, were arrayed across the top of the wooden surface. Thomas was meticulous, eschewing even the tiniest mistakes. His current project, though early in its assembly, was no exception.

"Could you hang those up for me?" Thomas asked it casually, flicking a nonchalant gesture at the basket of clothes. He tried to sound relaxed, but Daniel could hear the tremor.

"Thomas . . ."

"Come on, it's my birthday." Then belatedly and half-heartedly, "Please?"

"All right."

Pulling a hanger from the closet, Daniel slid the first shirt deftly onto it and secured the top button before returning the pair—shirt and hanger—to the wooden bar. "Are you all right, son? You seem stressed."

That was always a dangerous question. Usually Thomas would simply ignore it, but occasionally it would cause him to angrily pontificate on his life as a Mirror. Rarely—far too rarely—he would open up and share something new. Though those moments of insight were few and far between, that chance was still enough to keep Daniel asking.

"I asked to Reflect Father Sean today."

Daniel's hand slipped, and he dropped the shirt he was holding to the floor. "And?"

"He turned me down."

Picking up the fallen shirt, Daniel's mind raced to find an appropriate response.

"Being Reflected is hard," he said carefully.

A moment of silence passed between them, then Thomas let out a derisive snort. "You've never been Reflected. Not fully."

"I don't have to drop a brick on my toe to know it's going to hurt."

"Everyone knows the Reflections hurt, but only the Reflected know how much. Aren't people supposed to endure pain for the ones they love?

"It hurts me, too," Thomas went on. "I hate ripping off these glasses, but I was willing to 'drop a brick on my toe'—to borrow your colorful metaphor—for the opportunity to have one of my biggest supporters tucked up in my head. I hoped that someone might be willing to bare their soul to me, to volunteer to serve as my crutch, even if it hurt. I've learned my lesson."

Daniel slid the last pair of jeans onto a hanger and tucked them into the closet. Snatching up the basket with one hand, he shut the door. Turning to continue this conversation with Thomas, Daniel took a final glance around the floor to make sure he had not accidentally dropped something.

"I wish it were that simple, but people don't always—"

Raising his eyes, Daniel caught a split-second flash of something silvery cross his vision; by the time his brain processed what he was seeing, it was too late.

With a thunderous roar, a billion pinpricks of life blasted into existence, searing their image upon Daniel's consciousness with impossible speed. In a fractured instant, everything Daniel Ross had ever lived rushed to the forefront of his mind and lodged there, waiting to be seen.

It was as though every moment of his life chose to replay itself for him at the same time. The sound was an incomprehensible din. Tastes and smells became confused. He couldn't place images or feelings in any kind of rational order. For that instant, it went from *what was* to *what is* as if his whole being had been pressed into this infinitesimal moment of time.

It was over just that quickly. His connection with Thomas's eyes broke. Thomas slumped over at his desk, and Daniel crashed to the floor, knocking over the basket of laundry.

Heart pumping, Daniel gathered what little strength he had and crawled for the door. With a grunt of effort, he pulled it closed behind him. Then, gasping, he leaned against the hallway wall, staring at the ceiling as his brain short-circuited.

He'd been wrong. It wasn't over. It was all still there in his head. Everything he'd ever lived begged for his attention. It was so much he didn't even know where to begin.

He'd let each of the children meet his eyes once before their power had matured. That experience had been odd but not horrifying. Afterward he'd had a single moment restored. An isolated memory had been ripped from relative obscurity and made real again.

This was something else entirely.

A low moan of horror escaped his lips as he sat there. He couldn't comprehend it; it felt as though his mind were packed too full. His brain was ready to tear apart at the seams.

In a blind panic, he grabbed at the first image he could find. He was in first grade and crying. He'd been teased again. He felt the crushing pain all over again, experienced it as he had when he'd been a child.

That wasn't all, though. That image linked to another, this time from eighth grade. Only this time he was the bully, mocking a sixth grader because his clothes were obvious hand-me-downs.

Part of him remembered the satisfaction he'd drawn from ridiculing that little boy. Now, though, his mind had linked to the emotion of his first grade self, and he suddenly realized exactly what he'd done. The pain of his grade-school years impressed itself into the image of him in middle school, and Daniel gave an involuntary sob.

It didn't stop there. Every moment of derisive teasing in his life came along as part of that chain—those where he'd been the butt of the joke and those where he'd been the instigator. He'd always remembered being bullied, but until today he'd forgotten those moments where it had been him playing the tyrant.

The flood rushed onward, seeking out new emotions and linking them to other scenes in ways he'd never seen before. He saw his own loneliness and then saw it contrasted with the loneliness in others he had ignored. He lived great joy and then lived those moments where he had downplayed others' joy.

Every memory he scanned filed itself back into his mind, but with everything laid out all out once, he knew his brain was sorting it all back into different places. Memories he'd built grudges over suddenly became his fault instead of the other way around. Heroes he'd worshipped in years past suddenly seemed less heroic. He was changing, he knew, at the most basic level, and he could do nothing to stop it.

Daniel realized suddenly that tears were dripping from his cheeks. He furiously scrubbed at his eyes, but the torrent continued unabated. Everything his mind touched drew a tempest about it as it sought out connections; there was no eye of calm within this storm.

Lying in the hall, arms wrapped protectively around himself, Daniel Ross fought despair as he discovered who he truly was.

-CHAPTER 28-

Sounds of harried travelers echoed inside the terminal as passengers scurried to and from their gates. Carrying books or briefcases, coffee or children, the nameless swarms bustled past in a steady stream that had barely slowed and never abated in the hour that Sally had watched them. The lines at the coffee shop across from her gate and crowds in the tiny bookstores whispered promises of a teeming throng, but at gate 30, almost every seat stood empty.

Naively, Sally had initially believed she and Ashley were the only passengers scheduled to fly to Denver. Careful observation had stifled that notion quickly.

Many of those waiting stood next to the windows, assiduously watching the planes. Too assiduously, she realized. Few turned away from their study of the tarmac. Those who did never swept their eyes where she, Ashley, and the new Shepherd, Julie Morse, sat. Other passengers waited at the coffee shop, lingering uncertainly just far enough from the gate so as to not be immediately connected with it. Some paced back and forth, and a few waited at other gates, ignoring the calls for those planes but listening intently to every word issued about flight 1037. It was only then that Sally had recognized the tacit quarantine. Busy as the airport was, no one walked within ten feet of them; none dared sit within twenty.

Maybe that was justified. The world didn't know about Carol's Reflection, of course, but they'd heard about Calleigh's. Based upon the twins' stories, though, the world had shunned them even before that. Having proof that Mirrors were loose cannons had not helped the situation any.

Ashley sat wedged sideways in a chair, back to the armrest and knees pulled up to her chest. The girl's slim arms were wrapped around her legs, and her chin rested on her knees. Those silver eyes were shaded, of course, and Sally wondered, not for the first time, if her daughter had drifted off to sleep. Exhaustion had seized her after the Reflection, and she'd needed Sally's support to walk through the airport.

Julie had asked about it as soon as they had met her just past the security checkpoint. She didn't have anywhere near Carol's thirty years of experience, but she'd been a Shepherd long enough to immediately recognize the aftereffects of a Reflection.

Sally had filled her in, giving only the most basic of details. Ashley had offered no explanation of her own, but that hadn't been surprising. She'd said almost nothing since the Reflection and hadn't even offered any defense when Julie had pressed her on it. Eventually the Shepherd had just shrugged and asked if Ashley was going to Reflect anyone else today. When Ashley had shaken her head, the woman had nodded and taken them to their gate without another word.

And so they'd sat in silence for the past hour, waiting.

Abruptly, Julie stood up. She looked at Ashley, then at Sally, and said, "I need to use the restroom. You will keep an eye on her?"

"Of course," Sally said, trying to keep her voice neutral. On the surface, the request seemed innocent enough, but she could sense the unspoken question: "If I leave you alone for five minutes, can you keep her from causing another national panic?"

Julie nodded and strode away. People parted around her. She wasn't a Mirror, but her special glasses trumpeted her association with them. That was enough.

Sally turned back to her daughter. "Are you asleep?"

This wasn't her first attempt to draw Ashley out. She'd tried to engage her in conversation several times since they'd reached the gate. Any simple question was met with a mere nod or shake of the head, though, and any question requiring a more verbose answer was simply ignored.

This time her daughter sat a long moment in a deep silence Sally took as an unspoken yes. Just as Sally gave an understanding nod and returned to her magazine, Ashley surrendered her wordless thoughts and said, "You have to be Carol now."

Startled, Sally dropped the magazine. "What?"

"With Carol gone, you have to play her role."

Icy fear crept into Sally's stomach, but she worked her face into a soothing smile. "You have Julie."

Ashley shook her head. "You've met her. She's not the same. She's competent, but that's about it. This is her job, and that's how she treats it. I'm not a person, I'm a responsibility."

Sally opened her mouth to ask how Ashley could so easily judge a woman she had known for all of sixty minutes, but the words died on her tongue. The Reflection. She silently chastised herself for forgetting so quickly. Carol's knowledge and opinions were now etched in her daughter's mind.

"She seems fine," Sally lied. "I know you like Carol, but . . ."

"And you hate her," Ashley replied smoothly.

"I don't . . ."

"Yes, you do. You told her you did. March 16th of last year, when she dropped me off." Then, with just the barest pause, added, "Were you lying?" There was no malice in the question; Ashley simply wanted to know.

Sally's smile slipped, and she barely held back a dark grimace. "I was angry. We'd had a fight."

"I know." That voice was frustratingly calm. "I'm pretty sure I remember that argument better than you do. You accused her of caring about her reputation more than she did me. It wasn't the first time you threw that at her. It wasn't the last, either."

Sally remembered those arguments too. Half a dozen times, perhaps more, she and Carol had squared off over this one point. It burned her that the Shepherd denied what was so obvious, but she'd never extracted the truth from the woman, no matter how often they shouted at each other.

The opportunity, though, presented itself now. "You've seen her whole life. Isn't that what she cared about? She wants to go down in history, Ashley. You have to see that now."

Uncurling, Ashley shifted her feet to the floor, turned her body straight, and slouched down into the chair. Her shaded gaze left Sally to rest on the coffee shop across the way, and the few people whose eyes had strayed toward them turned abruptly away.

"Pride goeth before destruction," Ashley whispered, and Sally wasn't sure her daughter meant for her to hear it or not.

"Yes," Ashley continued in a slightly louder voice. "She wanted glory, and she judged success in the years her Mirrors lived before . . ." Her frail voice faded, and her head seemed to twitch toward Sally as if judging her mother's reaction. With a sigh, Ashley gave a terse nod.

"Yes, she pushed them through each obstacle with her own place in the histories on her mind. Carol Raines is probably the most arrogant person I've ever known. She became a Shepherd specifically because she felt it gave the best chance at immortality."

"And what do you think about her now that you know?"

Ashley dropped her head back down. Her voice was broken, her fatigue obvious. "I wish I didn't know. I pulled back the curtain and revealed a woman so steeped in herself that everyone else fades into the background. I miss the ignorance. I miss it so much."

"Then why. . . ?"

Ashley shook her head, cutting her off. "Do you really think her Mirrors lived longer just because she wanted to be famous?" Ashley asked. "Whatever drove her, Carol played her part well. In three years of being dragged from Reflection to Reflection, I never doubted that she cared about me."

224

Shaking her head, the girl's head turned toward the window. One of her hands moved up and swept under those dark glasses, wiping a tear away.

"I'm not sure I doubt it now. Deep down Carol understood that fake compassion would never command the loyalty she needed. She twisted herself, squeezing out every ounce of love she could summon in order to bind us to her. Whether her motives were pure is inconsequential; most of us never had reason to wonder."

"What about now?" Sally pressed. "Now that you've seen what she really wanted, doesn't it change anything?"

Ashley turned back slowly, mouth quirked in a weird, contemplative grimace. Sally felt the weight of that gaze through the shaded lenses and fought the urge to instinctively retreat from her daughter's scrutiny. Ashley opened her mouth twice, each time twisting her tongue as if looking for the proper words before lapsing back into stillness. Eventually she bowed her head, ducking back into the protective cavity of her knees.

"No." Pause. "Yes? Maybe." Ashley's words were muffled. "I don't know."

Long silence dominated. With a sigh, Ashley continued. "Yes, learning Carol's motives hurt. But they're not the only thing I learned today.

"When I collapsed in that hotel room after the Reflection, I finally understood what was changing: Carol wasn't there to catch me this time. It was the first time I hit the floor after a Reflection; even in the airport with Calleigh, when she wasn't expecting it, her instincts were to break my fall.

"In the hotel . . . you didn't step into take her place. I needed you to catch me, and you couldn't do it. You couldn't do it because you were so furious with her you didn't even think of me. That wasn't the only reason, though." She paused, gave a small sob, and finished in a trembling voice, "You're scared to touch me."

"No, baby, I . . ."

Ashley raised her head and shook it vehemently. "You flinched as I grabbed on to you when we left the hotel, and you frowned when I leaned on you for support here in the terminal. Carol wasn't afraid to touch me, Mom. She wasn't afraid of my eyes. She wasn't afraid of *me*. Does it matter why? To her, I'm still a girl lost in the mazes the world has erected for her. To you, though, I'm just a constant reminder of what's gone wrong. You remember fondly what was, and you're scared of what will be. You've don't love me as I am, only as I was."

Sally tried to find the words to fight. Ashley's voice had strengthened as she spoke, and spectators hanging in range of her voice hesitated in their purposeful strides to cast surreptitious glances at the pair.

"I'm going to die," Ashley continued firmly. Sally flinched as if struck, and Ashley responded by repeating it again as a shout. "I'm going to die!" People froze in their passage, searching for the proclamation's source. When their searching found those shaded eyes, all hurried on. The furtive listeners who'd gathered at the edge of earshot scrambled away, and the empty zones around mother and daughter doubled in range.

"I'm going to die," Ashley repeated again, the words still hard but quiet this time. "You have to be able to think it without cringing and say it without crying. Carol knew the ending to my story before she ever knocked on our door, but she never cringed. She's never surrendered a single child until death finally stole them. I'm not dead yet, and I don't want to die."

Ashley's placid expression faltered, giving way to a near sob. She shrank back, head bowed. With a short whimper, she drew a deep breath, clearly fighting the tears that would pool inside her glasses if she let herself cry.

"Carol may have been driven by selfish goals," she managed, voice shaking a bit, "but at least it led her to act like she cared. I believe you love me, but little you've done in the last three years shows it. Is it any surprise my Shepherd's strength has endeared me to her more strongly than your terror has drawn me to you?"

Ashley shifted to face Sally again. She held a hand in front of her, palm up. "You can focus on her drive for glory and say she was too proud. You can point out that all her ends were self-serving and that she likely would have sacrificed us in a heartbeat if necessary. You'd be right." The girl held up her other hand in the same fashion. "Or you can see her tender side and strive to duplicate that." She dropped both hands back down and sighed. "It's your choice, Mom. Having you absent in this fight would be worse than having Carol totally driven by selfish ego. Especially since your actions would be driven by love for me."

"I'm going to die." The words rang through Sally's mind. It hurt to think about it. *I should reach out and hold her; she needs comfort. She needs* me.

Despite this epiphany, she couldn't stop nervously wringing her hands. She ached to reach out and touch her daughter, to stroke her hair, to hug her tightly. Ashley should be resting her head on Sally's shoulder, not cringing alone at the edge of the row of chairs, but the thought brought no strength. Sick with fear, Sally wrenched her gaze away from her daughter.

She's not dead yet. That was better, but still hard. *She's not dead yet. She is my daughter.* Warmth tinged that thought, but not enough. Her hands still twisted nervously in her lap, and she made no move toward Ashley. *She's not dead yet. She's not dead yet.* The words echoed numbly in her mind, but she forced them on. Strength would come when she could face this; it would have to.

"Flight 1037 with service to the Denver International Airport is ready to board. There is a Justice Department asset on this flight; general boarding will begin after she has been secured. Passenger Ashley Ross and escort, please report to gate 30."

"That's us," Ashley said stoically.

"Julie's not back yet," Sally said, looking around.

"She's over by the gate," Ashley noted, pointing. "I guess she was willing to let us finish our conversation in private." She cocked her head. "Maybe Carol was wrong about her. I hope so."

Ashley uncurled, dropping her feet off the chair to the ground. Her shoes clunked on the floor, and she pushed herself up with agonizing deliberation. Her face screamed the fatigue of post-Reflection, and she barely maintained her balance. Steadying, she grabbed her bag and pulled it over her shoulder.

"I can make it to the plane on my own. You don't have to support me," Ashley said quietly, but Sally could read her face. Everything there cried out to be helped, to have someone hold her up and share her burdens. She wanted her mother to object, to offer the help she so obviously needed.

And yet Sally sat there, still petrified. *Help her, you fool!* screamed a voice inside her head, but the words that passed her lips were a barely audible "All right." She picked up her fallen magazine, grabbed her own bag, and stood beside her daughter.

Disappointment crossed Ashley's face, but she said nothing further about the weakness, instead marching in deliberate strides to the gate with her ticket. Sally followed a few feet behind, shame bowing her head.

Just after handing over her ticket, just as she started down the ramp to the plane, Ashley stopped, turning to look over her shoulder. In that too-quiet voice, she said, "Think about what I told you, Mom. Just because I had Carol never meant I didn't need you, too. Now I need you more than ever."

With that, she faced forward again and shuffled in an unsteady gait down the incline. Julie stepped up beside her. With an encouraging smile, the Shepherd wrapped an arm around her, offering support. Sally stood frozen a moment, then followed them, still at a distance.

She's not dead yet. She's not dead yet. She's not dead . . .

-CHAPTER 29-

United States attorney general Susan Dubois started as a knock at the door pulled her attention away from the most recent case file splayed in front of her.

Darkness draped her office, driven back only by the light of a small desk lamp. Night had crept up on her again.

How long had it been since she'd finally sent William home? Instinctively, her eyes flicked to the ancient grandfather clock and she swore as her mind processed the information. Already past ten; she hadn't come up for air in hours.

"Come in, Cole," she called with more energy than she felt.

As expected, Cole Bryant slipped inside; only the Mirror specialist stopped by at this time of night without calling first. Despite the hour, his suit was immaculate and his posture unbent. Clutched in his left hand was a small drink carrier with two coffees tucked inside. His right hand carried the ever-present briefcase Susan had never seen him without.

"May I have a minute?" he asked calmly, raising the libations in a conciliatory gesture.

"Of course." He knew far too well that she would forgive any-one who came bearing coffee.

Susan had little time to devote to following the latest gossip, but even she was aware of this man's reputation. Cole Bryant, the brilliant but isolated man who had devoted his life to study-ing Mirrors and thus had no time for love, friendship, or social niceties. It was an easy portrait to paint but one Susan constantly had to reevaluate.

The specialist was terse, blunt, and seemed averse to learning tact, but as Susan shared many of these qualities, she found it refreshing. A life immersed with lawyers and bureaucrats had driven her to adopt their despised doublespeak as a matter of course, and, in a way, she admired Cole for his stubborn resistance to the natural order of politics.

It won him few other friends, though, and she had wondered before if she might be his only confidant. They would go to lunch together, open up, share small talk, and even laugh. It was a unique relationship for Cole; she'd never seen him interact with anyone else like that.

Within the department, the man had a reputation as a loner. None of her assistants and aides—even William, who seemed to like everyone—enjoyed his company. She'd heard rumors that Cole was interested in her romantically, but his curt refusal of her advances more than thirty years ago seemed a definitive answer for Susan. As near as her experiences proved, he was a machine powered only by his eternal quest to maintain Mirror justice.

Gratefully taking the steaming cup her guest held out, Susan leaned back in her chair as Cole removed his own drink from the holder. Collapsing the thick paper, he shoved the crumpled tray into the trash before setting down his briefcase and taking a seat opposite her.

"How did the Ross girl's meeting go?" she asked. "I'm sorry I couldn't be there."

"You had more important matters to attend to," he said. "I knew you would want a report, though."

Sure enough, he reached into his briefcase and slid a thin folder onto her desk. No doubt he'd typed up a thorough transcript of the event and included his own analyses.

"Long day, Cole. Can I get the abridged version?"

"Why do you think I came by?"

Susan smiled. "And you brought coffee. Anticipating my every need. You should have been a butler."

Cole snorted but did give a tired smile of his own.

"The very short version is that the board fired Carol Raines."

"That much I heard."

"It was probably closer than you'd think, particularly since Beverly voted to keep her."

"Really?" Susan was genuinely floored. "I was sure they hated each other."

"They do, but the only thing Beverly hates more is losing Reflections. The longevity of Carol's Mirrors is statistically significant, and the good doctor knows her math. Firing Carol costs us an average of thirty-five Reflections for each Mirror she'd have had. Additionally, we're now short a Shepherd with no immediate replacement looming. That means we've had to postpone several appointments and have thus lost even more Reflections in the long run. It was a perfect storm for Beverly to side with her longtime rival."

Susan paused, considering. Maximizing Reflections per child was a common topic of conversation in these halls. Almost all of them focused on psychological evaluations, Shepherd training, and other similar means. No one ever talked about the obvious, though.

"You could remove the suicide dispensation," Susan suggested.

Cole stiffened immediately. She'd heard he took the matter seriously—he was the one who had pushed it through Congress, after all—but she'd never actually brought it up. Apparently the stories were true.

"No." His voice was iron.

"If you're concerned about losing Reflections, that is the simplest way to address it."

"So we tie them down, stick them in straitjackets, keep someone watching them twenty-four hours a day?"

Susan shrugged. "Why not? We don't let normal suicidal people take their own lives. This way we can keep them alive *and* get the maximum number of Reflections out of them."

"When we prevent normal people from killing themselves, we're not usually torturing them once a week, are we? Keeping Mirrors alive against their will just to subject them to Reflections is cruelty beyond even what I can condone."

"You're willing to have them Reflect each week but not keep them alive to do it?"

"Mirrors Reflect. It's what they do. I've never heard of a Mirror who made it to fifteen without Reflecting *someone*. For those outside government control, it's almost always a family member or close friend. I'm convinced more than ever it's that bond that destroys them in the end.

"So, yes, I have them Reflect, but it's something they're going to do anyway. I merely direct their powers toward more productive candidates."

"But you won't keep them alive to do it?"

"Do you want that job?" Cole shot back. "Picture it, Susan. You've brought a criminal to a seventeen-year-old girl who is literally begging you to die. She's sobbing, knowing what's coming. And then you're going to physically pry her eyes open to force her to look at another criminal? I know I'm a monster, but that's horrifying."

Susan leaned back, processing that image. "Okay, maybe that's a bit much."

"Death is a Mirror's indication that she is done Reflecting. You can force her to comply, but that's the only way it'll happen. Death is a small mercy, but it's the only one I can offer."

"All right," Susan said, raising her hands in surrender. "You're the expert." She took a sip of her coffee. "Anything else important?"

"I think Hanover is leaning Liberator."

"Well, he's been headed that way for a while now."

"Seeing Ashley today may have pushed him over the edge. Keep an eye on him."

"I guess I'll start a list of candidates to fill a vacancy."

Cole nodded. "Good. I'm fairly certain you'll need it."

"So, why did you bring her here?" Susan asked.

"Who? Ashley?"

"Yes. I saw the preliminary reports. This wasn't complex. Ashley clearly did it, and knowing you as well as I do, I'm guessing your analysis of her state of mind is solid. Since we've never seen an event like this, Thomas Ross seems a more likely foundation for the girl's strength than Carol Raines's influence. It would have been an easy vote. Even if Hanover were leaning Liberator, you'd have had her in a government facility with a vote of four to one. Three to two at worst.

"You didn't do that. Instead you made sure to bring her here, which you had to know was a recipe for disaster. It's an easy choice to make on paper, but a lot harder when you have a mother and her daughter sitting across from you, pleading for leniency."

"Does it seem right to make a decision on a case such as this without at least speaking to her?" Cole asked.

Susan frowned. "Don't give me that. The board has made plenty of decisions about Mirrors, even in specific cases, without so much as a phone call to the family beforehand." She leveled a finger at him accusingly. "You're dodging the question, Cole, and it's not like you. What's really going on?"

For a long moment, he studied his coffee cup, obviously lost in thought. For the first time, Susan noticed the dark circles under his eyes and the almost haunted look they bestowed. Her friend's features were haggard, his demeanor grim. Perhaps it was the dim pool of light from the desk lamp playing tricks on her mind, just the shadows painting fables with their dark fingers. She hoped it was. If Cole grew tired of fighting this war, there was no telling how Mirror justice might change.

"The Ross twins have proven remarkably resilient," Cole said finally. "I had intended their case as an experiment in whether Reflecting Mirrors raised by their own parents would live longer than those raised in government homes. That data is muddied by the fact that we have two Mirrors in the same household. While I believe their placement with Daniel and Sally Ross has an impact, it has become clear that the support system of living with another Mirror has proven even more beneficial.

"From a purely academic standpoint, I need to get as much data out of this as I can. The traditional wisdom has been that housing Mirrors together is a disastrous idea since they could Reflect each other and die. The Ross twins are providing strong evidence against that hypothesis. Perhaps the advantage of raising Mirrors together outweighs the risks, but until I see this to the end, I won't know."

Susan frowned. "And the Reflection of Calleigh Kershfeldt?"

"Dangerous, I agree. Further incidents like that have the potential to undermine the entire system. Perhaps it was an isolated incident. If so, then the benefits clearly supersede the expected risks. If, however, events like the Detroit Metro Reflection are normal, we can know that the Ross experiment is a failure."

Leaning back in her chair, Susan finished off her coffee and tossed the cup into the trash can by her desk.

"An excellent argument. It's exactly the kind of answer I expect from you. Why didn't you just tell me that at the outset instead of dodging the issue?"

Cole frowned, then shook his head. "I should make a point not to befriend people as smart as I am."

"Well, that wouldn't have saved you from me," Susan replied with a smile. However much she wanted to believe otherwise, the Mirror expert was far, far smarter than she could ever hope to be.

"I guess," Cole said haltingly, "I'm tired of being the only one who's damned."

"What?"

"We walk a very fine line, Susan. At least we should."

He leaned forward, his face blooming with lamplight. "I see these children constantly. I watch them grow up, and I watch them break down. Most of the people here, even the board, see them as nothing more than pawns in a game of chess. Every decision we make is rendered in a vacuum.

"Of course, all the Liberators see is the other side. They've never lost someone to a maniac and don't understand the driving need for justice. All they see is a child slowly wasting away as the Department of Justice and its cronies poison her mind with unspeakable horrors. They see a government that pays blood money in exchange for heartlessly murdering children. To them, we are the criminals.

"For decades I've walked a tightrope, surveying both sides but part of neither. I've sought to find the perfect balance between manipulating Mirrors as the valuable tools they are and providing them the dignity worthy of a human being. It's an impossible problem, and I hate it.

"I've decided, though, that what I hate more is being the only one to acknowledge it. I'm tired of watching a board that hasn't even bothered to meet their charges."

Susan frowned. "Did you ever think that might be for the best? I mean, look at Hanover. You're worried about him being a Liberator; is there any doubt why? Did you really expect that showing them a Mirror face-to-face wouldn't turn some of them?"

Cole frowned. "Of course, it's for the best . . . as long as we define 'best' as 'using Mirrors until we've ground them to dust.' It's not that simple, Susan. I've seen both sides of this conflict, and I've had to make my own peace. I think it's time the rest of those involved do the same."

"Why not just let things continue as they have? Is it worth destroying the entire program?" Susan asked, incredulous. "Would you turn your back on everything Mirror justice has accomplished? What about all those victims?" She hardened her voice. "What about my sister?"

"I've not forgotten what was done to your sister," Cole said gently. "I'm not turning my back on anything. I still support the use of Reflections."

Susan frowned. "Then why force everyone else to answer these questions?"

"Destroying someone should cause us pain, Susan, no matter how justified our actions. That pain is what keeps us from becoming monsters." He leaned forward. "If we can slowly destroy these children without a tear shed, why would we assume we are morally capable of determining what is just?"

She scoffed. "You know I still get letters from Mirrors' foster parents complaining about you. They say that you're distant, detached. If you feel pain for feeding their children to the wheels of justice, they certainly don't know that. Trust me, Cole, there's no love lost between you and those you claim to protect."

Cole leaned back, his face descending into shadows again. His eyes were hard, burning with a dangerous fury, and Susan suddenly wondered what had possessed her to say it.

No. No, she didn't wonder. She'd said it because it was true. He was lecturing her on what the people in the department should and shouldn't feel while he ignored his own actions. He didn't get to take some moral high ground and pretend he was immune. If he was going to be blunt, well, so could she.

Silence stretched between them, and she felt her muscles tense; this wasn't a game she liked playing with him. He was better at patiently waiting for his opponents to collapse. Still, she waited for an answer, refusing to let any of her discomfort show on her face.

"I know the fruits of my labor better than anyone. I'm dispassionate, and people hate me for it. So be it. At least I've analyzed my choices. I think the rest of the board should too."

"At what cost?"

"Peace of mind. Most of the board will lose a few nights of sleep over this and then find their balance. If necessary, Hanover will be replaced. Justice will roll on, but perhaps those who dispense it will be wiser."

"You can't know that."

"No, I can't."

Susan ground her teeth. At times, Cole's openness could definitely be as irritating as it was refreshing. It was very hard to argue with someone who so freely admitted the merits of his opponents' case. She could get angry now, declare his move a mistake, and he would calmly acknowledge all her concerns. In a public forum he would bring all his gifts of oratory to bear, slicing apart her protestations with ease. Here, in the sanctuary of her darkened office, he would simply nod agreement to her misgivings.

"Fine," she said. "It's already done, so I won't waste time worrying about it. Was there anything else?"

He shook his head and stood. "It's been a long day, and I'm exhausted. Let's do lunch later this week, though. It would be nice to talk about something other than work."

"Yeah."

Picking up his briefcase, Cole gave her a final deferential nod, then turned and left the small island of light. His last steps to the door garbed him in shadows, and she could barely make out his outline even as she traced the progress of his footfalls in their egress. A sharp click, and a crack of light broke around the door as the specialist pulled it open. Susan saw him in silhouette, tall and proud, coffee cup still clutched in one hand and ever-present briefcase in the other. With another click, he was gone and the evening shadows rushed in to replace him.

– CHAPTER 30 –

Water dripped languorously from the eaves of the house as Mom turned into the driveway, the bulk of the cold rain having passed before their plane even touched down. No lights burned in the front windows, and the darkness wrapped the house in an inhospitable cloak. Ashley hadn't held out hope for an energetic homecoming, but the black stillness was eerie.

Behind them, the garage door rumbled noisily down in its track. Ashley pulled herself from the car with a tired groan. The acute exhaustion that followed a Reflection had receded into mere fatigue; she no longer had to struggle for every step, but each movement bore reminders of what she had done. She didn't bother to grab her luggage from the trunk before heading inside and wasn't really surprised to notice Mom didn't either.

What did surprise her was that the house was just as dark inside as it had looked outside. It was almost ten, but surely Dad had waited up for them. His car was here, so he was definitely home.

Flipping on light switches as she penetrated into the heart of the house, Ashley shuffled out to the living room. Mom followed her that far, then broke off toward the master bedroom. Opening the door, her mother took a single step before stopping abruptly.

Ashley could just make out her father's form on the bed. He raised his head lethargically, then dropped it back down. Without a word, Mom backed out and closed the door. She strode stiffly toward the back of the house. A second later, Ashley heard the office door open and shut.

Ashley waited a few seconds to see if Dad would come greet her, but there was no sound from his room. With a dejected sigh, she made her own trip to the back hallway.

The light slipping through the crack under Thomas's door was the first encouraging omen since she'd gotten home, and the barest of smiles creased her weary features. She gently rapped on the door—a single staccato knock so that he would know it was her—but didn't wait for an invitation.

Thomas sat hunched over his desk, a model Corvette set out before him. Unlike most of his work, the tiny vehicle showed clear signs of distraction. Bits of glue had squeezed out of the joints and several pieces were clearly misaligned. She had caught him in the act of painting, and colors overlapped or blended in odd patterns. The entire project was a disaster, and to Ashley it was an immediate sign that something was awry.

"What happened? What's wrong?"

She studied her brother intently, seeking the source of his discomfort. It hit her almost immediately. She read it in his labored movements; she heard it screamed by his wrinkled forehead. Every muscle seemed to betray his secret. She knew too well what a Reflection's aftermath looked like.

"Who?" she asked quietly, shutting the door behind her.

"You Reflected someone too," he said, ignoring her query.

She nodded woodenly. "Carol Raines. They fired her and told me I couldn't see her again. What about you?"

Thomas said nothing, instead turning back to his model. Suppressing an angry growl, Ashley took a spot on her brother's bed. She waited a long minute while Thomas swirled his paintbrush in a small tub of red paint, studiously avoiding her gaze.

"Dad," she said eventually. "I thought it was weird that he didn't greet us. Well, me at least."

"Yeah."

"Why?"

Thomas hesitated, casting his gaze at a point somewhere between Ashley and his desk. Then, taking a final moment to visibly battle the traces of fatigue, he said, "It was an accident." The words were casual. "I was working on the model, and I took off the glasses for a second to get a better look."

His response was calm, the tone nonchalant. Unfortunately, that was precisely the problem. Such pretense with her was worthless; it was almost insulting. They saw each other after being dragged through the streets of hell each week. Most days they spoke in the weary droning that swallowed all feelings and never apologized. Now, though—hours after absorbing their father's world—he sat opposite her and drew the required energy to feign unconcerned normalcy?

Something about her brother brought forth the emotions the world never saw. Usually it was an unexpected surge of joy or a sobbing moment of catharsis. Today, fire bubbled inside her. His lie infuriated her, and though she hated to admit it, she relished the way it made her feel alive. She grabbed the sensation and rode it, drawing it in and feeding on it.

She grabbed his arm forcefully and spun him to face her. "After all we've been through, after all we've done for each other, don't you dare lie to me, Thomas Ross!"

He quailed before that gaze, shrinking into the chair. She'd seen him rant many times, both before the Reflections started and after. His fuse was short and his explosions loud. He, on the other hand, had never seen her truly angry.

"We don't accidentally Reflect," she snapped. "Fifteen years of training, 150 infusions of foreign lives, and I'm supposed to believe you made an amateur mistake? We don't even open our eyes when we wake until the glasses are on, and you expect me to believe that in the middle of the day, with Dad in your room, you cast all caution to the wind and actually removed the only shield we have against the world?"

Thomas's face had paled and his mouth worked silently but furiously. Finally, he clamped his teeth shut, took a deep breath, and swallowed.

"Tell me why," she demanded tersely.

"I was mad."

"Mad? At who? Dad?"

Thomas shook his head vigorously and slumped back in his chair. "At Father Sean. I wanted to Reflect him when I saw him today. He turned me down."

"Why'd you want to Reflect Father Sean?"

"Why'd you want to Reflect Carol Raines?"

"I'm not going to see Carol again," Ashley said quietly. Her voice didn't shake, but she feared that was because the apathy was creeping in again now that the brief surge of fury had passed. "Are you not going back to see Father Sean?"

"It's not like that. I wanted his view of the world. He's so . . . positive. He never seems to regret that I'm dying." He paused and shook his head again. "That didn't come out right. I mean, that sounds awful, but it's not like that."

Flustered, he waved a hand as if clearing away what he'd just said. "I just mean that Father Sean sees me as I am now and wants me to live in the present as best I can. That's all he expects. He wants me to find purpose in my Reflections. He has all these simple beliefs that seem to give him peace, and I wanted that."

"Thomas, I've been trying to tell you that for years. We make a difference."

Her brother leaned back in his chair and crossed his arms over his chest. "I know that. I know *you* think that. *I* don't. I thought if I could really see that perspective, really see it lived . . ."

"We've Reflected plenty of people. Surely one of them was an optimist."

Thomas gave a bitter laugh. "We've seen through the eyes of the worst of society. Maybe from someone like a priest it would be different. Someone who, you know, hasn't killed someone?"

"Some of them haven't, Thomas. Some of them didn't commit the crimes . . ."

"They're all guilty!" her brother roared suddenly, slamming his fist just inches from his model. The small car jumped from the force of the blow. "They're all so flawed. Even the ones we acquit. I thought that surely Father Sean would be different. He'd be . . ."

Ashley arched an eyebrow skeptically. "Perfect? You know better."

"I do now. He refused." His face crumpled, and his voice broke. "There was evil in him. In him!" His right hand clenched around the edge of the desk. "Evil in the man who has shown me so much kindness. So much evil he was scared to show me." Opening his fist, he drew his hands to his face and drew a deep breath. "If he . . . if he was . . ." The words were muffled, barely clear enough to hear.

Ashley walked over and put an arm around him. "I'm sorry, Thomas. I am . . . Maybe he just didn't want to be Reflected. It's not easy."

He cut her off; his voice was weak, but he spoke with determination. "Carol let you Reflect her, though."

Ashley balked. "Sort of. She said I could, but once I'd done it, I realized that she only said that to win an argument with Mom. She never actually intended for me to Reflect her."

Thomas lips curled up in a dark sneer. "Sounds selfish."

Ashley nodded sadly. "She's a selfish woman. Pride drives Carol more than anyone else I've ever seen. Everything she did was a calculated move to establish a legacy."

"So Mom was right."

Ashley shook her head. "She did care about me, Thomas. She just cared about her legacy more."

"Mom was right," Thomas insisted. "That's what Mom always accused her of."

"It doesn't matter."

"It matters to me," he whispered.

"But . . ."

Thomas plowed over her before she could finish. "It matters because it's proof that everybody fails. Dennis Carson didn't really want to hit his son. But he did." He shuddered, and she knew he was fighting the parade of lives. Opening the gates like this was dangerous. "Rudolph Keller wanted to molest that girl . . . and he didn't want to. He screamed at God for an hour the night before, begging for some kind of release. Michael Pater cried when he'd killed his family and threw up everything he ate for three days. But fear got him more than the horror, and he lied to hide it and ran away. Now Carol Raines isn't the great champion of Mirrors she pretends to be."

"And what did you learn today?" Ashley asked, trying to direct the conversation away from all that. She was certain Dad hadn't killed anyone, at least. "What did Dad show you?"

"Why we Reflect."

Ashley's heart froze. It was an answer they'd sought for years. Every other Mirror raised at home was free from the burden. Only the Ross twins were raised by their birth parents and also served Justice. The two of them had speculated dozens of times over the past three years, but it had always ended in a mystery.

"What did you see?"

"Bryant came and tried to buy us. There was some haggling, but ultimately Mom and Dad *chose* to do this to us. There wasn't even paperwork for this kind of deal, so they had to trust Bryant when he said he'd make it work. And so we get raised at home but still pulled away to Reflect once a week."

Ashley shook her head firmly. "No. We've gotten that far on our own. I want to know *why* they did it."

"Lots of reasons. Dad was actually on board with giving us up to the state. Start over, try for a new family without Mirrors. Mom wouldn't give us up. So they compromised."

"No. You're not telling me something. Why? Why not just keep us and not have the Reflections as part of it?"

"They get paid to take care of us," Thomas said bitterly. "That was definitely a part of it."

"Really? It can't be just that because I'm pretty sure Dad's been burning through that money the last couple of years." She leaned forward, jabbing a finger in her brother's face. "What aren't you telling me?"

Thomas batted her hand away and leaned forward himself, placing his face inches from hers. "Fine! Bryant told them we'd live longer if we Reflected. He claimed it's his expertise that keeps us alive. Bryant hammered it hard. Mom wanted that but couldn't bring herself to give us up. As time was running out, she made a deal: we Reflect, and Bryant does his best to keep us alive as long as possible."

Ashley slumped down onto his bed, suddenly confused. "That's not so bad. They wanted to keep us alive. Even if they made the wrong decision, that's not something I can hate them for."

"I knew you'd see it that way!" Thomas spat. "I knew you'd want to wrap it up all nice, but it's not that simple!"

"Why not?"

"Because even if you're right, that was just Mom's position. Dad really did want to give us up. The money tempted him. The normalcy tempted him even more."

"So? He didn't give us away. We're Reflecting, but he and Mom raised us. We're here! We're together! Why are you focused on what *might* have happened?"

"Don't you care that he almost abandoned us?"

"But he didn't!"

"Doesn't it matter that he wanted to?"

"Of course it does, but if I'm supposed to hate him for twenty-four hours of weakness, why can't you love him for fifteen years of strength?"

"You didn't see what I did."

"No," Ashley conceded. "If I did, do you think I'd agree with you?" Thomas opened his mouth to speak, and she immediately reminded him, "*Don't* lie to me."

"I wasn't going to," he shot back. He didn't answer immediately, though.

"Probably not," he conceded glumly. "But it doesn't make you right."

"I didn't say it did."

"You thought it, though."

Ashley forced a smile. "Well, yeah."

Thomas stared at her for a long minute, then sighed and picked up his paintbrush. To her dismay, he didn't return the grin.

"I'm tired of arguing. I just want to finish my model."

"No."

Dropping his brush into the cup of water, he turned an irritated look on his sister. "What?"

"No. We're not done."

"Yes, we are."

"Today was different, Thomas."

She heard him suck in his breath. His fingers were shaking slightly, and she could almost see his lip quivering. He was trying so hard to be strong in front of her, but she saw past it all. They'd Reflected two very different people today, but one important factor was the same.

"We didn't Reflect strangers," Ashley continued quietly. "These are people we loved. People we trusted. And they let us down."

Thomas didn't say anything. Instead, he took his quivering fingers, grabbed the brush in his fist, and dipped it forcefully into the red paint.

"Bryant was right; government Mirrors live longer, but I don't think it's his intervention. Not directly, anyway.

"It's one thing to see strangers stripped down, with every secret laid bare. We didn't know them before, so the only impressions we can form are the ones we get from the Reflection. There's no image to shatter; they're always going to be exactly what we know they are.

"But not today. Today you Reflected our dad, and I Reflected a woman I trusted my life with."

"And they failed," Thomas said bitterly, daubing paint onto his model.

"At least they haven't killed anyone," Ashley replied.

"They still failed, Ash. Did you know that Dad . . ."

"I don't want to know, Thomas."

"Neither do I!"

"Then I guess you shouldn't have Reflected him."

Thomas scowled. "Maybe he should have just tried harder."

Ashley rolled her eyes and opened her mouth, but Thomas spoke over her. "Whatever. You've proven my point. You don't want to know because their failure hurts. Don't pretend it doesn't."

Ashley sighed and nodded. "I'm not. It *does* hurt."

"So it hurts, and it shatters the image, and we wonder who we can trust," Thomas said, quickly rattling it off, following the path to its conclusion. "And as our world breaks down, we lose our supports. And, let me guess, you believe that now we're closer to killing ourselves."

"Don't you?"

Thomas said nothing, instead drawing an unsteady line of red onto his car. She knew he was thinking it, though. He'd followed the line of her logic too quickly not to have seen it already.

"I always wondered what kept you going," Ashley continued. "I think I know now. You want to find someone who measures up. Someone who hasn't failed.

"The criminals were never a good place to start, but you held out hope that the people around you were better. Sam, Sean, Dad, me. As long as you believed that, you could keep doing this."

Thomas nodded. "I thought that maybe you were right. Maybe we were making a difference. If everyone's broken, though, then there's no way it can matter. Lock up some of the evil and let the others go free."

"So you had to Reflect someone you trusted. To see that they were different."

"And they weren't," Thomas said, voice shaking.

"And now . . ." Ashley prompted.

"And now . . ." Thomas repeated in a whisper, "I guess, why bother?"

"You're giving up?" Ashley asked, heart sinking.

"Why shouldn't I? I'm supposed to be locking away the criminals so the rest of the world can live in a better place, but if they're not any better themselves . . ." He trailed off, shrugging. "Instead I'm torturing myself each week for a world that doesn't deserve it."

Ashley's hands were shaking now too. She heard the despair tormenting her brother and knew the end was coming. If he'd run out of reasons to keep Reflecting, he'd run out of reasons to live.

"Please don't leave me," she begged. "Please."

He finally turned to face her. "I should have known. You want to keep doing this? Of course you do. Even after Reflecting Carol?" She cringed as he gave a mocking laugh. "What's wrong with you? When is it enough?"

"Carol was flawed, but she wasn't a monster."

"Failure," Thomas spat back, some fire returning to his voice. "She failed you."

"You think she's like Spencer, then?"

"Aren't they all?"

A derisive laugh escaped Ashley before she could stop it. "She wants to be a legend; she's not raping children. To equate the two is stupid."

"And you deny she'd have thrown you under a bus if it suited her goals?"

"She probably would have," Ashley admitted. "I guess I'm glad she chose a profession where compassion furthered her aims better than cruelty."

"How can you defend her?" Thomas demanded.

"Because I can't reduce a woman I've admired and respected to a single trait."

"Well, I can."

Shaking her head, Ashley's tone grew sad. "What are you going to do about it?"

This time he hesitated, and Ashley felt her spirits raise just slightly. He was dispirited, broken, and giving up, but some part of him still wanted to live.

She needed to take advantage of this hesitation. Before he had a chance to voice it, to say it and make it real, Ashley interjected, "What if you're wrong?"

Thomas snorted. "Sure. I've seen 151 people, Ash. They're useless."

"And what about me?"

He froze, clearly not anticipating the question.

"What about you?"

"Do you think I'm all a failure, too?"

"No. I mean, I know you. We've spent our entire lives together. If you were like them, I'd know."

"What about me? Can't you make the world a better place for me?"

Indecision painted Thomas's face. Ashley slid off the bed and gripped his shoulder, staring into his shaded glasses with pleading eyes.

"Please, Thomas. I'm not ready to go, and I don't want to be alone."

She didn't mention it, but she hoped it made him think of his promise a year ago. She didn't think he'd break it if he remembered, but he might not appreciate it if she used it as a pair of shackles, either.

"I don't know . . ."

"Give me tonight. Please. We can talk about it in the morning. Just stay alive tonight."

He sighed. "We're going to go through all this again then, aren't we? I know you. It'll always be 'just one more day.'"

"Then you can always say no tomorrow."

Thomas pushed away from her, dropping his eyes to the desk.

He cocked his head to glance over at the poorly made model and then swept it into the trash can by his desk with an irritated motion. Ashley watched him without a word, silently imploring him not to abandon her.

"Fine," he said eventually. "You get tonight."

She hugged him weakly, barely able to keep from falling into the chair with him. He returned the embrace just as weakly, then pulled away.

Thomas opened a drawer in his desk, apparently planning to pull out another model to work on, but Ashley said, "Wait. Can't we do something together?"

"Like what?"

"We could play Stibium," she suggested, referencing their trivia game.

"I don't know," Thomas said. "Long day."

"We could play 'no rules.'"

Thomas brightened a bit. He loved playing without the rules since he felt it was a better chance to show off. Ashley was encouraged by his sudden interest but saddened a bit as well. It showed her what she'd suspected; despite Father Sean and her attempts to push Thomas into something more meaningful, he still derived his greatest joy from impressing others.

Tonight it was enough, though.

—CHAPTER 31—

Daniel raised his hand to knock on the office door, then hesitated as he noticed the light leaking from the crack under Thomas's door. Ashley's door was still open and her room dark, so it was almost certain the twins were together. He longed to rush in there and hug his daughter. A part of him wanted to be sure she had really returned home, to know definitively that the board hadn't taken her away. A stronger force welled up and destroyed those urges, though; no matter the urgency at seeing Ashley, he wasn't ready to face his son again.

Turning back to the office door, he gave it a soft tapping. Surprised silence greeted him for a long moment. Then, just as he was about to walk away, Sally's voice drifted out to him.

"Come in."

He stepped quickly inside. His wife watched him warily from her place at the desk. One of the photo albums was spread out before her, and Daniel barely managed to suppress the sigh that rose unbidden from the exhausted depths of his soul. Her desire to lose herself in the past had played a prominent role in their emotional separation, and he'd come to hate the bound collections for all they represented. Still, he had expected this when he found her here. It didn't change what he had to do.

With lethargic steps, he made his way to the padded leather chair in the corner of the room and collapsed into its comfortable familiarity. Sally's eyes hadn't left him. Curiosity painted her features almost as clearly as distrust did. It had been a long time since they'd initiated such an encounter without the kids as an audience.

"I'm sorry," he began.

"For what?"

"For a lot of things. For everything." He paused, struggling to put into words the wealth of regrets he sought pardon for. His thoughts were less roiled than in those horrible moments immediately after the Reflection, but he still had trouble focusing. Bits of his life would drift through his mind seemingly at random, and he could easily get caught again in the rapids of his past.

Her response was cold. "Oh. I see you've put a lot of thought into this."

This wasn't going at all as he had hoped. Placing his head in hands, Daniel started where he should have.

"Thomas Reflected me today."

Stunned silence greeted that pronouncement. He didn't need to look up to feel his wife's eyes boring into him. He felt the weight of her questions even though she left them unasked. They would have been his questions had their positions been reversed. He hadn't come to talk about that, though.

"I've made a lot of mistakes. I saw that very clearly." He drew a deep breath, trying to steady his fraying nerves. "I've wanted to blame all our problems on you, on how you've reacted since the kids started Reflecting. I can't do that anymore.

"When you started to pull away from the twins, I let you go. I was disgusted with how you wouldn't even acknowledge our new situation. You buried yourself in the past, holding on to the scraps of a lost reality, and you let our children face the new reality alone.

"I . . . I couldn't forgive you for that. After all we'd been through together, after twelve years of facing the difficulties of being a Mirror family side by side, I suddenly felt like you'd failed us. Failed *me*."

He heard Sally open her mouth to speak and quickly cut her off. He hadn't come to fight, and everything to this point was decidedly negative toward her. He'd had to set it up, though. She needed to understand why he'd taken the paths he had. What was important, though, was what he still had to say.

"So I abandoned you," Daniel said miserably. "I saw your pain, and I dismissed it. I was so angry with you that I never paused to consider what I could do to help. I was so caught up in doing more for our kids I forgot how much better it worked when we fought this battle together.

"As I pushed you away, you reacted exactly as I should have expected: you retreated. I didn't understand why you wouldn't step up and address our children's fears instead of burying yourself in daydreams.

"I get it now. You didn't know how to react, and the only one who could possibly understand what you were going through had turned his back on you. I've felt isolated and alone a lot over the past few years, but I at least felt I was making some kind of progress with Ashley and Thomas. I can't imagine the horror you've felt as you single-handedly fought something you saw as insurmountable.

"I'm sorry. I know that's not enough for three years of scorn and neglect, but I wanted you to know it. I'm truly, deeply sorry."

An uncomfortable hush settled on the office with those final words. He raised his head slowly, afraid of what he'd see written in Sally's features.

A single tear ran down her impassive face. She reached up absently to brush it away. Her features betrayed nothing, but he saw some deep internal struggle behind her eyes. Eventually she looked away, her body slumping.

"I'm sorry too," she said finally. "I've done a terrible job communicating what I want. What I need." She paused, sadly looking down at the photo album. "I've spent too much time not even knowing what I need."

Scanning those weary eyes and the taut face, Daniel's mind jumped to a conclusion. "Were you Reflected, too?"

Sally paused, thinking, then shook her head. "It felt like it, though. Ashley confronted me at the airport. Threw in my face all my inaction over the past few years. I kept telling myself that I wasn't that bad. I wanted to believe I was still helpful, but I guess I can stop lying to myself."

She barely finished that statement before sobs overtook her and the tears started in earnest. His protective instinct toward his wife had dulled over the previous years, but the Reflection had re-kindled the tiniest spark of it. Daniel pushed up from the chair and knelt next to her. He didn't embrace her as he once would have but instead took one trembling hand into his steady ones.

Those gasping sobs ripped at his soul, reminding him again how far he had fallen from his vow to take her "for better or for worse." He had shed all his tears that afternoon, though. He was an empty husk of a man now, but one ready to start over. He whispered soothing words until she finally slipped out of the chair, gripped him tightly, and cried into his shoulder.

He lost track of time as they sat together on the floor, wrapped in each other's arms. A part of him—buried deeply now but definitely still there—wanted to curse her for her weakness. He shoved it down, remembering how raw his own emotions had been after he managed to crawl away from Thomas's door. He feared that the immediacy of his guilt would fade as time passed, but he hoped to build a foundation here that could withstand that erosion.

As Sally's tears slowed, Daniel's attention was drawn to the desk. He'd glanced at the photo album in passing as he entered, but he hadn't actually looked at the book. It was only now, kneeling with his wife beside her work, that he realized which volume she had pulled out.

"Those pictures are from after the Reflections," he said dully.

He felt her nod against his chest. "I . . . I can't go on pretending. I have to be stronger. Ashley begged me."

"Then we'll be stronger. Both of us." He said it with more confidence than he felt.

254

"I'm not there yet," Sally cautioned. "I'm not even close. My hands shake when I hold the pictures."

"It's okay. I realized today I'm not there yet either. I *am* ready to take the first step, though." He paused, uncoiling himself from the floor as his limbs protested. "We can do it together."

She took his proffered hand and ascended far more gracefully than he had. She settled back into the desk chair, still looking defeated. A twinge of fear gripped Daniel's heart, but he thrust it down. She *would* find her strength this time. He'd see that she did.

Drawing up a second seat, Daniel sat opposite his wife as she shuffled through a year's worth of photos. There was still a wall between them, but the first steady strikes of the chisel had created the tiniest of holes.

—CHAPTER 32—

Father Sean Murphy's woodworking kept him strong for a man his age, but it was clear he was no match for the much younger man standing nearby. Sean's jaw ached from the jab he'd taken, and his side burned where the man's knife had slipped in under the ribs. He had at least managed to distract his assailant long enough for the man's victim to escape; hopefully the young lady was calling police.

"What made you follow me to the park?" the armed man spat.

"I recognized you," Sean said.

"Recognized me?" the man asked incredulously. "From what? The news?"

"I saw the story when Thomas Ross cleared you."

"Yes, cleared me! I was innocent!" The man stressed each syllable of the last word, driving home its meaning. "Do you often stalk innocent people, Father?"

"Actually, Mr. Ragen, I have a friend who has seen the very core of your soul. He assures me that you *will* kill." Sean gestured to his wound. "Perhaps tonight."

"You could have just walked on by," Jayce Ragen hissed. "Would have been the smart thing to do."

There was no denying that. Sean had been out for an evening stroll, a way to sort through the chaos of the day, when he had noticed Jayce walking the opposite direction. He still couldn't pinpoint exactly what had inspired him to turn and follow him to the park. As he trailed along, though, he had known that whatever happened might be dangerous.

In a way, he was glad he'd ignored that voice of self-preservation. Without his intervention, it would have been the woman Jayce had tried to rape who would have been the man's first victim. At least she'd gotten away.

"Goodbye, Father. Should have left well enough alone."

The young thug darted forward, covering the distance between them in a few short strides. He brought his knife up, and Father Sean grabbed the wrist with both hands, forcing it back. His attacker brought the free arm around and punched the open wound in Sean's abdomen. With a grunt, Sean's arms gave way and the man's blade found its way into his chest.

The last feeble hope of surviving this fight left with the blood flowing from his new wound. That certainty of death brought a clarity of its own, though. He'd made his choice in full understanding of the likely outcome. He had not died in vain; his actions had spared a woman's life. If God willed, perhaps his death could serve a second purpose.

With a final surge of strength, Sean gripped the man's hand, squeezing hard enough to make the bones creak. His assailant yelped, releasing the knife handle. With the blade still buried in his body, the priest brought up his other hand and grabbed the man's face, drawing it close.

"I need one small favor from you" Sean said quietly, blood tinting his lips.

He whispered his last words quickly to the shocked man before collapsing. He felt a tug as the knife was pulled free, then heard the sound of rapidly retreating footsteps. With a terrible sadness, he noticed there were no sirens.

— PART V —

Sixteen Years Old—Changes

America has been very fortunate in regard to runaway Mirrors. We've never lost a single scheduled Reflection to an escape attempt, which puts us ahead of most other countries that use Mirrors in the pursuit of justice.

Many have noted the mutual extradition treaties with our northern and southern neighbors as a deterrent to any such attempts. This analysis isn't wrong, per se; lack of an easily accessible safe haven certainly factors into the decision for those seeking to run, but it's hardly the only factor in play.

Instead, I believe the placement of our Mirrors with foster parents provides the greatest boost to security. Unlike a child's birth parents, these guardians are federal employees who have been carefully screened for any hint of Liberator ideology. By choosing who these children live with, we limit the number of people who might help them run.

It's not a perfect solution. The Liberator movement is slowly gaining strength. As more former employees share embellished or outright false versions of their experiences here, it's generating a groundswell of interest in the lives of Mirrors.

We know they are well cared for. Given how carefully we screen applicants and how thorough our routine inspections are, I'm confident we provide an environment for our Mirrors as good or better than the traditional nuclear family. Those opposed to our cause, of course, will be unmoved by any evidence of that care.

Even with this growing sense of disdain among our detractors, I know adding ankle monitors to our Mirrors seems excessive. At this exact moment, it probably is. Unfortunately, such a move is always excessive before the event where you needed it. If we wait until after a Mirror has vanished off the grid, we've waited too long.

I don't know where the threat will come from. Perhaps new parents who have signed over their child have second thoughts. We've certainly given them the money to strike at us to steal their offspring back if they have the inclination. Or perhaps it will be a well-meaning member of the Liberator community who breaks into one our houses and kidnaps a child in the middle of the night.

Regardless of the eventual culprit, my fear is the same. Someday, someone will believe he has sufficiently good reason to take a Mirror and run. Let's decide right now to give them a stronger reason to stay.

—Dr. Cole Bryant addressing the Mirror Review Board on the decision to add ankle monitors to all government Mirrors

— CHAPTER 33—

"M r. Ross, please have a seat."
Thomas flopped listlessly into the chair between Sam and his mother. The leather squeaked and the springs protested the sudden addition of his weight. Idly, he wondered if this was the same chair that had held his sister during her battle with the Mirror Review Board a year ago.

With a distasteful twist of the lips, Thomas scornfully surveyed the five men and women that comprised the board. Four of them he could place from Ashley's descriptions, but the board member second from the right, a clean-shaven man in his forties with long blond hair, didn't fit. Unsurprisingly, the sympathetic Dr. Hanover seemed to be the missing member.

Bryant sat to the right of the board with just enough distance between them to indicate he wasn't a member. Thomas had expected his presence. Also as expected, Thomas could no longer even bring himself to really hate the man. There was distaste there, perhaps a bit of anger, but too many years and too many Reflections had drained most of Thomas's feelings away.

A second stranger sat on the other side of Dr. Bryant. The woman's position also clearly separated her from the board, but her self-assured posture made it clear that she belonged here in some capacity. Thomas figured she was likely some politician who wanted to watch these bureaucrats do their work. He supposed he should be curious, but he wasn't. His antipathy toward the Mirror specialist wasn't the only emotion he'd lost. These days he never felt anything strongly.

That wasn't entirely true. Ashley was one of two obvious exceptions. For the past year she'd used that connection to keep him alive, to drive him forward even as the rest of his life fell apart. Part of him wondered how much longer she could keep it up.

The other obvious exception provided the reason for this hearing.

"Mr. Ross, my name is Maria Perales. I'm the head of the Mirror Review Board, and these are my peers and fellow members." She went around the table introducing each of them in turn, but Thomas listened with only half an ear. The board would do what it would do, and unlike his sister, he had no drive to fight them. What a difference a year made.

Thomas barely spared a thought when Ms. Perales introduced the unknown woman as Attorney General Susan Dubois, but Mom sat up straighter. He couldn't read his mother's reaction completely—both parents had started wearing sunglasses after he'd Reflected Daniel—but she was obviously surprised and a little unnerved by the presence of a member of the cabinet. No reason was given for her attendance today, but Thomas thought the long-suffering look the woman gave Bryant implied the specialist's involvement.

"Do you know why you're here?" the head of the board continued.

Thomas contemplated saying, "So the board can feel useful," but decided in the end that he didn't have the strength for the firestorm that comment was certain to set off. Shaking his head would only convince them that he was being difficult since he'd been told about fifty times what this was about. Acknowledging the meeting's purpose would probably require his side of the story, something he was loath to give since it would require taking the energy to present his case.

In the end, he decided that if he simply admitted everything up front, the meeting might at least be brief.

"I'm here," he sighed, "because I tried to kill Jayce Ragen."

"You did a good job," the white-haired lady—Urich?—said coldly. "He's still in a coma."

Thomas actually took some small amount of pleasure in that. Not much, but he'd really hate to think he'd thrown away everything only for Jayce to recover.

"Why did you do it?" This was another member, the colonel.

"He killed my friend. He killed Father Sean."

"The priest you used to visit." This was from Bryant, and a statement of fact rather than a question of clarification. His face registered genuine surprise, though.

"Jayce was accused of a convenience store holdup gone wrong that ended with a shotgun blast to the face for an unfortunate clerk." Thomas's voice was quiet, but remembering the incident returned some of the fire. Not much, but enough to drive him on. "He didn't do that, so by his Fourth Amendment protections, he'd walk. He did kill Father Sean, but since no one even suspected him, he'd never stand trial for it."

For almost a year, Thomas had wondered what had transpired that night. Father Sean's body had been found in a small park near his home. He'd been stabbed twice, but beyond that there was little to say what had happened. Rain had washed away most of the evidence by the time he was discovered the next morning. Police had seemed interested in solving the crime but never managed to find a solid lead. When Thomas found himself in a police station opposite Jayce Ragen—again—he'd already given up all hope of knowing the truth.

Truth was crueler than any of his expectations. Father Sean's death hadn't been random; the old priest had purposely followed his killer in an attempt to prevent the man from harming someone else. Moreover, that killer was the very man Thomas had tried to put behind bars with his lies, only to find himself unable to speak the words. In a way, Thomas felt a responsibility for the priest's death.

263

Almost three and a half minutes after Thomas had broken contact with the murderer, he had regained enough of himself to realize what this all meant. Immediately after the Reflection, the DA had asked the pertinent questions about the convenience-store murder, and Thomas, unable to answer anything else in those crucial first seconds, had spoken the truth, which would set Father Sean's murderer back on the streets.

By sixteen, most Mirrors were completely docile. They were led to Reflections, did their required duty, and went home. They rarely talked, never smiled, and took very little independent action. Thomas was a week and a half shy of that mark when he Reflected Jayce, but he wasn't a typical Mirror. With a willpower buttressed by his sister's support, Thomas Ross still felt *something* occasionally. That day he had remembered what it meant to hate.

Pushing himself to his hands and knees, adrenaline had coursed through his body. Pure, blind rage had consumed him. Rage at the system that would now twice—twice!—have sent a violent and dangerous man out to kill. Rage at himself for being too weak to stop it the first time. Mostly, though, it was rage at the man who had stolen one of his only friends. When Thomas had finally found his feet, he'd leapt across the table and bowled straight into the murderer, carrying them both backward.

So shocked were those present that for the first few seconds no one had moved to stop him. Taking advantage of that moment of surprise, Thomas had grabbed Jayce by his collar and slammed the man's head repeatedly into the tile floor, all the while screaming, "You killed him! You killed him!" By the time they'd dragged Thomas off, Jayce was unconscious on the floor in a thick puddle of his own blood. As they'd forced him back, Thomas had spit on the unmoving form before him. Then, the adrenaline spent, his body suddenly remembered the fatigue that had been so easily forgotten only moments before. As his weakness drew him to the ground, he'd almost pulled Sam down with him.

He'd not managed to work up the desire to research it, but Thomas was certain that no Mirror had ever reacted like that so late in their cycle of Reflections. Unfortunately, he couldn't duplicate that emotional high. For those few crazy seconds while attacking Jayce, he'd felt exhilaration, anger, and raw fury. He would rather have experienced profound happiness than profound hatred, but it was nice to feel *anything* so strongly after month upon month of nothingness.

Guesses were all he had as to why the response was so strong; he doubted even Bryant could have offered a sufficient explanation. Thomas's pet theory was that despite all evidence to the contrary, somewhere deep inside he still possessed a connection to people like Father Sean. Layers of apathy blanketed his emotional land-scape like several feet of snow, but buried beneath that wasteland waited personal connections that everyone—including Thomas himself—had long believed dead.

Abruptly, he realized the entire board was watching him.

"What?"

"I asked if you had anything else you wanted to add," replied one of the men. Based on Ashley's account, he matched the bespectacled face with a name: Peter Lane. "This is your last chance to make your case."

Thomas shrugged noncommittally, and to his left Mom shifted uncomfortably. His dad had wanted to accompany him, but after the Reflection last year, Thomas had avoided contact with the man when possible and refused, point-blank, to have him along today.

"May I speak on his behalf?" Mom asked. Her hands shook, but the words were surprisingly steady.

"Since the purpose of this hearing is to examine the events of the day—which you were not present for—I am afraid I don't understand what you hope to add," Urich replied, her face smooth.

"If only the events are in question, then why are we here?" Mom demanded. "You have reams of paper detailing the event. You didn't fly us all the way to Washington, DC, to make small talk."

"She makes a good point, Maria," Lane said. "We wanted to see the human side of this. She seems a good candidate for that."

"That's why *you* invited them," the white-haired woman shot back icily. "I was ready to vote."

"The purpose of the board is to regulate Mirrors in the legal system," Maria Perales said slowly. "I think most of us realized a year ago that we were watching only one side of the problem." Her brow furrowed, and she looked pensive. "We're not dealing with automatons here."

Turning to Mom, she said, "Please. Go ahead."

With a grateful nod, Mom began her defense.

"A year ago, I sat here as you considered taking away my daughter." Her words were still steady but hardly firm. It was almost certain that she'd written this speech over the past week, and it showed. Her tone carried the plodding, stilted performance of a memorized presentation being delivered by an amateur public speaker.

"You chose not to take one of my children, but it was obvious you'd evaluate it later. You fired Carol last year as a compromise. It was a warning, too, though: as long as my children toed the line and stayed out of trouble, we could remain a family. What Thomas has done is even worse than what Ashley did, so I'm guessing you're going to take him away from us. I'd like to explain why you shouldn't do that."

Mom's recitation wasn't the least bit convincing. Her wooden delivery removed any emotional power her words might have had. Even Sam was grimacing; he could see it too.

"We haven't even begun discussion on the proper response to this action," Mrs. Perales said calmly. "Perhaps your plea is a bit premature."

"Is it?" Mom scoffed. "Wasn't Dr. Urich just saying she was ready to vote? Ready to vote on what, precisely?"

Though her prepared speech had fallen flat, this off-the-cuff remark certainly drew attention. A couple members of the board looked a bit sheepish, and Maria grimaced distastefully. Quite obviously his fate had been discussed in the preceding days and what was happening here was a formality. That was probably why they'd been willing to let Mom speak; anything she said would make her feel better but was unlikely to change the outcome.

Mom seemed to realize this too as she stared angrily at the board members opposite her. They stared back, stone-faced and silent. For an instant it looked like she would back down. Her resolve faltered, and she drew a heavy breath. Then, right when it looked as though the meeting would press along, she shot Thomas a final, pained glance. Her jaw pushed out stubbornly, and she seemed to find new life. Groaning inside, Thomas shut his eyes—so much for this being over quickly.

"I will not stand idly by and let you whisk my son away," she declared.

"Thomas Ross has provided plenty of reason to support such an action," Bryant said, his voice neutral. "He attempted to murder a man . . ."

"That man killed a Catholic priest!" Mom exclaimed.

"Vigilantism is illegal," the attorney general said. "Jayce Ragen's actions are immaterial."

"I agree," Maria Perales said. "Whatever Jayce's crimes, Thomas would be in a detention center if he weren't a Mirror. Attempted murder is unacceptable under any circumstances."

"So why not send me off to jail?" Thomas asked wryly over his mother's attempts to shush him.

Arching an eyebrow in surprise, Bryant seemed to consider this for a moment. "First, because I honestly don't believe you're likely to do this again. Finding the priest's killer was an isolated incident. Second, I'm not so naïve as to believe you'd exist peacefully in a cell."

"You think I'll kill myself if you take me away from my family."

"Do you want to die?"

The question was so direct and so unexpected it caught

Thomas off guard. Saying yes would indicate it really didn't matter what the board did. Saying no would mean they could strip him from his home without worrying whether he would kill himself in despair. Taking several long seconds of careful consideration, Thomas finally replied, "Not as long as I'm with my sister."

"They clearly lean on each other too heavily," Urich said. "Ashley's hearing a year ago was proof of that, and now we're seeing it again." She shifted to look at the Mirror specialist. "You're the expert here, Cole. Talk."

Bryant frowned, drumming his fingers on his coffee mug. Like everyone who worked around Mirrors long enough, his eyes were hidden behind glasses, but his mood was obvious even without being able to read them. Thomas felt the specialist's gaze on him, weighing him, trying to read deeply his motivations and fears. Silence stretched as the expert clearly sought the proper words.

"In some ways you're right, Beverly. It is almost certainly the empathy of an understanding soul that has provided the Ross twins with their strength. I've never encountered Mirrors so strong and so defiant this late in the cycle, even if that strength evidences itself only in intermittent stretches. In light of that, it would seem that the obvious answer is to separate them. It is reasonable to assume that slicing that bond would bring them in line with the rest of their brethren.

"If that were the only consideration, then it would make this decision simpler. Instead, the issue is complicated by its timing. We are reaching the end of their life cycles. At the moment, they still have not fully submitted to the total despair I would expect at this age. They even display occasional signs of sympathy. Given what I've witnessed from the Ross twins compared with every other child I've studied, it is not unreasonable to believe they will make it to eighteen, possibly much later. It is impossible to deny they are decaying, but they do so at a noticeably arrested rate.

"I can only posit guesses as to how their situation might change if we remove that link. Would they collapse at the expected rate, or might they implode immediately? I can't predict that. If we leave the Ross family together, we likely get another two years of Reflections from each of them.

"Given that the purpose of this board is to maximize the potential of Mirror justice, it is reckless to test the question. If we remove Thomas from his home and he chooses to die rather than be stripped from his sister, we lose up to two years of work from him. If his sister follows him in death, we lose her Reflections as well. That's up to two hundred Reflections lost—a staggering blow.

"Even Thomas's testimony, brief as it has been, has reinforced this idea. He's told us point blank that he wants to live so long as he's with his sister. His implication is that he will not live without her."

Each of the members absorbed this differently. Most seemed thoughtful, and Beverly Urich seemed clearly torn, which was surprising. Emotions warred on her face, and she hadn't fully stilled them when she asked, "What about the incidents that require this board's attention? If we leave them together, will we see one of these kids again next November for some other unexpected action?"

Bryant frowned deeply. "I don't know." The words sounded ripped from him, the admission of ignorance an obviously painful act.

"Losing two hundred Reflections would be difficult," the colonel said carefully. "However, another incident might bring the entire program into question. Congress chose not to enact anything major after Ashley's Reflection, though it was close. We've kept this indiscretion as quiet as possible, but there's no guarantee the Ross twins' next action won't be as public as the airport Reflection of the Kershfeldt girl."

"He's right," said the new board member. "Every time this board meets to resolve an issue like this, we hand the Liberators a new weapon."

Urich gave a frustrated sigh. "Even worse, we have to wonder what the next incident will look like. While some may want to overlook a charge of attempted murder because the victim wasn't a saint, it demands we ask what he might do as an encore. Rape? Armed robbery? Anything like that would cause a divide unlike anything we've seen."

"I can guarantee those aren't a concern," Bryant said coolly. "No Mirror has shown such tendencies. Even Thomas's attack was one born out of sense of justice."

"Oh?" the white-haired woman shot back. "Why should we believe that? You've already told us the Ross twins aren't normal Mirrors. Can you honestly say you know for certain that they *won't* commit some heinous crime?"

Bryant opened his mouth, but Peter Lane spoke first, disgust evident on his face. "Please. I don't even need an expert opinion to dismiss that one, Beverly. Look at him. The boy's beaten down. He's not even fighting us as we decide his fate. He's not going to go on some sort of crime spree."

"Are you sure of that?" Urich demanded angrily. "Would you gamble everything on it?"

"Yes," Lane said, rolling his eyes. "If Thomas Ross robs Fort Knox, I take full responsibility."

"This is getting ridiculous," Perales said, and there were nods of assent from around the table. "We have the facts. Brief closing arguments, and then we'll vote. Peter, you have anything to add?"

Lane nodded, then cleared his throat and sat forward, pushing his glasses up on his nose as he did so. "This is madness. Removing Thomas from his house won't make the world noticeably safer, and in the process we isolate a boy from the only home he's ever known, potentially lose Reflections, and weaken any case the board has of supporting parents raising their own Mirrors.

"Jayce Ragen's a criminal. We have every reason to believe he murdered a priest, but if he survives this coma, he'll be free to live however he wants. Thomas meanwhile, who has grudgingly but consistently given his services to us, risks spending his remaining months separated from his family. How is it that a board dedicated to the proper distribution of justice can't see the injustice here?

"We have to stand for these kids at some point. Liberator ideology is too strong a stand: it is a breach of decency to allow the powers of a Mirror to go completely to waste. Beverly's ideals are too weak. Ashley's review last year taught me that if we stop seeing Mirrors as children, we've lost the right to dispense justice. The proper view of this board should be to find that balance; we need to find where we can use Mirrors as necessary and still treat them with dignity.

"That's all I'm asking for here. Send Thomas home, let him complete his assigned Reflections, and let him finally die with his family. It's nothing less than any of us would expect."

Lane fell silent, and Thomas saw Mom silently mouth "Thank you" to him. More surprising, though, was that Bryant was nodding silently in support of all the bespectacled man had said.

"Mr. Ross, would you like to add anything?" Mrs. Perales asked. Thomas shook his head, convinced it would be a waste of energy. The head of the board turned to Mom. "Mrs. Ross? What about you?"

Obviously surprised at being allowed to make her case, Mom opened her mouth twice before finally managing to speak on the third try.

"Parenting a Mirror isn't easy," she began hesitantly, "and parenting two is impossible, but I tried my best. I've watched my kids leave every Thursday morning terrified. They come back every Thursday night weighed down with lives they should never have had to see. I've watched those lives eat at them for years, driving them away from certain music, or food, or . . . or everything. It's hard, at times, to find the core of my children that I can still trace back to the pre-Reflection years.

"My little boy has grown into a distrustful and angry young man who dislikes spending time with anyone except his sister. My little girl barely moves from her bed anymore and speaks less and less often. They've been twisted and warped by the tasks this board has set before them, and in each I see only the tiniest spark of who they were and what they might have—should have—been.

"The Reflections have already taken away my children's future. You've crippled them, made them mere shells of the children I raised, *but they are my children!*" She emphasized those last five words, staring at each board member in turn. Some, like Urich, returned that gaze; others, like Hanover's replacement, looked away. "Don't take them away from me. Not yet. Someday I'll lose them completely, someday they'll be torn away, but for now just let me have the shreds you've left me." She drew a deep breath. "They're all I have."

Lane frowned, clearly embarrassed. Bryant watched emotionlessly, while the colonel stared stubbornly at Thomas himself, carefully avoiding Mom's gaze. Hanover's replacement looked decidedly uncomfortable, and the attorney general looked oddly discomfited as well. Even Maria Perales grimaced uncertainly as she turned to Bryant and asked, "Do you have anything to add, Cole?"

The specialist hesitated, weighing something. Eventually he shook his head. "No. As I've said before, I'm not here to pick a side, only to provide facts. I've given you all that I can."

"I guess that leaves me," Urich said. "I have no emotional plea to make. Instead, I can only point out the truth we know: Ashley Ross has Reflected an unwilling child, and Thomas Ross has attempted murder. Neither child has even tried to deny this.

"Ashley mind-raped a young girl. She violated a level of privacy that makes us all shudder; who here would volunteer for a Reflection? Instead of Ashley being held responsible, though, it was Carol Raines who paid the price.

"Can we afford to shift the blame again? Thomas Ross may yet get the murder he intended. Maybe he won't act that way again, but I'm unwilling to bet the lives of other people on this belief. The stakes are simply too high. If he does commit more crimes, it would fall on us. If that didn't kill the program outright, it would almost certainly cripple it.

"We can't afford that. We suffered an almost fatal blow with the Reflection of Calleigh Kershfeldt, and if we survive Thomas's rage, it's only because so few people know. The public is terrified of Mirrors, and repeated incidents like this will not help that fear.

"Over the course of their lives, the Ross twins have been afforded special treatment. If they were not Mirrors, would we still be so hesitant to take action? If any other fifteen-year-old girl so grossly violated the bounds of privacy as Ashley did, would she have been let off with a slap on the wrist? If any other sixteen-year-old boy so boldly proclaimed his attempt to kill someone, would we avert our eyes? Of course not.

"We can't be turned from our duty by emotion. This board was formed on the belief that the needs of a society are greater than those of a single person; we have to uphold that foundation now or we risk losing everything."

A few seconds of awkward silence passed before Perales finally said, "Thank you all. If there are no further objections, we will vote. A vote of 'yea' will be in favor of removing Thomas Ross to a government facility. 'Nay' is a vote in favor of leaving him with his family."

"Nay," Lane said immediately, and Urich followed on his heels with a "Yea."

The colonel contemplated and shot a final look at Thomas before finally nodding and announcing, "Yea."

At the center of the table, Maria Perales stared fixedly at Thomas. No malice walked in that gaze; she seemed simply to be studying him. Deep beneath the layers of uncaring, a spark of surprise ignited in Thomas as he realized she was torn. Her face was perfectly still, but in her eyes he could see she was weighing what to do.

He wasn't the only one who noticed either. Bryant was leaning forward to look at her, his tie trailing dangerously close to his coffee mug. At Perales's side, Lane was cocking an eyebrow in startled amazement. Mom had slid forward to the edge of her seat, gripping the table. Even Sam, who had done little more than sit quietly for the past half hour, now leaned onto the table expectantly.

Perales's lips barely moved as she finally delivered her verdict. "Nay."

Attention immediately shifted to Hanover's nameless replacement. Clearly the man had hoped the motion would pass or fail without his intervention. In his eyes there was true sympathy for Thomas, but something else lay buried in that gaze. Only as those blue eyes flicked nervously to Urich did Thomas understand. The white-haired woman had been the one who'd gotten him a spot on the board. She'd either offered up his name, supported his candidacy, or both. He was weighing his conscience with his debt to her.

With a sad sigh, the man practically crumpled in his chair. "Beverly's right. We can't risk everything on this. I vote yea."

–CHAPTER 34–

Ashley lay curled up on the long green couch in the living room, head resting peacefully on one of the pillows. She was so still she might have been sleeping, but her eyes were open. Across the room the TV droned a recap of the previous night's football game, but it was clear she wasn't processing any of that information. Her almost vacant stare indicated she was once again lost in some dark daydream.

Seeing his daughter's eyes was still a shock to Daniel. In the early years it had been vitally important to keep the children's eyes covered for their own safety. Not old enough to understand the threat they posed to each other, the parents had been vigilant in keeping them both bound in shaded glass. It was such an important part of normalcy that he and Sally had never even questioned it once the twins were old enough to understand the consequences.

It was only after Thomas Reflected him that Daniel had fully understood the danger. He'd ordered glasses for Sally and him only hours after that invasion. Still, it was almost two months before he thought to ask his daughter if she would prefer to go without her own protective glasses for a while. Her tears of gratitude had been so unexpected he was ashamed he'd never thought of it before.

Only one of them could go unmasked at a time, but those moments of freedom were coveted. Thomas tried to downplay it, but Daniel knew better. It had taken some adjustment, but Daniel now wished he had considered this years ago. Though there would always be a barrier between their gazes, he still felt closer than ever to his children now that he could sometimes read their eyes.

Most of the time those windows were depressed or haunted. Occasionally, though, he caught a glimpse of something still burning inside their young minds. Those sparks were proof of life. With their glasses on, he thought he might have missed them completely, instead believing that all vitality had fled. Those brief glimpses into a living soul, even one weak and ravaged, gave him the strength to fight on.

From the kitchen, the phone rang, and father and daughter shared a glance. Ashley's face was impassive, but he caught the barest hint of fear buried in her eyes. She knew what this was as well as he did: Sally was calling with the results of the board meeting.

"Hello," he said quietly, picking up the receiver.

"They're taking Thomas away. They've got a house ready for him in Albuquerque."

Sally had offered no preamble, no warning. She sounded empty. They'd both been expecting this outcome, but he could never really have prepared himself for this. Sighing heavily, he slumped against the counter.

"They have a place ready to go? So they were prepared."

"They say that the foster parents were set up to receive the next Mirror baby. Now they're getting Thomas instead." She paused. "I think they created it specifically for Thomas, though."

"Will we be able to visit him?"

"Yes. You and I get supervised visits, but he won't be able to see Ashley."

Daniel considered their options. "One of us could move down there, get an apartment. At least we'd be close."

"I proposed that. He doesn't want it. He says we should stay together for Ashley's sake."

A conflicting stream of emotions swept Daniel. He and Sally had slowly rebuilt burned bridges over the last year. Matters were far from perfect, but they were moving forward. The thought of being alone with Ashley—it would have to be Ashley; Thomas would never let him be the one in New Mexico—tore at him. He loved his daughter, but he needed his partner.

"Okay. I love you."

"I love you too," she said, her voice cracking. "I've got to go. Our ride to the airport is leaving."

Stepping from the kitchen, Daniel saw Ashley watching him, the question obvious. With a sigh, Daniel gave her the bad news. She processed this silently for a long moment, then gave a slow nod as if coming to some agreement with herself.

"Thomas and I made a promise," she said hesitantly. "Two years ago, on our birthday."

She paused, clearly summoning the energy to speak. Ashley had already spoken more than she normally did. Her interactions had become increasingly reticent over the past few months, and it was obviously taking a supreme force of will to continue.

"I was scared of the end. I knew that I might pull away from Carol or that she might be gone. I knew that I might withdraw from you and Mom. I knew that when the end came I might be all alone because I had pushed everyone away. Everyone except Thomas."

Daniel's insides froze as he realized what she was saying. "You promised to die together."

Ashley nodded. "I'm . . . I'm sorry, Dad. I'm not really ready, but I don't want . . . I don't want to be alone that day. Today. If he's leaving . . . I have to . . ."

She trailed off, and Daniel was at her side in an instant. Tears leaked down her cheeks, the most emotion he'd seen from her since the summer. He pulled her up in an embrace, and to his surprise she held him back, her arms gripping him with all the strength she could muster. He felt her body shake against him, heard the gasping rush of breath that punctuated the sobs.

"You don't have to die," he said.

"I'll never see Thomas again," she said quietly, still holding him. "You know it. They won't let me."

"Maybe we could get a special dispensation. One last visit."

His daughter pulled away enough to look him in the eyes. The shadow of a sad smile tugged her lips. "And if we can't, then I've wasted my last opportunity."

Daniel knew she was right. He didn't say so, though.

Leaning away, Ashley scrubbed at her eyes. Daniel dropped next to her on the couch. She folded her hands lightly into her lap, then studied him for a long time. He saw more emotion there than he had before. Death's imminence seemed to have shaken her to the core, dislodging the feelings she felt she had to share before it all ended.

"Do you ever regret keeping us?" she asked.

Blinking in surprise, Daniel leaned back into the sofa. It was about the last question he had expected. Part of him wanted to lie, but she had certainly spoken to Thomas about the Reflection. She knew already.

"Yes. Not often, but sometimes. When I realized that there would be no grandchildren, when my parents and my brother walled me away. I love you both, but sometimes the price just seemed so high." He knew the shame was plain on his face. "Why ask me that now?"

"Because you've tried to so hard. You always wanted to connect with us, to give us the life everyone said we couldn't have." She drew a harsh breath. "I'm just afraid that when we die you'll blame yourself for the life you and Mom didn't have."

"No." He shook his head and repeated it more firmly. "No. I love you, Ashley. I love you both."

She gave a sad nod. "I know that, but how do you conquer the specter of what your life could have been if you'd acted differently?"

Understanding came abruptly. She wasn't asking for his sake, she was battling her own lost opportunities. "What do you regret?"

"I'll never know anyone in this family as well as I know

strangers." She saw his involuntary tic and said soothingly, "I don't want to Reflect you. I just want to expunge all these other lives."

She continued, her eyes gaining a faraway look. "I regret that there was only one Calleigh Kershfeldt in my life, that I never helped more people with my . . ." She trailed off, and he knew she was wrestling whether to call it a gift or a curse. She ended up choosing neither and plowing ahead.

"I regret that I never got to Reflect someone who benefited from my work, people who only saw closure because of what I do. I think it would have helped me, knowing what my sacrifice meant to them.

"Mostly, though, I'm sad I'm not strong enough to do this forever."

Daniel frowned. "The way the board has used you has destroyed our family."

"My being born a Mirror destroyed our family," Ashley corrected. "Look at other countries. Mirrors do not live happy lives anywhere in the world. If they're not used for good or evil, they're recluses too scared to look into the world for fear they would be moved to act."

"Are you bitter?"

"I'm sorry it was me who fulfilled this role, but the world as a whole is a better place with Mirror justice."

It wasn't a straight answer, but Daniel figured it was as close as he would get.

"You are taking this calmly," Ashley said.

"I've been expecting this moment for sixteen years. I never wanted this day to come, but . . . I've seen how you suffered every step of the way."

"You're relieved," she said.

"Yes," he admitted guiltily.

"Good. Remember that." Her voice was almost firm. "Even if I'm not ready to go, dying will be a release."

That was easier said than done. Daniel felt as though he were tied up in knots. His chest was tight, and he'd been fighting tears of his own since she had started crying. So many emotions warred within him that he couldn't even decide which he wanted to win. Was it wrong to feel happy that she'd be freed from pain? Was it wrong that he didn't want to surrender her, even though her continued existence would promise her only more and greater pains?

"I want to remember good times," she said abruptly. "Facing death so clearly has revived emotions I thought were gone. I want to use that."

Nodding, Daniel stood. "I'll be back." Hurrying to the back of the house, he slipped into the office and grabbed a handful of Sally's photo albums from the shelf. He went with earlier years, knowing they would host the happiest times the Ross family had lived. Returning to the living room, he dropped them next to his spot on the couch. Ashley curled up next to him, and he protectively wrapped his arm around her.

Flipping open the first collection, they were greeted with a picture of Thomas on his sixth birthday. He'd tried to shove half of the slice of birthday cake in his mouth. Smeared with frosting, the boy still managed to look remarkably pleased with himself. Ashley produced only a weak smile, but something sparkled in her eyes. These were her last hours, and she was drinking in the joys of her life as though she were dying of thirst.

They flipped through every single album together. Ashley never managed more than the occasional turn of the corners of her mouth, but that weak glimmer of life never left her eyes. Daniel sobbed openly now, the fullness of his loss displayed in color across every page. He had to pause occasionally to remove his glasses, but through it all he still remembered how to laugh. Every hesitant chuckle seemed to give his daughter a measure of peace. She seemed to draw comfort that he would remember the happy times as well as the bad.

As he closed the last album, Ashley laid her head against his chest. She craned her neck to look at him, and as he watched, the spark that sustained her through the morning finally began to fade from her eyes. Apathy and indifference stole over her soul, and he realized he was losing her for the last time.

Wrapping his arms around her in a hug, he whispered, "I love you, Ashley."

"I love you, Daddy."

There was warmth in those words, a final gift to him.

Then the moment passed. Her mouth drew taut, and her eyes drained of the vigor that had sustained her. She was lost again, pulled away once and for all by the ravages of her curse. There was abject hollowness in her. She was still breathing, but in every way that mattered, he knew she was already gone.

-CHAPTER 35-

Susan Dubois often found herself dining at restaurants with linen napkins, fine wines, and renowned chefs. These were the selections of the capital's elite, and she indulged them. The food was always good, but she felt that it was the status such choices afforded more than the fare that prompted the selection. Thus, when given the opportunity to choose for herself, she often elected for something that hearkened to her formative years in the Midwest. Today it was a burger and fries at a rundown little shack on the Maryland side of the line.

Conversation while they waited for their order had been light. She talked about her niece's upcoming marriage and an old friend's invitation to visit the middle of the country. Cole talked about a book he was reading; she had expected something dry and informative, but he'd surprised her by announcing a love for sci-fi. Even after all these years, she was constantly reminded of how little she actually knew about him.

As enjoyable as these rare moments were, she hadn't invited him out for the harmless chatter they'd engaged in so far. The morning's events had shaken her to a degree, and she wanted to pick the brain of the only person who could answer her qualms. She was certain he suspected as much, but he'd said nothing about it so far. It was unusual; he normally would have brought it up immediately to get it out of the way. Eventually, she decided she would have to broach the subject.

"I want to talk about Mirrors."

It was a clumsy opening, but it was direct. Cole would at least like that.

"I figured as much," he said as he dipped one of his fries in ketchup.

"So why not bring it up before now?"

"To be honest," he said with a grimace, "I've been thinking over the morning's events. I needed time to analyze before offering conclusions. Ask what you wish, and I will answer as best I can."

Susan cut directly to the point. "Do you believe Thomas will kill himself?"

Cole frowned and stared at the french fry he still held as it dripped a dollop of ketchup back onto his plate. "I honestly wish I knew.

"On their last birthday, Thomas Reflected his father," Cole continued. "Ashley Reflected Carol Raines. When Mirrors start Reflecting those they care for, it is a harbinger of a sudden decline. That's always been true, regardless of whether they work for the government or are raised by their families.

"I estimated at that point that they had only a 50-percent chance of making it another three months and less than a 5-percent chance they'd make it to this birthday. I was obviously wrong.

"Based on what I've seen from the Ross twins lately, those Reflections did hasten their decline, but not as precipitously as any of my modeling predicted. Given what I saw today, I would guess that Thomas probably won't take his life, but I've learned that I just don't know. It's very possible that removing his sister's support will cause a catastrophic collapse."

"Wait," Susan said, processing that answer. "Are you saying you think another Mirror would press on after something like today?" Susan asked curiously. "He seemed empty."

"Compared to a Mirror at the end of life, he was still quite active."

"They get worse than that?"

Cole finally got around to popping that fry into his mouth. "At the end, they are almost completely catatonic. They rarely eat unless forced and say little to nothing. The mind has shut down. Unable to process any more pain, they seek to escape."

"That's . . . awful." He arched an eyebrow at her, and she continued. "I guess I can see why you wanted me to come today."

Something bothered her, though. She raised her burger to her open mouth, stopped, and lowered it. "Why? I think most kids who were as distraught as Thomas was today would end it now. Why do Mirrors wait so long?"

"Because Mirrors aren't regular children."

"Well, obviously, I didn't mean to . . ."

"It's more than just the Reflections," Cole interrupted, leaning in closer, his attention focused now. "Every Mirror I've studied, and every foreign Mirror for which I have reliable data, show higher than average IQs. The lowest I've seen was around 120. Among the general populace, about 10 percent test that well, but among Mirrors it's 100 percent.

"I've always wondered why. Does being naturally intelligent put you at greater risk of being a Mirror, or is it the other way around? Does the condition itself make someone naturally brighter? Right now we don't know; we may never know.

"That's just one of the oddities we can track from before Mirrors begin Reflections, though it's one of the more surprising traits. Once they start Reflecting, though, the situation gets even muddier."

He was in his element now, eyes focused on hers. He loved to share knowledge, but so much of what he knew went over people's heads or was tedious. He had learned long ago not to ramble at an audience, even a captive one, if he wanted to have any kind of social interaction with people. He had told her as much several years ago, but she wondered who he had been talking to; this was fascinating.

"Every Mirror I've interviewed has told me that the lives they absorb are seamlessly integrated into their own memories. They

285

believe that their Reflected's lives are just as real as their own. They fully believe that the memories gained through Reflections are just as much a part of them as the memories they've actually lived.

"On the other hand, every Mirror has also told me how much they treasure memories that are truly their own. If they do something one of their Reflected has already done, they still hold their own memory in greater regard than they do the external one. Whether it be reading a novel, watching a sunset, or sitting on Santa's lap, they all tell me their own memory is best."

"Why wouldn't they?" Susan asked. "I'm sure they want their own memory to be more important to them. Even if it does all blend together, they'd assign extra meaning to their own as a means of fighting against being overwhelmed by other people's lives."

Bryant shot her a genuine smile. "An excellent theory."

"Yours as well, I assume?"

"Partly. I labored under that impression for years."

"It's not true?"

"I seriously doubt it. I've worked with these kids too long, seen them too often to miss the clues. There is something that separates out the real from the Reflected. Even if they don't know it consciously, there *is* a difference."

Susan frowned skeptically. "How can you be sure?"

"Two reasons. First, no matter how many lives they take on, Mirrors never identify as one of their Reflected. In fact, they always worry that their Reflected have influenced them in some way. That seems an odd concern if there isn't a core part of them that is unchanged. If every Reflection's memories are as real as their own, they would simply shift their core beliefs to accommodate each new life. That doesn't happen."

"You're sure they don't?"

"Yes. Even after taking on the lives of hundreds of criminals, the Mirrors I've worked with maintain the moral code they display before their first Reflection. To Reflect more than a hundred murderers who justified what they did and *still* think it's a terrible crime? Clearly something has survived."

Nodding, Susan said, "That makes sense. What's the other reason?"

"The Ross twins. They defy all my expectations, all the norms established by Mirrors."

"So?"

"Every Mirror in government employ follows a very precise cycle. Initially they suffer, then they figure out how to adjust. This leads to a moderate recovery for the two-year bounce before they decay and kill themselves sometime over the next few years. The exact timing of this cycle varies, but the steps are very clearly defined. With Thomas and Ashley Ross, I cannot say that."

"How does that fit into this discussion?"

"Because they are the only Mirrors who can count another Mirror as a confidant. "Sympathy is important. Why do you think Carol Raines's girls lived longer? Whether Carol's compassion was pretense or not, her charges were each completely and totally convinced she cared for them. That effect is multiplied greatly by having a companion who truly understands what it's like to absorb a life each week."

Susan sighed. She still couldn't see how this proved his original point. Sometimes it was hard being friends with someone much smarter than yourself.

Apparently sensing her frustration, or possibly just caught up in the excitement of discovery, Cole rushed on.

"At this point, the Ross twins each have completed more than two hundred Reflections. If their assumption is correct, then each of those two hundred extra lives has equal weight with their own life. If that were true, though, why would it matter that they have an empathetic companion who understands just *one* of those lives? It wouldn't . . ."

". . . unless that one life were the true one." Susan finally understood. "Despite thousands of years of memories, the most powerful support they have is someone who understands the shortest of their lives, their real life as a Mirror."

"Exactly."

"Is it possible to isolate those true memories? Let them see themselves without the Reflected's memories?"

Cole shrugged. "Yes and no. We don't have any technology even remotely close to what would be necessary, and we don't understand the brain nearly well enough to utilize it even if we did. We're likely centuries away from such a breakthrough.

"Right now the only technology we possess that could perform such a feat is a Reflection."

Susan nodded slowly. "Ah."

Twenty-eight years ago in a California airport, several flights were delayed because of weather. What should have been a simple inconvenience became something more when it put two Mirrors in the same place at the same time. Jason Williams and Ben Hart had been passing one another in the terminal when—for reasons still unknown—they decided to Reflect each other. The contact lasted only a few seconds, but both boys died.

"So, Jason and Ben were able to see themselves as they truly were for that instant before it killed them," Susan said.

"I believe so, yes."

It was remarkably cruel. It wasn't hard to imagine that there had been an instant of joyful celebration as the boys watched the chains of other people's lives drop away. It was particularly cruel since that freedom then cost them their lives.

"Could . . . could it be fixed? Could Mirrors Reflect each other and live?"

Cole shrugged sadly. "No. I've asked several of my contemporaries around the world, and none of us even knows where to start. Dr. Gabrielle Micheau has proposed a formal theory on why dual Reflections are fatal, and the elite specialists all agree she's probably correct, but we can't even begin to fathom how to stop it."

"Why? What's happening?"

He hesitated. "I'm still preparing a paper on it. I'm waiting to read the final results of Dr. Micheau's tests on the physical after-effects of Reflections."

Suppressing another sigh, Susan reminded herself to be patient. Asking anyone to be succinct when discussing the topic of their doctorate was an exercise in futility, but Cole was worse than most. Maybe it *was* best that he tended to keep this to himself.

Luckily, he quickly cleared his throat and moved on. "The short version is that when a Mirror Reflects anyone, it causes odd changes in the Mirror's body. The heart attempts to alter beating to match the rhythm of the other person's heart, digestion patterns adjust, and pretty much the entire body shifts for a split second to march in time with the impulses of a stranger.

"This doesn't last long. The heart recovers almost immediately, the stomach in an hour or two. Some of the glands can take days to revert to proper function. It's only the Mirror who sees these changes, though; the Reflected's body continues to function as normal.

"It is assumed that the Mirror survives principally because a typical Reflection is only a fraction of a second. There isn't time for the body to adjust any more than that. We suspect strongly that it is the Reflected's mind that kills the connection. Between two Mirrors, though, there is no signal to disconnect the minds. When they are pulled apart, each heart is now beating in time with the signal from someone else's body. It's likely that two Mirrors who are Reflecting reach a sort of symbiotic state. When that link is severed, neither can live without the other. By that point they require the other's mental commands for even basic autonomic functions."

"If there were a way to limit the length of a dual Mirror Reflection, could they be saved?"

Cole's burger was growing cold on his plate, forgotten. His eyes were far away, lost in another world. "It's been theorized but not tested. I'm not overly hopeful, though.

"Ten years ago a pair of Japanese Mirrors Reflected each other when they wound up together due to a paperwork error. Their handlers figured out what was happening immediately, and estimates of the exposure are less than a second. In fact, their exposure was so brief no one even realized they'd actually Reflected until they discovered the children were dying.

"When I asked about the event, Dr. Yamamoto put forth a theory that the connection between Mirrors builds stronger and faster than in a normal Reflection since both their bodies know what to expect from the event. It's reasonable, but it would be hard to test without violating some ethical standards.

"All I can say for sure is that at this point, we don't have enough evidence to produce an unassailable hypothesis."

As if suddenly remembering that he was supposed to be eating, Cole grabbed his burger and took a large bite. That mouthful of food suddenly broke whatever spell stole over him during these academic moments. His brow furrowed as he chewed, and Susan watched his happiness fade. She could almost feel his mood darkening as the discussion left the ivory tower and crashed back into reality.

"You wanted to keep them together. The Ross twins, I mean."

He chewed silently, feigning interest in something on the street outside. That was unusual for Cole; normally he'd just tell her he didn't want to discuss something.

"You could have offered them Sam. They threw Carol to the dogs last year."

"I tried."

Cole's voice was unusually tight with emotion. He pulled his gaze from the window but didn't look at Susan, instead focusing his attention on the burger he'd barely touched.

Uncertainty gripped Susan unexpectedly. She'd known Cole Bryant since they were both children. She, Cole, and her twin sister had been in school together for a few years until he'd jumped several grades. He'd been stoic, almost cold, his entire life. She'd learned how to read those empty glances, could detect sadness that no one else would see, but this was the first time she'd ever seen it so openly. He was close to tears, and she felt the pedestal she'd set him on cracking.

"You tried?"

"As Urich so foolishly admitted, the board had been discussing the vote for several days. I floated the idea of firing Sam, but no one seriously considered it. They could see that the Ross twins' behavior is unpredictable because of the sibling relationship. They're worried about losing the whole program should Thomas or Ashley undertake another unexpected action. That said, I was surprised by the final vote today; until this morning it was four to one. Maria changed her mind at the last second."

Susan frowned. "Why was this so important to you? The board has a point: another incident like Ashley's heroics last year and we might well watch a terrified public seek to shutter the program.

"Besides, the Ross twins are sixteen. Even if they stay together, how much time can they reasonably have left?"

Bryant shook his head fiercely, the emotion in his eyes swapping rapidly from sorrow to anger. "This is what I'm fighting against," he said sharply. "Why does everyone assume these children can be treated as objects? They're people, Susan. If they have three hours or three years left, it should be their decision, not ours."

Cole's tone triggered something in Susan. Being in politics gave you a thick skin, but you never stopped wanting to defend yourself. Here in a small burger joint with a friend, she wasn't simply going to be attacked.

"And if they don't care? Thomas didn't seem to."

"You're wrong. He does care. I know him better than you do."

Susan opened her mouth to speak, but Cole plowed ahead. "What about his sister? What about his parents? Do they not count either? Even if you can toss his feelings away, what about theirs?"

Her mouth was open, her tongue poised to berate him before she realized she had nothing to say. He was right. She hadn't considered them. Deep down she knew she didn't want to consider them. It complicated what seemed like such a straightforward solution. She'd fallen into exactly the trap he had warned her about last year.

Mirrors were vital to the American justice system. They'd destroyed organized crime, ensured the right person was punished, and all but guaranteed convictions for the worst offences. They had taken an imperfect process and made it work.

More importantly, they had given Susan closure; she knew who had killed her sister, a court had sentenced her sister's murderer to die using the certainty a Reflection provided.

She needed these things. Personally and professionally, she needed Mirrors to be a part of the system. So, just as the board had done, she'd distanced herself from them. They were pieces on a board, pawns to sacrifice to take the queen.

Bile rose in her throat as she suddenly realized just how much she was taking for granted. Appetite vanishing, she shoved her plate away.

At the sudden ache inside her, she remembered their conversation from a year ago.

"You're tired of being the only one who's damned."

Across the table, Cole nodded solemnly.

Susan scowled at him in frustration. "Why couldn't you just let me have my neat little package? Justice all tied up and simple?"

Cole smiled sympathetically, an odd gesture from such a stoic man. Perhaps he finally found something he could actually sympathize with. Shaking his head, he said quietly, "When justice becomes easy, it stops being justice."

—CHAPTER 36—

In a life increasingly marked by unwanted change, Sally had drawn an unexpected shred of comfort when she realized that gate 30 had remained unaltered during her absence.

She rested tiredly in the same chair she'd chosen after Ashley's hearing, and Thomas slumped in the same seat his sister had occupied. Around the edges of the gate's waiting area, the same bubble of tacit quarantine left them mostly undisturbed. Across the aisle, the same coffee shop and bookstore dispensed their wares to bored and exhausted travelers.

Today's version of gate 30 was not a true replica, of course. Where Ashley had protectively curled in on herself, Thomas's posture announced his silent distaste for the world. Slouched in his chair, he sat barely high enough for the top of his head to crest the seat back. Arms folded over his chest, Thomas stared out the window, face completely devoid of expression.

Sam shadowed Thomas, standing beside him as a rather large reminder of the second major difference. The Shepherd's posture hinted at the relationship they had built. He was protective, wary, and perhaps, guilty.

That spoke to the most important change: today was the last trip home for her child.

Sally's gut wrenched thinking about it. She'd cried a lot after the meeting, and on the trip to the airport. She'd done her best to say goodbye to Thomas, but he'd all but ignored her. Sam had encouraged Thomas to talk about it, but he'd just shrugged and looked out the window of their car.

Everything was still raw, and Sally still felt searing pain every time she looked over at her son. She was running out of tears, though, and all that was left was a bitter emptiness. She just couldn't feel the acute horror anymore. Maybe it was because she'd started pulling away four years ago.

"May I join you a moment?"

Startled, Sally almost fell out of her seat.

While she had been musing, a man had broken the barriers of imposed solitude and now stood a pace to her right. Raising her eyes, she gaped.

"Mr. Lane?"

Nodding solemnly, the board member said, "Please. Call me Peter." He gestured at the seat opposite Sally. "Do you mind if I sit?"

"No, not at all." Doing her best to gather her thoughts, she took a deep breath as Lane sank gratefully into the chair. "What . . . why . . . ?"

"I just want to talk a minute. I promise I won't take much of your time."

"Okay."

"For what it's worth, I wish I could alter the board's decision. Whatever else we do, tearing apart families should never be on our agenda." He paused, regarding her sadly. "I resigned in protest."

Sally almost gaped in surprise and struggled for the right words. "I . . . I don't . . . Thank you." She swallowed, fighting back tears; Peter's presence stirred up all the emotions she thought she'd suppressed. "I appreciated your words today."

Lane nodded absently. "They weren't worth much." He shrugged and leaned back, pulling off his glasses.

"You didn't come here to tell me that," Sally said.

"No. I suppose I didn't. Well, not just that, anyway," he replied. "I wish I could even say that I came here for you, but my motives are more . . . selfish, I guess."

Sally regarded him coolly for a second, and he pushed the glasses farther up on his nose and hurried on.

"I worked as a member of the Mirror Review Board for thirteen years. My expertise was in logistics; I scheduled each Reflection and made sure we had proper transportation for both Mirror and Shepherd. I've booked all of Cole's flights around the country and arranged rental cars and hotels. I'm a numbers person, living life behind a computer screen. My data is my daily companion.

"To be honest, I only half understood what I was doing. I've known for years the impact Mirrors have on criminal justice. Until I sat for Ashley's hearing one year ago, though, I had never even met a Mirror. I saw them as pieces of an enormously complex puzzle. I was always figuring out which Mirror went where on what day for what criminal and at what time. It was chaotic sometimes, but I was good at my job."

"I don't understand . . ." Sally began, but Lane held up a hand.

"I'm sorry. I'm not being clear.

"You see, I never doubted that what I did was right. To be honest, I don't know that I doubt it now. I'm not a Liberator. There are dangerous criminals in the world, and Mirrors alone can make sure we prosecute the right man.

"That doesn't make it easy to do this. Watching Ashley explain her life to the board shook me. Seeing Thomas today shook me again. I still believe in the good of the faceless Many over the good of the faceless One, but giving that One a face makes it much harder."

"Peter, I still don't understand."

He sighed, gritted his teeth, and forged ahead. "When I took this job, all three of my daughters had been born. The youngest was six. The threat of having a Mirror was past.

"My oldest daughter is twenty-four now, married, and expecting my first grandchild around the end of March. She's still a bit early for the prenatal Mirror test, and I have no reason to assume a positive result, but . . ."

"You're afraid she'll have a Mirror," Sally said, finally understanding. Lane nodded.

"The odds aren't good. Cole says it's about one in every 750,000 births. I shouldn't be worried."

"Except that you're talking to the woman who gave birth to twin Mirrors."

"I'm sorry," he said, and he sounded sincere. "I'm trying to convince myself there's nothing to fear, but I'm doing so in poor company. I am sorry." He grimaced and shook his head.

"What did you come here for? Forgiveness? Absolution?" Sally asked.

"I came here because I'm trying to grasp what I've helped do.

"What if my grandson's a Mirror? Can I look my daughter in the eye and tell her I'm proud of what I've done? That her son will live and die in a hell I helped maintain?"

"Those sound like questions you should have asked years ago, Peter."

"I agree. My soul-searching comes far too late, and so most in the Liberator community see me as a monster. I'll get no answers from them. I came to you because I feel you've seen both sides of me. I've played the role of jailer, but I have not, and never would, support Urich in the removal of your children."

She shook her head. "That's a small comfort."

"Is it? Are you telling me Thomas's last goodbye tonight is a small thing?"

Sally said nothing.

"I didn't think so."

"I still don't know what you want." Sally didn't even try to hide the heat that tinged her words. She was grateful for the former board member's vote to let her keep Thomas at home, but that alone—especially since the vote failed—proved insufficient goodwill for Sally to overlook his place in the bureaucracy.

Lane shook his head. "Proof that I've been in the government too long, I guess; I can't even give a straight answer." Leaning forward intently, his eyes fixed on Sally's, he said, "I want to understand what part I've played in destroying your children and the dozens of other Mirrors like them. I want to clear my conscience so I can sleep at night. I want to know that I'm on the right side."

Sally laughed bitterly. "And you think you'll get an unbiased opinion from me?" She didn't even bother to hide how ridiculous she thought that sounded.

"You won't give me the party line," Lane replied firmly. "That's all I've gotten in thirteen years. No one on the Hill talks about Mirrors as people. Other than perhaps Bryant, they certainly don't talk about them as children."

"Why should I tell you anything?" Sally demanded.

"Because I'm willing to listen. As I said, I'm no Liberator, but I'm not heartless. I've always stood for using these kids because if they're going to die young anyway—and they do—then we should make use of that amazing gift of theirs."

"Curse," Thomas offered stoically. He had wrenched his gaze from the planes and now stared at Sally and the former board member. "Gifts don't hurt."

"Curse, then," Lane amended. "Whatever it is, it has great potential for good. I've worked to harness that potential and funnel it into improving society. If my grandson's a Mirror, though, I don't think my idealism would be enough to allow me to nod, smile, and gush philosophically about the merits of utilitarianism."

"You sound like you want me to convince you to be a Liberator," Sally said.

"Maybe I do. I don't know. I just want to be able to sleep at night." He closed his eyes and massaged his forehead. "Your children were dragged to hell each week, Mrs. Ross, but at least you can say you didn't help the devil build his domain. I did."

"How can you look at my kids and not want them set free? Don't you see how much they've deteriorated in just one year? Look around you, Peter. There's evidence everywhere!"

297

Lane said nothing. His eyes fixed on Thomas, though, who had resumed staring out the window. From behind Thomas, Sam was watching closely.

"Why is it so hard for you to grasp this?" Sally pressed.

Lane opened his mouth, shut it, and then leaned back in his chair. He removed his glasses, wiped away the beads of sweat on his forehead with a white handkerchief, and then turned his uncertain, myopic gaze back to Sally.

"Tell her, Peter," Sam said suddenly, drawing looks from everyone. Even Thomas broke his plane-watching just long enough to shoot the Shepherd a disinterested look.

"Tell me what?"

Lane frowned. "There's not really a rush of people clamoring to work with Mirrors. The only reason we can find Shepherds is because we have the whole country to pick from. Some Liberators try to slip in, but we only hire people willing to submit to the board's position." He shot Sam a meaningful look. "More than 90 percent of all board members and Shepherds since the establishment of Mirror Review have had direct contact with Mirror justice before their appointment. It's not a coincidence; most of us have sought out the work because we were changed by an event in our past, and the politicians calling the shots want to make sure we're going to agree with continuing the program.

"Sam's son was a Mirror. Maria Perales lost a sister to a serial killer who was eventually convicted with the assistance of Mirror testimony. Urich lost her father to a random robbery in the days before we used Mirrors; the man arrested for the murder wasn't convicted due to a lack of evidence, and she's never forgotten that.

"It's unfair, I guess, but Sam's the only one of us who has ever been related to a Mirror. The rest of us came from the other side of the aisle. We witnessed loved ones destroyed by evil and found solace in the presence of a Mirror's justice. Needless to say, those I work with are heavily biased in favor of keeping these children where they are."

"And you?"

He hesitated, obviously uncomfortable. Drawing a deep breath, he began an intent study of the coffee shop at the edge of the gate. Bringing a hand to his face, he quickly wiped tears from each eye before forming a response.

"I'm bound by Rachel, my middle daughter. She was kidnapped, raped, and murdered; she was only eight. As happens too often, the only reason we nailed the man who did it was because of Mirror testimony."

"What about fingerprints?"

"He was a smart; I'll give him that. Circumstantial evidence was all we had. Footprints that matched his shoe tread, stuff like that. Enough to convince the DA to try the case but probably not enough to eliminate the shadow of doubt."

"And you managed to get a Reflection?"

"I was on the board by that time. I'd sought to join soon after Rachel was murdered, and I was working with them by the time the Reflection came up for consideration."

"No one saw a conflict of interest?"

"Approving cases for Mirror review wasn't my area. Urich did that; still does. I argued my case aggressively, though. I don't know if I swayed her or if she was planning to approve it anyway, but we got the Reflection. And through that we got the conviction.

"Yes, Sally, I can see what these Reflections have done to your family, but I know what a Reflection did for mine. Rachel's spirit can rest at peace, and I, my wife, and my two living daughters found some closure. That's why this isn't so easy. That's why I've never been a Liberator.

"For every Thomas Ross in the country there are dozens of Rachel Lanes. The victims of human weakness number far more than the victims of the board. More families than just yours seek comfort, and it isn't just Mirrors who die young."

He broke off, pulling his gaze from Sally's as he searched for words. Noise from the glut of travelers spilled in from all sides in

299

a resounding cacophony, but it seemed to Sally that the world had shrunk to contain only the four people assembled within the circle of isolation. She watched Lane struggle, finally find his strength, and continue.

"I always knew Mirrors died. What I didn't understand—what I spent years actively ignoring for the sake of ease—was that they weren't just dying; they were living several years of the darkest torture I can fathom and then dying.

"And yet, after meeting Ashley, I did my best to ignore that. I went about my business as always and shoved down all doubt."

"So you decided to simply forget about what you'd seen? How could you?"

Peter didn't balk this time. He plowed ahead, meeting her gaze. "Do you ever see people begging on the side of the road as you drive around town? They stand holding their signs looking beaten down. They are the very embodiment of despair. Do you stop? Do you give them money? Or do you pretend you don't see them, looking away so you can continue living in a world where that kind of sadness doesn't have to exist?"

Sally looked away, licking her lips. Peter continued, though. "Starving children in Africa, victims of famine or genocide. Orphanages in eastern Europe. Places where . . ."

"I get it," Sally interjected tersely. "We don't see what we don't want to."

"Yes."

"Yet here you are. You resigned."

"Sometimes we can't help but see." He sighed and bowed his head.

"I've created a world that might destroy my own grandchildren in the name of my daughter. I don't even know how to reconcile that." Peter choked back a sob.

"I realize now that the only time we are forced to see the broken of the world . . . is when we realize we could become them.

300

"I don't know if this is a world where we need people who can maneuver Mirrors like pieces on a chess board. I remember Rachel, and think it might be. Even if it is, though, I know I can't be that man anymore. I can't destroy your child as someone destroyed mine."

Finally looking back up, he said again, "So . . . I'm sorry."

Before he could continue, a female voice crackled through the speaker overhead. "Attention: flight 2401 nonstop to Atlanta will now begin preboarding at gate 27."

"That's me. Since I have some free time, I figured I'd spend some of it with my daughter."

"That sounds like an excellent plan," Sally said, forcing a smile.

"I really intended to just listen, but I got to talking and . . ."

Sally interrupted him. "It's okay. I learned something too."

"Oh?"

"The Many have faces too, Peter, not just the One."

"Thank you."

With a final weary smile, he turned away, hurrying off to catch his plane.

— CHAPTER 37 —

Ashley watched Mom quietly slip out the door to her room. This goodbye had been harder than the one with Dad, though not in the way Ashley had expected. The earlier trip through the photo albums had sapped her emotions, leaving little to share with her mother. Thus, the past half hour of farewell had been comprised mostly of Mom hugging and sobbing while Ashley sat stiffly, unable to summon the proper responses.

As expected, Thomas sidled into the room almost as soon as Mom was truly gone. He was wringing his hands nervously; honestly, it was more emotion than she had expected from him. As withdrawn as he had been lately, she expected he would embrace this end. At the very least, she expected he wouldn't fight it.

"We made a promise two years ago," Thomas said.

His reminder was unnecessary, of course. Ashley remembered the day vividly. Watching a sunset without the shaded glass to block it, she had promised Thomas she'd be with him at the end if he'd do the same for her. The promise had sustained her as a sheltering rock in a storm. Hopelessness could assail her, but the knowledge that she wouldn't face the end alone had been a much-needed boon.

Now, though, the tables were turned. The board's decision changed everything. For them both to remain true to their word would require her to die now. She didn't want to die yet. Well, part of her did, but she didn't think she should give in; there was so much she hadn't done. So many she hadn't helped.

That didn't matter. She had a promise to keep.

"I'm . . . I'm ready," she said quietly.

"I'm not."

Ashley's mouth dropped open in surprise.

Thomas looked empty, hollow, but was a force behind those words. She couldn't see his eyes, of course, but she knew immediately that he wasn't lying; Thomas was holding on to something.

"If you're ready to die," he whispered, "then I'll go with you. You won't have to force me; just say the word and we can end it all. If it's my choice, though . . . well, I'm not ready."

She barely avoided gaping. "Why?"

He looked away now, chewing on his lip as he wrestled with the words. "Father Sean's last words to me. They . . . I . . ."

"When he refused to let you Reflect him?"

"No. After that."

"But, he died that night," Ashley said, confused. "You didn't see him again."

"I didn't, but I Reflected someone who did.

"Father Sean left me a message. When Jayce Ragen stabbed him, he knew he was going to die. He grabbed Jayce and spoke to him, but he was really speaking to me. Even addressed me by name. As he bled out and died, he passed on a message, hoping that I would Reflect Jayce again."

Ashley was too stunned for words. Across the room her brother stood stiffly, his muscles taut, hands drawn into fists.

"Father Sean got stabbed so that a woman could live. He traded his life for hers, and as he died, he grabbed the man who was murdering him and thought of me. Me! He told me that our conversation that morning, that his refusal to allow the Reflection, had made him question whether he was doing enough good in the world. It spurred him to follow Jayce, and in doing so, he got killed.

"His last words were, 'Thomas, thank you. I've learned so much from you. Remember how much we care about you. Find your purpose.'"

"Thomas," Ashley said slowly, her voice as tender as she could make it. "I'm sorry."

"No. It was . . . positive, I think. I didn't realize how much I missed him until I saw him again. He never backed down from believing I was worth something, that my existence meant something. He wants me to find purpose in life, and I want to. I owe him that much, don't I? If he can think of me as he's dying, shouldn't I think of him?"

"Yes."

It was the hardest word she'd ever uttered, but Ashley couldn't hold it back. Her brother was finally embracing something more, giving up the comfort of her presence to find meaning for himself. It meant she would die alone, but now she could do it believing that Thomas had embraced something larger than himself.

"This is goodbye, then, isn't it?" she asked. She was wrong; she hadn't drained all of her emotion earlier. A weight settled in her chest, and a single tear leaked out into her glasses. She felt more building in her eyes. Severing ties with her brother had opened the vault of emotions that always seemed reserved for him.

Relinquishing the safety of the bed, Ashley crossed the carpet, dodging the sundry bits of clutter between her and her brother. Wrapping him in a hug, she battled the realization that this would be the last time they'd see one another. Dwelling on that would make this unbearable.

For his part, Thomas returned the embrace. There was no sudden strength in that moment; instead, she could feel the weakness his body language implied. It only made her more scared. Alone, they had been so weak, but together . . .

Thomas broke away, and the bulwark collapsed. "Goodbye, sis." Then, awkwardly, he added, "I love you."

She wanted to look away but forced herself to meet his shaded eyes. "Take care of yourself." It was a stupid thing to say, but she still meant it. News of his eventual death would reach her when it came, but she wanted to delay that moment as long as possible.

Knowing he was alive, even hours away, would be the last scrap of comfort left to her. Then, as her parting declaration, she offered, "I love you too."

He nodded numbly and wrenched open the door. In seconds, he was gone.

Halting footsteps carried Ashley back to the relative security of her bed. Climbing atop the mattress, she pulled the blankets up to her chin, removed her glasses, placed them on the bedside table, and rolled over to face the wall. Despair flooded her, burning away the apathy in fiery torture. Mom, Dad, and her Shepherd, Julie, might still be there, but in every way that mattered, Ashley felt suddenly alone.

As the pain sank deeper and she yielded to tears, Ashley replayed her final conversation with Thomas. What words could she ever speak that would be more valuable than her goodbye here?

It was foolishness, but she told herself that if those words of affection to Thomas remained her last, she might still keep the promise in a way. Die to the world today, let her last communication be her sorrowful goodbye to him and it would be close, so close, to dying with him. It was foolishness, but it was the kind of foolishness that allowed humanity to survive.

Embracing the idea with every cell of her being, Ashley knew that for the rest of her life, however short it might be, she had nothing more to say to this world that had stolen her best friend.

-CHAPTER 38-

Thomas slipped out of Ashley's room and slouched down the hall. Sad, whispering voices drifted from the entryway. Sam and his parents were waiting for them to die. Thomas's stomach turned over; he felt sick.

Tuning them out with effort, he took a final look around the house he had called home all his life. These walls had been his prison the first twelve years, his fortress the last four. How odd that the walls he cursed for holding him in had become the place he treasured for keeping the world out.

He wandered through his room, touching each of his models, remembering the time he spent assembling each one. He looked at the twin bookshelves against the western wall and shook his head. Four years ago he couldn't read, and today he had hundreds of books he'd torn through. He stared a long time at his stereo system, lingering over his CD collection. He opened his closet and took stock of his neatly arranged wardrobe.

This was all his. Trappings of the life he'd lived, and memories of the life he loved best. He supposed now that he'd decided to keep living he should pack some of it up. It felt meaningless, though. These things weren't what made this all tolerable. Not really.

Leaving his room behind, he headed toward the front of the house. Before he reached the living room, his eyes landed on the small stand positioned at the end of the hall. A tall blue lamp with a dingy white shade rested atop it, standing a silent vigil over four small wooden picture frames. From behind those oak borders and glass sheets, the Ross family peered back at him.

Thomas strode to the end table and picked up the picture of his sister. Ashley's grin was tired but genuine. He remembered that afternoon, an island of hope in the two-year bounce. The pictures were shot beside the tree in the backyard with their parents taking turns at the camera; most professional photographers feared working with Mirrors as much as anyone else.

Setting down the picture, he took a single step away before drawing to an abrupt stop. *Maybe there is something I want to take,* he thought.

Grabbing Ashley's photo again, he gave it a brief glance, just long enough to make sure it was the right one. Flipping it over, he gripped the frame by its edge and fiddled with the tiny clasps holding the backing in place. Pressure held them tight, and he quickly grew tired of fussing with them. Surrendering to brute force, he clutched the wooden edge tightly and swung the glass pane hard into the corner of the end table.

Glass shattered and cascaded to the floor with a light tinkling; someone in the dining room gave a muffled cry, but no one approached. Righting the frame, Thomas examined the picture. The damage to Ashley's image was minimal; it would do. Shaking out the last dusty shards, he pushed his fist in the picture. The clasps on the back strained against the additional force, then popped free. The wooden rectangle slid over his left hand; in his right he clutched his prize.

Casting backing and frame to the side with a disdainful toss, he stole a final glance at the picture before stuffing it unceremoniously into his pocket. As he stepped into the living room, he saw everyone assembled in the dining room. They looked at him with obvious surprise.

"I'm ready now," he muttered.

"Thomas, I thought . . ." Dad left what he thought unsaid.

"We're still alive. Now I'm leaving, just like the board demanded." He cast a look at Sam, who was clearly as stunned as the parents. With a frustrated huff, Thomas pushed his way past them all and through the door.

—CHAPTER 39—

Outside the window, inky shadows slid past as an indistinct blur. Beyond the slicing scope of the headlights the world faded to impenetrable gloom, and Thomas imagined that even without the sunglasses he'd be unable to make anything out.

He gazed outside not because he hoped to actually see anything but because it was preferable to talking to Sam. Leaning against the seat and facing the window, he had feigned sleep for the last hour. The Shepherd had posed questions a few times, but Thomas had ignored them all. So they rode on with the gentle rumble of the road providing the only rebuttal against the silence.

"I know you're awake," Sam said.

It was true. Thomas hadn't really tried to regulate his breathing and was relying solely on his lack of response to convince the Shepherd to leave him alone. Sam's statement did nothing to prompt Thomas to respond, though.

"Are you planning to ignore me the whole trip?"

Yes, Thomas thought, but still said nothing.

"You're mad at me; I guess you've got a right to be."

Thomas chose to respond to that. "I hate you." There was no heat in it; it was just a statement. Thomas wasn't sure it was true, though. Hate was what he had felt while he slammed Jayce Ragen's head into the floor of the police station. Nothing like that burned against Sam. All he felt toward the Shepherd was emptiness.

"Because I didn't say anything at the hearing?"

"Genius," Thomas muttered, managing to force a bit of cynicism into his voice.

"Do you want to know why?"

"C-Y-A. You saw what they did to Carol last year."

"To an extent, but I think the board had already made up their mind."

"So? Some people fight even though they know they're going to lose. They say the battle's more important that the outcome."

"Like your sister?"

Thomas chose to ignore that. "So why not fight? Am I not worth fighting for?"

"You are."

"You expect me to believe that now?"

"Do you really want an answer, or do you just want to blame me? If you want to lay blame, go ahead. I won't stop you."

Thomas considered that for a minute. Part of him wanted to let loose at the man with a list of all the grievances stored up over the past four years. More of him didn't want to expend the energy necessary. In the end he shrugged and said, "I don't care."

"You're not my only Mirror, Thomas."

Thomas finally moved, shifting to watch the Shepherd. "They're younger, aren't they? Happier? Easier to get along with? Two more years—at the most—and you're rid of me for good. Why end a good thing?"

Sam gripped the steering wheel tightly, focusing on the illuminated swath of road stretched out before him.

"Why do you think I do this?" Sam demanded suddenly. His voice was hard, almost angry.

"It's a paycheck."

Sam shook his head firmly. Even in the dark, Thomas could make out the gesture. "I told you the day of your first Reflection that I could make more money doing something else."

Memories of a conversation floated to the surface, and instinctively Thomas pushed them away before realizing that this time the memory seeking his attention was his own. He remembered sitting in the plane, talking after that first Reflection.

"To make a difference," Thomas said. "And you don't think you'd have done that today."

"Yes, Thomas. Someday I'll lose this job by caring too much for one of my kids, but it wasn't today. I'm not going to sacrifice everything when it won't make any difference."

For a long moment, Thomas processed that. Then, quietly, he said, "It would have made a difference to me."

Shifting to stare back out the window, Thomas closed his eyes. Sleep was the furthest thing from his mind, but he wanted to block out the world. He could still hear the steady thrumming of the engine, though, could still feel the sedan cruising resolutely down the highway. He shivered against the frozen chill that fought to infiltrate the car and heard the Shepherd flip a switch on the console. The dusty scent of the car filled Thomas's nostrils even as the first tendrils of heat licked at his face and hands. He opened his eyes.

On the dashboard, the LCD clock recorded midnight, and another birthday—another year—passed from life to memory.

— PART VI —

Seventeen Years Old—Goodbye

The data available is quite clear: Mirrors raised in government foster care live almost eighteen months longer on average than Mirrors raised by their own families. Despite Liberator propaganda to the contrary, being forced to Reflect does not actually decrease a Mirror's lifespan. Instead, regular Reflections lead to a marked increase in life expectancy.

Questions remain as to what specifically is responsible for the difference. Theories principally focus on two possibilities: the foster family environment, or the Reflections themselves.

Those who argue for the family element posit that the removal of natural parental instinct plays an important role. Mirrors who have Reflected do not behave traditionally, and the relationship with parents is often skewed. While a biological parent may have difficulty shifting roles so quickly, a foster parent—particularly one who has been on the job only a few years—is much less emotionally steered toward such rigid functions. Thus, the assumption is that the flexibility of the relationship is more important than the stable, emotional foundation of a traditional parent-child relationship.

The second theory holds that it is the Reflections themselves that provide the boost. While this seems counterintuitive to anyone familiar with the pain of Reflections, the theory has some merit. The major tenet of this theory is that the more Reflections a Mirror engages in, the better he or she is able to handle them. The first is always a tragic experience, but with practice many Mirrors manage to adapt, if only temporarily.

If that is indeed the case, then forcing Mirrors to perform Reflections each week isn't a tragedy . . . it's a treatment.

—Excerpt of Dr. Cole Bryant addressing the Senate Judiciary Committee

-CHAPTER 40-

Though the hour still hovered on the early side of six, Thomas was dressed and plodding out the front door toward Sam Barton's waiting rental car. Wrenching open the passenger-side door, he slumped into the seat and grimaced at the thick blackness of pre-dawn. Sam shifted the car into gear, hit the accelerator, and they sped away from the place Thomas wryly called "The Orphanage."

"Morning," Sam said.

Thomas offered no reply, instead staring out the window through his dark lenses. The world beyond the car sped by as nothing more than the occasional blur of light, but Thomas wasn't really paying attention to the scenery anyway. Instead, he was building up the strength for a conversation he'd been planning for months.

"I was surprised to see you didn't request off today," Sam said quietly.

Thomas bit back the sarcastic retort that immediately leapt to mind. He still needed a huge favor from the man beside him. Insulting Sam would be a poor introduction to a request for help. Besides, the Shepherd had just provided the perfect introduction.

"Because of my birthday?" Thomas asked.

"You usually take this week off."

"Do you know if Ashley's off today?"

"You know I haven't seen your parents in a year. Does it matter?"

Thomas frowned. He'd waited for today for months, but none of that patient planning would matter if Ashley hadn't taken vacation on their birthday.

Sam cleared his throat and repeated, "Does it matter?"

"It matters a lot."

"Why?"

Thomas leaned his head on the window, feeling the cool glass press against his scalp. He'd always known he'd have to tell Sam what was going on; the man's involvement was vital, but now that the moment had come, he discovered he was ashamed.

"I'm going to die," Thomas whispered to the darkness outside. Over the hum of the engine and the flush of the heater, he didn't think the Shepherd could hear him. "I can't take it anymore, and I'm giving up."

"Thomas?"

He looked over at Sam, opening his mouth to explain, but nothing came out. A dark hollowness filled him, and he felt everything crashing down. He'd felt this a lot recently, this miasma of oppressive emptiness, but he'd hoped that today would be the exception. He still had one last thing he needed to do.

On a desperate impulse, Thomas thrust a hand deep into the pocket of his jeans. Trembling slightly, he drew out the photo of Ashley he'd claimed as he left home. Twelve months of journeying between pockets had left long creases across the surface and rubbed it pale in several places. Mostly untouched by the damage, Ashley's face smiled back at him from beneath her own shadowed glasses. That smile dated the photo and served as his constant reminder: this had been taken within a few weeks of sharing that sunset on the back fence.

"I need to see my sister," he said hoarsely. "I have to keep that promise."

Sam drove in silence for a few seconds, then said, "You know I can't."

"Why?"

"Thomas, illegally transporting a Mirror away from a Reflection is a felony. It's a federal crime."

"I'm dying today, Sam. At my home or at The Orphanage, I'm finally done."

Sam seemed to soak this in. At any rate, he didn't interrupt.

"I need to see her. You know I promised I wouldn't let her die alone."

"Are you sure she's ready to die?"

"No. But I know I am. I at least have to give her that chance. I broke our promise last year, and now I have to make it up to her."

Sam paused, processing. Thomas figured he was more than a little surprised. He'd never told anyone that it was him and not his sister who had called off their suicide pact. He didn't figure it mattered.

"You got into this business to help Mirrors." Thomas had worked on this speech for months, planning every word. Trying to find the best way to prod the Shepherd into helping him. Today he sought for all the emotions he'd buried long ago. He wasn't sure how well he succeeded, but he at least managed to avoid slipping into the monotone he had dreaded.

"I think you wanted to save us. Help us live better lives. In some small way to make your son's death meaningful.

"You can't save us. Bryant's right about that; we're broken. Nothing we do changes our fate. We burn out and die young. It's the Mirror curse. You can work as a Shepherd the rest of your life, and you're not going to get the opportunity to save us.

"I kept looking for meaning in my life, and I never found it. People just kept letting me down. I was never satisfied with all of this like Ashley was. But maybe I can make today mean something."

Sam didn't reply. He stared straight ahead, watching the road, never turning in Thomas's direction. As Thomas waited, he felt the fire draining out of him. Had the Shepherd shouted back, or become defensive, or shown just about any defiance at all, he might

319

have been able to keep the fire kindled. Sam's silence only sapped the energy from him.

An experienced Shepherd had to know that. Give an older Mirror plenty of quiet and they'd sputter out, unable to sustain any plea for longer than a few minutes. It felt like betrayal to Thomas; he felt used. That realization should have provided some new fury, but all he felt was a profound sadness. Rather than empower his words, it drew him in and consumed the last sparks of hope.

Sam threw on his turn signal and drifted off the highway. After a year, Thomas was familiar with the route to the airport. Fighting down a sob, he leaned against the window and, head down, pulled into a ball as much as the seat belt would allow.

He'd been so sure Sam would listen that he hadn't even bothered to bring a means of killing himself on the trip. Would he have to go through one more Reflection? Take on one more life before it was all over? Surely he could find some way to escape before that happened.

Instead of making the next turn, Sam drove through the intersection and pulled into a gas station. Perplexed, Thomas turned to look at the fuel gauge. Full.

Nosing into a space along a dark wall, Sam opened his door. Light flooded the interior of the car, illuminating Shepherd and Mirror clearly. An answering light flickered on in a dark hatchback parked beside them. Thomas caught a glimpse of the two figures inside as the other car's doors opened.

Carol Raines emerged regally from behind the wheel of the other vehicle, a wry smile creasing her face. From the other side emerged a boy several years younger than Thomas wearing a gray, hooded jacket and dark sunglasses. Another Mirror? What was going on here?

"Hello, Carol," Sam said amiably, apparently not surprised by her presence.

"Hello, Sam. I take it you were right?"

"Yeah. He wants to see his sister one last time."

Turning toward Thomas, who was still sitting in the dark sedan, she called out, "Come on, we haven't got all day."

"What's happening?" Thomas asked, confused.

"She's taking you home," Sam said solemnly. "I'm sorry for not telling you sooner; I needed to know how badly you wanted this. Once they figure out the switch, I'm in quite a bit of trouble."

"Who's the Mirror?"

"Not a Mirror at all," Carol said. "My grandson, Chase, who volunteered to help us out. Boy's a Liberator like his grandmother."

Thomas had heard that the woman had joined the Liberator movement. He'd heard she'd even made a play to be the face of the movement by claiming deep, inside knowledge of the workings of the Mirror Review Board. Her prior occupation had earned her a few supporters but also spawned an equal number of detractors. Given what he knew of her, Thomas had no doubt that her intention with this stunt was to make another play to gain influence.

Sam picked up the explanation where Carol left off. "If I don't show up at the airport on time with a Mirror, someone at the board's going to get a call. If that happens, you'll never make it home before they nab you. With Chase pretending to be you, no one will think twice. Who looks closely enough at a Mirror to tell one from another?"

It was true. Most people would have no way of knowing it wasn't Thomas Ross sitting with the large man. Maybe there was advantage to the disposable way the board treated them: who noticed a tool?

"Hi," Chase said shyly, waving a gloved hand. "I hope everything works out okay."

His youthful innocence burned Thomas. It was clear Sam and Carol hadn't told the boy why this trip home was so important. It was touching, and Thomas desperately wished he could summon the grateful words this clearly deserved. Instead, he merely nodded to the boy as he unlatched his seat belt and stepped from the car.

321

He trudged over to Carol's hatchback, slipped inside, and shut the door.

They reassembled, each "Mirror" with his new driver. Before either car could pull away, Thomas rolled down the window and motioned for his longtime caretaker to do the same. Sam did so and leaned out expectantly.

"Thanks." The word was empty, flat. Thomas tried to put all his gratitude into that word, but instead it collapsed dully between them.

"Don't worry," Sam said, smiling. "I understand." The grin faded. "I'm sorry I can't do more."

Thomas pulled back, collapsing into the seat. Beside him, the sedan pulled away, gliding off into the darkness, back on its familiar trek toward the airport. This time, it wasn't him being carted off to the trenches; he was going home.

–CHAPTER 41–

Daniel jumped uneasily at the knock on the door; in the kitchen Sally dropped a pan. She recovered from the shock first, ignoring the fallen cookware and dashing toward the entryway with Daniel so close behind he almost ran into her as she stopped and wrenched the front door open.

Carol Raines stood smiling on the stoop, Thomas at her side. Their son was pale and thin, his shoulders slumped. He had grown some since they'd seen him last, but he was still small for his age. Hands shoved deeply into the pockets of his jacket, he sidled inside. He'd barely crossed the threshold before Sally grabbed him, drawing him close and squeezing him as tightly as she could. Thomas didn't try to break the hold. He accepted the embrace stoically but didn't even raise his arms to feign returning the emotion.

Daniel took his turn, pulling his son close. Nearby, Sally watched them and gave a single wrenching sob. Other than that single sign of weakness, she held strong.

"I'm sorry it took so long," Carol said idly as she checked her watch. "Wreck on I-25 coming into the city." She turned to Daniel. "Best let him go. If Sam's flight left on time, the board will realize what's happened any minute now."

Thomas escaped Daniel's grip and trudged listlessly toward the back of the house. As he vanished from sight, Daniel felt his heart plunge to his stomach.

He and Sally had said their goodbyes to Ashley earlier that

morning. It had been a very different experience from last year's farewell. Unwilling to get her hopes up in case something went wrong, they hadn't told her Thomas was coming. He and Sally had played off their obvious catharsis as a reaction to her birthday. They hadn't explicitly said goodbye. It didn't matter; they'd been saying it implicitly every day for the past twelve months.

Daniel turned back from watching his son retreat just in time to see Sally move forward and grab Carol in a tight hug. The usually unflappable ex-Shepherd was so shocked that for a moment she stood rigid. As Carol finally returned the gesture, albeit hesitantly, Sally said, "Thank you for bringing him back."

"You do know why I'm here?" the older woman asked with an arched eyebrow. "He's going . . ."

"He's going to die today," Sally interrupted, her voice hard. "I know. At least I got to see him one last time. At least he'll get to see his sister."

Silence filled the entryway for a long moment as Carol Raines examined the woman opposite her. She tapped her chin thoughtfully, as if analyzing a particularly difficult puzzle. Eventually she said, "You're not the woman I knew."

"No, I'm not. I became what I always should have been."

Carol nodded slowly, the barest hint of admiration evident in her features. "I'm sorry I didn't meet this side of you years ago."

"I am too."

A tense silence hovered between the two women for a long moment, then Carol straightened her coat. "Well, if everything went according to plan on Sam's end, he dropped my grandson off with relatives as soon as the plane landed. There will be nothing to link me to this little kidnapping plot . . . unless I'm still hanging around here when the police show up, of course."

"I understand. Go. And thank you again."

With a parting nod, Carol turned to face the frozen November morning. She managed a single step, froze, and stumbled back into the house as another figure mounted the steps to the porch.

Cole Bryant strode up to the doorway, paused at the welcome mat, and stood waiting for an invitation. Shocked, Daniel instinctively motioned the new arrival in. The specialist didn't hesitate, springing from the blowing wind into the relative safety of the house with an alacrity that seemed out of character for the dour man.

Carol stayed at the edge of the room and watched the doctor. Her clean getaway had been spoiled, and she was evidently working up an excuse for why she was leaving a house she'd been expressly forbidden to visit.

"It's Ashley birthday, and Daniel and Sally were kind enough to let me . . ." she began, but Cole raised a hand to stop her.

"You brought Thomas?" he asked simply.

Carol nodded weakly.

"Good. Go. I never saw you."

Without another word, Carol gripped the collar of her thick coat and plunged into the cold outside. Daniel and Sally watched her through the glass in the front door until she had slipped into her hatchback and driven away.

Sally let out a long breath. "I hate her so much."

Daniel's first instinct was to laugh, but he suddenly remembered everything else happening around them, and the sound caught in his throat.

He turned to the specialist. "How did you know about Thomas?"

"He didn't ask for the day off. He'd never subject himself to a Reflection he didn't have to. Still, I have to confess it was merely a solid hypothesis until I saw Carol."

Daniel nodded. If you knew the twins and Sam, it was pretty easy to follow the logic. Indeed, it was exactly what Sam had done in arranging this.

A sudden fear gripped Daniel. "The board sent you? You're here to stop them?"

Bryant shook his head. "No, I doubt the board has any idea what's going on. Peter Lane would have noticed it; he knew the twins always took their birthday off. His fellow board members drove him away, though, and his replacement is not nearly so astute. I imagine they are blissfully unaware." He glanced down at his watch. "At least for a few more minutes."

"So, why are you here?"

"I think I know how they intend to die," Bryant said, pulling out a pad of paper. "I need to record what happens."

— CHAPTER 42 —

Thomas knocked on his sister's door. When there was no answer, he tried again. After getting only silence on the third knock, his heart started pounding in his chest, and he felt his stomach drop in terror. Had Ashley taken her life before he could get there?

Steeling himself, he pushed the door open and stepped into the darkened room. Little, if anything, had changed in the past year. Perhaps a blouse or a pair of jeans had shifted position in that time, but certainly nothing more drastic than that. Thomas shivered slightly as he surveyed the familiar scene; the spark of life had already left this place.

Ashley sat on the edge of the bed wearing her pajamas and sunglasses. She looked terrible. Her hair had grown past her shoulders, but it was apparent it saw no daily care; large snarls and tangles dominated. Even from the door, Thomas could see it hadn't been washed in a few days. Her cheeks were sunken, and she was painfully thin. If the prior twelve months had been hard on Thomas, it was nothing compared to what his sister had seen.

After their conversation a year ago, Thomas had expected surprise, or at least confusion. By all accounts, he shouldn't be here. Neither registered on Ashley's face, but whether it was a silent certainty of his return or the apathy instilled by Reflections, he couldn't be sure.

Shutting the door behind him with a soft click, Thomas moved toward the center of the room. "I came back." His sister nodded weakly but said nothing. "Because I promised." Still no response. "You know why I'm here."

On the far side of the room, Ashley showed no expression, and his heart sank a bit. Still, she pushed herself off the bed and strode toward him with a resolve that belied her disheveled appearance. As gaunt and pale as she looked, the fortitude that had seemed synonymous with his sister in years past wasn't completely gone. Once she reached him, she fiercely wrapped those thin arms around him and pulled him into the best hug he'd ever received.

"Thank you." Her voice was raspy and thin, but he could hear the genuine appreciation. Without thinking, he reached up and returned the embrace.

They stood there for a long minute, and Thomas felt his lips quirk up into a weak smile for the first time in a year. It was a bittersweet final meeting between two friends. He felt the lines of despair around his heart unraveling, but this couldn't last, and it wasn't why he had come.

"Are you ready?"

Stepping away and watching him warily, she gave no response. Thomas grew cold. He'd fought so hard to get back here. He had come back for her. She didn't want to die alone, but if they didn't do it quickly, they might not get the chance.

"Five years of hell is more than enough," he pressed. "Whether we end it here together or I find a good knife back in Albuquerque doesn't really matter to me. I did my part; I came back.

"I remember a promise I made three years ago on the back fence, a promise that I said then wouldn't matter today. But it does. It does because you were there for me more than anyone else, more than even Sam. He'll probably go to jail for what he did today so that I could choose where to spend my last moments. But he won't give up his life so I don't die alone.

"Please . . ." Thomas begged. "Please don't let me go alone . . ."

Ashley finally answered, her expression sad. "I thought . . . you wanted a purpose."

"I was foolish," Thomas answered honestly. "Some people don't have a purpose."

"You have a purpose," she whispered. "You just never embraced it."

"You're wrong. They used us. They drained us. And for what? Some illusion of justice."

"You never did accept the idea of innocence," she said in that quiet, raspy voice.

"In everyone I looked at, I saw evil," he shot back.

"In everyone I looked at, I saw good. Maybe you weren't looking in the right places."

"They don't cancel each other out," Thomas retorted.

"I didn't say they did."

Thomas shrugged and frowned at her. "Whatever you think, nobody is worth this pain. Nobody deserves my sacrifice. Everybody is broken."

"Everyone?" She arched an eyebrow in question. "Then why did you fight so hard to come back?"

Thomas paused. He'd asked himself that question almost every day for the past three months. In August he'd been ready to die, ready to escape from the continued influx of pain. He'd even planned it out. Then, at the last second he'd changed his mind. Instead, he'd waited until he could see his sister. It made no sense, really. Dying with Ashley was ultimately meaningless since neither of them would live long enough to appreciate the act.

He'd come anyway.

"I guess sometimes I'm stupid," he said with a scowl, and Ashley sighed.

"You're not even honest with yourself, are you?"

Thomas didn't bother to answer that. "Whatever. Are we doing this?"

Ashley turned back to the window. "Even if I choose not to die, this is really the last time we're going to see each other, isn't it?"

"Yes."

"Maybe it's for the best," she allowed. "We did promise, and I'm so tired . . ."

She shook her head and walked over to the window. Gripping the cord on her blinds, she gave it a hard tug. With a whoosh, they climbed to the top of frame and rested there. Bits of cloudy sunlight spilled over the room, transforming the odd-sized shadowy lumps strewn across the floor into recognizable shards of the past.

"We lived most of our lives in darkness," Ashley said. "We shouldn't die that way."

Returning to the center of the room, she gazed at him a long moment through the mirrored glasses before finally dropping her head. "I'll do this. For you. For us. We do it my way, though. One last Reflection. If I'm going to die, I want to know who I really am."

Thomas felt his insides go cold, but he saw the determination in the set of her jaw. He'd wanted to die today to avoid any more Reflections. He opened his mouth to refuse, but then he hesitated. What did it matter? It was an escape.

Besides, he'd believed in her. Had she really been worth all the pain?

"Okay."

Thomas unlocked and stripped his glasses from his face. Tossing them to the floor, he stomped hard on them, and gave the briefest of smiles as they crunched beneath his shoe.

Ashley stepped forward, grabbing him in another hug.

"Goodbye."

"Goodbye, Ash."

She released him and took a short step back as she unclipped her glasses, then lazily cast them over her shoulder onto the bed. Face still directed at the carpet, her breathing was rapid, scared. He saw the hesitancy in every gesture, heard it in every gulp of air.

"Today was always supposed to be in the future," she whispered.

Thomas opened his mouth to offer some final piece of comfort or encouragement, whatever would be necessary to drive her to the end. But she was stronger than she seemed, and with a final hard breath, Ashley's head shot up and their silver eyes locked.

-CHAPTER 43-

Daniel sat in a large green chair, massaging his temples. Sally stood at the back of the room, wringing her hands and occasionally shooting a nervous glance down the hallway. It was hard to tell how much either was paying attention, and Cole worried that choosing to explain himself was a mistake. He was losing time!

"Why does this matter so much?" Daniel asked finally.

"Do you know how rare two Mirrors Reflecting is?"

Cole couldn't be 100-percent certain it was how they'd choose to die, of course, but the decision to be together on this final day certainly pointed heavily in that direction. Boosting the case was the fact that Ashley had long wanted to Reflect herself to see if she had been changed. Thomas was a bit of a wild card. He both wanted and desperately didn't want to know if his sister was the person he hoped she was.

"Since you're here, I'm going to guess it's pretty rare."

"The United States has seen it happen exactly once. Worldwide, I know of maybe four incidents with any kind of academic write-up on them. In none of those cases was a Mirror specialist actually present to record data.

"We can't study the situation in a lab, either. Since the experiment would kill both children, ethics concerns preclude researchers from setting up any such encounter on purpose.

"However, by the laws in place in our country, we cannot prevent a Mirror from taking their own life. If your children choose a dual Reflection as their method of suicide, it would create an ideal situation from which I could gather the information I need. It won't be in a controlled environment, and I'm lacking some of the equipment I'd like, but it's still something I have to see."

Sally shook her head. "We thought they were going to kill themselves last year. You weren't here then. Why today?"

"It took me time to discern what their intentions were. It didn't really become clear to me until later that day when I was having lunch with the attorney general. That evening I thought I'd missed an opportunity. When Sam called early the next morning to confirm Thomas had been delivered to Albuquerque, I realized I might get another chance."

Daniel barked a derisive laugh. "And what possible incentive could we have for letting you crash their final moments together?"

"You have two, actually," Cole admitted.

"First, according to the paperwork you signed when they were born, you have to grant me reasonable access to the twins. They're wards of the state, and I'm one of their caretakers. You don't legally have the means to stop me.

"I understand that's probably not very motivating. So the second incentive is that Sam Barton, Carol Raines, and both of you were involved in a plot to move a Mirror away from a Reflection and bring him to a place he was not permitted to be. That's a felony offense."

"You can't prove we had anything to do with it," Daniel replied testily.

Cole sighed. Why did people assume he was an idiot?

"They had to let you know. There's no reason to bring Thomas all the way up from Albuquerque and risk you being gone. You've not been able to keep the tradition, but in the past you tried to go out on their birthday. That would have been disastrous today since they'd have broken the law with nothing to show for it.

"I'm willing to bet that if we subpoena your phone records, we can show contact between you and either Sam or Carol, neither of whom would have had cause to contact you otherwise."

"Circumstantial," Daniel said dismissively, but Cole could see the fear creeping into Sally's face.

"For you? Yes. Carol and Sam are a different story. They're definitely guilty. However, if I get something out of all this, then it was worth it. I'll convince the board to forgive everything if I can get firsthand data that no one else has."

Daniel finally stood up, jabbing a finger toward Cole. "As I recall, we made a similar deal with you seventeen years ago. A better world for all of us and your word that their lives would be improved. Maybe we won't be taken in so easily this time."

Cole glanced nervously toward the back of the house. He expected that the twins would talk for at least a bit, say their good-byes and whatnot, but he was running out of time. He needed their parents to make a decision.

"I want to give you the opportunity to do the right thing, but I need to act now. Yes or no?"

"Helping you isn't . . ." Daniel began.

"Yes," Sally said, suddenly overriding her husband. Daniel turned to stare at her, clearly shocked, but her eyes were fixed on Cole.

"We agree. Get your information." She took a step forward, and he watched with surprise as her eyebrows drew down and her words grew harder. "In return I want you, the board, and the Justice Department out of our lives. You get nothing else from us. You take your information, and you leave."

"Done." Cole didn't even have to think about it. After today, he wouldn't need the Ross family anyway.

"I'm coming with you," Daniel said, standing. He cast a wary look at his wife. At least he didn't argue with her about it. "I want to keep an eye on you."

"If you must. Stay back and keep your glasses on."

"Sure," Daniel replied angrily.

Permission given, Cole pushed past Sally and hurried to the back of the house.

-CHAPTER 44-

Thomas raged, clearing a shelf of books in Father Sean's office. The sound of tearing paper blended with the musty scent of old books as the colorful tomes cascaded to the floor with a thundering crash. Fury lit Thomas, but there was despair there as well. He wanted answers. He *needed* answers, and Father Sean was supposed to have them.

Thomas laughed as his sister chased him around the living room. He barely missed the leg of the coffee table as he hurtled past, his stocking feet sliding out from under him as he took the turn too tightly. His right hand hit the carpet, keeping him from falling over completely, and he was off again, darting toward his room. Behind him he could hear both his sister's joyful giggle and his mother's exasperated shouts. He didn't pause, though. If he let up now, Ashley would catch him before he got back to his bed.

Thomas sobbed, emotions he had thought long gone suddenly restored in ways he didn't want. The officer on their doorstep was frowning anxiously, but Thomas barely noticed. Father Sean was dead, found stabbed to death in a park near his home. Tears leaked from his eyes, filling up his glasses. His world was collapsing.

The feel of this Reflection was familiar, even if the context was not. The rush of a single life, the destruction of self in the flood of another person's memories. These were familiar corridors to a Mirror.

Then everything changed.

Ashley leaned weakly on Carol Raines as they walked through the Atlanta airport. Exhaustion swirled in Ashley's every muscle, her mind sluggish. Another Reflection done, she wanted to sob openly. Her emotions were rubbed raw, and she felt as though she had been scoured of all hope. Tears welled in her eyes again, and she felt Carol's grip tighten in encouragement.

Just that quickly, the world seemed to collapse. A Reflection was supposed to be a single perspective delivered in intimate detail. With this second set of memories intruding, the experience shifted in new and dramatic ways. Prompted by this fresh recollection, self-awareness budded. Minuscule at first but steadily growing stronger, the spirit of Ashley Ross began to fight against the flow of images.

For the first time in any Reflection, she knew herself. Ashley knew she was drawing her brother's life into her, experiencing everything from his perspective. Unlike all her previous Reflections, though, she was getting something else: all her own memories poured back into her mind with perfect clarity.

Utter chaos dominated. Memories from both lives were strewn about with no connection. There was a sense of self but no cohesion of thought. Seventeen years of life with no index wasn't a person; it was pandemonium.

Fortunately, instinct took over. With skills honed by years of repetition, Ashley began sorting all the stray experiences crowding about her. She grabbed those images she wanted and set aside what she didn't want. Without the weekly infusions of memories, she was sure she couldn't have parsed this one. Two hundred and fifty-two Reflections, though, made for a lot of practice, and part of her knew exactly how to arrange it all. Even as proficient as she'd gotten at this kind of mental filing, she was becoming more practiced with every second.

She sorted Thomas's life off to the edge of her awareness. At first this process was manual, but every passing moment provided new insight, and soon she was able to automatically set aside any such memories. With a blend of curiosity and fear, she then pulled up her own memories and rapidly assembled them chronologically. Bracing herself for the truth, Ashley relived her own life.

She watched herself pout for no good reason, blushed at childhood immaturity, and gaped at her own laziness. It became difficult not to keep a running tally of every mistake. She cringed as she realized just how often she'd been selfish, and weak, and wrong.

It should have crushed her. The truth in their souls was the unconquerable monster that haunted all people after Reflections. For Ashley, though, there was an even more powerful realization.

The lives of her Reflected weren't here.

She saw herself being dragged to police stations and court-houses, looking the accused in the eye, and leaving. That was the end of it, though. No actual memories of those Reflections existed in this space. The only images passing between brother and sister were the ones they had lived themselves.

It was glorious. The emotional chains she'd forged over five long years shattered were without thought. This Ashley Ross, the one who existed free of other people's sins, was almost a foreigner. She was drawn to this creature, to this child she was sure she had never known. Pulling away was impossible; she couldn't focus on anything but this stunning vision of freedom.

This is me? she thought in disbelief.

After her very first Reflection, she had sought to know if she had become like Spencer Duncan; only now did she finally get her answer. Twelve-year-old Ashley Ross was scared and exhausted . . . and a flawed human.

In some ways it was terrifying. She saw within herself the means to become like Spencer. She saw the same cruelties, the same dark self-ishness that lived in everyone. What set her apart, though, were the decisions she had made. She wanted more; she wanted a better world.

She wasn't like Spencer Duncan because she chose not to be.

The fear that had dominated her so much since that first Reflection was blown apart in light of this truth. She understood now just how much her fear of Spencer's evil had shaped her. She'd lived in terror of what she might be, of what she might do. Ashley had become a terrified shell of herself. With each new infusion of memories over the years, she'd grown to fear that dark potential more and more. It was only here, watching the construction of herself in strokes of harsh reality, that she was able to cast off those fears completely.

This is me. This time the thought was triumphant, joyous. Exhilaration roared through her. Ashley Ross was reborn.

"No . . . please . . ."

Ashley's mind jerked to a sudden stop. Those words weren't from her memories. Where . . . ?

Thomas.

In a normal Reflection, she would have absorbed all the memories of a life, and the connection would end. Afterward, her Reflected would react to the experience, but she'd never see those memories; the link would already be broken. Here, in the infinite recurrence of two Reflections, that didn't happen.

She was receiving her brother's whole life, including what he was experiencing right now. He was reacting to the Reflection, and the thoughts he formed were transmitting to her as part of the link they shared.

"Thomas!"

It wasn't really a spoken word, but speech was how her mind interpreted the sensation. They lacked throats or tongues in this image, but she still heard her voice as though she were physically speaking.

Their connection was far more than words, though. She felt her brother's response almost immediately: pure shock. Apparently his initial communication had been accidental. He had always learned quickly, though.

"I don't want to see any more." It was a plea. She could feel the despair, practically hear the need to be away from the onrushing cascade.

"No! Look at it!" Ashley replied excitedly. "We're alone!"

She sensed his confusion. Of course they were alone. Then she felt the moment of awestruck elation as he understood.

She waited with almost quivering anticipation. She expected to feel his burst of joy as he explored his life without the interference of their Reflected. Instead, she only felt his dread grow.

There was no victory for Thomas, and Ashley felt growing terror in his realizations. He was drowning in the reality of who he was. Shame burned at him, and sorrow choked back any hope of freedom in this deluge of truth.

Sadness engulfed Ashley as she came to understand. Thomas was doing what he had always done: finding the worst and magnifying those faults to override all else. Freed from the shackles of his Reflected's lives, he realized he had no one but himself to blame for his petty resentment, his bitterness. He was sinking in a trap of his own devising.

Unlike Ashley's experience, losing the Reflected's lives wasn't liberating for Thomas. He'd always known he was flawed but comforted himself in the belief that it was the Reflections that had made him that way. Stripping away that lie left him vulnerable to the same disdain he poured on everyone else.

"I'm just like them," he said. "I'm a failure too."

"No! We're all flawed, but those flaws don't have to define who you are!"

Silence. Despair. Drowning.

Ashley considered what words she could wield to tear down his walls, to fight through the pyre of self-loathing he was building over himself. What could she say? Nothing. How could words hope to overcome such pain?

Desperately, she changed strategies. Instead of trying to communicate with words, she pushed herself beyond the realm of physical capabilities. Ashley pulled on the beliefs and hopes that formed the foundation of her world. She gathered them and held them there, knowing that her brother would receive them as he drew on her life.

Abruptly, the nature of their communication changed. He had received Ashley's first volley in this fight and was responding. Images from their lives intertwined, their conflicting viewpoints battling. His cynicism crashed relentlessly against the bulwark of her optimism. She felt him change, felt his angst and pessimism melting in the strength of her hope. Even then she could sense his brutal honesty dulling her impossible dreams. Both sides gave ground, and time seemed to stop as their war reached its climax, but neither was experiencing any shift in its foundations.

Ashley suddenly understood: she couldn't win. Her brother was self-destructing because on some level he *wanted* to. No matter what tactic she chose, he could ignore her.

In desperation, she clawed open the mental box where she'd stored his impression of this dual Reflection. It became immediately apparent how differently they'd approached this. While her first response had been to shove her brother's life aside so she could focus on her own, he'd headed the other way. He'd separated out her life and watched it with rapt fascination.

Today, Ashley had jumped at the chance to finally see who she was. So had her brother.

For years he'd held a perfect image of her, an ideal that couldn't possibly exist. Even once they'd started Reflecting others five years ago, even as he'd given up hope on everyone else, he'd believed she might be different. When he'd Reflected their father, he'd fought off the urge to commit suicide because he comforted himself with the belief that surely his sister wasn't like that.

Today he'd seen that she was.

Thomas was destroying himself because he couldn't handle that reality. As soon as he'd seen her selfishness, her sloth and her malice, he'd fled, locking her memories away. He'd given up on Ashley and then focused on himself. At first he'd clung to the belief that the Reflections had ruined them. Then Ashley had pointed out that wasn't the case. With his excuses burned away, Thomas now saw every failing as proof that he deserved to die.

Despair gripped Ashley like a vise, crushing the hope she had just discovered. She couldn't help him if he was determined to run away from her.

The answer suddenly came clear. He was running away from *her*.

With new hope, Ashley changed tactics one last time. She grabbed the perfect picture of herself Thomas had clung to for so long. She showed it to him, showed him how he had idolized her, how he had adored her. Then, with barely a shift, she showed him how she had seen him all these years.

It wasn't a perfect match, but it was close enough. The love he held for his sister was the same love and admiration she held for him. Thomas recoiled from the image. In confusion, he hurled back every shortcoming he had ever possessed. Ashley braced against the mental onslaught, holding on to her glowing image of him even as he attacked it.

"That's not me!" he insisted.

"Isn't it?"

"You know it isn't! You've seen my failures!"

"And you've seen mine. But you fled. Look again."

Ashley felt a sudden crush of emotions plow into her that she couldn't begin to work out.

"No! I'm not . . . I'm not going to . . ."

"You don't want to see the real me, do you?"

"Why couldn't you be perfect?! Why couldn't you have been worth all of this insanity?"

"You've always known, Thomas. You knew me better than anyone. The clues were always there. You remember how I woke you up early the morning of our first Reflection? How I refused to let you sleep just so I wouldn't be bored? That was me being selfish. You knew it then, and you pretended it wasn't. I've always been that way, you just overlooked it.

"That's not true!"

"You've lied to yourself for years. Not about you, but about me. You made me out to be better than I really am."

Thomas was crying now. His body might not be, but she could feel the rawness of the tears. In this state, a physical manifestation wasn't necessary for it to be real.

Ashley pushed forward, still holding the image of her brother as she wanted to see him.

"You couldn't look away from other people's failures. You were quick to point out Dennis's, and Dad's, and even Father Sean's. They were all too weak, and you searched for the proof. But me? My failures have been shoved in your face, and you're running away from them. For the first time in your life, you *don't* want them to be true.

"No," he begged. "Please . . ."

"You don't want to see me as I am, but I'm a failure too. You know that with certainty now, and you still want to believe something better about me. Look at me. Look at how I've seen you. Thomas, seeing someone as better than they truly are isn't weakness. It's love."

She felt his despair, stronger now than even in the midst of the darkest days after a Reflection. He saw who he was framed against how she saw him. He knew he could never live up to that. Panic surged in him.

"Stop," she said gently. "This isn't a test. Loving someone paints an image of them you can believe the best of," she continued, "and being loved makes you want to live up that image. I know what you are and what you're not, and I don't care. I love you, brother. Do you love me enough to try to be what I see in you?"

The destruction paused, and for a long moment there was nothing. Then, Ashley felt something surging deep within her brother. A powerful light. A hope.

His resistance to her touch crumbled. He relaxed, and a flash of joy burst through their connection. Relieved, Ashley pulled Thomas from his prison of shadows into the light.

With the last barriers gone, their souls touched.

-CHAPTER 45-

Thomas and Ashley stood knee-deep in a cool mountain lake. Trees lined the water's edge closest to them, and craggy, snow-capped peaks towered at the other end of the pool. He saw little hiking paths crisscrossing up the dark cliffs while a thin waterfall crashed over an outcropping a few thousand feet above them.

"We're not really here," Thomas said, looking around.

"I don't think so," Ashley said. She was wading barefoot through the chilly water. "But I always wanted to go someplace like this."

"Really? I always wanted to play on some beach in the Caribbean."

Suddenly their little pond of water transformed into a cove at the edge of a vast ocean. Instead of standing in a cool pond with smooth rocks beneath their feet, they now braced against waves of salty froth that flowed around their calves and over the sun-warmed sand.

The newly made beach transitioned almost seamlessly into the evergreen forest, and the water now lapped at the feet of the mountains that formed Ashley's part of this shared dream. Even at first glance, Thomas knew this place could never exist in the real world. Beholding the impossible beauty made him smile.

Without warning, Ashley took off at a run, splashing water behind her. Thomas followed, chasing after her with unnatural speed. They practically skipped across the surface of the bay, then raced up the mountain passes. They ascended quickly, climbing above the clouds and reveling as the high mountain winds slashed at their skin.

Cole rapped a staccato knock on Ashley's door. Getting no response, he pushed his way into the room. He froze the instant he crossed the threshold.

As expected, Ashley and Thomas were facing each other, only inches apart. Their glasses were off, their silver eyes locked together.

With a sense of awe, Cole crept into the room. He had brought a notepad but immediately discarded it. Not daring to pull his gaze from the pair, he drew a small tape recorder from his pocket. Thumbing the record button, he slowly circled the twins.

Out of the corner of his eye, he noticed Daniel lurking just inside the doorway. Cole raised a warning hand, urging him to stay back. Surprisingly, the man heeded the gesture, stumbling back into the hall. Cole couldn't be sure whether it was his motion that prompted obedience or if Daniel simply had a hard time watching his children's final moments. Either way, it left his study unhindered.

How long had this been going on? A few minutes, perhaps? It was impossible to tell. He'd hoped to catch it right at the beginning. Then again, there was no way to know. Perhaps he'd done just that. He frowned. Too many unknowns.

No. Focus. Note what can be recorded now and deal with the rest later.

He recorded relative body temperature, pulse, and breathing. Both twins were flushed, and their hearts were beating dangerously. Breathing was rapid, and sweat was breaking out across their foreheads.

In every previous double Reflection, the Mirrors had been pulled apart by those present. It was a natural reaction by their caretakers, he supposed, but it created a gap in his knowledge. Today he wanted to learn what happened if you didn't separate them.

Thomas basked in the sunshine and squeezed his toes around the pristine white sand of the beach. The splash of water around his legs was a joyful feeling, but it was also unnerving. He still wasn't sure why they were here.

"What is this place?" Thomas asked cautiously. He wasn't sure he wanted to know. "Are we dead?"

Ashley shook her head as she walked deeper into the water, spreading her hands to welcome a fresh wave. "We're still very much alive. Focus on yourself."

Puzzled, Thomas arched an eyebrow at his sister. She gestured impatiently, and he closed his eyes. Clearing his mind, he looked inward. With a lurch, he was suddenly aware of the real world.

He was standing in Ashley's room, dappled sunlight lighting the messy floor. His sister stood opposite him, silver eyes locked open and staring directly into his. Behind her, he saw Cole Bryant moving, watching them, speaking into a small recorder. Movement at the edge of the room may have been one of their parents, but he couldn't get a good look at the figure out of the corner of his eye, and if he turned to look, it would break the connection and kill them both.

As he studied the scene, though, he balked. This was more than just awareness of their real surroundings. He felt their hearts beating in perfect time. He felt his muscles working to keep him standing, his digestive system churning, and wondered why he hadn't eaten that morning. For the first time in his life, he was aware of his autonomic nervous system working to keep him alive.

He was perfectly aware of all that he was. It was probably where this illusory world had come from. His body and mind were fully attuned, connected to the point that he could detect individual neurons. He wasn't really on this sandy beach, but he could insert perfectly the sensations he'd be experiencing if he were. Sight, sound, smell, taste, and touch. Nothing was left out.

If he could so perfectly manipulate his senses, could he also change other parts? He imagined stopping his heartbeat for just a second, and . . .

The steady lapping of the ocean at their feet stopped. Everything went still, and for a long moment the tide seemed frozen in place. Nothing moved around him, and even the waves far from shore stopped their undulations in that single terrible moment.

Thomas gasped, then released control, allowing his body to resume its regular functions.

Just that quickly, sanity reasserted itself. The horrible, unnatural stillness of the waves broke, and water swirled in around their feet again.

"I guess I should *not* do that again," Thomas said with a laugh.

To his surprise, Ashley didn't join in his mirth. Standing waist-deep in the crystal-clear ocean waters, she was watching the horizon. She turned back to the mountains she had created and stared sadly at the towering peaks.

"What?" Thomas asked.

"It's already failing," Ashley said quietly.

"It is?"

"Yeah. There are signs, but they're still subtle.

"Our minds know something is wrong," she continued, "so it's showing in this illusion. Watch the waves. The tide is going out, slowly ebbing away. My waterfall at the other end of the bay is slowing. A little less flow every second. Eventually it'll stop. Or maybe the ocean will recede till we can't see it. That'll be the end of us."

"At least we got to really say goodbye," Thomas said. "That's better than nothing."

"I've changed my mind," Ashley said. "We're not going to die."

"That's why I came home!"

"Are you telling me you still feel the same? That you've given in to despair?"

Thomas paused, looking around their shared utopia. He looked back on his life, remembering too many days spent sobbing in his room or just hiding from the world. There was so much he hadn't done, and he realized he still wanted to go out and do it.

"No, I want to live. I want to . . ." He shook his head. "But what does it matter? This is going to kill us."

"Always the pessimist. Well, it's good to see you haven't changed too much," Ashley said with a smile. "Still, haven't you learned anything? I'm not giving up yet."

Thomas shook his head, but he returned her grin and felt a surge of optimism at her certainty. "Of course you're not. What's the plan?"

She hesitated, then nodded, steeling herself. "Bryant suspected that in this kind of Reflection, our bodies develop a need for the second mind. Without it, they shut down or go haywire or something. They need that connection."

"Right. So, can we break that link?"

"I've been looking at it, and I don't think I can. Not safely, anyway. I just don't know enough."

Thomas frowned. "Then what are you going to do?"

"What if one of us slows the heartbeat? Maybe if we can create enough dissonance, our brains will give up trying to reconcile with each other and the connection will break on its own."

"I don't think that will work," Thomas said skeptically. He opened his mouth to argue further, when he suddenly understood what she meant.

"One of us would die," he said accusingly. "This is the plan? Right after we decided to live?"

"Yes," Ashley said quietly. "Maybe if the mind feels the other heart stopping, it'll force some kind of failsafe. If it realizes the other body is dying, there's a chance it will break the connection on its own."

"That's insane! It might just kill us both anyway!"

"Yes, it might," Ashley admitted. "But if we don't do anything, we'll *definitely* both die. At least this way one of us might survive." She paused. "Unless you have a better idea?"

Thomas shook his head. "No." He kicked at the water angrily. "No, I don't." He swore loudly, then took a deep breath, trying to calm himself.

"Fine. Let's just figure out of which of us is going to die."

Ashley smiled at Thomas, one of those genuine beaming grins he'd missed so much. "Oh, Thomas. I've already started."

Bryant noticed the irregularity in heartbeat and began to speak into his recorder with even more haste. He'd always theorized that such an event would be impossible, but Ashley's heart rate was definitely slowing relative to her brother's.

He thought her skin was growing paler too, but it was hard to tell. The sun had wandered behind another cloud. With an exasperated sigh, he reached up and flipped the locks on his glasses open. With caution born from years of experience, he carefully kept his eyes directed well below the twins' faces. He pushed the glasses down to the end of his nose and peered over the top to glance at Ashley's skin, all while speaking quickly into his recorder.

He slid the glasses back into place but didn't lock them. He'd need to compare her skin tone again in a few minutes.

Taking great care not to jostle her, Cole reached down and gripped Ashley's wrist to take her pulse again.

All around Thomas and Ashley, their utopia was crumbling. Sections of mountain were breaking free, crashing into the ocean or smashing into the forest. As she'd predicted, the flow of water over the waterfall was visibly thinning. Around them, the needles on the remaining trees were bleeding from green to a lifeless brown as Thomas watched.

His pocket of ocean fared better but was clearly suffering. The flow of waves was irregular, and the tide was still receding. Where the water had once been a pristine greenish blue, it was sliding slowly to a muddy gray.

"You have to stop!" he insisted.

"No," Ashley said, weakly. "It's our only hope."

"It's not working!"

She shook her head. "Our heart rates are different. That's a step in the right direction. It means we *can* keep them separated."

"Yes, as long as we're here, connected. As soon as the Reflection ends, I won't have this level of control. I won't be able to maintain it."

"We don't know that."

Thomas grabbed her by the shoulders. "Stop! Please. Don't throw your life away. Let's just spend these last moments together. I'd rather enjoy this time than know we gave it all away for nothing." He watched as she stared at him dully, and he realized she was quickly fading. "Please, Ashley."

She opened her mouth to respond but abruptly slumped forward before any sound came out. Thomas darted forward, catching her before she slid to the sand. He collapsed to his knees, cradling her in his arms. He could *feel* her getting weaker, could sense her heartbeat slowing.

"I feel weak," she said thoughtfully. "Weird. This is just a mental image."

"Does it matter?" Thomas asked, then shook his head irritably. That question was useless. "Come back. Don't leave me yet. Please."

"I always wanted to Reflect him," she said absently. She was staring beyond Thomas.

"What?"

"Bryant. He was Reflected once. He told me so."

She was fading even faster now. It seemed to Thomas she was growing hazy, less opaque. He was running out of time. Sobbing, he drew her close, hugging her with all the strength he had.

"I wouldn't want to share his thoughts," Thomas said. "I can only imagine he's worse than all the rest."

"Maybe you could change his mind," Ashley said, smiling up at him feebly.

"Not me. I don't have the will."

"Mmmm." Her eyes were closed. He could see his own arms through her image.

To his left, the mountains shook, and enormous sections of dark rock crashed into the sea. The water surrounding them fled as if running away. The whole world seemed to darken as if the sun itself were fading. Perhaps it was.

Refusing to waste his final moments, Thomas immersed himself in Ashley's life one last time, savoring her presence as he waited for the end. He probably didn't have time to relive it all, so he focused on their birthdays, drinking in those days, working backward from today.

He saw his removal from their home, then her fight with the board and Carol's firing. In his memories of her, Ashley grew stronger and more confident with each year he jumped back. He watched the promise at the fence, the moment that had drawn him back here. He watched her sick with the flu on their thirteenth birthday; she worked crosswords and talked to Bryant.

Suddenly it all clicked.

All his life Thomas had hated being a Mirror. After every Reflection he'd downplayed the good he might have done and instead drawn all the hatred and distaste he could muster. From that first day with Dennis to this final Reflection with Ashley, he'd fought the assertion that any of this chaos could have meaning. By extension, he'd rejected that any part of his life could have purpose.

He thought of Father Sean. The man had made time for an angst-ridden teenager each week. Then he'd died alone to save a woman he'd never met. As a final act, he'd commanded Thomas to go out and to make his life matter.

With a sad smile, Thomas finally understood what Sean and Ashley had been trying to teach him: if you didn't care enough to give of yourself, you never really understood what life was about. He'd never felt his life was meaningful because his power had been taken by the government rather than given.

Now he was finally ready to give freely. And so it was time to find purpose.

"Well," he said to his sister's fading form, "better late than never."

Cole was examining Ashley with a careful eye. She was definitely paler, and her heartbeat was dangerously slow. Her eyes were still open and locked with her brother's, but she was obviously flagging. He expected her to drop any second now.

He was about to turn back to Thomas to check on the boy's progress when a hand shot out of nowhere and grabbed his face. Cole was so shocked he didn't even have a chance to resist as another hand rose up and knocked his glasses free.

With a startled yelp, he felt himself being dragged sideways.

Ashley was dying. She felt it. Her heartbeat had slowed enough that she'd soon collapse, breaking the connection. She hoped it would be enough.

It was getting harder to concentrate. It was hard to think. Thomas was still talking to her. She heard him, but she couldn't respond anymore. She tried to smile for him.

His sudden burst of joy was a surprise. Was it working? Was he breaking free of her mind's control? She hoped so. Maybe one of them could survive this ordeal.

Then something strange happened. She saw motion in her bedroom. Thomas suddenly yelled, and Bryant's face appeared abruptly in front of Thomas's. Before she could think, before she could even react, her contact with Thomas was severed and he was replaced by Dr. Cole Bryant.

Her brain lurched as the new Reflection began. It was a brutal moment, a harsh explosion of mental energy. It was like shifting a car cruising at highway speed into reverse. She felt her mind fighting, resisting the new contact.

She received a life. An instant passed. There was darkness.

-CHAPTER 46-

Ashley Ross woke up.

That was a pleasant surprise. On the other hand, the dull ache pounding in her skull and the bruises she felt along her right side were less welcome. They did indicate she was still alive, though.

She wondered where she was. As she had done for years, Ashley kept her eyes tightly shut even upon waking. It wouldn't have mattered in this case. A strip of gauze had been wrapped tightly around her head to prevent her from opening her eyes. At least she could still hear.

To her right she heard a rhythmic beeping. She also heard the muffled sound of automobiles through a window. At her left, she caught a soft rumbling sound.

Lifting a hand to her left temple, Ashley stripped the makeshift blindfold from her face.

Careful to keep her gaze down, she cracked open one eye. She was ready to squint against an invasion of light but was surprised to find her room dimly lit. Casting a glance at her surroundings, she discovered her glasses had been set out next to her bed within easy reach. An odd blend of exhilaration and relief swept her as she locked them into place.

Properly safe, Ashley surveyed her surroundings. She quickly confirmed now what her other senses suggested: she was in a hospital room, likely at the children's hospital. An IV pierced her arm, and a heart monitor stood to her right. A window behind them showed her the setting sun and the city. To her left, slumped in a particularly uncomfortable-looking chair, slept Mom.

The small rumbles Ashley had first detected on waking were her mother's delicate snores. It was touching to see she had refused to leave even to rest. Mom clutched her own pair of shaded lenses in a tight fist. Ashley smiled; she knew how hard it was to sleep with those on.

"Mom." The word was soft, but it was enough. Her mother startled awake, glancing around, clearly confused about her surroundings.

As soon as she saw Ashley, she gasped and raised a shaking hand to her mouth. Mom stood hurriedly, and a single step brought her to the bedside. She reached out a hand, taking Ashley's in a firm grip as if confirming it wasn't a dream. Then, with a sharp cry of joy, she leaned over and pulled her into a stifling embrace.

Ashley gave an exhausted but appreciative laugh and returned the gesture, encircling her mother in a weak hug. "It's good to see you too, Mom." She paused, released the embrace ever so slightly, then repeated the pressure. "And that's from Thomas. He was sorry he didn't give you a proper one this morning."

She felt Mom tense at the words, and Ashley's heart fell. Part of her hoped Thomas had survived to deliver that hug himself, but she'd known deep down that it was an empty dream. Mom's reaction was all the confirmation she needed. Her brother was gone.

It made her even happier that she'd been able to deliver his final gift of love. They hadn't specifically talked about it, but Ashley had shared his whole life. When he'd come home for that last goodbye, he'd seen their parents as an irritant to be avoided. Near the end of their Reflection when all the other lives were stripped away, she'd felt his deep regret at how he'd spurned them.

Mom was clearly looking for the words to break the news.

"Where's Dad?" Ashley said to avoid the topic for the moment.

Mom checked the clock on the wall. "He was going to deal with some paperwork, but he should be back any minute."

As if cued, the door to the tiny room opened and Dad stood framed in the doorway. He stopped abruptly, then broke into an excited smile. He thrust two coffees toward Mom, who grabbed them and set them on the counter with a tearful grin.

In an instant, father and daughter were together. Ashley gave a small laugh, but Dad just held her quietly. He shook slightly, crying. She held him tightly, so happy to see him again, so thankful she could finally show the proper emotion for all he'd done for her over the past few years.

As he let go, Ashley pulled him in for a second hug as she had with Mom and again emphasized it being from her brother.

"Ashley," Dad said quietly, "Thomas . . ."

"He's gone. I know." She *had* known, but saying it opened a new wound. Her smile faded, and tears ran down into her glasses. She pushed back against the sickly ache rising inside her, though. Part of her wanted to explore the pain, to wrap herself in grieving for her best friend.

Now wasn't the time. Her parents were still in shock. She could see on their faces the inner turmoil. Thrill that she was alive battled the pain of losing Thomas.

Forcing a smile, Ashley decided now was a time for joy; they'd weep together later.

"Do you know why . . . you're still here?"

Mom was prone to euphemism, as always, but Ashley knew it would be an even longer conversation if they kept dancing around the subject. "You want to know why I'm alive."

"Yes," Mom said, obviously steeling herself. "And . . . do you still want to die?"

Ashley smiled at her, then shook her head firmly. "No. I'm past that. I've seen who I am. You're going to have to put up with me a little longer."

They positively beamed at that, and she felt a rush of joy from deep inside.

"But *how* did you survive?" Dad asked, finally retrieving his coffee.

"Cole told me several years ago what causes two Reflecting Mirrors to die. Every Reflection is a bond between two people, and every connection causes odd physical changes in the body. The bodies want to sync up. Heart rhythms align; digestive patterns and endocrine glands adjust to function in parallel. In the end, the Reflected's mind breaks the connection after only a fraction of a second. The process is hard on a Mirror's body but ultimately changes little because the contact is so brief.

"We react differently when we Reflect each other. There's something unique in Mirrors that means we don't end the connection like a normal person does. As the connection continues, our minds have a chance to match far more closely. Basically, we become a single body controlled by two minds acting in perfect harmony. It's such a complete conversion that we can no longer live without both minds working in concert. We die because when the connection breaks, it is as if half of our brain is suddenly removed.

"It's why pulling Mirrors apart has killed them every single time. Leaving us alone, though, wouldn't have worked, either. We were dying even before we could be separated. I just don't think two minds are meant to control a person that way.

"The secret is what Cole told me all those years ago: the Reflected's brain is the one that lets go. In a normal Reflection, it's what releases us and allows us each to go back to our lives. Whatever signal it sends to end the Reflection is what resets the Mirror's body.

"Thomas realized it before I did. The only way to save one of us was to switch the double Reflection to a normal one so the Reflected's brain would reset ours. He grabbed Cole and dragged him into my line of sight."

"Thomas sacrificed himself," Dad said, voice hushed.

"I know this doesn't help, but it really was his choice. I was going to die. I even tried something else, but . . ." Ashley trailed off again, fighting the tears. "At the end, it was his decision."

An awkward moment passed as everyone processed that. Then Mom got up and moved over to the edge of Ashley's bed, hugging her again. Dad walked to the other side. Between them, Ashley said, "I'm tired, but I honestly think I'm okay. Is there any chance they can get us out of here before McMurray's closes?"

"It's a hospital, so probably not," Dad said with a short laugh, "but I'll check. If they can't, I'll grab food and bring it here."

He stood and walked to the door but stopped as soon as he opened it. Waiting just outside was Cole Bryant.

"Get out of here." Mom said firmly. "We made a deal. You got to see them Reflecting. Now you get out of our lives for good."

Cole didn't even flinch. Instead, he calmly set his briefcase down on a nearby cart, flipped it open, and extracted a stack of papers. He then thrust them at Mom and said, "Indeed. This is a new contract, officially voiding the last one and freeing Ashley from Reflecting for the Justice Department. As I am the only authorized representative of the board within a thousand miles, it made sense for me to deliver it."

Mom went silent, mouth gaping. Dad looked as though he were going to say something, then simply shook his head. He did reach out and take the offered papers, though.

"Let me see those," Ashley said. "I want to know what we're signing."

Ashley read it, carefully analyzing every line. She'd never Reflected a lawyer but had done a paralegal. It was Cole Bryant's knowledge that proved most useful, though. The man might not be a lawyer, but his only real friend was the attorney general. He'd picked up quite a bit from her. Even better, since he was the one who got the custody contracts signed, he'd learned the intricacies of these exchanges long ago.

"It's good," Ashley said, handing it back. "It provides indemnity for any illegal actions committed in allowing Thomas to come home, releases you as house parents from the Mirror program, and transfers me from state control back to you. It even offers a severance bonus for your years of faithful service." She turned to the specialist. "You work quickly."

"The board counts many lawyers and judges among its friends," Cole noted as he held out a pen.

"I'll bet it does," Dad muttered as he hastily scrawled his signature at the bottom of the document.

"You're being awfully nice," Mom said suspiciously, looking toward the specialist.

"He's not being nice," Ashley said. "He's trying to be clever."

"I don't understand."

"He promised you he'd let me go, but that wasn't really binding. You were denying him his legal right of access at that point, anyway. So his deal was just to get you to give him what was legally obligated. You didn't have anything to bargain with in the first place."

"So why offer this?" She held up the new contract.

"Because Ashley has something I need," Cole said simply. "She's the only Mirror to ever survive a dual Reflection, and I want her account."

Dad glanced at the specialist in surprise. "You're sure being up front about this."

The specialist shrugged. "As Ashley has demonstrated, she knows my motives. Dissembling is useless."

"So, you offer us our daughter in exchange for her story?"

Ashley answered that one. "Essentially. He knows he can't use the existing contract as a bargaining chip."

Cole nodded. "If I force her hand, she could lie about what happened between her and her brother. I have no way to corroborate her information. She has to be willing to give it to me. This seemed a good start."

Mom took all of this in, then signed as rapidly as Dad had. Perhaps she was worried Cole would suddenly change his mind. Ashley didn't think he would, but she understood their concern. After all she'd endured, she could understand why they would have trouble trusting him.

Of course, they didn't know him like she did.

Thrusting the paper back to Cole, Mom asked, "Do we need a notary or witness or something?"

Ashley answered that one. "No. Because Cole's usually alone when he handles these negotiations, he's authorized to act unilaterally on matters like this. His signature is enough."

Taking the pen, Cole stepped up and, after a moment's hesitation, signed in a single swift motion. The knowledge he'd gain from picking her brain was easily worth more to him than the fifty Reflections she would have given him before being released on her next birthday, but he clearly still hated giving them away. Every Reflection was precious.

"It's done," he said, tucking the pen back into his jacket pocket. He handed Dad one copy of the documents and stuffed the other in his briefcase. "Now, will you give me what I need?"

Despite being Reflected only a few hours ago, the man was as stoic as ever. Ashley hadn't had much time to dig through his life yet, but his reaction didn't really surprise her. Mental discipline was the hallmark of Cole Bryant's life. He was almost certainly still wrestling with his brutal self-examination, but he wasn't about to let that struggle undermine his attempt to secure what might be the most important work of his entire career.

Ashley shook her head. "You're not done yet."

Pulling back the blankets, she revealed her right ankle. Strapped to it was the monitoring device she'd been forced to endure even before she'd performed her first Reflection. More than anything else, she saw it as the symbol of her slavery and the board's unbreakable control. The contract they'd just signed was the act that would legally free her, but it wouldn't feel real until her shackle was gone.

Bryant nodded wordlessly, slipping around her bed to stand next to the device. He disabled the alarm trigger, then pulled out a key and unlocked it. Ashley had to stifle a nervous laugh as it fell away into the specialist's hands.

"Now get out," Dad said fiercely, pointing to the door.

"Will you . . . ?"

"We'll be in touch," Dad interrupted, now smiling. "If we feel like it."

Ashley was so busy exulting in her newfound freedom she almost missed the exchange. It was only when Cole picked up his briefcase with obvious irritation that she realized what was happening.

"Wait."

Everyone turned to face her. Mom and Dad were clearly confused, but the sudden blossom of hope on Cole's face was an unusual show of emotion from the specialist.

"Yes," she said, looking directly at him. "I'll tell you everything you want to know about the Reflection. It won't be today, though. It won't be a short conversation, and I'm doing dinner with my family tonight."

Cole nodded as he reined in his enthusiasm. Ashley understood him well enough now to read the gesture. He was excited for this opportunity, but he was determined to hide exactly how excited. He didn't want them to know just how much more they could have wrung out of him. With his classic stony demeanor, he simply said, "Thank you," and turned to leave.

"Why?" Mom asked, clearly crestfallen. "Why give him anything after all he's done to Mirrors?"

"It's a long story. And I promise I'll tell you everything, but like I told him, not tonight."

"Okay."

Ashley could tell she wasn't convinced. Wringing her hands nervously together, Mom eyed the specialist, then Ashley. The gesture made Ashley smile a bit. At least some things never changed.

This wasn't finished, though. There was still something Ashley had to do. "Cole and I do still need to talk tonight, though. Some things won't wait."

The specialist froze, hand on the doorknob. He turned back to look at her, a single eyebrow arched quizzically. Mom and Dad were more open in their disbelief.

"Are you sure?" Dad asked. "Your mother's right. Why not just be done with him?"

"I wish it were that easy," Ashley said to her parents. "Can you give us a moment? See if you can get me out of here? Or maybe call in an order to McMurray's?"

Her parents shared a look that clearly said that they doubted the wisdom of this, but neither complained. Instead, each came back to her bed, offered another round of hugs, then filed out of the room without a word to the specialist.

"If we are not discussing your Reflection, I'm not sure what we have to talk about," Cole said as the door clicked shut.

"We're discussing my Reflection," Ashley said. "Just not the one I had with Thomas."

"So you did receive my life," Bryant said musingly. "I wasn't sure. Compared to all I know of Reflections—including my own—this one was an aberration."

Ashley nodded. "It was definitely that. I don't even remember the Reflection itself. That's never happened before.

"I can confirm that I received at least some of your memories, but I'm not sure yet if I received everything. I haven't been awake long enough to dig more than a handful up. I got enough, though."

"For what?"

Ashley chose not to answer directly. "You killed a man when you were fifteen."

"Yes. I told you that on your thirteenth birthday. It was self-defense."

"You didn't tell me how much you enjoyed it."

Cole stood silently, staring at her from behind those dark glasses. There were no overt changes in his expression, but he raised a hand to his head and massaged one of his temples. Ashley also thought the briefcase shook slightly in his other hand as he laid it atop the nearby counter.

"I really didn't mean to kill him."

"I know."

"After it was over, I remembered the exhilaration of victory. I remembered dominating another person in the ultimate struggle, in the fight for one's life."

With a long sigh, he dropped his gaze to the floor. She knew he'd never spoken to anyone about this, and now he was confessing to a seventeen-year-old girl who had just tried to kill herself. That was probably a lot to come to grips with.

"I wanted to do it again," he said finally. "To do it on purpose, to execute a plan, to get away with the perfect murder."

Ashley leaned forward. "You didn't, though."

He dropped the hand rubbing his forehead. He looked up, dark glasses meeting dark glasses, and straightened to his full height. There was pride in that stance. "No. I did not."

"Instead, you helped establish a system meant to prevent that perfect murder. It's not foolproof, of course. Someone would have to suspect you, after all, but if it got to that point . . . well, even a super genius can't fool a Mirror's eyes.

"Four years ago you told me you've worked on the Mirror program to protect innocent people. That never rang true to me. It wasn't until today I understood what you meant. You aren't trying to protect innocent people like yourself who have been falsely accused. You're trying to save the people who might end up dead by your hands."

"Not just mine." He sighed again, and some of his proud determination fled. "I'm driven to protect the Mirror program because I know what children like you are actually fighting against."

"So you buy children for the government, remove them from their homes, and chain them to a weekly Reflection."

"Yes." There was no apology in that voice.

"You seem awfully certain about all of this," Ashley replied.

"What's the alternative? Should we end up like countries that have banned Mirror justice? You want a strong organized crime presence? Or gangs that run the streets? Perhaps you want to go back to days when our murder rates were double what they are now? Perhaps you liked the part where we locked up innocent people for decades?

"Mirror justice moves us beyond all of that, and through it all, Mirrors live longer when they Reflect anyway. It's a win/win situation."

"Then why does it torture you?"

"Because humans are weak, foolish creatures who attach destructive emotions to necessary tasks."

"Agreed," Ashley admitted. "But you've lived your life resisting a literal homicidal urge. You've trained yourself to ignore the feelings you have. You've become a veritable stone, and it's driven away pretty much every person who might have been your friend.

"Yet, when it comes to Mirrors, you almost inflame those dangerous emotions. You don't fight the tears when we die. You have fled from human weakness in every other aspect of life, but here you've done everything you can to maintain those feelings.

"What do you expect me to say?" he demanded, crossing his arms over his chest. "You Reflected me. You know all my answers already."

Ashley leaned forward intently. "Not quite. The one answer the Reflection can't give me is what you're going to do now.

"You've been living a lie, Cole. On the one hand, you're the single most powerful voice for Mirror justice in this country. You've fought hard for the right to buy children and strip them away from families in the name of justice. You've done everything you can to ensure that they have no hope of normalcy, instead languishing in a system where kids are given new guardians an average of every three years.

"On the other hand, you've maintained an emotional connection to those children when you've done your best to shut out everyone else. We never see it, but you cry for every Mirror who dies. You feel like you're damned because of what you've done, and you've embraced a life of loneliness because of it.

"You've reconciled all this as your penance. You draw the pain of Mirror's lives into you, because you've told yourself that if it hurts you, you're not a monster. It's not as easy as that, though. Over the years, you've convinced yourself the pain is enough. As long as you hurt, you can do whatever else you need to do.

"It doesn't work that way. You can't condemn us and then love us and hope the two cancel each other out. Either we're tools to be used and discarded or we're children to be treasured and nurtured.

"I don't know which of these positions is the lie. I'm not sure you do either. But one of them *is* a lie, and if there's one thing a Reflection does well, it's destroy the lies we tell ourselves.

Cole simply watched her, posture unchanged. The whole time she'd spoken, he'd barely moved. Only the slightest twitches in his cheek had given away the internal turmoil she knew he must be trying to reconcile. Stoic to the end, his demeanor offered nothing until he finally answered.

"Why can't I be both? There's no immutable law that a man can't do what is necessary and still regret it."

Ashley shook her head. "That's not what is happening here. You're grinding to dust the children you say you care about."

"No. You're framing it incorrectly," Cole shot back, emotion finally rising in his voice. He wasn't exactly angry, but there was a definite flush of irritation. "I'm a general, sending my soldiers into combat. I know there will be casualties, but there are victories which must be secured regardless of cost!"

"And what general knows every lowly grunt as well as you know us? What general expects to lose 100 percent of his troops?" She paused, drew a deep breath, then asked, "What general has an army of nothing but conscripts?"

Cole actually shook his head at that. "What am I supposed to do? Ask for volunteers?"

"That's *exactly* what you should be doing."

He actually laughed at that, a startled sound of utter disbelief. "You must be kidding."

"I'm dead serious. Use only those of us who volunteer or none at all."

Cole's mirth vanished, and he almost growled. Shaking his head, he slammed his fist down on his briefcase. One of the coffees her father had brought rested beside it and rattled with the force of the blow. His face had grown red, and his mouth was set in a stern line.

"Mirror justice must happen!" He emphasized each word. "We're fighting against evil and chaos, and Reflections are the greatest weapon we've ever been handed! You don't understand! You don't know what you're fighting against!"

They'd finally arrived at the crux of it all. This was where Ashley had been directing the conversation, but she had to steel herself in the face of Cole's sudden fury. Thomas had died for her, died so she could live her own purpose. It was time to do just that.

"Don't I?" she asked quietly.

"I remember killing hundreds of people. The horror and exhilaration.

"I remember raping children. The lust and burning need.

"I remember abusing people. Hurting those I love with my own fists or worse.

"I remember it all, Cole. I've seen the darkest scum of humanity, the ones who *didn't* stop their unspeakable desires. I've felt the aftermath of things you only dream you understand.

"Through the entire time I Reflected, you and I have been driven by the same things. We need to stop this darkness from overwhelming the world. You've been forcing Mirrors to do this when we're the only people who really understand it the same way you do."

Cole processed this silently for a moment, then shook his head forcefully. "It doesn't work that way. Fifteen minutes ago you had the choice to keep Reflecting, and your only focus was to flee from all the good you're doing."

"No. Today I decided not to be your slave anymore. There's a big difference."

Ashley swung off the bed and stepped over to the specialist. She was still weak, and her knees almost buckled. It was more than just the Reflection; she'd spent a long year of neglecting her health. Still, this was important. She needed him to see her intensity, see that she wasn't simply spouting words.

She reached up and unlocked her glasses. Pulling them from her face, she tilted her face up to his, silver eyes boring deep into his own shaded gaze.

"I see what you see. I know what I do has helped countless people." She took a deep breath, steeling herself. "That's why I'm promising to finish out my term of duty and Reflect until my eighteenth birthday."

Cole gaped at her and took a step back. He looked over at the contract her parents had just signed. "You're not serious." He looked at her again, then shook his head. "You *are* serious. You're volunteering?"

"I had to prove to you that someone would. I needed you to know that this was my choice."

"But why? You know what this will do to you."

"Actually, I'm not sure anymore. I learned a lot today about storing away memories. The Reflection with Thomas gave me plenty of practice." She shrugged. "Even if I'm wrong, though, it doesn't matter. It's the choice I'd have made five years ago, and I make it again today."

She softened her expression and reached out for the coffee her parents had abandoned as they left. It was still hot enough to drink. She held it out to Cole.

"You call yourself a general. That makes me your soldier. It's an appropriate metaphor. What you forgot, though, is that people do volunteer for that work. Even in war, when the chances they could die are highest, people want to fight for something bigger than themselves."

He accepted the drink and took a halting sip. He was clearly buying time, thinking through all the possibilities. It was the way he did things. Think first, and there would be fewer problems later.

"You are unusual," he said eventually. "Even your brother would never have volunteered. You can't count on every Mirror to approach this job with such zeal. Or any Mirror, really."

"I wonder why." Ashley didn't bother to hide her sarcasm. "Did you ever think your marketing might be the problem?"

"I don't follow."

"You sell the program to the parents of prospective Mirrors as a chance for something great and wonderful. Their children will be heroes. They'll have a deep and abiding sense of purpose. You don't believe it, though. You believe that our lives are so terrible it's something you should torture yourself for.

"We can all see how you really feel. And because you're the smartest man in the room, the board, the Shepherds, and the house parents have followed your lead. Pretty much all of them whisper what an honor being a Mirror is, but few of them believe it.

"What's funny is that you've got it backward. You've spent your whole career selling something you believe is a lie, when it's actually true.

"I'm a hero. We all are. Mirrors have done more to reduce crime in this country than any other change to the justice system. Instead of parades, though, we're prisoners in our own homes. You've treated us like slaves, and society has seen that. Instead of accolades and gratitude, you've fostered an environment of distrust and loathing."

Cole stood a moment watching her, then shook his head and turned away. He strode slowly around the bed to the window. In a single abrupt motion, he pushed aside the blinds, revealing the buildings of downtown Denver framed against the fading sun.

Ashley followed, standing beside him as he silently watched the light fade and sipped his coffee.

"We currently have eleven Mirrors Reflecting," he said eventually. He didn't look at her, instead keeping his eyes on the sunset. "Two of whom I expect to lose in the next six months. So, if I went to each of them tonight and freed them from their obligations, how many do you think would sign back up?"

"None of them."

Cole nodded approvingly. "So you're not totally delusional."

Ashley turned to face him. "I can't save them from a broken system."

"So that's your strategy. You have changes in mind."

"A few."

"Ah." Cole sounded doubtful. "More dual Reflections?"

"I think it's worth exploring, but my experience with Thomas would be hard to duplicate. We were already close, which set the tone for the whole experience.

"Eventually we will get there, but there will need to be other adjustments first. We'll probably have to change the frequency of Reflections. Maybe more early on to give us practice sorting them, then fewer later. Maybe the opposite. I'm not sure. But my years of practice were vital to surviving my Reflection with Thomas. I'm sure of it."

"I might be able to convince the board of that," Cole said slowly. "What else?"

"Stop locking away your Mirrors. Let them visit malls, go to movies, and maybe even an amusement park. Send them on vacations. Let them swim in the ocean."

Cole scoffed. "I don't believe the public will like that. I'm sure the board won't allow it."

"Then you, as the nation's foremost expert on Mirrors, need to educate them on why it's so important."

Cole considered it. "Is it?"

"You know it is. You've said as much yourself: our own lives are more real to us than those of our Reflected. Right now we're remembering all those very interesting interactions and meanwhile we're basically prisoners. I can guarantee it's affecting our worldview."

Ashley shrugged. "You've got to find ways to encourage us to live, and this is the simplest."

He frowned. "People don't like having Mirrors in their midst. Airlines have repeatedly lobbied to force us to use private planes. It will be a difficult fight."

She turned to face him and pulled him to look at her again. "Yes, it is, but you might save us a lot of heartache."

Cole held her gaze for a long moment, then turned back to face the window. He stared out into the growing darkness with his hands clasped behind him, never saying a word. Ashley watched him for a bit, then grabbed her glasses; it felt weird to be unsafe for so long. As she slid them on, she slid back into bed, still watching the specialist contemplate his dilemma.

Not turning from the window, Cole asked quietly, "Are you certain you can work with me?"

Ashley smiled at him. "What? You don't think I was won over by your personality?"

Turning away from his city gazing, Cole fixed her with a stony scowl. "I know who I am. After the Reflection, how could I not? I tend toward stoic indifference and an air of superiority in my social interactions. I've isolated many people because I'm afraid to make connections.

"More importantly, you are correct. The emotions I've shown for Mirrors are mostly to assuage any guilt I feel for the situation I've created." He shook his head. "Even I must confess it's not a compelling résumé."

"So what?" Ashley asked. Cole traded his angry frown for a furrowed brow. "You think those matter? Yes, you're aloof and arrogant. You know who else was? Thomas. You're moved to compassion for all the wrong reasons? So is Carol. I loved and worked with both of them.

"You've made mistakes in the past, Cole. Honestly? I care more about what you're going to do tomorrow to fix them."

Cole stared at her for a long time. She instinctively wanted to look away from his fierce, shaded gaze, but today she met it with her own determined mien. They held their silent contest for several long minutes.

"Change isn't easy," he finally said.

"You don't have to do it all at once," Ashley replied. "All you need to do today is to take the first step."

He considered her a long moment, then sighed. Without warning, he spun on his heel and stalked away. Crossing the room with long, purposeful strides, he grabbed his briefcase and marched out. He didn't even pause to say goodbye.

Ashley's heart fell to her stomach, and a sob slipped out before she could think about it. She felt tears well in her eyes. Her revision of Mirror justice had never been a sure thing, but she'd hoped they could at least come to *some* sort of agreement, even if it wasn't the one she wanted.

It didn't matter now. Without Cole's help, the program would continue as it always had. Ashley knew her side in the fight, knew her purpose, and that helped. She'd serve her year. Maybe she could still convince him. Maybe they didn't have to be enemies.

"Ashley? What's wrong, sweetie?"

Mom stood at her bedside gripping her arm as Dad waited at her feet. She hadn't even seen her parents return, but, of course, they'd just been waiting for Cole to leave.

"Long day," she said with a weak smile.

They both nodded, but Dad frowned. "Did he hurt you?"

"Not exactly. Don't worry about him. What did you learn?"

"They're going to release you," Mom said. Her smile was forced, but the one Ashley returned was genuine.

"Ha! I didn't really expect that." At least the news wasn't all bad.

"Well, I think they wanted to get you out of the hospital," Dad said uncomfortably. Then, with some false cheer, he added, "Being a Mirror worked in your favor this time."

"It's about time!" She was done running from herself. It was time to embrace her abilities and status. Take the advantages where she could.

A nurse came by to remove the IV, and the doctor returned to give some last-minute instructions. His spiel was hurried, though, and she realized Dad was probably right. While she couldn't change things today, this was exactly the attitude she'd fight to abolish.

She'd just finished zipping up her jacket when Cole Bryant suddenly reappeared in her doorway. He was holding his briefcase, a new cup of coffee—and a pack of colorful socks. The rainbow hues of the socks clashed with his dark suit, and he held them with obvious embarrassment.

Ashley blinked in surprise, and Mom and Dad wordlessly got out of his way when he pushed forward. He dropped the socks on the foot of her bed, licked his lips nervously, then said, "I agree."

He hesitated, seeming to fight for words. "I don't like our odds, to be honest. It seems insane. Still, I have to make a choice." He stopped abruptly, clearly not sure how to proceed.

"Those are for you," he said tersely, pointing at the socks.

Ashley stared at the gift for a long moment, confused. Reaching out, she pulled the package to her and suddenly understood. Three pairs of neon-tinted knee-length socks. Exactly the kind she couldn't wear over her ankle monitor. These weren't just a random gift; they were a symbol of her new freedom. Ashley felt a wide smile split her face.

Cole gave a final jerky nod as the corners of his mouth gave the barest tick up. He strode toward the door, but right before he vanished from sight, he turned back and said, "We'll talk tomorrow. About your Reflection and where the program is going. Is 10:00 a.m. good for you?"

"I'll check my calendar, but that should work," Ashley said, grin turning wry.

"Good." He hesitated. "Get well soon," he added in a rush.

And he was gone. Mom gaped after him and even walked to the doorway to stare down the hallway after him. Dad stood, completely flabbergasted, looking back and forth between Ashley and the socks.

"What just happened?"

Ashley laughed. She couldn't help it. The image of the eternally stoic Cole Bryant awkwardly carrying the brightly colored socks was just too much.

"No, really. What the hell just happened?"

"I think," Ashley managed between giggles, "it's a good first step."

NOTE TO THE READER

Thank you so much for taking the time to read my book. I hope you've enjoyed the adventure. If you did, it would mean a great deal to me if you'd leave me a review on Amazon and Goodreads—and, of course, spread the word!

With deepest gratitude,
WILEY

ABOUT THE AUTHOR

Wiley A Haydon III was born and raised in Texas. He's worked in a wafer fab, been an engineer, spent time as an over-the-road truck driver, and is extremely happy to add author to that list of professions. He lives in west Texas with his wife and two cats. *Soul Mirrors* is his debut novel. You can connect with Wiley and see some of his short stories at http://www.wileyhaydon.com.